CURSE OF THE NEPHILIM

THE HEALER CHRONICLES
BOOK ONE

ELEANA JAYNES

RAVENSWOOD
PUBLISHING & GOODS

Tanya...
Oh, Daddy....

COPYRIGHT

This novel is entirely a work of fiction. The names, characters, and incidents portrayed in it are the work of the author's imagination. Any resemblance to actual persons, living or dead, events, or localities is entirely coincidental.
Copyright © 2023 by Eleana Jaynes.
All rights reserved. No part of this publication may be reproduced, stored or transmitted in any form or by any means, electronic, mechanical, photocopying, recording, scanning, or otherwise, without written permission from the publisher. It is illegal to copy this book, post it to a website, or distribute it by any other means without permission.

First edition Hardcover October 2023
ISBN: 9781739452308
Edited by Paige Lawson and Tanya Hagel
New Cover by Black Phoenix Covers
Formatting and original Cover by Ravenswood Publishing
& Goods ravenswoodpg@gmail.com www.
ravenswoodpublishinghouse.com

Curse of The Nephilim

Eleana Jaynes

TRIGGER AND CONTENT WARNINGS

This book has dark sexually explicit scenes. Bondage, knife play, blood play, and sexual violence. There is some crude and degrading language that some may find offensive.
There is a *sexual* Dom/Sub relationship. Daddy kink! Praise Kink! Enemies to Lovers! Forced proximity!
Some scenes may cause distress. Including the death of a child.
This is a slow burn, so please do not expect sexual content from the beginning. But it is worth the wait!
Fayolan is an unapologetically dark, sadistic bastard, and that will not change!
If you are still with me… Enjoy!

Solis
Braylor
Stidahl
Fayspire
Grimfell
No Man's Land
Ustraya
Trenmont

CHAPTER ONE

Tempest

A strong breeze ran through the meadow, bringing with it the spirits of the dead. Their eerie melody called out to me.

"War is coming. Run, sweet child, or you will dance with us!"

The wind grew stronger, and my body tingled with excitement as the air condensed. *A storm was brewing.* I could sense its unease as it made the hair on my neck bristle.

The first drops of rain drew me from my musings. The storm called out to me, speaking in riddles. *I wish it would just tell me what it wanted me to know.*

I remember the first time I heard the storm talking to me. Gods, I must have been only about three years old. Since then, we discovered that no other Nephilim could. Although some could hear the spirits, whilst others could only see them. No one knew why I was different.

A defiant smile crossed my lips as I held my arms wide above my head, mocking the storm.

Forks of lightning tore through the sky. I closed my eyes, counting. *One... Two... Three*. Thunder rumbled, making the ground quake beneath my feet.

"Tempie, come inside," Maeve called from behind me, the wind sweeping away her words. Her hands flew up as a bolt of lightning sizzled across the sky.

"Go home, little sister. I will be there soon."

Maeve crossed her arms over her chest in a huff. "You're going to catch your death one of these days." She turned away, slipping on the muddy ground.

"The *irony* alone would be worth it!" I shouted over the rumbling thunder. I hauled Maeve up, catching her before she could slip again.

"Seriously, I mean it Tempie. You know how mother worries when you put yourself in danger."

She was right, and my mother's concern was well-founded. Fifteen years ago, mercenaries found me playing amongst the trees and kidnapped me. Intending to collect a bounty from the King of Stidahl.

"Tempie?"

I snapped back from the dark memories. "I promise I will be okay. Go!"

Maeve clenched her fists and sighed. Turning back, scurrying towards the safety of our cottage.

Who are you? The storm called as it raged around me.

"My name is Tempest. I'm the daughter of Sirus. I do *not* fear you," I yelled into the storm.

You are like me, Nephilim. Lightning ploughed into the earth, leaving scorched grass in its wake. *Death is hunting you. He will destroy you! Destiny will not be kind to you.*

Ha! When wasn't she fucking me over? She wrecked my life by allowing my parents to fall in love. My father, the disgraced son of the Goddess of Destiny herself, and the God of War. They'd cursed me to a life of suffering. Hunted and killed just for existing.

Heading back towards my family's weathered cottage, I saw Mother glaring at me from the window. I smiled at her as I slipped inside.

She looked me up and down. Her mouth tightened into a thin line as she took in my dishevelled state. "Tempest Fern Bellmont!" Her cheeks turned red as she glared at the puddle forming at my feet.

"Sorry, I…"

"You and the whispers of the storm, Tempest," she said with a sharp sigh. "They bring nothing but trouble." She was right, but she'd never understand my connection to the storm. *I must have inherited that from my father.* "Get changed and sit by the fire before you catch your death." I saluted with a grin, which only got me another chastising look.

Mother knew I wouldn't get sick. Fortunately, Nephilim never do. As we can heal others, but not ourselves.

I climbed the stairs to the room Maeve and I shared. She grinned as I approached the old, withered wardrobe and got another long-sleeved dress.

"How many names did Mother use?" she asked with a knowing smirk. I held up three fingers. "Ouch," she said, chuckling as she got up.

"It's not that bad," I said, poking my tongue out at her. "Can you go watch Lily whilst mother cooks? I will be there soon." With a nod, she closed the door quietly.

I struggled to untie my corset and remove the sodden skirt with freezing fingers. The dress dropped to my feet, soaking the floor. As I stood up, I glimpsed myself half-naked in the mirror.

Purplish-red scars ran across my body. They grew darker

and ached in the cold. I couldn't bear to see them, so I tossed a blanket over the mirror.

They were a permanent reminder of the cruelty the mercenaries had shown me. I was just a child, but they had beaten and lashed me. Leaving me scarred and unable to endure touch.

Men from my village tracked the mercenaries and saved me. When my mother saw me, she ran and hugged me tight, but I howled in pain until she finally let me go. I'd let no one touch me since. *Well, except Lily...*I endured the pain for her. She was too young to understand.

I slipped into a soft underskirt and a simple dress that hid the hideous scars. It hugged my curves, showing them off to any man who looked my way. My mother had purchased this dress to prove a point that, at twenty-three years, I needed to settle down.

It wasn't like I didn't want to... Many men had tried to court me, but I knew my scars would repulse them. *Hell, they disgusted me, and if I couldn't love myself, how would anyone else?*

I uncovered the mirror and saw myself staring back with blue and magenta eyes. They marked me as Nephilim, as did my flared ears and the blue strands throughout my chestnut brown hair. A midnight streak appeared each time a Nephilim healed someone.

However, I was much smaller than most of my kind, who stood over seven feet tall. My growth had always matched that of a human, and by the age of seventeen, I had stopped growing altogether. I was a freak even amongst the Nephilim.

The distinct clanging of pots and pans pulled me from my musings. *Mother would need more help with dinner.* I straightened my dress and headed downstairs.

Maeve looked up when the first step creaked under my foot. She sat near the flickering fire with Lily in her arms, crooning to her. My mother was setting the table, and she glanced up. "Give me a hand, Tempie." She placed the cutlery down as she returned to the kitchen.

The delicious aroma of stew made my mouth water. Living in a hidden village, we enjoyed a simple life. A small forest spread out around us, offering shelter from the outside world.

I positioned one of Maeve's vases of flowers at the heart of the table as I placed settings for three. Maeve was always bringing home the wildflowers from the meadow. She said they reminded her of my eyes. I arranged several more vases around the cottage, their sweet aroma filling every room.

Lily moaned, and I glanced across at Maeve. "I'll take her." I smiled as Maeve carried her through to the kitchen.

"Thanks," she said as she grabbed bowls and set them around the table.

"You are getting so big, Lily." I grinned as she grabbed a strand of blue hair, wrapping it around her fingers. She wasn't like Maeve and me. We were both feisty and strong willed. But Lily was soft and innocent. She was the spitting image of Maeve, though, with curly blonde hair and startling blue eyes.

Pulling out a chair, I perched Lily on my lap and grabbed another bowl for Mother to dish out the stew. I patiently waited for her to be seated at the head of the table. Leading prayers to the Gods.

Maeve's lips moved as she mouthed the words. But I never joined in. Mother gave me a disapproving look, but I wasn't budging. I refused to pray to powerful beings like my father, who mated with mortals, only to abandon them and their offspring. My father left before I was even born.

After eating, Mother scooped up Lily and sat in her comfy chair by the hearth.

I swung a cauldron over the fire to heat the wash water. Maeve and I cleared the table and swept the kitchen while waiting for it to boil as Mother started singing to break the drudgery of washing dishes. Soon we were all joining in with her melody.

A drop splashed on my face, and I stepped back. I noted the spot where the drips continued to fall. After the storm blew over, I'd ask Serrin to help me fix it. I slid a pot into position to catch the rain.

Our cottage was the largest in the village, but it was run down. The thatched roof needed fixing, and the old hinges could do with some oil, but it was home. I grabbed a rag, stuffing it into the gap between the sash and the window to keep it from rattling.

I remained staring out into the turbulent night. Longing to be out there.

"Tempest… come sit by the fire," my mother said, drawing me away from the storm.

CHAPTER TWO

Tempest

I nestled on the wooden chair in front of the fire. Listening to it crackle and pop as it warmed my chilled skin. My arms slumped on the armrests, my head resting back, as my mother ran the brush through my hair. She blamed herself for what happened to me as a child, so I allowed her this slight contact, knowing it comforted her.

Loud hammering on the door startled us, causing my mother to drop the brush. "Maeve take Lily," my mother said as I stood, grabbing my carved wooden bow from beside the fireplace.

My mother slipped a dagger from its sheath by the door as it shuddered. I raised my bow, notching an arrow. "Who's there?" My mother raised her voice above the pounding.

"It's Serrin!"

She relaxed as she freed the locks, pulling the door open. "What's happened?"

Serrin looked pale as he flew past her, just fitting beneath the door frame. "We need you Tempie. It's my Father…" His words tapered off as he ruffled his copper hair, tilting his head towards the door.

Without pause, I dropped the bow and hurried across the room, gathering my dress so I did not stumble. He bolted into the storm, keeping close enough to shield me, but never coming into contact.

"What happened?" I asked, yelling over the howling wind as it battered against us.

His voice shook as he spoke. "He got struck by lightning. My mother is going to heal him, but it's bad, Tempie." His mother and I were both Nephilim, but I was stronger. The mightier the parent, the more potent the Nephilim. *And my sperm donor was one powerful son of a bitch.*

We rounded my cottage and his mother's cabin came into view. Men and women had gathered outside. A wave of voices greeted us as they moved out of our way.

Serrin flicked his head so his floppy fringe moved out of his face, swinging the door open. Men filled the cabin; many I recognised as being part of the village council. "Come on." Serrin cleared a path for me as we moved through the crowd.

"Morgaan," I said, darting to the table, where she held her hands over Charin's chest. Lightning had left his face charred and his shirt had melted into his skin. The stench of burnt flesh was sickening.

"You have to pull me out if it gets too much," she said, her blue and magenta eyes met mine.

"Let me heal him, Morgaan." My hand hovered above her shoulder, but I could not allow myself to touch her. "I'm stronger and if I need you too, you can pull me back."

She shook her head as tears dripped down her cheek. "I love him more than life itself, Tempest. I am not strong enough to let him die."

Several rules applied when a Nephilim healed. If

Morgaan lacked the strength to finish healing Charin, they would both die. But I could break the contact between them and save Morgaan's life. No one else in the room could. As when healing, we draw the injuries into ourselves, but if we make contact with anyone… the injuries pass to them.

"Are you sure about doing this?" I asked. She nodded, placing her hands on Charin's bare flesh. Nephilim needed direct contact with the skin to heal. And although it caused me pain, to save a life, I endured it.

"Wear these." Serrin handed me a set of suede gloves. If I had to pull Morgaan away from Charin, they would make it less unpleasant.

"Are you ready?" I asked, taking position behind her.

"Yes." Morgaan's breath shuddered as her magic swelled around us. The air thickened, and those that lingered in the cabin stepped back. Charin's burns were deep and his chest wheezed as he fought to draw breath.

Wings unfurled from Morgaan's back as she transformed. They were delicate, shimmering as if made of glass. Her skin took on a bluish tinge as she leant over the table.

I remained ready as the tremor of her hands spread through her body. It would take a lot more power to heal Charin's internal injuries. A soft whimper escaped her lips.

"What's happening?" Serrin remained at my side. His eyes transfixed on his mother and father. *If I failed… he would lose both of his parents tonight.*

"She is doing okay. The lightning has damaged his heart and liver, but the worst injury is to his brain." Morgaan's heart raced as she absorbed Charin's injuries into herself. *She'd have one hell of a headache in the morning.*

I let my magic mingle with hers, sensing the throb of brain activity within Charin. Morgaan's teeth clenched as a stifled scream pierced the air.

"Tempest?" Serrin edged closer to his mother.

"She's fine… I promise." The pressure in the air grew as Morgaan's body spasmed.

"Pull her back," Serrin said, barking his command. But I stayed in place, waiting. She was fine, for now at least. Morgaan wailed as she fought to keep hold of Charin as they both convulsed under the strain. "I said pull her back, Tempest."

"She can do this. Just give her a minute." Serrin squared up to me, standing tall as he glared down at me. My teeth clenched as I stood my ground.

"Get. Her. Back. Now, Tempest! Or so help me…" Serrin lunged, trying to grab me, but I stepped aside and he sailed past. He caught himself before he sprawled across the floor. I stayed put. His mother's life depended on me being ready.

"Restrain him." My command echoed through the room. Two men rushed forward, grabbing his arms as they dragged him back. "I won't let her die, Serrin."

He watched on as Morgaan's wails got louder and he fought against those holding him.

"Tempest…"

"*Quiet!* Or they will both die." Silence fell around me as I watched. *Come on, Morgaan… you can do this.* A screech reverberated from her throat, and she collapsed over Charin.

Everyone waited tensely to see if they had survived. But I could already feel the steady beating of both Charin's and Morgaan's hearts. "Let him go." I cast a quick glance over my shoulder at Serrin. He shoved the men aside as he pushed his way towards me.

He hesitated as I scowled at him. "Are they alive?"

"You're welcome." I barked as I stormed away towards the cabin door. "Try to touch me again, Serrin, and I will *rip* your dick off!"

"Tempie… I'm sorry," Serrin said, his voice fading as I rushed out into the storm. I balled my hands, charging into the onslaught of rain. I ran until I reached the meadow, knowing no one would be brave enough to follow me.

The storm comforted me as I howled, carrying away the sound. *Serrin had tried to touch me!* He was my best friend, and he betrayed my trust.

I lost track of how long I stood alone. Men trickled out of the cabin, but not one spared a glance in my direction as they hurried to their homes.

Candlelight beamed on the porch of my cottage, illuminating my mother. She watched and waited until I crossed the meadow. The light fading as she returned inside.

CHAPTER THREE

Tempest

I stepped onto the porch, sensing Serrin's presence, before I saw him leaning against the old railings.

"Careful you don't fall." My brows pinched, and I pursed my lips. "It'd be a shame to have to *fix* the railings." He pushed off them with a chuckle, stepping towards me.

His wet clothes clung to his skin, showing off his sinewy muscles as he shivered. With drooped shoulders, he edged towards me with a blanket clutched in his hands.

"Please don't rip my cock off." He grinned as he placed the blanket over my arms, being careful not to touch me.

"I would have sent the women of the village into *mourning.*" Even as he laughed heartily, throwing his head back, I could see the dullness in his eyes. "Serrin I…"

"Tempie, I am so sorry." He cut me off. "I lost my Gods damned mind back there. It's no excuse, I know… I just…" His smile vanished when our eyes met. I bit my lip to hide its tremble. I knew he didn't mean to hurt me, but it still stung. "Please, I'll do anything to make it right."

I wanted to be mad at him... but Serrin was family. Whenever I was in trouble, he was the first person I turned to, and he never let me down. Even when I got lost in my mind, he could make me smile. I was tough and prickly, yet Serrin didn't care. *But I wouldn't let him off the hook so easily.*

"Anything?" I asked, with a smirk teasing the corners of my mouth.

"Just name it Tempie." *Oh, this was going to be fun.*

"I'll need some time to consider it. *But...* I could use a hand fixing the roof. *Oh*, and the doors are creaking, and a nice, cooked meal sounds good. Maybe you could be my hired muscle for a week... no, a *month*."

He shook his head as the familiar glint returned to his dazzling blue eyes. "Anything else, my Queen?"

I couldn't help but chuckle as he bowed. "*Well...*"

He is almost here, Little Nephilim. Run! The storm called. Lightning illuminating the sky, splitting the meadow, causing me to jump.

"They're speaking again, aren't they?" Serrin turned towards the storm with a scowl. They only ever brought bad news. "What is it saying?"

"It's telling me to run. Death is coming for me." I sighed, stepping towards Serrin as his jaw tensed.

"Are you going to?" he asked without turning towards me.

"No." I shrugged. "Who would make *you* fix the roof if I left?" As if in response, lightning struck again, chasing the shadows from half of his face. His hand slid across the railings, stopping just shy of mine.

I gazed at his calloused hand. My finger twitched, almost brushing against his. Thunder crashed, stirring me from my trance.

The absence of touch often left me feeling alone, but I could never bring myself to allow it. My heart raced, and I pulled away as I removed the soft suede gloves. "Please give these to your mother." I placed them over the railing before heading to the door.

"Tempie," Serrin muttered, but I kept walking. I gripped the handle, resting my head against the door. The wood creaked as Serrin leant against the cottage. "Are you okay?"

I swallowed as I felt the heat of his gaze. "Yeah." He didn't back away as I angled my head to look up at him. "Ever craved something you don't really want?"

"I once craved Mac's pickled herrings?" I almost wretched at the thought.

"Gods Serrin… I hope you didn't..." I shuddered.

"Hell no." His chuckle was infectious, and I stifled a giggle with my hand. "Please do not suggest I eat one to make amends. You mean the world to me, Tempie. But I won't, not even for you."

"Hey, I'm not *that* mean!" I pouted.

"Seriously though, Tempie, are you alright?" I nodded, sighing with a smile.

"I'm good, *really*. It's just there are moments, when the loneliness gets bad, that I wish I could be closer to people and feel them physically. But I still don't want anyone to touch me," I said, clicking the handle and pushing the door open.

"I wish I could take the pain from you, Tempest. If I can do anything, just ask, okay?"

I nodded, turning away from him. "Will you come by in the morning?"

"Sure." He smiled as he rested his hand on the door. "I have to make things right, remember?"

"*Oh*, I won't forget it." I poked my tongue out as he gave a playful salute.

"Goodnight." I watched as he sauntered into the darkness,

closing the door behind him. I hurried to my room before my mother could chastise me again.

Maeve was already dozing, so I shut the door without making a sound. Troubling thoughts swamped my mind as I crawled onto my bed, uncaring that I was soaking.

In a moment of madness, I came close to touching Serrin. *What had I been thinking? Gods, I need to get a grip.* I stared up at the ceiling as I let my mind wander.

Once I had pulled myself together, I slid off the bed and freed my corset. Checking, Maeve was still asleep as I shimmied into a satin nightdress.

I took in the sodden bed, shuddering as a chill set in. *Damn it, Tempest!* Clutching my blankets, I crept across the room to avoid waking Maeve. Careful not to slip as I made my way downstairs.

The candles had gone out. Only the flicker of the dying fire lit my way. I flopped onto the chair beside the hearth, wrapping the blanket around me to ease my shivering. The rain's patter was the only sound as I drifted off.

Lily's soft wail roused me from my sleep. I threw the blanket aside before climbing the groaning stairs. The door whined as I slunk into my mother's room. Inhaling the familiar lavender incense.

"Tempest?" she asked.

"I've got her," I said, lifting Lily from the carved wooden crib that was once mine. I ran my fingertips across the mahogany. The familiar enchantments within the timber sent a warming sensation through my body. It was the only thing my father had ever given me. He'd left it in my mother's bedroom the day he disappeared.

I shimmied towards the door. "Get some more sleep." It was pointless for both of us to be awake.

After I sat down, Lily snuggled into me and I wrapped my blanket around her. Her eyelids drooped as she drifted in and out of sleep until I heard the floorboards creak above me. Maeve and my Mother were awake.

I tucked Lily into her bassinet before heading to the porch to gather firewood. The air was fresh now the storm had passed. An uneasy feeling crept over me as I scanned the forest. As if something lurked beyond the trees. Watching and waiting. *Now I was imagining things.*

"I'll sort breakfast." Maeve startled me as I crossed to the fire.

"Shit! Maeve." I almost dropped the logs. She had a habit of making me jump.

"Sorry," she said, trying not to grin. "What do you fancy? We have oats or some leftover bread and I swear I saw some bacon."

I tossed the logs into the fire, striking the flint and watching as flames flickered to life. "I wouldn't turn down some bacon." As if in response, my stomach grumbled.

"Oh, you should probably change. Mother needs you to go hunting." My mother always avoided entering the woods after a storm, so I wasn't surprised that she would ask me to go.

My mother had not left her room as I slipped into mine. I threw on a soft linen blouse and my favourite leather hunting trousers. Before pulling my hair into a tight bun, leaving a few loose wisps to frame my face.

"Tempie," my mother said, rapping on my bedroom door as she passed.

"I'll be right down." I fastened my leather waistcoat into

place and hurried down the stairs. Almost groaning out loud as the aroma of bacon and eggs reached me.

"Is Serrin coming by this morning?" Mother asked. *Here we go again...*

"Yes," I shovelled the bacon down as I eyed her suspiciously.

"You should invite him to dinner," she said with a smile, ignoring the subtle shake of my head. "Maybe you should cook for him."

"What are you up to today, Maeve?" I changed the subject before my mother could make me feel anymore awkward. Regardless that I told her a million times that Serrin and I were just friends, she always insisted on trying to push us together.

"I don't know." She shrugged. "Can I come with you?"

"Not this time." She pouted as she finished the last of her eggs. "You could pick some vegetables from the garden to help me out."

"*Okay...*" she drawled. Getting to my feet, I gathered the empty plates from the table. Before I slipped on my leather boots, tightening the laces that ran from my foot to my knee.

"I'll be back soon," I said, scooping up my bow as I swung the quiver over my shoulder.

"Be careful out there Tempest." I blew my mother a kiss as her eyes drifted to the window.

"Aren't I always?" Obviously, my mother did not think so as her brows rose.

"Serrin's here." Maeve waved through the window as he climbed the steps of the porch. I pushed the door ajar to meet him.

"My mother asked me to give you this." He held out a small box decorated with gold inlay.

"There's no need for payment. I literally did *nothing*." I crossed my arms across my chest.

"You did, and you know it." I went to argue, but he shook his head as he sighed. "Take the *damn* box, Tempie." He shoved it into my hands before I could refuse. I never liked accepting gifts in return for healing, especially when I was only there as a precaution.

I knew Morgaan well enough to know she'd insist, even if I told Serrin to return it. So, I released the ornate clasp to find the most beautiful ear cuff I had ever seen. Thin gold twisted like a vine with leaves. The moment I touched it, I felt its magic stirring beneath my fingertips.

"Where did she get this?" Serrin lifted the cuff, unaware of the power it held.

"Her father gave it to her, along with a heap of other useless trinkets," he said, scowling. Morgaan's father had split, just as mine had.

Serrin secured the cuff around my left ear, framing it as the enchantments permanently fastened it in place. "It suits you."

"Thanks. How is Charin doing?" I asked, and his smile slipped.

"He is alive because of you."

"Don't you dare get all emotional on me." I wiggled my finger at him with a playful wink. His dimples appeared as he smiled. That's probably why all the girls pursued him. *Not that he minded, of course.*

"You had to go and hurt my ego. Now I will have to prove my masculinity," he said, and I stifled a laugh.

"*Well,* I have just the thing… Fancy a hunt?"

CHAPTER FOUR

The village was bustling. Children played in the streets as men and women scoured the market stalls.

All three races made their homes here, creating a unique blend. Fae, the elites, with ferocious magic that raised them above the rest. They were beautiful, fierce, and arrogant. With a few exceptions, of course. *I was nothing like them. Just a forbidden reject of their kind.*

Then there was the lesser Fae. They looked human, but had magic of their own. And the lowest race was the humans. Their vast numbers were the only notable thing about them. *I only wished to be one of them. Just another nobody in the crowd.*

We had everything we needed, right here in Grimfell. Our village was hidden in No Man's Land. A small wedge of land that separated two countries. Stidahl to the north and Ustraya to the south. We were safe here as long as we avoided crossing the barriers into either country. The only thing they agreed on was that Nephilim deserved to die.

Very few people dared venture into No Man's Land. My mother blamed it on the fact magic was weaker here. *But it was home to me.*

"Sooooo, my mother wants to invite you for dinner," I said as I walked beside Serrin.

"She's *still* trying to set us up?" he asked with a chuckle as he made his way towards the stables.

"Yep." I grimaced. "You should hurry and ask Molly to court you, then she will stop." I glanced across at the bakery her father owned. Despite flirting with Molly for years, Serrin never committed.

"Should I now?" He grinned, flashing his dimples.

"I thought you liked her? Besides, she is head over heels for you." I bat my lashes as Molly often did when speaking to Serrin.

"I do… It just hasn't been the right time." Serrin beelined for the stables, no doubt to avoid our conversation.

"Hey Sammy, bring us two horses." He signalled towards the small grimy stable boy.

"Hi, Tempest," Sammy said with a grin as he held out his hand to Serrin for payment. "That's twenty-four coppers."

"That's steep… You're not trying to fleece me, are you, Sammy?" Serrin asked with a frown.

I stifled a laugh as Sammy stuck his tongue out. He was a good kid, but he was sneaky.

"*Fine*. Eighteen Coppers."

"Make it sixteen and we will clean the horses down when we return." Serrin held out his hand for Sammy, who scrunched up his nose as he considered the offer.

"For Tempest it's a deal."

I smiled, thanking him as Serrin handed him the coppers. I glanced around the market as Serrin followed Sammy to collect the horses. Until I noticed a misty spirit trying to gain the attention of a young man.

"War is heading this way, Dylan. Run, son. Before it's too late." She sang out in her attempt to reach him.

"Tempie?" Serrin asked, making me jump. I had been so focused on the spirit I'd not heard him return with the horses.

"I think we might need to warn the village." The warnings were too prevalent to ignore.

"Okay," he said. I had expected him to argue after the last commotion I had caused. But he had a sombre expression as he watched the villagers milling around.

"Let's hunt, then we will speak to my father."

"Is he well enough to see me?"

"Yes. My mother mentioned something about receiving warnings, but she is still recovering." Morgaan rarely heard the spirits, so if she had… we could be in serious trouble.

Serrin handed me the reins of the smaller chestnut mare. It nuzzled me as I stroked her glossy fur. Thankfully, my dislike of touch did not extend to animals.

I hauled myself onto the saddle as we guided the horses through the village and across the meadow. My skin prickled with goosebumps as I still sensed someone watching me from within the trees.

"Keep your eyes out," I said as we ventured deeper into the forest.

"Everything okay?" Serrin pulled up beside me, gripping the hilt of his dagger.

"The storm has me on edge. I swear I am losing my mind." I faked a smile as we headed on towards the river that divided the forest. Serrin and I had visited it often, but I had never learnt to swim. So, I would sit on the banks, dipping my toes in the cold water as Serrin swam.

We positioned ourselves downwind, as animals often congregated by the river to drink or fish.

"Look, there…" Serrin pointed towards fresh deer tracks. A twig snapped, and I spun my head, just glimpsing something as it disappeared behind a tree.

"What was that?" I watched for whatever I saw to pass the tree, but nothing appeared.

"I didn't see anything." Serrin led his horse the way I had seen the blurred creature. Or it could have been a person. It all happened so fast I couldn't be sure.

"Right there. I could have sworn it ducked behind that tree."

He shrugged as he scanned the area. "There's nothing here now." That did not ease my concerns.

"Let's get this over with and get the fuck out of here." I was eager to leave. Regardless of whether my imagination was running wild or if I actually caught sight of something.

"Just stay close to me." Serrin led us through the forest, tracking the path until we could hear the roar of the river.

"Over there…" Serrin whispered as he pointed towards a deer as it grazed in a clearing. I lifted my bow, drawing in a breath as I notched an arrow. *Easy Tempest…*

"Run! Death knows you are here, Nephilim!" I startled as a spirit wailed. The arrow sped away, missing the deer and giving away our presence.

"Fuck, *Tempie*!" Serrin cursed. I grabbed a second arrow, drawing the bow strings taught and releasing it. It sank deep into its flank before it could vanish out of sight.

We bolted through the trees after it, and Serrin tossed his dagger. Hitting its mark and bringing the deer down.

"What happened back there?" Serrin asked as he dismounted his horse, retrieving his dagger.

"A spirit…" My words dwindled as I grimaced. I felt stupid jumping at every little noise.

"Should we be worried?" Serrin asked as he dropped beside the deer. Resting his hands on it, he mumbled prayers to thank the Gods for the plentiful hunt. *Why did he even bother?* Serrin hated the Gods to the same extent as me.

"*Tempest.*" He shot a stern look at me as I failed to recite the prayers.

"*What?* I'm not doing it, and neither should you." My mother would have thrown a fit if she had heard my sacrilegious words.

"It doesn't matter what I think of the Gods. I won't risk their wrath." *Seriously!*

"I think we should say thanks to the deer instead. Its sacrifice means we will have food on the table. That one animal has done more for my family than the Gods *ever* have." Serrin rolled his shoulders, turning his back on me as he hefted the deer over his shoulders. *Show off!*

"If you want to risk it, be my guest," he chuckled. "Now scoot back. The deer will take up my horse." I slid back in the saddle as he secured it.

Serrin mounted before me, leaving enough room that we were not touching. Over the years, he'd learnt how to make me feel close to him without physical contact.

I tightened my grip on the saddle as we rode back through the forest. Avoiding the area I had seen the wailing spirit.

The village was still busy as we crossed the meadow to the porch of my mother's cottage.

I pushed the door wide open. "We're back."

I heard my mother calling to Maeve as I returned to help Serrin.

"Oh *Tempest*," my mother said as a smile creased her lips. "Well done, both of you. Serrin dear, why don't you join us for dinner? My way of saying thank you."

"I would love to Mrs Beaumont." I shot Serrin a frustrated look, making him chuckle.

"You two go have fun. I'll take care of this."

"We'll be back soon, anyway. I just want to check on

Morgaan and Charin." I knew if I told her the real reason for my visit, she would worry. So, I smiled and took the reins of my horse, heading back towards the stables.

Sammy was waiting by the time we got there, with buckets filled with brushes. I set to work, running a grooming brush over the chestnut mare as my mind wandered over how I would tell Charin.

The last time I'd been mistaken, it hadn't gone down well with the village council. They made me clean their meeting rooms for over a month as punishment.

"You're doing the right thing," Serrin said.

"Huh?" I had been so lost in thought I had not noticed him watching me.

"I know that look on your face. You're worried about telling my father about the storm and the spirits." He knew me too well.

"I don't want to cause a panic if it's nothing."

"And if it's not… you would never forgive yourself." I could only hope they *were* wrong!

We finished grooming the horses and took our time scouring the market, buying a few supplies along the way. Serrin remained at my back, using his body so no one would brush against me in the crowds.

By the time we got to Charin's the sun was setting and I hesitated, fidgeting with my fingers. "Maybe we should just wait till the morning," I said, but Serrin rolled his eyes, hauling the door open and calling to his father.

I followed him inside as Charin took a seat at the end of the table. He appeared significantly healthier than he had last night. By looking at him, you'd never have known he had almost died.

"I'm glad you stopped by, Tempest. We owe you a debt of gratitude for what you did for us last night." I pulled out a chair, hiding my hands beneath the table as they trembled.

"I'm glad to see you're looking much better. How is Morgaan doing?" I glanced towards the stairs. The cabin seemed empty without her.

"She is resting, but doing well. Now, I'm guessing you wanted something?" Charin asked as he glanced between Serrin and I.

I explained everything the storm had warned me of. "Do you believe it?" he asked, and I shrugged.

"I don't know, but I couldn't ignore it." I watched as Charin rubbed his jaw as he contemplated. A long silence prevailed, and when he next spoke, Serrin and I both jumped.

"I will meet with the council in the morning. But in the meantime, Tempest… please be careful. Morgaan also warned me that Death, whoever he is, wants you."

"I will," I said as Serrin helped him to his feet.

"I should stay with Tempest until we know more." Serrin grabbed a pack that sat by the stairs as he followed his father.

"I am not some damsel in distress." I pouted.

"Of course, you're not. I feel *sorry* for anyone that tries to get to you. But an extra pair of hands to help protect your mother, Maeve, and Lily can't hurt."

I sighed, grateful that he cared enough to want to protect them. It had been just the four of us since Maeve and Lily's father died.

I said my goodbyes to Charin, and we headed home. The deer was no longer on the porch and the aroma of cooking venison reached me as I stepped inside.

Lily was the first to spot us and she ran to Serrin, who scooped her up in his arms.

"Are you staying, Serrin?" my mother asked as she raised an eyebrow at me from the kitchen. "Why don't you freshen up before dinner? Tempest, fill the tub." I pouted as he smirked at me. *Ass!*

I made an obscene gesture, being careful my mother did

not see as I slunk to the bathing room, knowing Serrin was loving this. *So much for him making amends.*

I warmed water in a cauldron over the small fire before pouring it into the bath. *Hmmm...I wonder.* My mother's scented oil collection sat on a shelf and I searched through them, sniffing each one. *Perfect... Serin would smell lovely after his bath.* I added more drops than was necessary as I smirked to myself, hurrying downstairs.

"Your bath is ready, my Lord." I curtsied with as much sarcasm as I could muster.

"*Tempest*!" My mother frowned as she chastised me. Serrin stifled a laugh as he headed upstairs.

"I might go foraging in the morning," Maeve said when I joined her at the table. She straightened her skirt as she flicked her untamed locks.

The flush of her cheeks showed she was plotting something. Either she would come home with bunches of flowers insisting I give them to Serrin, or she was sneaking off to see Tamas, the son of the blacksmith.

"Foraging, *huh*?" I asked, chuckling as she turned away, trying to hide her face as her cheeks reddened further. *Tamas it was.*

"Can you gather some more mushrooms whilst you are at it?" my mother asked as she placed the venison on a platter in the middle of the table. I bit back a laugh as Maeve rolled her eyes.

CHAPTER FIVE

Tempest

I woke as something solid jabbed into my side. "Tempest!" Serrin hissed as he pressed a finger to his lips. I jolted upright, rubbing my bleary eyes.

"What's going on?" I asked in a whisper as I clambered from the bed, looking around. *Maeve's was already empty!*

Serrin crossed the room, nudging the curtain as he peered out, keeping his back pressed against the wall. *What was he looking at?* I edged towards him, peeking out the window, but saw nothing unusual. "What the hell Ser…"

"Sush!" He darted across the room, signalling me to follow him. We crept down the stairs to find my mother, clinging to Lily as she stood in the darkness.

I opened my mouth to speak when a shadow crossed in front of the window by the door. As the handle twisted, my heart started racing.

"Stay back!" I hissed to my mother as I snuck to the fire-place, clutching the bow and taking aim. I remained hidden in the shadows, holding my breath. Serrin gripped his dagger as he took position between my mother and the door.

The locks held, and the sounds of a scuffle echoed from outside. Staying out of sight, I edged closer. Pressing my ear to the door as I heard voices.

"Fayolan's orders are to hunt and kill all the Ustrayan scum." The voice was gruff and deep.

"And the villagers?" a female voice asked.

"They are nothing more than criminals and vagrants. Locate the Nephilim and kill everyone that gets in the way." *Fuck! They knew about me!*

The voices faded as heavy footsteps creaked down the porch steps. *We had to get out of here!*

I spun to my mother. "Where's Maeve? We need to go… Now!" Panic flared across my mother's face.

"I thought she was upstairs," she said as she clutched Lily tighter. *Dammit!* Her basket was gone… she was in the forest!

"I think Maeve has gone foraging… I'll go find her. Serrin, get my Mother and Lily out of here!"

Serrin darted for the door, blocking me before I could wrench it open. "Like Hell you are Tempie!"

"I…" My mother cut me off, attempting to hand Lily to me.

"You will do no such thing!" she snapped, as her piercing gaze locked with mine. "Take Lily and go with Serrin to safety. I will look for *my* daughter."

I motioned my head from side to side, facing them both. "Lily needs her mother, and if they catch you all with me, you're as good as dead. Serrin, *please* take my mother to safety. Charin will need you as well. Whoever they are… they know there are Nephilim here."

"I'll come with you," Serrin argued.

I spun on him with a huff. "No, I am faster alone and I

refuse to put you in harm's way. Get my mother to safety and help your parents. Right now, *they* need you more. I *will* bring Maeve home!"

Serrin flung the door open, stepping away so I could glance outside. Around forty men clashed in the meadow. The white and blue sigil of Ustraya mixed with the yellow and red of Stidahl. But one man drew my gaze.

He carved through the Ustrayan soldiers as if they were nothing. *Death!* My pulse quickened as several of them bolted for the forest, with the man closing in behind them. *They would not get far.*

As the man disappeared into the trees, I took off, my mother crying after me. I hurried down the porch, slowing as I reached the boundary of the cottage. I panted heavily as I glanced around the corner, seeing the chaos as men fought desperately to guide their families to safety.

"Help!" a woman screamed as a large soldier in silver armour advanced towards her. I drew my bow and shot an arrow, piercing the soldier's leg. He howled as he stumbled, allowing the woman to escape.

I bolted before he could gather himself. Stidahlian and Ustrayan soldiers were everywhere. I dodged and weaved through the village as I navigated my way to the stables.

The chestnut mare was still in its stall and I swung the gate open, grabbing the reins as it reared up. The horse bolted, and I mounted on the run, but it snorted and bucked.

"Calm," I said, letting my magic soothe it. "I can't heal myself, so I would appreciate you not *killing* me." We burst from the stables, and villagers fled before they could get trampled beneath the horse's hooves.

I spotted Serrin shepherding my mother and Lily away, with Charin aiding Morgaan. He scowled as our eyes met, the blue of his now much darker. Serrin lifted his hand, clutching my large dagger in it.

With a nudge of my knee, I angled the horse towards him. Plucking it from his hand as I charged past. Not slowing as I crossed out of the village.

I stared across the meadow. The small battle was still waging, blocking the most direct route to the forest. Yesterday, the meadow had been serene and filled with beauty. Today it ran red with blood and spirits that still did not realise their fate.

I yanked the reins, guiding the horse past my cottage, sparing it one last glance. It quickened its pace, barrelling through the outskirts of the meadow. I clutched the reins tighter and pressed myself against the mare's neck.

"It's the Nephilim! Stop her!" someone yelled. Men in Stidahlian armour reacted, converging on me. An arrow whizzed by, the feathers brushing my cheek as it missed me by a hair's breadth.

I kept going, just focusing on breathing as we reached the trees. They creaked and groaned as if trying to warn me of the danger that awaited. Not that I needed it… *I knew who was coming for me!*

"Go Little Nephilim. Death is here!" A wail echoed around me, causing the horse to rear up, dumping me to the rough ground. I landed on my back, knocking the breath from my lungs with a huff.

I rolled to my stomach, curling up as I gasped for air. Stars shimmered at the edge of my vision as I lay motionless, watching my horse flee further into the forest.

"Come on!" I threw a handful of dirt after the vanishing horse. *Just what I fucking needed.* I pulled myself up, shaking the dirt and leaves off me.

"Death has you in his sights, Nephilim. Get as far away as you can," the spirit called out again.

"I *heard* you the *first* time," I said through my teeth as I watched the spirit weaving amongst the trees. His face distorted as he phased in and out. Edging closer. I'd never seen the spirits behave this way.

I shuddered as he vanished and goosebumps broke out across my skin. *Where had it gone?* A hand gripped my shoulder, and I shrieked. Spinning to see the spirit's empty black eyes staring into mine. *He was right in my face. How...* I uttered a cry as he entered my body.

Visions swirled in my head. I was no longer stood in the forest but inside a magnificent palace with large wooden doors. Gold inlay that matched my ear cuff decorated the old mahogany.

My boots clanged against the marble floor. Heavy metal armour clad me from head to toe, and the helm I wore restricted my vision.

"Ramos!" a voice bellowed. I whirled around, gripping the sword sheathed at my side.

"I knew you would come for me eventually, Fayolan," I said. My voice was deep and male. *Was I witnessing the spirit's past?* My heart pounded in my ears, and sweat drenched my clammy palms.

"You should have escaped whilst you had the chance." The voice echoed down the corridor. I squinted into the darkness, but I couldn't locate the man the voice belonged to.

"Show yourself!" I commanded. Something darted towards me from the shadows. Piercing through my chest armour, and I roared in pain. Until it subsided, becoming an all over cold and my sight dimmed. The last thing I glimpsed was the talons of a feathered wing.

I gasped as I woke, finding myself alone in the forest. My fingers shook as I clasped my shirt, examining my chest where I had been impaled. *I was unharmed. It had all been in my mind.*

"What the *fuck*?" I grumbled as I took a step forward on shaking legs. Scooping up my dagger from the ground where

I had dropped it, I threaded it through my belt, securing it in place.

I suppressed the eerie feeling of being watched as I edged deeper into the trees. If Maeve was foraging mushrooms, she would have headed for the grove near the border to Stidahl.

A scream reached my ears, and my heart pounded in my chest. *Maeve!* I bolted towards her cries for help until they cut off. *Shit!*

I reached the spot I had last heard the screams. Her basket lay upturned, its contents scattered across the forest floor. "Gods no!" My breath came in heavy gasps as I fought the rising panic. *She had to be close by...*

My mind swam as I searched for any clue. Then I spotted it… a scarlet handprint. The blood was smeared on a log close to her basket. I rested my hand over it. The crimson print was barely smaller than my own. *Clever girl… Maeve was leaving me a trail.*

I lifted my bow and strung an arrow while I tracked the tiny beads of blood scattered across the leaves. I clenched my jaw and persevered through the throbbing all over my body as I advanced farther into the woods. My back ached from falling from the horse, and a mild trickle of blood ran down my neck.

The sound of wailing spirits grew as I felt the buzz of the barrier to Stidahl. I could feel it zapping my skin as I reached out. The moment my fingers touched the wards, a painful jolt of energy ran through my hand, making my guts roil. *Gods! Please tell me Maeve had not crossed the boundaries?*

Looking beyond it, I spotted another smeared bloody print upon a boulder. My legs gave way beneath me, and I sank to the ground. There was only one reason Maeve would have crossed the barrier. *Stidahlian warriors had her!*

"Argh!" I dug my hands into the soil as I howled. If I

crossed and they caught me, I was dead. *If I didn't go, Maeve was.*

I clambered up, my bow drawn with an arrow notched as I rammed my way through the barrier. A sharp pain ripped through me, blurring my vision. I staggered ahead with clenched teeth, pushing against the agony until it eased.

A refreshing breeze kissed me as I stepped away from the wards. The magic in Stidahl was overpowering as it tingled against my skin. My mother had not been mistaken about how weak it was in Grimfell.

The majority of residents in my village were human, so it had no effect on them. Of course, there were exceptions. Morgaan and I were Fae and Serrin was a lesser Fae, although he showed no signs of magic. Maybe here in Stidahl he would have.

After several moments, the dizziness, and ringing in my ears settled. I pushed on until I reached a clearing with a lake. *It was beautiful!* The sun's rays made the water glisten. I drew a deep breath, inhaling the scent of damp grass... *and sweat?*

I almost failed to notice the man dressed in black leather. Darting towards the nearest tree, I pressed my back firmly against it as I stole a glance. He dipped his hands into the lake to drink. His flared ears were barely visible amongst his raven black hair, which cupped the edge of his muscular jaw. *He was a Fae like me.*

Something about him held me, mesmerised by the contours of his thighs. The black leather trousers clung to him like a second skin. My brow arched as I admired him. *He was definitely well-defined in all the right ways!*

A spirit shrieked, but the presence prowling behind him chilled me to the bone. A hulking figure bearing the symbol of Ustraya lurked in the shadows. His beady eyes fixed on me.

CHAPTER SIX

Tempest

The Ustrayan soldier held his bow ready as he advanced. His lips curled as his gaze darted between me and the man at the lake. He edged closer, bow raised towards the unsuspecting stranger.

Adrenaline surged through my veins as he pulled the drawstring taught. I turned to run, but stopped dead in my tracks as I noticed figures moving in the trees. Ustrayan soldiers were closing in, blocking my escape.

I had one option left… Pray the man at the lake would help me. *Here goes fucking nothing!* I glanced back towards him as he crouched, enveloped in shadows. Sweat trickled down my neck as I raised my bow.

I felt the tension of the strings in my hand as I released a slow exhale and loosed the arrow. It flew past the man. He whirled and giant wings burst out of his back. Smoke coated his hand, and he hurled a dagger in my direction.

The world lurched and white-hot pain tore through my

shoulder as I fell to the ground. My hands shook as I reached up to pull the dagger out, howling as it came free. The storm had not lied this time. Death was coming for me... *and I just found him!*

I hoisted myself up as voices rang out around me. But only one made me pause and listen. "Tempest!" Maeve screamed.

"I'm coming!" I pitched forward with a loud cry of pain. My body trembled, and my arm hung loose at my side. "Maeve?"

A heavy mass collided with me. Well-muscled arms wrapped around my chest, dragging me to the ground.

"Don't touch me!" My heart stopped as I realised it was Death who had me in his clutches. He clamped his hand over my mouth to silence me.

"*Shut up!*" His pale golden eyes burned into me. "Do you *want* them to find us?"

"Stop, tou..." He pulled a rag from the shadows around his hand. *How could he do that? I had never heard of magic like it before.* Death wadded up the foul-smelling rag, shoving it into my mouth. Gagging from the taste of dirt and horse that coated it, I fought against him. But he overpowered me, binding my wrists with rough rope.

He stepped back and gestured for silence with a finger to his lips. My chest rose and fell rapidly as I panted to keep from retching. *I had no desire to suffocate on my own vomit!*

"Get up," he barked at me as if I were a disobedient dog. I jumped up and bolted away from him. Pain flared through my shoulder as Death yanked on the rope, forcing me backward, stumbling into him. I bounced off him and landed in a muddy puddle at his feet. *Fucking asshole!*

The grunt he gave as he looked down at me held a hint of amusement. But his menacing expression as he violently dragged me up by my hair was far from humorous.

Death's wings spread wide as he brandished his dagger, already coated in my blood. "Walk or I will kill you, *Nephilim*," he said, spitting the word as if it tasted as foul as the rag in my mouth.

He spun on the ball of his foot and I stumbled behind him, struggling to keep up with his fast pace. Each time I tried to pull away, Death gave a sharp tug on the rope, making my shoulder burn with pain.

My head jerked up, realising he was dragging me away from Maeve as I felt the static of the barrier. *No!* I dug my feet into the muddy ground and hauled back on the rope with every bit of strength I could muster. My movement took Death by surprise and he staggered towards me. *Yes! I could do this!*

He planted his feet before pulling me back towards him. His fingers wrapped around my neck as he hissed in my face. "Stop fighting me. There is no escape for you."

My words were inaudible as I shouted again. Trying to get away from him. Maeve needed me and I had been foolish and saved the man that would soon kill me.

"*Enough!*" He bared his teeth, shoving me away whilst winding the rope around his arm. Shrinking the space between us. "Your resistance is futile. You do not stand a chance against me. Now *move*."

He yanked me forward through the barrier. The magic felt like molten fire burning through my veins. The pain sent my body into spasms. A scowl marred his expression as he saw me writhing on the ground, before he dragged me clear of the barrier.

I panted as the burning subsided and I cautiously brought my hands up to my shoulder. My fingers grazed over the wound and I groaned. Death lowered beside me, leaning over and batting my hands out of the way.

"Let me look at it," he said as he examined my shoulder. I

shuddered and pulled away as my back sunk into the cold mud. "You will live!"

He lifted me by the rope binding my hands and continued to drag me behind him without another word. Each forceful jerk of the rope pulled me further from Maeve. I couldn't bear to imagine her suffering at the hands of our enemies.

We soon emerged on to the meadow, where the last dregs of Ustrayan soldiers fought for survival. The putrid odour of blood was so overpowering that my stomach heaved. The rag flew from my mouth, landing with a moist splatter in a pool at my feet. Death scowled with disgust as I emptied my stomach again… this time at his feet.

When I had nothing left to wretch, he hauled on the rope, escorting me to a stake that was hammered deep into the ground. He bound the rope through a gigantic steel hoop, suspending me high enough that only my toes touched the ground.

Death gave me his back as he called out to a man stalking towards us. "Kalen, watch her!" The green-eyed man scowled as he bared his teeth. Drawing his sword as he approached, running his hand through his blood-soaked brown hair.

"Fayolan! Braedon just arrived with more troops. I sent them to clear the village." Kalen faced away from me as he spoke to Death.

"And the others?" Fayolan asked.

"Reed and Nix are out there," he said, glancing towards the small skirmish.

"Good. We'll spend the night here and move out in the morning." Kalen nodded as he watched Fayolan stalk towards the last of the fighting. "Have my tent put up around her. I want some privacy as I question her." Fayolan did not look back as he gave his commands.

My attention turned to the village, stifling a cry as I saw what remained of my home. Mother's cottage was ablaze with angry red flames. Thick black smoke coated the village and a single tear fell from my cheek.

"Bastards," I said under my breath, watching new spirits run between the burning buildings. Those that meant so much to me were now nothing more than wisps, unaware of their deaths.

I stifled a cry as I saw Morgaan. Her misty form stared at me from across the village as she floated towards me. The sound of her voice reached me as she phased closer. Just as the spirit in the forest had. Beads of sweat rolled down my back while I fought to stay upright.

Morgaan reached out to me. Her eyes were no longer the beautiful blue and magenta they had been. Instead, they were grey and white as mist roiled in them.

"I'm so sorry, Morgaan," I said, keeping my voice low so Kalen would not hear me. I braced and Morgaan slammed into me. Images played in my mind, telling her story from her eyes.

Charin was holding Morgaan up as they ran. Serrin and Mother were just ahead, with Lily wailing in her arms. Morgaan turned back, watching me charging across the meadow *as if I were some damn hero!*

"I'm going after Tempest," Morgaan said, pulling away from Charin.

"Don't be *ridiculous,* woman." He reached out for her, but she stepped away, avoiding him.

"Tempest is right. If they find you hiding a Nephilim, they will kill you all. It's better if I'm not here. I'll find Tempest and keep her safe until we can return."

"*Go!* I will follow soon," Serrin said, shouting over his shoulder. Morgaan sprinted back towards the meadow, ignoring Charin's yells for her to return.

She noticed four Stidahlian warriors charging towards the

village. *She knew she had to stop them!* To provide a window for others to escape.

She drew her sword, and in one swift movement severed the head of the first man. The others lunged, their sword's clashing with Morgaan's until one of them slipped behind her. Pain radiated from her chest. She glanced down as they pulled a sword from her, and everything went black.

My eyes flicked open as her brutal story ended. I struggled against my bindings as I called after Morgaan. "I will join you soon." She phased away, but I couldn't grieve for her now. War did not allow for such things.

"Be still or I'll end you now!" Kalen said with a deep rumble in his voice. He was watching Fayolan and did not glance back.

Fayolan tucked his wings into his back as he swung two black swords. For such a muscular man, he moved with grace and precision. Each swing ended a life. My stomach churned, and I looked away.

Men hurried to erect a large tent around me. They kept their distance. All except Kalen, who remained close by my side.

I dared not look up until a pair of black boots stepped into view. Fayolan had blood splattered across his face, and bits of Gods knew what, in his hair. He looked truly barbaric.

"Did she cause any trouble?" Fayolan asked. Without glancing away.

"Look at her… I could break her with one hand. How much mischief could a small woman like her cause?" Kalen asked.

"Why don't you let me go… then I'll show you just how much," I hissed, fighting against my restraints.

"Show some respect." Kalen's shoulders broadened as he loomed over me. "A creature as pitiful as you should be on your knees before your Prince."

"He is no Prince of mine. This is *not* Stidahl!" I snapped, unable to contain myself. If I were about to meet my end… I'd go out fighting. I knew who Fayolan was. *The Dark Prince of Stidahl… assassin… leader of Stidahl's armies. The King's only son.*

"Feral, isn't she?" Fayolan smirked. "I can take it from here. I require you to gather the others so we can plan for our return to Solis." Kalen dipped his head to Fayolan as he offered me one final scornful look.

Once Kalen had closed the tent flap, Fayolan turned his broad shoulders away. The shadows swirling around him pulsed as magic made the air heavy. A bed of furs appeared in the centre of the tent. It looked large enough to fit at least six grown men.

With another firm flick of his wrist, a polished wooden stand emerged from the shadows. Laden with jet-black leathers, and swords that hummed with power. A shudder ran down my back. Something about them felt unnatural.

Fayolan crossed the tent, tossing his sword onto the stand. His wings had torn through the leather of his Jerkin, leaving it in shreds. He disrobed without seeming to care that I was there.

What remained of the Jerkin landed in a tattered pile on the ground, soon followed by a crimson splattered shirt. I was certain most of the blood was mine.

His back rippled with powerful muscles that were just visible beneath his wings. Other than Morgaan and me, I'd met no one with wings. And none as stunning and lethal as his.

Fayolan grabbed an empty bucket and headed outside to fill it from a nearby rain barrel. I was relieved he had left the tent flap open. The air was thick and clammy, but the fresh breeze that came through was cool on my skin.

I watched as he poured several buckets of water over his

head. Thick rivulets of red ran down his body as the blood washed from his hair. I swallowed sharply as his wings flourished, flinging water off to each side. Fayolan was unlike any man I'd ever seen.

I gaped as his wings cracked and absorbed into his back. Black tattooed raven wings were all that remained in their place. Inked armour glided over his broad shoulders and back, interlocking like a puzzle. His skin looked shredded as if the realistic armour had ripped from within him, just as I had seen his wings do. And his arms were a canvas of tattooed chain mail and scales.

I tilted my head down when he turned, his gaze making my cheeks flush with heat. Even the slightest movement caused pain from my wound to flare. I sucked in several heated words. Fayolan heard them. His scowl deepened and, once again, the air became heavy.

"Heal yourself!" he demanded, and I laughed with a snort. *Was he serious?* Fayolan advanced on me, his closeness sending dread coursing through me.

"I can't," I bit back, returning Death's hateful stare.

"If you don't, you'll die." He watched me with a sneer.

"Then I'll die," I agreed with a haughty shrug. My body sagged with exhaustion, and I exhaled a frustrated sigh.

"We will see," he grunted, heading to the bed of furs. Fayolan lowered himself down and lay with his hands behind his head, observing me as if waiting for me to heal myself. *Did he not know I couldn't? How was it possible that he was unaware of my limitations? This could work to my advantage… If I didn't bleed out first.*

CHAPTER SEVEN

My eyes sprang open as I swung my arm out instinctively, my dagger halting just before it bit into Kalen's neck. He chuckled and swiped my hand away. "Do you have a death wish?" I asked as I lowered my blade.

"Just saying… if you plan to kill the Nephilim, at least put her outside. The tent will stink." My eyes shot to the woman. Her head hung limp, and the only sign of life was the gentle expansion and contraction of her ribcage.

"*Fuck!*" I leapt from the bed, stepping in the pool of blood at her feet. "I *told* her to heal." I brushed her torn shirt aside as I inspected the wound. *Stubborn woman!*

I pressed my fingers around the gash, and her head shot up as she glared at me.

"Don't touch me!" she screamed, writhing to get away from me. *Dammit. She was going to hurt herself more!*

"I will not hurt you." I knew from experience what some

men did to women like her… but that was one line I would *never* cross. But even with my promise, she did not calm.

I sighed, backing away just to stop her cries of pain. Her kaleidoscope eyes flared as she scowled at me. *She certainly had fight!*

"You're not as courageous now, are you?" I asked, enjoying the pout on her face. Few people had the gall to stand up to me. But she had more fight than any woman I'd met. *Well, apart from Nix.*

"She's so small. You should see the one in the village." Kalen smirked as his gaze roamed over the Nephilim. When Braedon had first told me he had seen her in the forest, I had not believed him. I had faced many of her kind and never once had I seen one of her size.

"She tried to kill me." I smirked, stepping closer so my breath fanned her face. Her long, thick lashes fluttered as she scowled.

"I *didn't* try to *kill* you!" she said, hissing through gritted teeth. "I saved you."

"So, you *didn't* shoot an arrow at me?" She rolled her eyes whilst letting out a sharp breath.

"If I had been aiming for you, I would *not* have missed." *I could never believe a word out of her mouth. She's a Nephilim, after all.*

"Enough of your lies. If you refuse to heal yourself, then I will stitch the wound!" Her nostrils flared as she pulled away.

Kalen searched his pack before handing me the small kit. She would soon change her mind about healing herself. She would not get the luxury of having the area numbed, and if she wouldn't do it herself, I would make her feel every stitch.

I snickered as she gave me a fierce look. She realised Kalen was closing in. "Hold her." The moment his hand met with her skin; a pained expression marred her face. It was as if his touch physically hurt her. The Nephilim let out an ear-piercing scream and Kalen jumped back, releasing her.

"What the *fuck?*" he uttered through clenched teeth. "You should just *end* her." The Nephilim's upper lip lifted in a snarl and she pulled away.

"We are not barbarians. I would kill any man that ravaged a woman's body. Now stand still and let me…"

"No!" She did not flinch as I towered over her. My fists clenching as my breath became ragged.

"*No?*" I asked, and she responded with a head shake. "You are in no position to refuse me. You *owe* me and I intend to take my pound of flesh."

"I owe *you* nothing." Her lips almost brushed mine as she glared up at me. "I was trying to save you."

"I do not need saving, I am…"

"Death!" she cut me off as she spat on the floor at my feet. I backhanded her cheek, leaving a red welt. I took a few deep breaths while attempting to calm myself. *She was starting to irritate me.*

"Heal or I'll do it. Choose now." She refused, shaking her head in defiance.

"I won't heal," she said as she blinked back tears. Not of fear… The little Nephilim wasn't afraid of me. But there was something else hidden in their depths… *Gods, why did it even matter to me in the first place? If she wasn't scared of me now, she would learn to be once we reached Solis.*

I freed the rope from the metal ring, allowing her to lower her arms as she dropped to her feet. Kalen remained ready, with his hand clutching the hilt of his dagger. Just in case the Nephilim tried to finish what she started back at the lake.

Employing a deft flick of my wrist, I pulled a wet cloth from the aether. I reached out, intending to lower her top, but the Nephilim hissed, pulling away.

"I can do it myself!" She slid her shirt aside, exposing the deep wound. She winced as she gently cleaned the area. Once she was done, she dropped the cloth to her feet with a subtle smirk. *Gods, help me! She seemed intent on pushing my buttons.*

She winced as I pushed the needle into her, careful that I did not touch her with my hand. The Nephilim's face remained cold and uncaring as I worked.

Kalen was on edge, clutching his dagger each time I pierced her, but she remained unnervingly still. The slight hitch of her breath was the only sign that she felt any pain.

"You're lucky I wasn't aiming to kill you." If I had been, my dagger would have pierced straight through her heart.

"You call this *luck*?" She snorted as she shook her head.

"Watch your tongue!" Kalen said as he slightly unsheathed his dagger. I extended my arm to stop him.

"Why didn't you?" she asked. "Aim to kill me, I mean." I intended to, but something had stopped me.

"You may have information I need." I wouldn't let a single Nephilim live. *Not even her.* She would eventually fall at my hand.

"Information like what?"

"How long have you lived here?" She shrugged, glaring ahead. She could fight me all she liked, but I had ways of making her talk. "*Answer* me, Nephilim." I dug the needle deeper, and she hissed as she bit back a small cry.

"Go to hell, *Death*!" I've been called much worse, but the venom behind her words almost stung. I intended to have fun breaking this one.

"Tsk! After I just patched you up? I will send you there first." She scowled as I finished up, holding my hand out for Kalen's dagger to cut the thread.

She remained still as I grabbed the rope and returned it to the ring. Her seductively veiled eyes met mine as I hauled her arms above her head. With a sigh, I slackened the rope. The last thing I needed was for her to rip the stitches.

She tested the extra leeway before lowering herself down the pole, resting her head back. I smirked as she wriggled, failing to find a comfortable position. *Good!*

She scowled as she noticed the expression on my face, and I could not suppress the chuckle that escaped. She made an obscene gesture, so I gave her my back, which would only frustrate her more.

"If you insist on keeping her alive… be careful. Female Nephilim are seductresses," Kalen warned, keeping a watchful eye on me. She let out a sharp laugh. It lacked the gentle tone you would expect from a woman as beautiful as her. She'd laced it with venom. Kalen spun, glaring at her as if he could not believe her insolence.

"Vicious isn't she?" I chuckled. "She *will* learn to show me respect." Again, she snorted. I stepped between her and Kalen before he lost his temper and killed her.

I signalled to the entrance, and he scowled, turning his back on her. "Don't *go* anywhere." Without looking back, I knew she was cursing me.

Silence filled the air as I stepped outside. I had managed to get enough men here to stop the Ustrayan's reaching Stidahl, but my main army lay in wait at the mountain pass. I had spies everywhere, but they almost missed the small force that entered No Man's Land.

Thankfully, we had Braedon. Without him to bring the soldiers here, we never would have made it. He had a… unique gift. He could displace. Moving himself and others from one place to another almost instantaneously.

I waved him over as I stalked towards the village with Kalen on my heels.

"We've cleared the area. But we don't know how many

villagers escaped into the forest," he said. I would deal with them soon enough.

"You need to return to the mountains. We can't be sure whether the Ustrayan's made it into Stidahl. So, arrange a few cohorts to return to Solis, searching as they go. But our primary force is to remain in position."

"And you?" Braedon asked.

"Kalen and I will leave in the morning by foot. General Tam will lead the men here behind us. Once you're done, take Nix and Reed and make your way to Fayspire."

"And the Neph…" I cut Kalen off with a snarl. The fewer people that knew about her, the better.

"The prisoner stays with me." She'd never make it to the palace alive if I left her with the men. "Show me the *other* creature!"

Kalen inclined his head towards the burning village. Bodies littered the ground, but I felt nothing but contempt. The people living here harboured Nephilim and paid the ultimate price for their treachery.

Kalen led me to the enormous body of a female as she lay with a sword wound through her chest. One of my soldiers crumpled beside her, his head no longer attached.

I cursed as I recognised the man… *Lupus*… I had trained with his son. I spat on the beast. "We cannot allow her to return to the Gods. Desecrate her body and burn *it*! And find the villagers."

Braedon stepped forward, placing a hand on Kalen's shoulder as he whistled for more men to join them.

"And when we do?" Kalen asked, with his dagger already unsheathed.

"Kill any Nephilim… and the villagers, too." I spared Lupus one last glance. *What the fuck was I thinking, keeping one of those creatures alive?* "On second thought, leave some breathing. I will make examples of them."

Braedon and Kalen displaced. The air rippled in the area they had just stood. *Now to deal with the Nephilim!*

"Fayolan," Reed rushed towards me, but I waved him off.

"Not now," I spat. Reed stepped aside as I blazed through the camp. My heart pounded faster with each step. *The Little Nephilim deserved no mercy from me!* I forced the tent flap aside in time to see the monster trying to free her hands.

Before she could react, I was on her. I grabbed her wrists, forcing her to the floor as she cried out, writhing beneath me. My hand forcefully covered her mouth while I gripped my dagger with the other. Raising it to her throat.

"I should have killed you when I first laid eyes on you," I hissed as she continued to thrash. The moment the blade bit into her neck, she stilled.

A trickle of blood ran down her tattered shirt. She scowled, glaring at me. "Then *do* it!" I saw what she was planning and as she went to lift her head, I tossed the dagger aside.

"You don't get to die. *Your* kind murdered my mother and now they have *killed* my friend." I shoved her head against the ground, climbing off her. "We *will* find the villagers, then I am going to make them suffer. They will beg for their deaths."

"You bastard!" The Nephilim's cry of anger grated on my nerves. Her people had betrayed mine, taking my mother from me before I even drew my first breath. I turned away before I could finish what I had started.

I retrieved my dagger, wiping her blood from it against my trousers. She scrambled back against the pillar, watching me with her arms against her chest. But I could see her body trembling, her muscles tense and on edge. I grabbed a shirt and sword, stalking past her. *She would watch as I tortured the villagers!*

Striding from the tent, I caught sight of a male ducking

behind another construct. He had not seen me and I knew who he was after. *The pretty little Nephilim.*

I moved away, ignoring his hiding place. I wanted to let her have hope—then I would destroy it. *She would break eventually.* Dodging out of sight, I circled around the small supply tent, where I could watch as he crept towards mine.

"Shall I kill him?" Reed asked as he crouched by my side.

"No. Let him find her. It'll be the last thing he does." I signalled for him to follow me as I stalked towards the tent. We watched as he slipped inside before creeping closer so we could listen.

"Serrin," she said. Her voice was soft when she spoke his name. She was fond of him. He would be the first to fall to my blade as she watched.

"We have little time. We have to go, now," he said, sounding hoarse. I raised my hand as Reed stepped forward. I would let her believe she had eluded me, and then I would send her a message. *She was mine now, and no one could save her from me. One...* I began to count.

"I can't... Go find Maeve. I almost had her, but I..." Her words trailed off. "Serrin stop. They took her into Stidahl. Please, you have to save her." *She was brave. I would give her that. Two...*

"You are coming with me," he said, huffing. *Three...* I signalled to Reed.

"He touched me, Serrin." Her voice trembled, and I swung my arm out to halt Reed. Something in the way she said it unnerved me.

"I'll *kill* him!" The boy hissed.

"You can't kill *Death*! And I can't escape him. Leave me here and track Maeve. She still has a chance." I released Reed, and we stormed through the opening.

Witnessing him being so near to her had an irrational

anger rearing in me. They were not touching, but I could see her hair moving as his breath fanned her face.

"*Run!*" she cried.

The male drew his sword to protect her. I smirked and all the colour drained from his face. She was right. *There was no escaping from me!*

CHAPTER EIGHT

Fayolan twirled his sword like it weighed nothing. It looked playful, as if he only intended to spar with Serrin. But that only made him seem more dangerous.

"What do we have here, Reed?" He glanced towards a tall, dark-haired man who stood blocking Serrin's escape.

"Looks like a frightened boy with a death wish." Reed grinned, making me feel nauseous.

"You murdered my mother!" Serrin snarled, keeping his attention on Fayolan.

"She killed my friend," Death countered. "Her kind are murderers, and death is what they deserve." Venom dripped from his words. Fayolan stepped forward with a powerful swing of his sword as he lunged.

Serrin lifted his, and a clang rang out as metal clashed against metal. Fayolan smirked. *The bastard was enjoying this.* Serrin pushed forward, and I gasped as Fayolan side-stepped, causing Serrin to lose his footing and stumble.

Reed's enormous frame blocked his escape as he shoved him back towards Fayolan.

My chest tightened as the men tried to kill each other. But even I could see Fayolan outmatched Serrin. Not only in size, but in skill. *I would never allow Serrin to die for me!*

I clambered to my feet, desperately waiting for my chance. My breath was ragged as I prayed Serrin would back up, and the moment he did, I slipped around him. Fayolan had already swung, and I covered my eyes as I braced... but the pain I expected didn't come.

"Move out of the way!" I glanced up to see Fayolan's sword hovering just above me.

"*No!* I *won't*." The muscles in his jaw ticked as I stood firm, lifting my chin as I refused to move.

Fayolan's towering figure cast a shadow over me as he leant down to meet my gaze. "Is that so?" His hand hovered mere inches from my throat. I heaved deep breaths, trying to steel my nerves.

"Let him go... please," I whispered. Our lips almost caressed as I spoke.

"Now, why would I do that?" A dark growl resonated around the tent.

"Because I will do *anything*."

Baring his teeth, he snarled, lowering his sword. "What makes you think you have *anything* to offer me?"

"Then let him go and I will suffer in his place." I swallowed as I met his stare, hardening my face.

"*You* are going to suffer anyway, Nephilim. I tell you what... Kiss me," he said. His words did not register at first until a dark smirk crossed his lips. He tilted his head towards me as a sickening grin teased across his face. "One kiss and I will let him live."

"Tempest, don't." Serrin tried to step around me, but I blocked his path. "He will kill me, anyway."

"I never break my promises." Fayolan's gaze returned to me, as if daring me to do as he asked. *He must have figured out I didn't like to be touched.*

Clenching my fists at my side, I braced myself. I raised up, brushing my mouth tenderly against his. Not even having time to register the pain before he pressed his lips against mine with a startling ferocity. I cried out as his touch burned. Fayolan slipped his tongue into my mouth, silencing me.

I kissed back as he explored me with a hunger I had never felt before. The taste of him had my stomach tightening as I craved more. *I'm going to hell!*

He pulled back, sucking my lip as he nipped it. I gave a whimper of pain and primal need and Fayolan's smirk grew as he released me. But he swung his sword out, sending Serrin's clattering to the ground.

"You *promised*!"

He grabbed Serrin, dragging him before me as Reed closed in. "I said I would not kill him… I *never* said he would leave unharmed!" Fayolan's fist collided with Serrin's face, but he remained standing.

"*Stop*!" I fought desperately against my bindings as Fayolan beat him. Serrin never stood a chance. He crumpled at my feet, blood coating his face, and only the rise and fall of his chest let me know he was alive. "I hate you!" I shrieked, but Death shot me a cruel smile.

He grabbed a piece of parchment and a quill to scrawl on it. Crouching over Serrin, he raised the dagger, his gaze fixed on me. He drove it into Serrin's shoulder, nailing the note to him.

"He will live as a warning for your people. Anyone that comes for you *will* die." I watched over his shoulder as Reed hauled Serrin out of the tent. Black flames danced in his eyes, sending a shiver down my spine.

"Where has that *feisty* Little Nephilim gone?" Fayolan

gave me a mocking smile. He tugged the rope that dug into my hands, ensuring I was still secure. "Get some rest. We have a long day tomorrow."

I sighed, leaning back against the pillar until exhaustion claimed me, and I dreamt of the million ways I could kill Death!

I woke to the now familiar yanking of the rope binding my wrists, hissing in pain as it rubbed my raw flesh. Fayolan sniggered as he hauled me upright.

Kalen was already waiting in the doorway, holding the flap. I stepped away from him as Fayolan hauled me outside, and he snorted in disdain. *What did I ever do to you, big guy?*

Kalen followed us as Fayolan led me through the camp. Neither of them stepped in as men jeered and cursed at me.

A soldier sauntered towards me, and a spray of spit flew from his lips. It landed on my cheek. But before I could wipe it away, Fayolan jerked the ropes, forcing my arms forward. *Animals!*

I glared at his back, picturing myself plunging a dagger into it. Fayolan didn't even glance back as more soldiers spat and cursed at me. I could imagine the look on his sickeningly handsome face. *Gods I hated him.*

As we reached the forest, Fayolan stopped and turned back to Kalen. Ignoring me as if I were too insignificant to waste his time on.

"Go check out what I spoke to you about earlier, then catch up," Fayolan commanded. "I doubt we will get far with her slowing us down."

"You could just let me go. Then I won't *be* a problem." He rolled his eyes with a sigh as he yanked on the rope. I winced as it tore at my skin.

I spared one final glance back towards my home… or what remained of it. All I could do was hope my mother and Lily had escaped Fayolan's men.

As we neared the barrier, I felt the usual tingle against my skin. "Move," Fayolan said as he crossed. This time, he pulled me through quickly behind him.

He did not speak as we trailed through the trees. The uneven ground caused me to tumble over a twisted tree root. I flung out my arms to stop myself, but Fayolan scowled as he yanked the rope.

My hands slipped from beneath me and my face hit the forest floor. Sharp pieces of debris jabbed my skin, and I groaned as a trickle of blood left a coppery taste in my mouth. *Bastard did that on purpose!*

"If you don't want me *slowing* you down, *stop* causing me to get hurt."

He cocked his head as his mouth slackened and one brow lifted. "If you can't walk, I *will* carry you." I scrambled up before he could get any other *stupid* ideas.

"Move out of my *way,* then." I stormed past him to avoid his lingering gaze. I headed in the direction Fayolan had been leading me until he jerked the rope back.

"Do not *push* me, Nephilim," he warned as he strolled past.

"Prick," I cussed. Fayolan spun, flicking his hand, making a cloth appear from within the shadows. I stepped back as he advanced toward me.

"What does your mother think of that wicked mouth?" he asked with an animalistic growl.

"I save it for those truly deserving, *Death,*" I spat the nickname I had given him. Fayolan lunged, grabbing my hair. My scalp pulled as he secured the gag around my mouth.

"You do not want to see me angry," he warned, hauling me deeper into the trees. *This wasn't him angry?*

I followed behind him until the heat of the sun and my exhaustion became unbearable. Causing me to stumble with each step.

Fayolan scowled as he stopped. "Sit." I attempted to lower myself, but my legs trembled. He stepped forward to help me, but I pulled away. His breath hissed between his teeth at my slight.

The shadows surrounding him pooled around his hand as he conjured a waterskin out of nothing. He held it out, but I turned away. I was not drinking that… *Gods only knew where it had come from.* His scowl intensified, as if he had believed I would trust him. *Nephilim are susceptible to poison and he knows it. At least he should.*

Fayolan took a sip before offering it back to me. I just stared at him. "Drink, or I will force you!" *Fine!* I pulled the cloth from my mouth, taking a sip of the cool water.

The gag had left my mouth dry, but I refused to show Fayolan even the smallest amount of gratitude. I took another long sip and offered it back to him as he took a seat. He gazed at me, looking at the state of my tattered clothes.

"Where are you taking me?" I asked. Silence… "*Now* you have nothing to say?"

Fayolan's head snapped left as he shushed me, looking towards the trees. He moved swiftly without making a sound, tossing the rope binding my hands over the lowest bough of the tree behind me. He secured it tight before wrapping it around the trunk, forcing me flush against it. The rough bark gouged my back, making me hiss. *What the hell?*

Fayolan lifted the gag and motioned for me to remain

quiet. His deadly black sword materialised in his hand as he crept towards the nearest tree.

I strained to listen and my heart leapt as I heard something moving within the shadows of the forest. If it was Ustrayan soldiers and they bested Fayolan, I was as good as dead. *Not that I wasn't if I remained with Death!*

He vanished into the trees, leaving me alone. All I could hear was my blood pulsing as I tugged on the rope, desperate to free myself.

Footsteps echoed through the clearing and voices grew louder. I glanced around, but Fayolan had fucking left me!

"What do we have here?" A man stepped into the clearing as he studied me. A sadistic look of glee on his face caused my stomach to churn and bile rise in my throat.

"Is that a Nephilim?" another asked. Five men emerged, mocking me with laughter as they fanned out around me. "Just kill it"

They approached, but the first man barred their way with an outstretched arm. "She is beautiful. It would be a shame to waste her without having a little taste." The soldier sheathed his sword and advanced nearer. The others offering sickening words of encouragement.

CHAPTER NINE

I tugged at the rope with all my might, but it cut into my skin. The gag was too tight, making it difficult for me to catch my breath. *That rat bastard had left me here as bait!*

The soldier was getting too close. I kicked out, sending dust and debris flying around me. The heel of my boot connected with his leg, and he stumbled back with a sickening chuckle.

"She's got fire!" He shot me a sleazy grin and grabbed his crotch. *Where was Fayolan? Had he really just left me?*

A cold shiver shot through me as a shadow moved behind the soldiers. Pale golden eyes stared back at me. *Death!* Sunlight glinted off his black sword as he swung.

As the others directed all their attention to me, the first man fell with a dull thud. *Poor bastards had no idea what was coming.*

I froze as the Ustrayan pushed my boots apart, spreading

my legs. "That's it… stay still, pretty girl." Disgust churned in my stomach as he unlatched his belt.

I stared past him, watching as Fayolan swung again, and a second man fell. *Just fucking kill them already!*

I did not take my eyes off Fayolan as he met my gaze, hardening his face. As if he offered a silent promise he would not let these men ravage me.

The third man fell. This time, the kill was sloppy, and he cried out a warning. Fayolan was not the type of man to make mistakes. *He did that for me!*

"What the fuck?" The soldier looming over me hissed. He grabbed at his belt as he spun to face Fayolan. Both remaining Ustrayan's brandished their swords whilst taking a step away from Fayolan.

"Move and I'll *kill* her!" The nearest man angled the tip of his sword towards me. Fayolan shrugged as he lunged, his wings bursting from his back.

With a swift jab, his sword pierced the other Ustrayan. "Bastard," the last soldier roared, thrusting his sword towards me. I winced as I waited for the blade to run me through. Instead, the sound of metal echoed in my ears.

A man in black armour held a sword across my body, blocking the Ustrayans. Fayolan darted towards us and cut down the last soldier. I leant my head on the tree trunk as my heart thumped in my chest.

Fayolan hauled the man's body from between my legs as he discarded it in a heap at his feet. He used his wings to shield me from more men lumbering towards us.

"Let me go!" a muffled voice pleaded for help. Fayolan spoke to the men approaching us, but I did not hear a word of it. All my attention was on Maeve, flung over a man's shoulder as she kicked and pounded him.

He ruthlessly dumped her on the ground and she scurried

back, holding her trembling hands up to shield herself. *Thank the Gods… she was alive!*

Maeve stilled the moment she noticed me bound to the tree. She opened her mouth to speak, but I gestured for her to keep quiet. I couldn't let Fayolan know she was my sister. I witnessed what he did to those I cared about, and I refused to allow him to do the same to Maeve.

The man that had saved me sheathed his sword as he nudged her with his boot. "This one was with a group of Ustrayans. We got to her before they roughed her up too badly." I searched her for injuries until I noticed Fayolan watching me.

My expression hardened as I turned away from her. My heart throbbed with a crushing pain as I hoped she understood why.

Fayolan crouched in front of her, tilting her head to look at him. Her lip trembled as she faced him with a neutral expression. Fayolan pushed her away as he turned back to me.

"She's probably from the village this *one* came from," Fayolan said without a trace of emotion.

"Is that a Nephilim?" The man scowled, pointing his sword at my face. "Why is *it* still breathing? You know the King's orders."

"She is my prisoner. She owes me a debt and I intend to make her pay it." Fayolan placed himself between me and the sword as he drew his own. My breath hitched as the two men stared at each other. But the soldier backed down. *That's a good little doggy.*

"The human girl is coming with us. Your father ordered us to bring back a new servant and she will catch his eye." Maeve whimpered and my heart ached. I couldn't do anything except watch.

"Remember the rules. The girl is to remain *untouched.*"

Fayolan warned, and the men dipped their heads, crossing their chests with their left arm.

The largest of them heaved Maeve over his shoulder and they retreated into the forest. She lifted her eyes to meet mine. The fear in them crushed me. *Hang on, Maeve… I will find a way to set you free.*

Fayolan waited until they were out of sight before he crouched beside me. His hand hovered above my cheek as his thumb almost grazed my skin. "I would never have allowed them to use your body like that." The softness in his voice caught me off guard. Deep down, something inside me believed him. *At least… it wanted to.*

Fayolan lowered the gag before releasing the rope from the bough. The tension drained from my muscles as I clambered to my feet. My legs trembled, but I kept pace behind him. My exhaustion made it impossible to fight against him.

The sun had dipped behind the trees as we reached a small clearing. Kalen had already started setting up camp when we emerged from the darkness.

"This way!" Fayolan grabbed my arm, forcing me down at the base of a large tree. He secured me to it, pulling my wrists tight above my head. The bark snagged my hair as I searched for a comfortable position, but my efforts were in vain. *The asshole enjoyed seeing me suffer.*

"Took you long enough." Kalen got to his feet as he crossed to us.

"We ran into trouble. Ustrayan's have crossed the border," Fayolan said. Kalen combed his hair with his fingers as he cursed. "There's something I need you to take care of." Fayolan tilted his head so Kalen followed him into the trees, where I could no longer hear or see them.

I leant back with a sigh as the silence allowed my mind to wander. Maeve was being taken to the King, and I didn't know if Mother, Lily, and Serrin were still alive. I had failed everyone I cared about.

I jumped as Fayolan dropped a bundle of logs onto the ground. A smirk tugged at the edge of his mouth. "Something on your mind?"

"Go to hell!" I glared at Fayolan and I felt my cheeks redden.

"Watch your mouth," Kalen said with a scowl plastered on his rugged face. Fayolan looked somewhat amused as he arranged the logs, preparing a fire close by.

"She can't help being uncivilised. It's what happens when you're raised amongst criminals and vagrants." *He was one to talk.*

"Opposed to liars and dictators I suppose. At least my mother taught to me be honest and value life. You're a murderer with the morals of a *gnat*."

Fayolan's grin slipped from his mouth as he sneered. "I never had a mother to teach me such humility. Remember that before you say another word!" The branch in his hand snapped under the strength of his grip. His nostrils flared, and I shut my mouth, swallowing the insult I had been about to hurl. "That's what I *thought*!"

I turned my head away from him. Focusing instead on Kalen as he held a curved piece of steel around his knuckles, striking it against a sharp piece of flint. A spark flew onto the shavings and an ember formed. He blew on it and it roared to life. I had not realised how cold I was in my tattered clothing until the warmth of the fire embraced me.

"Like what you see, Nephilim?" Kalen asked with a mocking grin.

"The fire is *delightful*," I said as I snorted. "It would be nicer with a couple of rabbits roasting over it. Unless, of course, your aim is to *starve* me to death." I had chosen my words carefully. Hoping the two men would leave to hunt, giving me a chance to free myself from these ropes. *If only I was that lucky!*

Fayolan glanced at me sideways as he pranced over to the fire. He bowed grandly before me, and with a flourish of his hand, his shadows gathered along the spit. Two rabbits appeared over the flames as Fayolan smirked. *Of course, he could conjure whatever his blackened heart desired.*

I expelled a huffed breath as I watched Kalen tend to the food as Fayolan took a seat close to the fire. He broke up some branches and tossed them into the flames, making them spit. I watched as embers flew towards the starless night sky.

When the rabbits finished cooking, Fayolan slid over to me, reaching towards the rope. I went to speak, but he held a finger up to silence me. "Now, my little Nephilim, if you promise to behave, I will free your hands so you can eat. I refuse to hand feed a creature like you."

I was too hungry to chance missing a meal, so I nodded my agreement. Fayolan loosened the rope so I could lower my hands. They felt lightweight from being suspended above me. I softly rubbed my sore wrists as Fayolan filled a bowl with the rabbit. He held it out to me and I snatched it before he could change his mind.

"Thank you," I said. My stomach grumbled again as the delicious smell made my mouth water. I wanted to shovel it down, but I couldn't be sure when Fayolan would next offer me food. So I took my time, avoiding his piercing gaze and the permanent scowl on his face.

"What's your name?" Fayolan broke the silence. He slipped off his gloves as he lifted some of the steaming meat to his mouth. "You seem to know mine, so giving me yours is polite."

I stopped eating, glaring at him with suspicion, before I turned away with a snort. *I owed him nothing!* A breath of wind startled me as a dagger sank into the tree beside my head. *What the fuck?* I spun to face Fayolan as he twirled a second dagger in his hand.

"The next *won't* miss!"

"*Tempest*," I hissed. He chuckled as he swiped his hand, and the dagger vanished in a cloud of black shadows.

"That wasn't so hard, was it?" I returned my attention to my food, dismissing him. "The name suits you. Your mouth is as vicious as a tempestuous storm."

Mocking me, he laughed, and I launched my bowl at him. He cursed, and Kalen was on me, his hand wrapping around my throat. He breathed raggedly into my face. "Do that again, and I will *snap* your pretty little neck." I whimpered at the pain, biting back the scream on the tip of my tongue.

"Let her go," Fayolan warned with a sinister growl. "She is mine to break."

Kalen slammed me back against the tree as he backed away. "Watch out Fayolan. We all know the Nephilim are dangerous. I will kill her myself if I think she's using magic on you." He stalked off, disappearing into the shadows.

Fayolan glared and I could tell from the set of his shoulders that he had not liked the way Kalen had spoken to him. He whirled on me abruptly. "Who's the girl?"

I shrugged as I pushed away the memories of what Fayolan had done to Serrin. I would not give him a reason to go after Maeve.

"So you won't mind when Kalen finds her and *kills* her," he said menacingly. I narrowed my gaze at him. But as his nostrils flared, and he rolled up his sleeves, I knew it was not an idle threat.

"She's a girl from my village. She is just a *child*." He stared at me a little longer before he nodded his head, pulling up a bedroll and laying down.

The shadows gathered around him, leaving in their wake lavish black furs. They reached out, washing over me, covering me with a thick blanket matching his. It was a kindness I had not expected.

Leaning back against the tree, I watched the stars peek out between the wafting clouds. *Did Maeve see the same stars? Was she wrapped in warm fur?* A single tear rolled down my face as I mumbled a prayer to the heavens. The first in fifteen years. "Please help my sister. She's always been faithful."

A howl in the distance gave me a little hope. Maybe wolves would catch our scent and kill us in our sleep. I would die happy seeing them maul Fayolan before they got me. But as the howls faded, a chill seeped into my exposed skin. *Maybe the cold would get me instead.*

"Sleep, Tempest. The girl is far better off than *you* are." Fayolan rolled over, his gaze meeting mine as if he knew my guilt was weighing on me.

He pulled the furs around him as he closed his eyes. The fire lit his face, flickering and hypnotising me. *Why was he so alluring? At least if he had been ugly, it would match his soul.*

The wind whistled through the trees, carrying another warning. *Beware Little Nephilim. Death has his claws in you. Run away before he devours your heart and corrupts your soul.*

"Thanks for telling me something I didn't *know* already!" Only a miracle would allow me to survive this man.

CHAPTER TEN

We awoke to icy rain the next morning. My bound hands made it difficult to cover my chest as my soaked shirt clung to my breasts. Leaving nothing to Fayolan's imagination as my nipples were visible beneath the now see-through fabric.

The mud sucked at my boots, causing me to stumble. And my hair clung to my face, forcing me to keep flicking it aside to see where I was going.

Fayolan stopped so fast that I slammed into his back. *Ouch!* His head snapped behind us. "What took you so long?" The crack of a twig announced Kalen's approach.

"I ran into a few... complications," Kalen said, with a snarl curling his lips.

"Did you take care of it?" Fayolan asked. Kalen nodded with a sombre look on his face. I gasped as I noticed the crimson splattered across his jacket, making my blood run cold. Fayolan's threat to Maeve ran through my mind. *Had he killed her?*

"No! What have you done?" My heart shattered, and I pulled back against the rope. Desperate to escape the men. *I had to find her, just to be sure.*

The rope was wet and slipped through Fayolan's fingers. "Stop fighting me," he snarled as he regained his grip. I yanked the rope again, but this time Fayolan was ready. He heaved me towards him and I collided with his chest.

Rain splattered my face as I glared with such hatred. My cheeks flushed. "You *murdered* her! She was just a *child*!"

"It's no different from the atrocities your kind have committed. She harboured you and that is a crime that comes with a death sentence. *You* did this to her!" Fayolan laced his tone with a cutting coldness. His eyes darkened with swirling shadows as he loomed above me. His teeth bared as a deep growl echoed from his chest.

"So, *you* say!" The words tumbled from my mouth without thinking. *How dare he compare me to him?* I've never taken a life. I save people… My kind are healers, not killers. "It seems to me like an excuse to hunt and murder innocent people just because you fear their fathers."

Fayolan's wings burst forth from his back, and he grabbed me, wrapping his powerful arms around my body. A cry escaped me as we shot into the air. My stomach lurched as the trees fell away from us. I scrambled for a better grip, fighting the pain it caused.

"Keep moving and you will fall," Fayolan said with a hiss. Fiery pain cut through me everywhere he touched my skin. Instinctively, I pulled back, and I slipped from his grasp.

"*Fayolan*!" I screamed as the ground raced towards me.

He grabbed my arm, jolting us back into the air.

"I told you to hold still."

"It *hurts*!" I screamed at him. Fayolan stopped fighting me as confusion played across his face.

"What do you mean?"

"It's painful when people touch me."

"Why?" he asked as he furrowed his brow. His grip loosening as I stopped squirming. He held me just tight enough to keep me from falling.

"It just does. Please… take me down."

Fayolan sighed, the anger ebbing from his features as he angled towards the ground. The beat of his wings resonated around me as he lowered us.

He released me the moment my feet planted on the forest floor, but he did not drop the rope. The wind his wings created buffeted against me as he stood looming down at me. His gaze lingered on my trembling body and heat rose in my cheeks as I noticed his eyes stop at my breasts. "*Fuck* you!" I folded my arms up to cover them again. *Pervert!*

Amusement lit Fayolan's face as he turned towards Kalen. "Find us shelter for the night." A sigh of relief slipped from my lips. I never minded the storms, but this icy rain had chilled me to the bone.

Fayolan looked back, about to say something. But as our eyes met, an uncomfortable silence prevailed.

A quick tug on the rope sent me falling into the mud. "You *utter* bastard."

Fayolan smirked, watching me scramble to my feet. *Ugh!* Mud dripped off me as I wiped the back of my hands across my face. Clearing the muck from my eyes, I blinked as something moved up ahead.

I shivered as an unnatural wind whipped at my clothing. A woman's spirit floated through the whirl, phasing in and out. *"Soldiers are coming. Beware, child."* Mud dripped from my lashes, making it difficult to keep track of her.

I gasped as she appeared just a hair's breadth away from

my face. *Shit!* My heartbeat quickened as I moved back, attempting to evade her grip as her frigid breath swirled against my cheek.

"Tempest?" Fayolan stepped closer as the spirit entered me. Flashes of smoke and fire filled my mind, along with the screams of villagers. Ustrayan soldiers stalked from home to home, cutting down men, women, and children, whilst burning down every house. Even livestock lay dead in their paddocks.

The woman was half lying in the crimson mud, clutching her dead son in her arms. Her husband's headless body leant against her, his blood soaking her scorched dress. I felt her heart fracture with the loss. *Oh Gods!*

It took several seconds for her to notice a person standing before her. She met the gaze of the Ustrayan soldier. Showing no fear, only acceptance… and a touch of gratitude towards the man that ended her suffering.

My heart clenched as the woman's life drained from her body. *At least he had offered her a quick death.*

My vision dimmed, and I felt myself collapsing. I gasped for air, clasping my chest, my legs still unable to bear my weight. The things the soldiers had done made bile burn my throat. I leant away from Fayolan and emptied my stomach.

"*Tempest!*" Fayolan bellowed. Gloves appeared on his hands as he reached out and pulled me into his chest, holding me upright. "What is happening? Talk to me."

"Ustrayan soldiers, they…" My legs gave out again. Fayolan scooped me up in his arms. His chest muscles flexed against the side of my cheek as he cradled me. He stared ahead with furrowed brows as he took off through the desolate, spirit filled forest.

I rested my head against him. Desperate for the pain to break through the images of the woman's death, replaying in my mind.

"Fayolan," Kalen said, yelling over the howl of the wind. Fayolan changed direction toward where Kalen stood, signalling for us to follow him. "It's not far." Kalen cursed as he looked over at me, clutched in Fayolan's arms. "What happened?"

"Her eyes glazed over, and I couldn't get through to her. Then she vomited and collapsed. I almost didn't catch her in time." Fayolan's chest heaved as he followed Kalen into a dark cave hidden in a rocky outcrop.

A fire already flickered and spat, lighting the innermost cavern. The reflection of the flames rippled across a large, sparkling pool. I could feel the water's magic coating me like honey.

Fayolan placed me near the warming fire. I lay listening to the crackling of the logs as they burned. The faint smell of charcoal comforted me as I attempted to block out the world. *Breathe Tempest!*

If not for Fayolan's men, would my village have met the same fate as hers? What if his men had found my mother and the villagers... would they have suffered like she did? I clamped my eyes shut as I pushed the dark thoughts away.

"Kalen, I want to know..." Fayolan's words trailed off. I glanced up as I heard Kalen move, edging closer to me. Raising myself a bit, I backed away.

"Know what?" I asked as Kalen reached out towards me.

"What happened back there? What did you see?" Kalen asked, stepping closer still.

"I... There was..." I couldn't find words for the horrors I had witnessed.

I sucked in a deep breath as I looked to Fayolan, waiting for him to stop Kalen from touching me. But Fayolan's expression hardened, and he did not say a word. "Soldiers attacked a village." I shrunk back, stammering.

Kalen's bare hand's reached out towards me. "What village?"

"I *don't* know. The spirit… she showed me…" My words failed as my back pressed against the jagged wall. I had nowhere to go.

"Do it," Fayolan said. He growled, baring his teeth as Kalen grabbed my temples. Using his body to restrain me as I cried out.

"Hold still and it won't take long," Kalen said, gritting his teeth as he battled to keep hold of me. "Stop fighting me!"

He slammed me back, adding more pressure to hold me still as the spirit's vision played out for all of us to see. I looked away, knowing the unforgettable horrors that would follow.

"You don't want to see this." They ignored my cries as they both watched the spirit and the echo of her death. "Let me go."

As the screams from my vision rose, filling the cave, I stilled, clamping my hands over my ears. It was pointless for them to see the spirit's memory… *we were already too late to save anyone.*

Once the screams of the villagers had died down, Kalen released me. His face had paled, staring at me with his lips parted. "You *saw* all of that?" he asked, stumbling over his words.

"I didn't just *see* it, I *felt* it. Every emotion that woman had ripped me apart from the inside out. And it's all for *nothing.* We *can't* help them!" *All I can do is bear witness to their deaths.*

"Do you recognise it?" Fayolan diverted Kalen's focus from me.

"No, but there's a village not far from here. Just beyond the forest." Kalen rubbed his tensed jaw as his other hand wrapped around the hilt of his sword.

"When did this happen?" Fayolan asked. I shrugged my shoulders. He lunged across the cave, gripping my chin in his hand. "I *asked* you a question."

"I *don't* know. You saw exactly what I did!" I pulled my face from his grasp and he backed away. *Asshole!*

"Scope it out and report back as soon as you can," Fayolan said. "Oh, and Kalen... be careful." He gave a curt nod before sprinting away.

I remained against the cavern wall as I stared after Kalen. Gods help any Ustrayan soldiers still in that village when the hulk of a man arrived. I would hate to be the other end of his brute strength.

I shivered, the warmth from the fire no longer reached me. But I refused to move closer to Fayolan. He inhaled deeply, shaking his head as he noticed me shivering. I watched him as he rose to his feet, his breath fogging the cold air.

His gaze locked with mine as he took his time removing his shirt, sending a wave of heat over my body. I looked away as a hint of amusement reached his lips. *As if I'd ever be interested in a man like him.*

A gentle laugh echoed around the cave, followed by a soft splash. I cast a brief glance behind me as Fayolan dipped his head below the water. My mind raced as I remembered the feel of his firm hands as he carried me through the woods. A dull ache spread between my thighs. *What the fuck was wrong with me?*

Lifting my hands, I realised that in the commotion, Fayolan had forgotten to secure me. I looked towards the cave entrance as he remained submerged beneath the water's surface. *Now was my chance!*

I scrambled to distance myself from the pool. Holding my breath as if it would be enough to alert him to my escape. I seized the rope in my hands, curling it up so I would not trip over it. *That would be just my luck.*

With one final glance back to check the coast was clear, I sprinted away from my captor and out into the woods. The breeze felt wonderful as it cooled my heated cheeks.

As the adrenaline surged through my veins, my heart pounded like a jackhammer in my ears. I was certain Fayolan would hear it. But I was free and there was no turning back.

As rain battered against me and the wind slapped my hair into my face, I couldn't gain my bearings. I needed to put as much distance as possible between me and Fayolan. Before he started hunting me.

My feet sank into the mud, leaving a trail behind me. *Great!* I spotted a dense patch of trees that would hide my tracks and I hurried towards them. Their branches snagged at my hair as I weaved, changing course several times. Although it delayed my escape, it was the best chance I had.

My already tattered shirt caught, ripping and exposing my breast. But I kept pushing deeper. Fayolan would have fun following me through here. I hoped the branches cut him to ribbons.

The ground gave way beneath my feet, and I tumbled down an embankment. My body was mercilessly tossed about as I rolled, colliding with rocks and branches.

Finally, I reached the bottom, ending up on my back in a clearing. "*Ugh!*" I pushed myself up, inspecting my body for any serious wounds. At least nothing seemed to be broken.

I glanced around and gasped... glowing eyes and deep growls made my hair stand on end. *Dire wolves!*

I spun back towards the embankment, but one had already blocked my retreat. It circled closer, forcing me to the centre of the clearing as the others closed in.

My mind raced as I watched them, my gaze darting

between the vicious beasts. I had two choices… *let the wolves rip me apart or call to Death and pray he's close by.*

The nearest wolf lunged, and I dropped to my knees as it sailed over me.

"*Fayolan!*" I screamed. My body protested as I rolled to a crouch as another hurtled towards me, it's razer sharp teeth bared. I lifted my bound wrists, jamming them deep into the beast's mouth. Its fangs sliced through the rope and into my flesh. I firmly locked my jaw, using all of my strength to keep the wolf's sharp canines away from my neck.

The sound of a sword whistled through the air and the beast dropped in two halves on top of me. *Death had found me.* The wolf's head still clung to the ropes by its fangs, as its blood and guts spilled over me.

I shredded what remained of my bindings and pulled my hands free before pushing the remains of the wolf off me. I glanced around to see several more lifeless beasts littering the clearing.

An ominous shadow passed over me, and fingers twisted in my hair. Fayolan dragged me up, hauling me backwards. My feet lifted off the ground, and I struggled vigorously to escape.

Fayolan stared down at me as he slammed my back against a tree, his naked body pressing against me. My own quivered in response as he pinned me in place. His chest rose and fell against me as shadows danced in his pale golden eyes.

"Are you done *running*, Tempest?" I tried to wiggle away from him as the pain roared through me, but he leant closer. His cock hard and throbbing against the exposed skin on my stomach. *Oh Gods! Don't look down, Tempest!*

His breath caught as my nipples, hardened from the cold, brushed against him. "What are you *doing* to me, Nephilim?" he spat as his hand flew to my neck, stifling my breath.

I struggled to speak as my airway closed. "You're the *naked* one… pressing your cock into me, *Death*!" I felt the strain on my neck as Fayolan tightened his grip.

I clawed at his chest, trying to free myself as my vision dimmed. But as my body weakened, all I managed was a feeble caress of his solid pecks. The blood from my shredded wrists trickled down his body.

"*Stop* moving!" he barked. His cock expanded as it pulsed. In response, my skin grew warmer and my thighs ached again.

"Then *stop* touching me!" I met Fayolan's gaze, and he took a deep breath. Lowering me down, he released my throat. His fingers ran across my cheek, his touch was tender, and I did not feel the usual pain.

"Get off me!" I bucked wildly. "What did you do to me, *Death*?"

Whatever spell Fayolan was under shattered and he lowered his gaze, hovering on my exposed breast before falling to my blood coated hands. He seized my wrists, lifting them so he could examine the wounds.

"*Ouch,*" I hissed, trying to pull away. His thumb caressed the deep, bloody abrasions from the rope, making me wince. *He did that on purpose!*

"You need to get cleaned up." He shoved my hands down and hefted me over his shoulder before I could stop him. His wings spread out behind him, and he took to the sky.

I slumped over him, and my hands skimmed over his iridescent feathers. His body tensed at my touch, and a growl reverberated through his chest.

The wind whipped my hair around my face, blinding me. So, I tucked my face into the crook of his neck, just beneath his jawline. He smelled of citrus and pine. His scent felt almost familiar.

I jolted back to reality when Fayolan landed with a jarring

thud. I almost fell from his shoulder, but he held me tight. He stormed into the cave, unceremoniously dumping me onto the ground beside the pool. I uttered a sharp groan as the force reawakened the aches and pains from my fall.

Dark shadows crossed a boulder beneath his hands and then receded. Leaving a beautiful lilac coloured gown in their wake. Intricate scroll work embroidered the belt, which was trimmed with fur.

"Get cleaned up and change. Don't get any foolish ideas about running. I'll be outside," Fayolan said with a growl, turning his back and stalking from the cave.

I stripped off my shredded clothing and tossed them onto the fire embers. My battered body felt so weak as I sauntered to the pool. I dipped my blood coated hands into the warm water. It seemed to be some kind of natural hot spring.

I leant over it as I looked for the bottom, but it was so deep I couldn't see it. My hands slipped, and I almost fell in. I caught myself and scurried back. I didn't go through all of this just to drown.

"Fayolan?" Silence… so I tried again. "Fayolan, I need a bowl."

A soft grumble reached my ears before he groaned. "Just get in the *damn* pool!"

"No. I can't. It's too deep." A mass of shadows formed at my feet before sinking into the ground, leaving a large wooden bowl, a cloth and a sweet-smelling block of soap. "Thank you."

Strong winds whipped through the cave, making me shudder as I scrubbed myself. My scars turned a deep purple in the cold. Even the thick layers of dirt couldn't hide them.

I hurried to wash, having to refill the bowl several times. Once I was clean from head to toe, I lifted the beautiful dress. My heart sank… it had short sleeves. I panicked.

"Fayolan?" I called out again; his growl echoed around the cavern.

"*What?*"

"Can I have a dress with sleeves… please?"

"I gave you an outfit. It's sufficient for you, Nephilim. Wear it," he called back into the cave. I slipped it on and stared down at my hideous arms as I fought back tears.

Small tendrils of smoke crawled down each shoulder of the dress, unveiling more fabric until each sleeve was wrist length.

I lifted a supple black leather corset vest that had appeared on the boulder by the pool. I slipped it over my shoulders, pulling the cords tight.

The bottom of the vest fanned out, sitting over my curvaceous hips. And my cleavage threatened to spill out in two well-rounded mounds.

I took in my reflection in the pool, and I gasped. The dress was luxurious, far more than anything I could afford. It clung to my every contour, and I regretted it would most likely get ruined as we continued through the forest.

I might have liked it if Death had not given it to me!

CHAPTER ELEVEN

My eyes snapped open, and I prepared to run from the beast hunting me, but I paused for a breath and listened. A drip echoed as it fell from the roof of the cave into the pool below. *It had only been a nightmare.* I relaxed as my vision grew accustomed to the darkness.

From my bed of furs, I could see Fayolan. His breath was steady and shallow as he appeared to be asleep. But still he clutched the rope that bound us together in his hand.

I sensed Fayolan's injury and directed my healing magic towards him. A wolf must have got him. Small twinges of pain littered his body as it tried to heal itself. I'd experienced nothing like it before. He appeared to recover faster than others.

I didn't need to use much magic to heal his wounds, so I would not transform. The gash across his abdomen was the most difficult to mend. My gut was on fire as I worked on it. I tightened my jaw to muffle a cry.

When we absorbed another's injuries, we suffered the physical pain of the wound. A broken leg was quick, but some injuries felt as if I were being torn apart from the inside.

A black inky tear dripped down my cheek, and I brushed it aside. At least now I had repaid him for saving me from the wolves. I refused to be indebted to a man like Death.

I stirred in the morning and found Fayolan watching me with an intense look. He pushed a bowl of fruit toward me. My mouth watered. I was starving, so I snatched it up. The fruit was juicy and quenched my thirst as I swallowed a groan.

Light shone through the cave entrance, and Kalen sat watching me with a scowl. I had failed to escape and now they would take extra care to ensure I couldn't do it again.

"So do you always see spirits?" Fayolan asked, and I glanced up without lifting my head, watching him through my thick lashes.

"Yes," I answered, popping a grape into my mouth.

"Do they speak to you?"

"Yes." I bit down on a ripe plum, and Fayolan watched me as juice ran down my chin and into the bowl. I rubbed it away, using the rear of my hand before Fayolan could make snide remarks about me being uncivilised.

"Do they speak to all Nephilim?" I shrugged my shoulders and almost laughed as he pinched his lips, giving me a glassy stare.

"My friend Morgaan could see them but almost never heard their words," I said to stop the burning look he was giving me.

"What do they tell you?"

"They warned me that *Death* was coming, and I needed to run before you caught me." I fixed him with an intense stare. "I guess I should have *listened* better."

"Yes, you should have," he confirmed with a dark smirk. I hissed at him before I returned my attention to the fruit. "Do they always give you visions?" He continued to probe. I sighed as the images of my last spirit encounter resurfaced. I pushed the bowl of fruit away, losing my appetite.

"What does it *matter*, Death?" The shadows around Fayolan grew, reaching out to me. I shuffled away until my back pressed against the wall.

"That sharp tongue of yours is going to get you into trouble," he warned. "You tried to kill me. The least you can do is answer a few questions."

"I was saving you. A decision I *regret*."

"Insolent *bitch*!" Kalen roared as he lumbered towards me. His jaw was rigid with hate for me as he slid his belt from his trousers.

He towered over me, leaning closer. His hand raised as he held the leather belt, ready to strike. I hardened my gaze, lifting my chin so I stared into the depths of his emerald-green eyes. He looked shocked that I had not cowered before him. I feared his touch more than the belt he held above me.

"It's about time you learnt your place. You're nothing but a prisoner at the mercy of the Prince of Stidahl." The belt cracked down; the sound echoed in my ears. Pain stung across my cheek as the leather struck me. I glanced over my shoulder at him, fighting to hold back tears, as I held my head high with a scowl. I hated him… and Fayolan. The first chance to be rid of them, I would.

He raised the belt again, and I refused to look away or flinch. "You are an abomination that steals breath you do not deserve!" Kalen struck me again, and I felt swelling as it heated my damaged flesh. *Fuck him!* I was worth far more than either of them.

"One more, and maybe she will think twice before using that vicious tongue of hers," Fayolan said as he crossed towards us.

I turned my fierce gaze on him. "Maybe if you want me punished, you should get your own hands dirty, *Death*," I hissed as I turned back to face Kalen. He could beat me and I would not show one ounce of weakness.

Kalen lifted his hand again, but Fayolan snatched the belt from his grasp. Kalen chuckled, taking a step back as he crossed his arms over his chest. Of course, he was enjoying this.

The leather belt stung my skin as it cracked against me, far harder than Kalen had done. I yelped as the force of the impact threw me to the ground.

"Don't make me do that again." Fayolan's breath fanned my ear as he leant in, reaching out to me. I trembled as his fingers wrapped around my chin, tilting my head and inspecting my stinging cheek.

"Like you need an excuse," I muttered beneath my breath. Fayolan ignored my comment as he skimmed his thumb over the raised skin. My breath hitched as his lips moved closer.

"Now *get* up. We're leaving." He shoved my chin to the side as he released me. I scowled as he hoisted me to my feet with a sharp yank on the rope. I was regretting healing him last night. Especially as my abdomen burned with every step I took. I stumbled with a groan, but Fayolan did not wait as he pulled me after him.

We stepped outside, and the sun burst through the canopies, almost blinding me. I squinted and relief flooded me as I spotted three horses grazing. Fayolan led me to the smallest of them and watched as I hauled myself into the saddle, adjusting my dress so I could get comfortable.

I reached towards the reins, but Fayolan snatched them away, taking them with him. "I won't give you another chance to escape." Maybe so, but I would not stop trying.

Fayolan led my horse as he mounted the largest of them. I clung to the saddle as he guided me through the trees until the foliage thinned. Revealing a dirt road that snaked through rolling hills. Enormous cliffs towered behind them, boxing us in. Even I could not deny the beauty of Stidahl.

"The village is just past those hills." Kalen pointed into the distance. "As far as I could tell, it looks deserted."

"When did the soldiers pass through?"

"Maybe a day or two ago. The village was smouldering when I arrived." Kalen's voice shook as his fists clenched.

"Tempest, hold on," Fayolan warned, and he geed his horse into a gallop. I struggled to grip the saddle as we took off through the hills.

As our pace slowed, goosebumps prickled my skin. An eerie silence left me feeling on edge. Something bad was coming… or we were heading right towards it.

"Tempest." Fayolan drew my attention to him. The rope securing my hands vanished as he held out a bow and quiver. "If you shoot me, Kalen will kill you."

"What's going on?" I asked as I took it from him, scanning our surroundings as I notched an arrow. I lifted it, taking aim for Fayolan, but he did not react. All I needed to do was release the arrow and run.

My heart pounded as I steeled my nerves. But Fayolan did not move or try to defend himself. *Come on Tempest… do it.*

"*Fuck.*" I lowered the bow, unable to murder him. A smirk teased on Fayolan's lips as he gave me his back, moving further ahead.

"Pathetic," Kalen said with a hiss. His attention remained focused on where we were going. I looked ahead, and that's when I saw it. In the distance, black smoke trailed into the sky.

I clutched my bow as the village came into sight and the woeful songs of spirits rang out around us. Their numbers created a deafening din.

I clasped my hands to my ears as we advanced, trying desperately to muffle the sound. "I'd rather not step foot in that place."

Fayolan smirked. The bastard enjoyed seeing me suffer. *I should have taken him out and haunted him in death once Kalen took my life.*

"Scared?" Kalen grinned as his horse pulled up alongside mine. "I thought *your* kind was used to death? It's the screams before they die you should fear." He leant closer to me. "Like the *pretty* little blonde."

"You *bastard*!" I screamed, grabbing his hands, digging my nails into his skin. Before he could stop me, I pulled his hands to my temples. The sounds of the sole crushing wails filled the air as his magic reacted to mine, drawing them from my mind. *See how you like that!*

"*Enough*." Fayolan yanked on my horse's reins, forcing me to release Kalen to stop from falling.

"What's the matter?" I scoffed. "I guess it's alright for you. You *murder* and kill and all they leave you with is a corpse. This is what you really leave behind. Maybe you would not be so merciless if you heard their suffering after snuffing out their lives."

Fayolan turned away with a snarl as he stared towards the desiccated village. I chuckled as Kalen moved further away, inspecting his hands. Somehow, I had made him use his magic. He gave me a wary look as I caressed the bow with narrowed eyes.

"Shoot him and *I* will kill you," Fayolan said as his shadows flickered menacingly.

We remained silent as we crossed into the village. The scent of death and thick smoke coated my nostrils, and I fought the bile that rose in my stomach.

Fayolan held out a silk scarf. "Use this. It will help with the smell." I wrapped it around my mouth and nose, pulling it tight before returning my hands to the bow. A tingling sensation spread through my body as the spirits tried to warn me. *Ustrayan soldiers were still here!*

I opened my mouth to warn Fayolan when he jerked on the reins and dismounted. A woman lay on the ground, blood pooled around her. But the gentle heaving of her bosom showed she still lived.

Fayolan rushed to her side and checked her wounds. "Tempest," he called, pressing his hand over her damaged stomach. "Heal her."

"Run little Nephilim, it's a trap!" A spirit wailed. I scanned the area as Kalen moved closer. "Now! Tempest."

"It's..." Movement in the tall grass just behind Fayolan halted my words. I raised my bow as I spotted the glint of a sword and I released an arrow. It sailed, narrowly avoiding Fayolan.

"You *bitch!*" Fayolan roared as he jumped to his feet and Kalen swooped in for the kill.

"Look up." The spirit warned, and I lifted my bow as a creak sounded from above. I loosed another arrow.

"It's a trap." My warning came too late, as Kalen collided with me. The impact knocked me off the horse. My head slammed into the ground as the weight of Kalen's large, muscular body landed on top of me. Expelling the breath from my chest.

Fayolan barked orders as more men rushed toward him and Kalen scrambled off me, charging into the fray. I rolled onto my stomach with a groan as I crawled towards the woman. She did not have long.

An arrow pierced the ground by my head and I shrieked as I scurried forward.

"Stay back," Fayolan snapped, but I had to save her. Enemy or not, she was innocent. I dragged myself to her side, resting her head on my lap as my magic unfurled.

Tears rolled down my cheeks as I watched her take her last breath. She was gone before I had a chance to heal her. "I'm so sorry."

CHAPTER TWELVE

Tempest's arrow shot past my head. "You *bitch*!" I roared as I jumped up before the Nephilim could attack again. Kalen leapt from his horse as Tempest looked up, notching a second arrow, sending it sailing towards an Ustrayan soldier hidden on a balcony above.

She did not kill him, but he stumbled forward and toppled over the balcony, finding death on the ground below.

"It's a trap," she warned frantically, but it was too late. Kalen dragged her from the horse. She hit the ground hard with a sickening thud as he landed on her tiny body.

"Get up," I commanded, pointing to the balcony. Kalen charged towards the house as men poured towards me. I cast a final glance at Tempest as she crawled towards the injured woman.

The first Ustrayan reached me, and I swung my sword. Slicing it across his stomach, bringing him to his knees.

Tempest shrieked, and I kicked him away as I spun to her. An arrow punctured the ground beside her head. "Stay back."

I plucked a dagger from the aether, and I launched it up at the man holding a bow with a second arrow trained on Tempest. He crumpled to the floor, his shot missing its mark as it bounced harmlessly off the ground.

My sword hummed as I raised it towards a man charging from the overgrown grass. It hungered for his soul. As I sunk it into his chest, my sword buzzed and devoured him. *His spirit would not haunt Tempest.*

"I'm so sorry." Tempest ran her hand over the woman's hair as tears rolled down her cheeks.

"*Fayolan*," Kalen bellowed a warning. I moved fast as I blocked an oncoming sword with my own. With a forceful shove, I made the soldier stumble backwards. Deftly avoiding another clumsy swing.

I raised my sword again as Kalen gave a second warning, but I was too slow. The blade of the Ustrayan lowered towards me. *Shit!* There was nothing I could do to block it.

The soldier's sword fell, clattering to the ground just beneath me, as I heard a cry. His eyes were lifeless as his body crumpled.

Tempest stood behind him with a bloody rock clasped in her trembling hands. Her face turned ashen as she stared ahead with a blank expression. I had seen that look before. *She was seeing his spirit.*

Tempest stumbled as her legs gave way. I dropped my sword, rushing to her side, catching her against my chest. She weighed almost nothing. I looked down into her face. It looked gaunt and weary compared to when I took her a few days ago.

"Do you think she saw his spirit?" Kalen asked as he drew his sword from the chest of a soldier.

"I think so." The memory of her haunted eyes stuck with me.

"That's three times she has saved your life now. Do you plan on admitting you know she wasn't aiming for you at the lake?" he asked, hauling a soldier from the long grass. Her arrow had pierced his spine, paralysing him.

"If she'd missed, it would have been me lying there." I glanced down at the pitiful man as he gurgled with every breath. "Besides, I've saved her twice."

I lowered Tempest to the ground. Before resting my sword against the soldier's chest as I pushed it through until I hit the ground beneath him. I sheathed it as I returned to Tempest. She remained unconscious, but her chest rose and fell and her breasts bulged in the dress I had given her.

"It's time to end her suffering, Fayolan." Kalen held out his dagger.

I seized his shirt as the beast within me struggled to break free. "She is *mine*!" My voice rumbled as I fought to remain in control of my body. Sharing it with an ancient being capable of ending the world was a constant battle for dominance.

Kalen stood his ground despite my snarling. "She is a *Nephilim*!" He glared at her, grimacing with the same disgust I felt towards her. I swung him away from Tempest, shoving him back against a tree.

"She will face death when I am satisfied she is what my father claims. Until then, I'll do with her as I please."

Kalen swung his arms, freeing himself from my grasp as he stalked away. "She has her claws in you already. Your cock has clouded your judgement. She may be pretty… but she is a demon." He may just be right. She was a monster, yet something about her captivated me.

"She could have killed me, Kalen. I gave her every chance to try, because I wanted to see if she would do it.

Gods *fucking* look at her. Does she really look dangerous to you?" He threw his arms in the air as he cursed, stalking back towards the horses.

I hauled the Nephilim from the ground and laid her over the saddle as I lifted her wrists to bind them. They were still raw and bloody from the rough rope. I was a bastard, but her kind were not innocent either.

"Let's check the rest of the village and then we can move on." We searched for any more Ustrayan soldiers lurking in the ruins. As I feared, they had made it into Stidahl, but I would meet them with death.

"Help," a weak voice called. I signalled Kalen to take the reins of Tempest's horse, inching my way to the nearest pile of debris.

"I'm here. Call out again so I can locate you." I listened as she pleaded for help. "I've got you." My muscles strained as I heaved burnt wooden beams, tossing them aside until I spotted the woman's arm. "Hold still." I lifted more from her until I exposed her blood coated head.

"The army…" she said as she struggled to point. "It's heading to Fayspire." I tried to pull her free, but her body lolled, and her chest stilled. She had lived just long enough to pass on her message.

"*Fuck*!" I banged my fist. Letting out a deep sigh before brushing my fingers over her eyes, closing them. "Rest now."

I sat back on my heels, running a hand through my hair as I stared at her. Fucking savages. I would kill them all. *I am Death and they will feel my wrath.*

"Fayo," Kalen cursed behind me. I glanced up as he lifted his hand from Tempest's head. Fresh crimson coated his hand.

Blood matted her loose hair as it hung over her face, leaving a trail behind us. "We can't risk patching her up now," Kalen said as he scanned the village. *We weren't safe here.*

He pulled off his blood-stained shirt, using it to stem the blood flow.

"We can take her to the lake and stitch her up there." I spared Tempest a fleeting glance and my heart raced.

"Do you really believe she can't heal herself?" Kalen asked as he secured Tempest. Before hauling himself onto his horse.

"I don't know. Maybe she is keeping her abilities hidden from us. But if you could heal the rope burns and the wolf bites, wouldn't you? Just to make yourself more comfortable."

"With her, it wouldn't surprise me if she suffered just to spite herself," he snorted. "Do you think your father lied about the Nephilim?" I'd been asking myself that since I met her.

"Either way, it's unlikely she will tell us what she can and can't do. She may be fierce and stubborn, but I saw genuine sadness when she failed to heal that woman. Nothing about her makes sense."

"She is still dangerous. The Nephilim used my magic against me," he warned.

"She was making a point," I said, chuckling as he scowled. "Next time, don't get so close if you insist on taunting her."

He cursed as he rode off. His temper often got the better of him. But he had not used his full force with Tempest back in the cave. I'd seen him do far worse to prisoners, but with her he held back.

I mounted and led Tempest through the village and back to the trail between the sweeping hills. She did not so much as stir as I watched her. *Who was this woman?* I knew under her cold exterior was someone that loved deeply.

My father had beat that out of me as a child. I was incapable of love. *I always have been.* Death was the gift the
Gods gave me and it served my father well. Hell, the closest I
ever came to giving a fuck about anybody was Kalen and my
elites.

As I reached the lake, Kalen was already there, with furs
spread out. "Get the suture kit."

I lowered her as she let out a weak groan. "I'm sorry
Tempest," I said, trying to soothe her as Kalen handed me a
damp cloth.

"The village is clear," he said as he hovered, watching me
clean the wound.

"Good. As soon as she is ready to move, we head to
Fayspire."

Kalen held out the kit but did not release it as I went to
take it. "We shouldn't wait. You've seen what those barbarians are capable of." Kalen scowled.

"Fayspire has its protections. They will not breach its
walls. In two days, we'll show Ustraya what happens when
they stray into *my* kingdom!"

"Let's hope you're not responsible for sacrificing innocent lives for a monster." Kalen released the kit as he turned
his back. He knew as well as I did Fayspire could withstand a
siege.

I breathed out a sigh as I stitched the Nephilim's head.
She would only slow us down if she was too weak to travel. I
swept her hair aside, exposing the purple bruises marring her
chest from the fall as she tried to escape from the cave.

She hadn't realised I'd already found her, even as she wasted time trying to hide her trail. It might have worked if I had followed her on foot.

I pulled a poultice from the aether and applied it to the stitches to avoid infection. She drifted off to sleep, and I moved away, taking a seat beside Kalen.

"We will take watch tonight," I said.

"For what? Her or Ustraya?" he asked as a sneer creased his face.

"*Fuck you!*"

CHAPTER THIRTEEN

Fayolan

Tempest woke screaming during the night, plagued by nightmares. But she refused to speak. She just glared at me with a scowl of accusation.

She didn't have to tell me she'd never taken a life before. I had seen that same expression on many men's faces. The first kill was always the hardest.

I turned back towards the night sky, my solace in the darkest of times. Her haunted look made my stomach tie in knots, yet I'd never experienced the pain she was going through. She called me Death, and she was right. But when it slipped from her vicious mouth… it stung.

The sun rose and fell again as she recovered. I watched over her as she slept, noting every contour of her body. She was so different from any other Nephilim I had seen. Not one compared to the alluring beauty she possessed. *Maybe she was a half-breed? That could explain why she hadn't healed herself.*

Tempest lay breaking, but I had no words of comfort. I couldn't find it in myself to relieve her of her burden. *She was, ultimately, a Nephilim.*

"You should eat." I held out a plate filled with succulent meat to tempt her. She had refused any food or drink since she woke.

"I'm not hungry." Tempest's shoulders slumped as she stared into the distance with a vacant expression.

"You still need to eat. I won't have you slowing me down any longer than you already have. There are lives at stake." I had tried the soft approach to get her to eat. But time was running out, and I needed her to pull herself together. *Gods, I would be content just to hear that smart mouth of hers.*

"Where are you taking me?" she asked as she took the plate, taking a mouthful. But her face remained blank, revealing no emotion.

"We are heading to Fayspire first and once I have dealt with the Ustrayans I'm taking you to Solis." She dipped her head and took another mouthful.

Kalen returned from the lake, pulling on a fresh shirt as he settled down next to the fire. His gaze fell upon Tempest and as she noticed a flicker of a scowl crossed her lips. *She was still in there.*

"How much longer are we going to waste time? She's awake, so what are we waiting for?" he asked as he tilted his face towards me.

I leant over and freed the Nephilim's hands from the rope, securing it to her ankle. "Bathe in the lake and change. We haven't got all day." I pulled a long-sleeved dress from the aether and tossed it towards Tempest. I did not have time to listen to her piteous sobs.

Tempest snatched up the dress, hugging it to her chest and shaking her head.

"No," she said as her gaze darted between Kalen and I.

"We will keep our backs turned. But since you insist on trying to escape, we are staying put." Her lips pursed as she shuffled back. "*Now* or I'll have to do it for you." I summoned a blade from the aether, pointing it towards her.

"Please don't make me." With a quivering lip, she scrambled upright and backed away. *Dammit!* She was going to make me force her. *Gods, I'd never met anyone as stubborn in my life.* "Now, Tempest."

"I can't," she cried. I leapt up as she shifted her gait, preparing to run. She bolted, but was not fast enough.

Kalen barred her way as I stalked closer. "Where are you *planning* to go, Tempest?" I asked with a smirk as I dangled the rope attached to her ankle. I stalked closer, giving her one last chance to submit. But her fingers clasped the dress tighter as she darted in the opposite direction.

She was swift, but I was faster. I clasped my arms around her midsection as I pulled her back against my chest, facing her away from me. "Nice try. Now, *cease* fighting or things will turn *ugly*."

I gripped her filthy dress, running my dagger through the laces of the leather corset. Tempest's chest heaved with every breath, and the vein in her neck throbbed as I gripped the sleeves of her dress.

"*Please…*" Her words tapered off as I cut the fabric away from her. She cried out as it fell around her feet. Raised, angry scars covered every inch of her arms and back.

My grip tightened as she fought to escape, causing us both to lose our balance. *Shit!* I toppled on top of her. My knee pressing into her back, pinning her firmly to the ground beneath me.

"Who the *fuck* did that to you?" I growled through gritted teeth. *I'll hunt them down and destroy them.* She cursed and thrashed beneath me as I trailed my fingertips down one of the long-jagged marks.

I had once seen a weapon leave scars like that. Disgust washed over me as I realised someone had used it on her. *A whip with razors along its tail.*

"*Let* me *go!*" Tempest bucked her hips to throw me off her.

"*Who.* Did. It?" I asked again, planting my hand between her shoulder blades as I forced her to stay still.

"*Fuck* you," she said with a hiss.

"Fine, have it your way. Kalen… show me." I needed to know what happened. She belonged to me now, it was my right.

"Don't you dare," she hissed as Kalen got closer. His face paled as he saw her scars.

I dug my knee deeper into her back. "Then tell me."

"It's my story, not yours. You don't deserve it." Whether she believed it to be hers was irrelevant. Now it would be mine too.

"Do it!" I gripped her hair, forcing her face into the dirt as Kalen lowered himself beside her. Enveloping her head in his enormous hands. "Now!"

Spectral visions appeared as I watched the memory from Tempest's perspective. She followed a spirit as it wove through the trees. Its voice drew her deeper as she laughed. Until a low hum of male voices caught her attention and she hurried to investigate.

Five men huddled around their fallen comrade as he groaned in pain. Unaware of the danger, she stepped out of the trees and offered to help.

The men's faces lit up with greed. But the emblem emblazoned on their armour filled me with an icy rage. Their chests bore the Stidahlian insignia. *Mother fuckers!*

Tempest dropped to her knees before the man, pressing her hands against his exposed chest. She touched him with no hesitation.

The moment she finished, they snatched her up. A hand tightened around her mouth, smothering her desperate cries for help. She seemed so small compared to them that no amount of pounding her tiny fists against them made any difference. *She was just a fucking child!*

I stared in horror as they made a game out of her, allowing her to run for a few moments before the sound of their footsteps closed in. They hunted her before dragging her to a small cabin. The wooden walls creaked as they tied her wrist to the sides.

They taunted her and brandished the weapon. The crack of the first lash made my blood boil. My hands trembled as I seethed.

Ten times they lashed her before a figure emerged from the darkness. A man I knew too well... *He was now the number one on my shit list.*

Kalen snarled as he saw Lacellus, the son of my father's top advisor. He held an ornate dagger in his hand, and Tempest screamed as he ran it down her arm. The cuts were deep enough to scar, but not to cause fatal bleeding. The prick wanted to keep her alive.

Lacellus' face twisted with hatred as he lashed her again, and a wave of nausea washed over me. The sound of the whip slicing into her flesh was almost unbearable.

Tempest's tiny screams diminished until they were nothing more than a whimper. Her head bowed and her eyes closed as the pain took over.

She stirred at the sounds of fighting. Men flooded the cabin and slaughtered the remaining Stidahlian warriors. They kept one alive, beating him until he told them all about

Lacellus and how he was the only one left, having gone to secure transport back to my father.

The men from her village cut her down, and she screamed as they carried her home. The first person she saw was her mother as she dashed towards Tempest and cuddled her. Tempest released a shrill scream akin to an animal's as she fought to get away.

I'd seen enough. "Let her go." Kalen nodded and released her. The horrific vision faded away.

"How old were you?" I asked, but she remained silent. "*Tempest?*" I gripped her hair tighter.

"Eight," she said with a hiss. My finger ran along a blemish marring her back as I freed her from beneath me. She used her hands to cover her exposed skin as she glowered at me with a fierce look on her tear-streaked face. "I *hate* you!"

I hurled the dress at her and retreated to the fire. Releasing the rope enough that she could make it to the lake.

"Do *you* intend to kill him, or shall *I*?" Kalen plunged his dagger into the ground beside him.

"He is *mine*." My voice rumbled, and he grinned. "I will show him the same *mercy* he showed the Nephilim." Lacellus would fall to my blade when we got back to Solis. But he would *fucking* suffer first. To torture a child was unforgivable, even if she was a Nephilim.

I kept my back turned until Tempest lowered herself to the ground beside the fire. I could not meet her gaze as the memories of her past lingered in my mind. "Let's go," I said with a cold bite to my words.

I released the rope from Tempest's ankle and returned it to her wrist. She scowled at me with a burning hatred so strong you would have thought that I had inflicted those wounds upon her.

"Are you happy now?" she asked, narrowing her eyes as a

scowl curled her lips. I deserved her anger, but I had no regrets.

"You hold no power here. I will take what I want from you. You're a *Nephilim*," I spat. *I was a cruel bastard.* But she needed to learn her place.

"So I am *Death*." Tempest would not survive long in Solis if she did not learn to keep her smart mouth shut.

CHAPTER FOURTEEN

I pulled away from Fayolan as he strode towards the horses. *He had violated me. I saved him… for what?* I would not do it again.

"Let me help you." Kalen stepped closer and held out a hand. I snorted as I shot him a hostile scowl and pulled myself into the saddle. I hoped he felt guilty… and I *fucking* prayed he choked on it.

We rode deeper into the hills, away from the village, and what I had done. Whenever my eyes closed, I saw the confused spirit of the man I'd killed. I had taken a life, and I could never forget it. I wasn't cold and heartless like Death. He killed without a shred of remorse, but I cared about life. *I saved it.*

"I'm sorry," Kalen said, making me jump as he pulled his horse alongside mine.

"*Sure,* you are." I gritted my teeth and focused my gaze

forward. His words were as meaningful as a wolf licking your hand before biting it off.

He chuckled as he glanced ahead at Fayolan. "Believe it, or don't. I won't waste my breath saying it twice."

"Your apology means nothing when I *know* if he ordered you to do it again, you would." *The Dark Prince's faithful mutt.*

"Enough, Nephilim." Fayolan dangled a cloth gag in his hands as his shadows pulsed around him. "I will not have you disrespecting my men. Unlike you, they know how to follow orders."

A deafening screech made me jump, and a flock of bright, colourful birds shot into the sky. "Eyes out." Fayolan signalled. The cloth in his hand vanished as his sword replaced it.

Kalen pulled away, heading towards a copse of trees. Disappearing from sight.

"What was that?" I asked, but Fayolan remained silent as he squared his shoulders. Keeping his attention trained on the trees.

Kalen burst from them, galloping towards us as he flailed his arms. "Run!" He kicked his horse's flank as he charged towards us.

I gripped the saddle as Fayolan geed his stallion on. But a roar followed behind us. I glanced back as giant wings lifted a creature bigger than anything I had seen before. *We were going to die.*

I stared as the beast soared towards us when arms gripped my waist. Fayolan hauled me from the horse. His body softened my fall as he covered my mouth with his hand.

"Be quiet," he hissed into my ear. The long grass hid us as our horses galloped away. The hideous creature with scales and a giant fanged snout chased them, plucking mine from the ground and carrying it away. I released my held breath as the creature vanished from sight.

Fayolan shoved me off him as he stood. "Looks like we're walking." I sprung to my feet as Kalen caught up to us.

"Did you see the size of that thing?" he said, a smirk playing on his lips. *Was he kidding? How could I miss it? I swear that thing was bigger than my cottage.*

"You're welcome by the way," Fayolan said with a scowl.

"For *what*?" I asked with a nonchalant shrug of my shoulders.

"For saving you."

"Oh, I *apologise*… Thank you, *Death*, for saving my life… just so *you* can take it at your convenience." I executed a bow with a heavy dose of sarcasm.

"Watch your tongue, Nephilim," Kalen warned, growling as he stepped closer. I crossed my middle fingers at him before striding off the way we were heading.

Fayolan jerked on the rope, pulling me back so I fell. I landed hard on my ass, sending a jolt up my spine. I glared up at him as he flashed me a cocky smirk. *Gods, I wanted to wipe it off his smug face.* Instead, I bit my tongue and got to my feet, dusting off my dress.

"Do you think it will come back?" I asked. Maybe it would return and devour Death. I doubt even he could survive that.

"I wouldn't worry about that one. It was female, so its mate is likely nearby," Fayolan warned as he strolled past me.

"Male dragons are twice the size," Kalen said with a chuckle as I stared towards the trees. That *thing* was a dragon? I had only heard of them in story books.

"Stay close, *Nephilim*." I hurried after Fayolan as the hair on my neck bristled. The rope hung loose between us, dragging on the ground. I tripped on it and Fayolan's hand flew out, saving me from unceremoniously sprawling across the ground.

"Thanks," I murmured as he exhaled heavily and distanced himself from me. He scooped up the excess rope and wound it around his wrist, keeping it off the ground.

I slowly rubbed my fingers over my arm where he had touched me, trying to ease the pain. He should have just let me fall.

Fayolan snorted as he directed a look of revulsion at me. "If I repulse you so much, stop touching me." I cocked my head, scowling at him. "It's not like I welcome it." Fayolan stalked away, rolling his eyes.

We walked in silence until the sun set. I winced as I dropped to the ground, rubbing my tight, aching calf muscles. I was not used to walking long distances over unforgiving terrain.

Kalen laid out some furs as I sat and hurried to eat the small meal Fayolan handed me. I placed the bowl down with a yawn.

"Get some rest, Nephilim." Kalen inclined his head towards an inviting pile of furs. I was so tired, I mumbled my thanks and lay down near the fire. Its warmth radiated over me as I shifted away from Fayolan, giving him my back.

I jolted awake, shivering from the chilly wind. Sitting up, I glanced around the camp. The fire was out, and Fayolan and Kalen slept so deeply that I felt uneasy. They were the type of men that slept with one eye open, but I could hear Kalen's soft snores.

I clambered up and crossed to the fire, poking it with a log, trying to stoke it. A tingle of magic brushed against me and I glanced up. Something moved amongst the shadows across the valley.

"Come play with us…" a whispery voice carried in the wind. *Sirens… it couldn't be. Could it?*

"Fayolan." I jabbed him in the ribs with the log, but he remained asleep.

"We're so hungry," the siren called. *Shit.*

"*Fayolan*!" I hit him with all my might, but he didn't even groan. I had to do something, or we were all dead. I crossed the camp, bringing the log down across Kalen's chest. "Wake the *fuck* up!" I yelled. I could not wake them. *Time to save myself.*

I dropped beside Kalen as I gripped his dagger, pulling it free from its sheath at his hip. My hands shook as I cut through the rope binding me, and I wasted no time in making my escape. But the siren's eerie voice called out again.

"You smell delicioussss…" My stomach churned at the thought of their fate in the hands of a siren. The vicious creatures would spend days stripping their victims' flesh with their barbarous teeth. All the while, they remained conscious and immobilised. *A fate I could not even wish on Death.*

I'm definitely going to regret this. I spun back to Fayolan, ignoring the pain as I straddled his abdomen. *Here goes nothing.* I brought my hand down across his cheek, feeling the heat of the strike. "Wake up!" I screamed in his face, but he did not stir. *Fucking dammit.*

What would wake Death if not pain? Oh, Gods forgive me. I leant over him and felt the warmth emanating from his body beneath my palms as I planted them firmly on his chest. My lips hovered over his and I took a deep breath as his musky scent washed over me. *Please let this work.*

I eased my lips against his as I kissed him. Fayolan's

body tensed beneath me as he responded, his tongue slipping into my mouth. His arm wrapped around my back, drawing me nearer.

His eyes snapped open, and he flung me back as he jumped from under me.

"What the *fuck* are you doing?" He glared as I lay in the dirt at his feet.

I scurried back and pointed behind him. "I couldn't wake you. *Siren.*"

He spun, cursing as the figure split into three. "Kalen," he bellowed, but it was no use. Fayolan's wings erupted from his back and, with a forceful leap, he ascended into the air. His soul devouring black sword clutched in his hand.

I scrambled over to Kalen. *I refused to kiss him, too.* "Wake up." I whacked him again with the log.

"Make him bleed," Fayolan yelled, and I felt the chill of his shadows as a dagger materialised at my feet. Tremors ran through my hands as I grabbed the hilt, nudging his hand open.

"*Please* don't kill me." Inhaling deeply, I ran the blade across his palm, drawing blood. His hand shot up, wrapping around my throat. I flailed as he lifted me off the ground, his gaze falling to the dagger I still clung to.

"Bitch," he cursed, squeezing my neck till I felt I would pass out. "Thought you could kill me, did you?"

"Sirens," I gasped, the air catching in my throat. I raised my hands in submission, tossing the dagger away.

His gaze darted past me as Fayolan roared. "*Shit.*" He threw me aside like a rag doll as he snatched up his weapons. He sprinted away, leaving me sprawled on the ground. Clasping my throat, as I gasped, desperate for air.

I crawled to Fayolan's dagger, taking it with me as I took off running towards the nearest trees. I had rescued them and now I had to save myself.

Gasping for breath, I ran faster, my chest heaving with the effort as I weaved through the trees. My best chance of escape would be to climb one. The thick leaves would hide me from Fayolan as he searched from above and Kalen from below.

I found a low-hanging branch, sturdy enough to take my weight, and I clasped it. Hauling myself up with gritted teeth as the tree's sharp needles pierced my hand. I ignored the pain as I climbed higher until I found a branch smooth enough to sit on.

I tucked my knees into my chest as I leant against the trunk. Waiting to hear the beat of Fayolan's wings. When I released a breath, it became visible, making me shudder.

"I see you," a siren whispered. I glanced down to see the creature baring its fangs in a horrific grin. It leapt towards the tree, scaling it with inhuman speed. I scrambled up, attempting to reach a branch from the nearest tree. But it moved too fast, and it's sharp, poisonous claws raked across my leg. "Come with me. I'm so hungry."

My vision blurred as the tree rocked. *No... it was me swaying.* I tried to clasp the trunk as my legs buckled, but my arms felt heavy and I fell.

I screamed as I plummeted, bouncing off branches that slowed my descent. But as I hit the ground, I felt no pain. My body wouldn't move, and I watched in terror as the siren slithered headfirst down the tree trunk.

Tears streaked down my cheeks as I faced the creature. This was it... the end.

CHAPTER FIFTEEN

Tempest's scent shrouded me as I woke. Her lips pressed against mine as I held my arm around her back. The heat of her hands pressed into my chest as our tongues intertwined. *What was she...*

I snapped to my senses with a jolt, flinging her off me. *What the fuck did she think she was doing?* She scrambled back, her lips trembling as she pointed behind me.

"I couldn't wake you. *Siren.*" Spinning, I watched a dark figure split into three creatures lurking closer. *Dammit!* I leapt to the sky as I ordered Tempest to wake Kalen, giving her a dagger to make him bleed.

Kalen roared as I swooped towards the creatures, my sword humming in my hand. Gnarled fingers gripped my wings as they tried to pull me down. I flailed, using my sword to slice the hands from the siren's body. Its high-pitched wails made my ears ring.

I flipped onto my feet, swinging as I removed its head.

My sword did not buzz. Even *it* did not like the blackened demonic souls of these creatures.

One of the sirens leapt towards me, smiling with rows of flesh-stripping teeth. I flew up, evading its claws, that dripped with a paralysing poison.

The loathsome creature twisted its gnarled limbs, which seemed too weighty for its meagre body to support. A sword pierced through its chest and it crumpled to the ground.

"Need a hand?" Kalen grinned as he swung again towards the third siren. I darted towards it, swooping from above, my sword cleaved into its skull. I kicked it away from me as I ripped my sword free, its acrid blood splattered across my jerkin.

"Gods that fucking smell." I almost wretched as I covered my nose with my hand.

"I've smelt sewers better than this," Kalen said, grimacing as he stepped over the body. "They don't normally come this far inland." Something was upsetting the delicate balance, and I suspected it was connected to the Ustrayan soldiers that defiled my lands.

"First dragons and now sirens… it's as if the Gods are turning against us." I spat on the nearest creature as I turned back towards the camp. It lay vacant. *Tempest!* The rope that had bound her to me dangled at my hip, sliced in half. In the chaos, she had slipped my mind. "She's running."

"She'll get herself killed if she bumps into one of these things," Kalen said. *Foolish Nephilim.* I raced towards the deserted camp. My dagger was gone, as was Tempest. "She'll head into the trees. It's what I would do."

A blood-curdling scream pierced the air and fear gripped me as we heard the snapping of branches as she plummeted from the trees. "Shit," I cursed, wrapping my arms around Kalen as I propelled us into the sky.

What was she fucking thinking? My pulse quickened as I

pictured her in the hands of one of those creatures. I pushed myself to my limits, my back muscles straining as I carried Kalen's weight beneath me. *Fuck, I wouldn't make it before…*

Tempest's screams cut off, making my heart hammer against my ribcage. *Hold on Little Nephilim.*

"There," Kalen said, pointing into the trees below. Tempest lay unmoving with a siren crawling up her body. I plummeted, dropping Kalen as he raised his sword and charged. Plunging it into the creature and hefting it over his head as if it weighed nothing.

The ground trembled as I landed beside Tempest. Her wide eyes met mine. Her breath fogged as she attempted to speak.

"Is she hurt?" Kalen asked as I lowered, mumbling an apology as I searched her body for injuries. Seeing that *thing* on top of her had left my stomach in knots.

"The bastard got her leg, but other than that and a few scrapes and bruises, she seems fine." Only Tempest could fall from a tree as tall as these and not break every bone in her body. "I'm going to lift you."

I placed my hands beneath her arms and legs while striving to support her head. Her body hung lifeless, with only the slightest rise and fall of her chest.

"You go ahead. I'm going to search for more. We need to avoid another surprise attack. Hell, they would've got us this time if not for her."

Kalen glanced down at Tempest. "Looks like I owe you one."

I carried Tempest back to the camp, laying her on her bedroll close to the smouldering fire. It was clear she'd tried to relight it with the log which lay discarded beside Kalen's furs.

I swept the hair from her face, tucking it behind her ear. "I'm going to re-light the fire. You're safe here with me." I hurried and soon it roared to life, illuminating her deathly pale skin. She looked terrified. This whole time, she'd never looked at me with such fear. Only hatred and contempt.

I settled beside her, extracting a small vial of glowing blue liquid from the aether. I considered leaving her immobile all night as punishment for running, but the creature had scared her enough.

With a pop, I uncorked the vial, running my thumb across her cheek, wiping away a stray tear. "This will not taste nice." With her head tilted back, I drizzled the antidote down her throat. "Drink."

She swallowed, and I pictured the curses she would have spewed if she could. "Get some rest, Nephilim," I ordered, but the word did not have the usual sting as I uttered it.

I covered Tempest in a thick fur blanket before leaving her to sleep. I hovered close by, watching the trees until Kalen emerged.

He dropped beside the fire, rubbing his chest as he glanced back towards Tempest. "Is she okay?" he asked.

"She is terrified, but will live. I've given her some moon blossom and she will be back to her *sarcastic* self by morning."

Kalen chuckled as he rubbed his chest as if in pain.

"Are you okay?" I asked.

His face lit with amusement. "I think she hit me with a log. I reckon she broke a rib or two." He unbuttoned his shirt to reveal a bruise swelling across his torso.

"I bet she enjoyed it, too," I said as I flicked a log onto the fire.

"I'm guessing she enjoyed *that* more." He pointed towards my cheek that I only just realised felt sore. "Wait…" he frowned, moving closer as he examined it. "She *touched* you. You are going to have a cracking handprint sized bruise by morning." He burst out laughing, tossing his head back-wards. *Damn Nephilim.*

I could still taste her on my lips. "She kissed me," I mumbled, glancing back at her.

"In her position, I would have run and let the sirens take us. *Especially…*" He did not need to finish his words… *after the way I'd treated her.*

"I won't release her, Kalen." Truth be told, I didn't think I could even if I wanted to. Maybe it was because of her breathtaking beauty, or the fiery glint in her eyes. But I wanted to figure her out, to learn everything about her. Maybe then I could end her life, freeing myself from her seductive grasp.

To me, food tasted bland and the world looked pale and dull. Yet when I looked at Tempest, I saw her vibrant colours. The midnight streaks that ran through her hair were radiant. And her captivating blue and magenta eyes reminded me of how Nix had described the galaxy visible in the night sky above Solis.

The day I had stolen a kiss from Tempest and our lips first touched, I witnessed true colour. Nix would often sit and describe the world through her eyes. But I'd not understood until the Nephilim. And I hated her for it… for giving me a glimpse of what I was missing when her fate was to die. With her death, I would never again see the world's iridescent beauty.

A soft whimper drew me from my dark thoughts. I glanced back to see slight movement beneath the furs. No doubt nightmares were plaguing her sleep.

Tempest screamed out, making me start. "*Fuck.* She'll draw any beast for miles." I got up, crossing to her side. She calmed the moment she saw me and I helped her to sit. I cupped her chin tenderly, lifting her face so she looked at me.

"I will not let them hurt you. You are mine, Little Nephilim and the only one you should fear is me."

She stilled at my touch, her lips parting as I leant closer, whispering into her ear. "Do not run from me again. It's too dangerous to be alone."

I expected her to pull away from my touch, but her face softened. Some of her fear leaching away as her gaze wandered to my lips. "You kissed me," I murmured, and the fire returned to her eyes.

"You wouldn't wake up. It wasn't like I *wanted* to." I tried to stifle the grin spreading across my face. *There she was. My fierce Little Nephilim.*

CHAPTER SIXTEEN

Tempest

I jolted awake as a cry left my lips. The siren's jagged, wide eyes haunted my sleep as it sniggered, sniffing my skin as it readied to strip my flesh. I gasped, clutching my chest, my heart palpitating in my struggle to catch a breath.

I sensed Fayolan's eyes on me before he got close. The taste of him still lingered on my lips. He'd reattached the rope to my wrists while I slept and moved his bedroll closer. Rousing me during the night when my screams became too loud.

"Fayspire is just over that ridge." Fayolan pointed to a large rolling hill in the distance. "You will be safe as long as you follow my orders. I cannot protect you if you run from me."

Glancing up, I gave a subtle nod. I'd learnt last night about the dangers that lurked in Stidahl. "Thank you for saving me," I said, meeting his gaze.

"Thanks for waking me *before* you ran." He smirked as he looked out towards the hills. It wasn't the cruel look Fayolan normally shot me, and my lips developed a will of their own, curling ever so slightly in the corners.

"I wasn't going to." I watched his face darken as he absorbed that information.

"What changed your mind?"

"Not even you, *Death*, deserve to die like that," I said as I studied his face. The subtle scar above his left eye. The way his raven black hair had a natural shine that reflected the sun's rays. Or the ring of black that surrounded his soft golden iris, pulsing as his pupils focused on me. He was mesmerising.

I snapped out of it, turning my gaze away from him. *He was my enemy.* I was not his friend. I doubted a man like Death even had any.

A bowl dropped at my feet, making me jump as Fayolan got to his feet, stalking over to Kalen. Several minutes passed as they kept their backs turned and voices lowered. I averted my gaze as I worried my bottom lip. *I'd been distracted all morning. As last night when I kissed Fayolan, it hadn't hurt.*

I finished my breakfast of fruit before I trailed over to them. Their conversation halted as I neared.

"Plotting my death?" I asked with a bite to my words. I was fluent in sarcasm, using it to keep people away. It hid how broken I was inside.

"I can as sure you it will start with me removing your tongue," Fayolan said with a snarl.

"That's right, you prefer your women silent with their legs spread, no doubt."

"She really does have a death wish." Kalen laughed. But Fayolan scowled, kicking a mound of dirt into the fire, leaving a smouldering pile of ashes.

A smile flit across my lips at his reaction. I knew I

shouldn't provoke Fayolan... *but he made it too easy.* Fayolan gave a powerful yank on the rope, dragging me along behind him.

"Do you still think he intends to kill you?" Kalen let out a throaty chuckle and shook his head.

"*Yes.* Being born was a death sentence, remember? I've done nothing bad in my life, yet *here* I am." I scowled. "Fayolan's taking me to a town filled with people that will want me dead. How is he *not* trying to get me killed?"

"For someone so smart witted, you can't see what is in front of your face." Kalen smirked as I pouted. "Tell me, what have you heard about the Dark Prince of Stidahl?"

"He is a merciless killer... the King's most skilled assassin. He's stealthy, and no one sees him coming until it is too late."

Kalen nodded as his gaze darted to Fayolan's back. "Does he resemble that man to you?" He raised his eyebrow as I turned my attention to Fayolan's back. From what I had seen, he was quick to anger, irritable and struggled to control himself. He wasn't the man I thought he'd be.

"The rumours are mistaken... *so* what?" I shrugged. It's probably some scare tactic used by the king to instil fear in his subjects.

"They *aren't* wrong," Kalen said as he leant in. A chill ran down my spine. *If the rumours were true, then why was he acting this way? Maybe he was used to people cowering before him.*

Kalen smirked as he pointed towards the ridge to Fayspire. "Not far now." I nodded as I began the tireless climb.

My legs protested as we reached halfway, and the sun beat down on us. As I peered at the top of the ridge, I wiped sweat from my forehead.

Half a day passed before we reached the summit of the

cliff. Fayspire spread out below us, surrounded by an enormous stone wall. So tall even the giants couldn't breach it. The streets crisscrossed the city in perfect symmetry. With enormous watchtowers lining the square wall.

On the outskirts of Fayspire, the smallest houses were located. The grander and more imposing abodes surrounded a castle-like structure at the core of the city. With its own barrier protecting it from the rest of Fayspire.

"Fuck," Fayolan said with a deep, resonating growl. His fists clenched at his sides as he stared. Not towards the city, but at the vast encampment of Ustrayan soldiers surrounding it. And the now smouldering ruins of the farmhouses they had set ablaze. *Gods I hoped those poor people made it into the safety of Fayspire.* "We stay until nightfall, then we go in."

"I am not going through *them*." I gestured towards the small army.

Fayolan smirked darkly as he continued to stare out at the army. "I didn't say through. We're going over." Before I could argue, a squawk echoed in the distance. The deep baritone suggested the creature was enormous. *Please don't let it be another dragon.*

"What was that?" I stammered as I searched the skies.

"That's my ride," Kalen said, grinning as he motioned for us to get down. Once I was flat on my stomach, hidden by the long grass, Kalen gave a shrill whistle. The creature responded with another loud squawk. I glanced up as it ascended from the central building in Fayspire.

"Is that a *gryphon*?" I asked with a gasp as it flew over the Ustrayan army. Its feathered wings sent debris scattering in all directions as it landed behind us, making the ground tremble.

The gryphon had an eagle's head, sharp talons, and a lion's body covered in coarse fur. Its beak alone could slice me in half. Regardless of the deadly sharp claws on its two enormous paws and taloned feet.

It's going to kill me! With my rising panic, I tried to scramble away. But Fayolan slammed his hand across my back, pinning me in place with his vice like grip.

"Stay still," Kalen warned as the gryphon prowled towards us. A coat of glossy black fur covered its lower body, rising and seamlessly blending into matching feathers. Its taloned feet clicked against the ground as it stalked closer.

The musky scent flooded my senses as the gryphon found me. Tilting its head for a better view. A scream built in my throat, but Fayolan's other hand clasped across my mouth. His brows knitted together in a warning.

I remained motionless despite the pain of his touch, locking my gaze with Fayolan's. One false move and I would be gryphon food.

The beast's head lowered, its beak prodding me as Fayolan clasped his hand tighter. Giant talons rested on each side of my hips as it nudged me again. The beak of the giant creature pressed against my cheek, pushing my head to the side. Its breath was hot against my skin.

Fayolan smiled as the creature chirped and backed off, returning to Kalen, who brushed his hand over the gryphon's back.

"She likes you," Fayolan said, removing his hand from my mouth.

"I don't think she does," I grumbled, pushing myself up. Kalen chuckled as he reached up and stroked the gryphon's feathers.

"Hey, girl," he said as she rested her giant head over his shoulders. *She was his.* Her eyes shifted to me as I stood up. "Come here." Kalen held his hand out to me. *Was he fucking insane?*

"You want me to go near her *again?*" I asked in utter disbelief.

A smirk creased his roguish face. "If she didn't like you, you would be dead already."

"Good to know." With bated breath, I stepped closer, each movement soft and slow. The last thing I wanted was to startle her.

I halted as I reached for Kalen's outstretched hand. He waited patiently as my fingers hovered above his palm.

"Here," Fayolan said, slipping beside me, his hand replacing Kalen's. As he skimmed his fingers softly across the palm of my hand, I let out my held breath. Focusing on my hand so it did not tremble. "Stroke her like this." Fayolan placed my palm against the gryphon's soft feathers.

"She's beautiful," I gasped as she spread her enormous wings. "Are all gryphon's black?"

"No, most are brown, but Saki is special. She's a rare breed. Aren't you, girl?" Kalen ruffled her feathers. She huffed in response. *Incredible… she understood him!*

"Are her family like her?" I asked.

"Her daughter is as black as Saki. But Ustrayan soldiers captured her a few years ago." My heart ached for her. I could still remember how hard my mother had taken my kidnapping. And if she were alive, she'd endure that pain again for Maeve and me.

"I'm so sorry Saki," I sighed. Her head dipped, and her beak clamped around my hand. "Ouch." She released me with another snort. Fayolan snatched my hand away from Saki. His grip was crushing as he raised it to get a better look.

I squinted, turning away just in case half my hand was missing. All I could feel was a burning heat where her beak had been.

"Did she just…" Fayolan looked stunned as he positioned my palm for Kalen to inspect.

"Did she just what? Is my hand okay?"

Kalen chuckled as he nodded. "Yes, it's fine. But…"

"But *what*?" I interrupted. "Please don't tell me I committed some *obscure* crime against your people." Fayolan laughed with a snort.

"A crime like *what*?" Kalen raised his brows.

"I don't know… like *tainting* rare breeds with my touch? I know how ridiculous your notions on Nephilim are."

Kalen sighed, running his hand down his face as he rolled his eyes. "She marked you as kin." His tone held a reverence to it I had never heard from him before.

I snatched my hand from Fayolan, inspecting the mark across my palm. "What does it mean?" I asked, as they shared a troubled look. "*What*?"

"It means something in you is familiar to Saki. Whatever you share has earned you the loyalty of her entire bloodline. Any gryphon in her family will treat you as kin." *Okay, that doesn't sound too bad.*

"That's a *good* thing, *right*?" I asked. I stared at the now glowing brand-like mark between my thumb and index finger, swirling around to the rear of my hand.

"It *should* be fine." Kalen grinned as he pulled himself onto the large black saddle on her back.

"Thanks for filling me with confidence," I called, stepping back as Saki stretched her powerful wings. Kalen was a brute of a man, but she was large enough to carry his weight.

After two mighty strokes of her wings, Saki shot into the air with ease. Catching an updraft, she circled before carrying Kalen to the central building in Fayspire.

"What now?" I asked as Fayolan returned to his position on the ridge, watching over the Ustrayan army below.

"We wait until dark."

CHAPTER SEVENTEEN

Fayolan was careful not to touch me as he settled a heavy velvet cloak over my shoulders. The clasp was of the finest gold, with the insignia of Stidahl intricately etched into its surface. It covered the black silk blouse and leather trousers he had created for me earlier, both smooth against my skin.

Fayolan leant in, uncoiling the rope from my waist. "Put these on." He tossed me a pair of supple leather gloves. They fit my petite hands perfectly. I remained still as he gripped my hands, binding my wrists tighter than before. The gloves created a barrier, stopping it from cutting into my skin.

"There are rules this time, Tempest," Fayolan said as he inspected my wrists, ensuring they were secure. "You're my *prisoner* and you are to behave as such. You will not speak, and you mustn't run." His eyes pierced into mine as if expecting a reply. I gave him a piercing stare, twisting my fingers by the edge of my lips as if turning a key in a lock and tossing it aside.

"This isn't a *fucking* game, Tempest. You are not safe here if they discover *what* you are. Listen to me for once and you might make it out alive."

"But will I survive *you*?" I scoffed.

"Not with that mouth," he countered, lifting a dark, almost impenetrable veil over my face. It settled just beneath the tip of my nose. "There will be consequences if you disobey me. I am not known for leniency and my reputation is worth more than your life."

My eyes rolled as I gave him a glare. "You *really* know how to woo a woman." The shadows enveloped Fayolan, pulsing as he advanced towards me.

"Just play your *fucking* part, and I won't have to make an example of you," he warned with a resonating rumble in his chest. "No magic, no healing, and for the love of the Gods keep your eyes and hair hidden."

He pulled the dark hood over my head, cloaking my face in the shadows. I was faceless, nothing more than a prisoner. That's all I'd ever been to him.

Fayolan unfurled his wings, his dark sword in its scabbard at his waist, demonstrating his might. The shadows that encircled him encompassed his well-defined muscular body.

When his arms coiled around my waist, I shuddered, pressing myself against his body.

"Please don't drop me," I groaned as he lifted my arms around his neck. I clung to him as he rose from the ground, carrying me with him. The ridge fell away, and I gasped, clinging tighter to stop myself from plummeting.

"I won't let you fall." My head rested against his shoulder as we soared above the clouds, making my head whirl. "Breathe, Tempest."

As panic gripped me, Fayolan's touch became torturous,

and I squirmed. "Tempest?" he asked, his fingers digging into my arms. He frowned, trying to steady me. "*Look* at me." I startled as Fayolan's voice rose. "The pain is *all* in your mind."

"I'm *going* to fall," I cried out. Fayolan rolled his eyes, pulling me closer.

"Never." The soft touch of his lips teasing against mine as he spoke caused the pain and fear to dissolve away. As I kissed him back, I could hear his heart beating in his chest.

Fayolan nuzzled my cheek, brushing away my hair as it whipped into my face. "Better?" he asked, and I nodded, relaxing as we dipped below the clouds and Fayspire came into view. The loud squawking of the gryphons grew louder as we neared the central tower and the platform above them.

Kalen stood waiting, encased in armour. There was no trace of his knowing smirk on his face. I'd never seen him looking so cold and menacing. Two other guards stood beside him, monitoring us as we descended.

The instant my feet made contact with the platform, Kalen ripped me from Fayolan, shoving me towards the two waiting guards. *Asshole!*

"She's dangerous and sharp-tongued. *No one* gets near her," Fayolan said, shooting me a look of disgust which made my stomach roil. He went from kissing me to being a complete and utter bastard once again.

The guard nearest to me, with shaved black hair, reached out. "Do not *touch* her," Fayolan warned with a snarl so fierce even I wanted to back away.

"Yes, my Prince," the guard said as he brandished his sword, pressing it against my back. The sharp point dug into my skin and I scowled.

"*Ouch!*" I scrunched my nose as I glared at the man.

Fayolan's venomous stare was like a weight on my chest as the men kept me in place. The swords never wavered as they pushed me forward. Grumbling, I trailed the second guard with curly locks tied into a loose man bun.

They led me to a set of stairs that curled in a corkscrew fashion to the platform below, where the gryphon nested.

Saki emitted a piercing shriek when she saw me. She had a fearsome glint in her eye as she barrelled towards us. Using her wing, she propelled the black-haired guard into a wall behind me. And with a swipe of her powerful taloned foot, she pinned him against the tower. He dropped his sword with an ear-piercing screech. It clattered across the platform, stopping by my feet.

"Thank you, Saki," I said, smiling as I nudged the sword, sending it skittering off the platform.

"Get her to *back* off." Man Bun unsheathed his sword, jabbing it threateningly towards me.

I chuckled as I turned my back on him, speaking through clenched teeth. "Do *not* point that at me unless you intend to use it."

"Watch your tongue!" Fayolan's hand collided with my cheek, sending me sprawling across the platform. *Dammit.* I hadn't seen him coming. His deep, menacing growl sent chills down my spine. "I warned you to behave. I will not do so again."

"Come on, girl," Kalen soothed, his hands pressing against Saki as he moved her back. She let out a raucous screech at the guard as she followed Kalen's orders.

I wiped crimson from my lip before pushing myself up. Fayolan struck me again, but this time I saw it coming and remained on my feet. I clenched my fists tight, refusing to give him the satisfaction of seeing me cower.

"Walk." Fayolan shoved me back towards Man Bun, who watched us with a look of shock.

"Yes, he *even* punishes women." My voice cracked like a whip. The guard snapped out of his trance, sheathing his sword and continuing down the stairs with Fayolan at my back. He ignored my sarcastic comment, as if responding was beneath him.

We stopped five floors down at the base of the soaring tower. The town spread out below us, but I could see the cobbled streets and the lamps flickering in the night, offering a soft glow to the building fronts.

Fayolan jolted me forward as I stopped to stare. We crossed to a large, intricate metal gate, and the guard knocked. It swung open, revealing a magical garden.

Moonlight washed over the decorative stone archways, casting a soft blue glow on the flowers that grew, weaving around them. White stone benches surrounded the garden and a relaxing trickle of water came from a large fountain in the centre.

A spectral woman floated between the archways, singing with a soft angelic voice. Along with a few other spirits that sang of peaceful times.

"Come sit in the Garden Of Souls, Little Nephilim. It's your home away from home. You can hide from those that seek to harm you. We offer you sanctuary here, Little Nephilim."

She glanced at Fayolan as she continued to sing, offering me peace and safety.

"I hate this garden. It gives me the chills," the first guard said, grimacing as he shuddered. His ignorance was infuriating.

"The beauty here is beyond what you're capable of seeing," I said in a sharp tone.

Fayolan closed the distance between us, his chest firmly against my back. "Are there spirits here?" His words caressed my ear.

"It's a shame you can't see them. They are different here… peaceful."

"Maybe one day I will," he muttered as he pulled away. "Now move." I almost stumbled as he jerked me forward. I caught myself as I crossed beneath the archway.

Five square stone buildings surrounded the Garden Of Souls. The largest was at the back and light flickered in its windows. Soft music and dainty laughter wafted from within it. *Fayolan's harem.*

I spun around furiously, and Fayolan smirked as he nodded for the guards to move in. The sharp edge of a blade pressed against my spine, guiding me towards the building.

"We have your residence waiting, my Prince. Where would you like the girl?" Man Bun scowled at me as he dug his sword a little deeper.

"He prefers me in his *dungeon*," I said with a smirk at the men's unease. I shot Fayolan a sly wink, ignoring the growl that resonated in his throat. A warning that sent chills down my back, but for all the wrong reasons. "He likes his lovers *bound* and at his mercy." I raised my hands with a seductive glance in Fayolan's direction.

He moved swiftly, his sizeable hand snapping around my neck, engulfing it as he jerked me closer. "You have no *fucking* idea." His thumb caressed my cheek as my breasts pressed against his chest. "Don't challenge me, *Pet*, or you'll learn just how tied up I like my lovers."

Forcing my head up, he grabbed my face and planted a hard kiss on my lips. One so deep and all-consuming, it displayed his ownership of me for all to see.

My hands pressed against him, trying to push him back, but he squeezed my throat tighter. Blocking my air as his tongue tasted me. I tried to back away, but Fayolan followed, cornering me against the building. With a gentle movement, his knee slid between my legs, settling at my pussy, and I gasped.

My cheeks flushed red at the ache he stirred between my thighs. A sensation no one had ever made me feel.

"Get *off* me," I hissed, but his kiss smothered my words from everyone but him. As he nibbled on my lip, his hand explored the soft fabric between my legs.

He gloated as he pulled back, his other hand remaining around my neck as his eyes bore into mine. Dark and wild, as if someone else looked back at me. "Don't play games you can't finish."

"As if I would *ever* want you," I spat. "You… You *disgust* me." With his fingers sliding down my leg, my words became knotted in my throat.

"Do you really believe I would *fuck* a monster like you?" Fayolan whispered against my ear.

"Then *fucking* let go of me." I writhed beneath the weight of his body, pinning me to the wall.

"You started this, remember?" A stupid move on my part.

"I would rather die than spend *one* second in your bed," I hissed.

"That can be arranged, Pet." He nipped my ear, chuckling as a groan escaped. *Bastard!* "She stays in *my* residence. *No one goes in or out!*"

"Shall we clear it out? The women are waiting for you," the first guard asked. Fayolan's smirk widened as he remained locked in a fierce stare off with me.

"Don't bother. She gets *furious* when she hears me *fucking* other women. And I enjoy bedding her angry," Fayolan said lazily as he released my throat and took another step back. "After you."

I pushed off the wall, breaking our eye contact as I hurried towards the door. I had to separate myself from Fayolan as much as I could. The heat he awakened in me wouldn't ease until I did.

The entrance room was lit with flickering candles, and

colourful scatter cushions littered the floor. "No magic, speaking, or leaving. Do you understand?" Fayolan asked as he shunted me towards the only chair in the room.

A gag appeared in his palm as he placed it beneath the hood of my cloak, wrapping it around my mouth. This one was different. Rather than a piece of cloth, he fastened a metal gag with leather straps around my head, securing it with a buckle at the back. The cold metal pressed against the corners of my lips and the taste of steel dried out my mouth.

"Now be a good girl, Tempest." I made a vile gesture behind his back, slumping down into the chair. "The women here mean a *great* deal to me and if you hurt them, I swear I will take you to the dungeons and show you how much I enjoy causing pain." I saluted mockingly as I rested my head back against the chair.

Fayolan gave a shrill whistle, startling me. He grinned as three beautiful women crossed into the room. Each wearing a sensual mesh gown that left nothing to the imagination. The material clung to their breasts, their nipples poking through the fabric as they noticed Fayolan. They were the epitome of sexual desire.

These women were purely there to fuck Fayolan. Well, they were welcome to him. I snorted as they dropped to their knees on the scatter cushions before him.

Fayolan ran his fingers through the hair of the youngest beauty. Her smile was radiant as she looked up longingly at him. "Later," he promised. She beamed as she dipped her head. Gods, if Fayolan thought I'd *ever* willingly be in his harem, he had *another* thing coming.

"It's time." Kalen stuck his head in the door. He did not even spare me a glance. Nor did he acknowledge the women. His gaze remained solely fixed on Fayolan. Maybe only Death himself was permitted to look upon them.

"She stays here." Fayolan tilted his head towards me as he

addressed the women. "She bites, so keep your distance." I scowled as he stalked across the room, followed by the two guards.

The door clicked shut, and the women turned their beautiful faces towards me. "I've never seen him bring anyone like *her* here."

CHAPTER EIGHTEEN

Tempest

The soft, mournful wail echoing through the room distracted me from the women of Fayolan's harem. The baby's cries were weak and hoarse. It sounded like it took effort just to make a noise. Fayolan's warnings rang in my head as my magic reacted to the pain of the suffering child.

To grab the women's attention, I stomped my foot on the floor. My jaw ached as I strained to communicate through the tight gag. But they remained stood at the opposite side of the room, scrutinising me. With a deep sigh, I rocked my arms, indicating the baby.

"The child is dying," a dark-haired beauty said.

"Shut up Reema," another said as she scowled at her. "She's dangerous."

I snorted as I showed my bound wrists.

"I don't think she is. Fayolan would never have left her

here if she were. The poor girl looks half starved." Reema smiled.

The babe wailed again, and I rocked my arms once more before pointing to myself.

"I don't understand," Reema said with a frown. I gestured toward the door leading further into the harem, then back to myself.

"We're not letting that poor babe anywhere near her," the oldest of the three said with contempt.

My magic swelled as the pained wails grew louder.

"You're a *healer*!" she gasped in astonishment.

I motioned to the gag, but the three women scurried from the room. *Dammit!* I could help if only they would stop being so… suspicious.

Exhaling heavily, I slumped back. *It wasn't their fault. Of course, they would be wary of me. Why did I even care? Healing was the only way to prove to myself, I'm not the monster everyone believes.*

"Will you heal my son?" A voice startled me from across the room. I rolled my head to the side and glimpsed a woman around the same age as me. As I raised my hands to the gag once more, she nodded, rushing towards me. She made a move to lower the cape, but I jerked away from her, shaking my head.

With a small apologetic smile, she reached beneath the hood as her fingers fumbled to find the buckle. She released it, placing it gently on the dresser.

"Thank you. Yes, I can try to heal your son." I smiled as I pushed off the chair.

"I'm Inaya," she said, extending her hand as she stepped towards me. Instinctively, I edged back.

"Sorry," I mumbled. "I don't like to be touched."

Inaya lowered her hand with a warm smile. "Not to worry, umm…"

"Tempest," I said, following as Inaya turned on her heels. She led me down a long corridor to a set of stairs.

"So how did you end up with Fayolan?" Inaya winced regretfully as she faced me once more. "Sorry, I shouldn't have asked that."

"He thinks I tried to kill him."

She took a tentative step away. "And did you?"

I chuckled, shaking my head. "No. I was *trying* to save him, but it didn't work out so well."

Inaya's shoulders relaxed as she continued up the stairs. "And being Fayolan, he was too stubborn to listen when you proclaimed your innocence." *She seems to know him too well.*

"Yeah, and if he knew what I was doing right now…" I muttered.

"*No one* here will say a word." Reema jerked the door open at the end of the corridor.

"There are a few conditions," I said. Crossing into the room with a small babe lying motionless in the crib. "No one can enter this room as I heal. My magic is temperamental at the best of times. The slightest distraction could make the boy sicker."

Inaya nodded as she lifted her son from the crib. "We understand. I can never repay you for this."

I took a deep breath and held it as she gently placed the baby into my waiting arms. "You're taking a risk allowing me to do this. Gods know what Fayolan will do if he finds out." Both women nodded without hesitation.

"Fayolan doesn't know my son is sick."

"Is it his?" I asked. Inaya and Reema shared an amused look.

"No. Fayolan doesn't sleep with me. He brought me here for my protection."

"Really?" It surprised me he cared enough about anyone to help her like that.

"Once you get to know him, he really isn't so bad." Reema frowned disapprovingly at me while I struggled to suppress a laugh.

"I've witnessed firsthand the actions of Fayolan…I know what kind of man he truly is." I pointed to my swollen cheek.

"You need to hurry," a voice said from behind the door.

"Go downstairs, Carlia," Reema snapped.

"What can I give you as payment?" Inaya asked.

I smiled at her, waving her off. "Maybe if one day I return seeking sanctuary, you can help me?" I would never ask her to put herself at risk to help me escape, but if I managed to, it wouldn't hurt to have a friend in Stidahl.

"When that day comes, I'll be ready." With a nod of my head, Reema ushered Inaya out of the room and closed the door, bolting it from the outside.

I let my magic wash over the babe. A wave of relief came over me as my magic found a small hole in the boy's heart. "I've got you, little one," I said, soothing him.

A trickle of black blood ran from my nose as his heartbeat became stronger. "Such a fighter. You'll make your mother proud." Colour returned to his rosy cheeks. His cries faded as the healing process continued. He gripped my finger and smiled.

Once finished, I wiped the blood from my nose on my sleeve where no one would see it. Lifting my hood to hide my hair. "You can come in now."

With a creak, the door swung open. Inaya rushed to her son's side. A relieved smile crossed her lips as she held him tight. "I can never thank you enough, Tempest."

"I'm just glad I could help the little warrior. If you wouldn't mind, I'm going to need you to replace the gag."

Reema cursed, muttering as she crossed the room with it in her hands. "I'm sorry."

Without removing my hood, she leant in and buckled it in

place, once again silencing me. "You look exhausted. Why don't you stay here and rest?"

My muscles did ache and my eyelids felt like weights, but if Fayolan found me here, we would all be in trouble. Fatigued, I struggled to my feet with a weary shake of my head.

"It's okay, we will wake you before Fayolan returns," Inaya insisted.

After weeks of trekking across Stidahl, I was exhausted, and I gave in, dropping back onto the luxurious bed. "I will lock the door. No one will come in unless it's me or Reema."

I mumbled an unintelligible thanks as I lay back on the pillow. My eyelids closed before they even left the room.

I groaned as someone burst into the room. I shot up, dragging the blanket off me. Reema slammed the door closed, locking it behind her.

"Get up, quickly," she commanded. Pausing for a moment, she reached out and straightened my hood, ensuring I remained obscured beneath it. "The guards are downstairs. They should never have entered."

Reema cursed as she hurried to the door. She pressed her ear to it, listening before turning the key. "Come on, we have to go. Now."

The sound of raised voices grew louder as we approached the bottom of the stairs. "Where the *fuck* is she?"

"She was tired. We just gave her a bed to sleep in." Inaya's voice raised as she clenched her fists. "You need to *leave.*"

"Not until we've seen her. So move aside, *Whore*."

Reema made way to let me pass. "See, she's right here. Now *get* out." She scowled.

I charged ahead, positioning myself as a barrier between the women and the two armed men. The head guard lifted his sword, pointing it directly at my chest.

"Where were you?"

"She was sleeping," Inaya said.

He sneered as he stepped closer. I held my ground and my heart raced. I would ensure the safety of these women after they had been so kind to me.

"Get out. No men can enter here without the Prince," Carlia said as she pushed past me. Thankfully, Reema pulled her back to safety.

"Take a seat," the head guard commanded, his expression sour. With a snort of contempt, I stepped forward. He followed, his sword at the ready. He untied the rope hanging from his belt. Shoving me into the chair, he grabbed my hands and began sawing at the bindings with his blade. I cried out at his touch.

"Get *off* her!" Inaya shrieked.

"Stay back," the second guard lifted his sword in her direction.

"Mmm hmmmp mmmph." I tried to curse, fighting against the guard as he secured my wrists to the armrests. He pulled each ankle to a leg of the chair and secured them.

"Not so tough now, are you?" he asked with a vile grin. "You must be a beauty if The Dark Prince is hiding you away. Let me see." He leant in and tugged on the delicate black veil.

No, you fucking don't. My forehead slammed into his nose, producing a sickening crunch.

"*Whore*," he screeched. I felt the sting of his backhand and the sudden loss of balance as my chair crashed to the ground.

The impact forced the air from my lungs. *What an idiot... Fayolan will notice the bruising. He'd struck my uninjured cheek.*

"You marked her." The second guard grabbed him, dragging him away from me. "He will kill us both, you *damned* fool."

He shoved his superior towards the entrance. Glancing back as he brandished his sword menacingly at the women. "Get her *cleaned* up." He stormed out, slamming the door behind him.

Reema and Inaya ran forward, setting me upright, still tied to the chair.

"Would you like us to clean you up?" Inaya asked, but I shook my head. I couldn't handle another person touching me.

"Fayolan will kill us all if he finds her like this," the fourth woman said. Her voice trembling as she stared at me.

"Don't be so stupid, Pilla. Fayolan knows we would never hurt her." Reema was right. He cared about these women; they were safe. At least, I hoped they were. *If I was wrong... I would defend them.*

Inaya grabbed a cushion, positioning it facing me as she took her son from Pilla. "We will stay here tonight in case they come back. Are you okay?" She pointed towards my lip and as I licked it, I could taste the distinct tang of blood.

She and her son nestled on the cushion, and the others followed her lead. Creating a barricade around me with their bodies.

"Move," Fayolan roared, bursting through the door. The sound of it slamming against the wall echoed around the room. He glared at me as he strode forward, forcing my chin up, inspecting the blood and swelling on my face. "*Who* the fuck touched you?"

I swallowed and glanced towards the door where the two guards stood.

"*Fuck*, Tempest." Fayolan gripped the arms of the chair as he cursed. "I told you to behave."

I scowled at him, his face mere inches from my own. The gore of battle still coated his body, and shadows materialised a black dagger in his bloody palm. He freed me from my restraints before storming towards the guards.

Fayolan stopped short. "Run me a bath," he barked at the women before slamming the door closed behind him.

We could hear the heated exchange between Fayolan, Kalen, and the guards outside. My heart raced at the unmistakable sound of two bodies hitting the ground.

The women jolted into action, scurrying away to run the bath.

Fayolan strode into the room, glaring as he wiped the blade of his dagger across his leg.

"You have some explaining to do." He flicked his hand, making the gag vanish. "*Where* did you go?"

"I fell asleep after the women offered me a bed. I'm so exhausted I couldn't refuse. You've dragged me across Stidahl on so little food that it's becoming an effort just to put one foot in front of the other. *Look* at me. I'm… just… so… tired."

"Those men died because of you, Tempest." Fayolan grabbed my face, his nails digging into my flesh. He turned my chin, examining the fresh bruise. "They hurt you to restrain you, and I had to set an example."

"They lied." I scowled and Fayolan tightened his grip.

"She's telling the truth." Inaya hovered in the doorway with her son cradled in her arms. "They tried to lift her veil, and she defended herself. That's when they struck her. They'd already restrained her in the chair. There was nothing we could do."

"She should not have left this room. Tempest knew better, but..." The babe stirred, drawing Fayolan's attention. He exposed his teeth as he looked between me and the boy. "Leave us."

Inaya jumped as Fayolan yelled again, "Get out!" She took off without a backward glance. *Fuck!*

"You healed the baby, didn't you?" Fayolan shoved my head aside as he released me. He slammed his fist into the wall, sending a shower of dust cascading to the ground.

"No one saw me do it."

"What have you done? I warned you not to hurt these women and now..."

"They know nothing. I was careful." *Gods. I can't believe I made such a foolish mistake.*

"So, you *lied* to me about sleeping?"

"*No,* I didn't. I swear to you, Fayolan... I was asleep upstairs."

Fayolan distanced himself as he paced the room. "You've put me in an impossible situation. I told you what these women mean to me. *Fuck*, Tempest... I can't deal with this right now. *Gods* if I get one hint they know what you are, I will *have* to kill them." Stopping to open the door, he let out a shrill whistle.

Pilla, Reema, and Carlia all rushed in, dropping to their knees at his feet. "Reema, warm my bed, I will join you soon." Fayolan caressed her cheek, smiling at her as if she were the most beautiful woman alive. My stomach clenched as I watched them together.

"I'll be waiting," Reema said seductively, batting her

lashes. Getting to her feet, she wiggled her hips with each step.

"Carlia, go to the bathing room. And Pilla, I will see *you* in the morning." Carlia rose from her seat, beaming as she reached out and took Fayolan's hand, leading him after her.

As he reached the door, Fayolan glanced back at Kalen. "Watch her. She is to remain bound and awake until I say otherwise." *Seriously?*

Soon the sound of water splashing and Carlia's shrill laughter echoed down the corridor. She screamed out Fayolan's name, begging for him to fuck her harder. *Great!*

Once she had finally quietened down, I let my eyelids close. But Kalen nudged my chair to wake me.

"*What*? They're done!" I lashed out, and he chuckled.

"I wouldn't count on it."

"Ugh," I groaned as Reema screamed his name in ecstasy. I fidgeted, struggling to block her out. *No one* would ever touch me like Fayolan did her.

The throb between my legs resurfaced as images of Fayolan and Reema's bodies intertwining filled my head. My stomach was in knots, as if I had some ridiculous notion he belonged to me. *Fucking have him Reema... I don't want him!*

CHAPTER NINETEEN

Fayolan

My erection pressed uncomfortably against my leather armour as I stormed from my harem. The Nephilim's wicked words taunted me. *He likes his lovers bound and in his dungeon...* She did not know how right she was as I imagined her chained to my wall as I fucked her. *Gods help me, I was under her spell.*

"Get your head on straight, Fayolan. We have an army to wipe out." Kalen's lips curved into a smirk as he observed me. *How was she doing this to me?* I fucked women all the time, but none made me lust over them. *Until her.*

My jaw clenched as I walked through the Garden Of Souls. I'd never seen the flowers here glowing under the moonlight. But as I reached up and plucked one from its thorny stem, it illuminated my palm. It reminded me of the Nephilim, beautiful beyond words but prickly.

Crushing the flower, I discarded the petals, letting them blow away in the wind. *I had to erase Tempest from my mind.*

As I reached the gryphons, Kalen had already organised their riders. Mal stood waiting with Saki at his side. He was the largest beast here, and he squawked as he saw me. I was the only man strong enough to ride him. When you enjoyed killing as much as Mal did, *Death* was the perfect companion to ride with.

He let out a sharp squawk as he nudged Saki aside. "Woman trouble, huh, boy?" I chuckled as I stroked my fingers over his thick brown feathers. "I know how you feel." Saki huffed beside me as she nipped at Mal's flank.

"At least these two are mates. Watching you and Tempest is giving me a headache." I scowled at Kalen as I crossed my middle fingers. "She's rubbing off on you," he said chuckling.

"Fuck you, *Kalen*."

He laughed as he went to make another smart-ass remark. "Don't say another word." I hauled myself onto Mal's bare back. He refused to allow anyone near him to place the huge saddle on. Several keepers had gone to their graves trying, but I did not require one.

I settled on his back, unfurling my wings just in case he threw me off. "Let's go boy." The other gryphons made way as we passed. Even they feared the menacing beast.

He was a vicious bastard, but Saki was strong enough to hold her own against him. She took position beside him and they spread their enormous wings, taking to the sky.

With a signal, I directed Kalen right as I veered left. Horsemen would flood through the city gates attacking from the front, whilst we swooped in from both sides. I had given the order that only one Ustrayan bastard would survive with a stark warning to his king.

With our fifty gryphons, we soared into position, and the soldiers below were quick to notice. Their warning cries came too late. They'd signed their death warrants the moment they crossed into my lands.

We navigated to the boundary of the encampment, and I gave a piercing whistle. With a deafening screech, Mal's taloned feet ripped through flesh as he dived into the waiting Ustrayans. With a sudden jerk, he returned to the sky, dropping the still screaming men to their deaths.

Warriors swarmed from the Gates of Fayspire, and flaming arrows shot into the tents from its walls. Gryphons waited for the rain of fire to cease before launching a second attack.

As Mal dropped again, I jumped from his back, my sword humming as it hungered for some action. I ran through the hordes of men. Each powerful strike stole the lives of those in my path. Blood sprayed across me as I roared, every step and swing bringing death.

"*Help*!" a woman screamed, and for the briefest moment, I pictured Tempest. A sword sliced across my cheek, but before I could react, Mal attacked, his beak slicing the man in two.

"Help me, please." The woman stumbled across the battlefield. Her hands were bound and her dress ripped and bloody. I charged towards her, piercing my sword through a man's chest as I kicked him aside. She fell forward, and I caught her.

Her body tensed, and I glimpsed a flash of steel as her arm raised. A dagger plunged into my shoulder as I pulled away, snapping the woman's neck before she could rip it free.

"The women are soldiers," I bellowed as several more appeared around the camp. *Fucking Ustrayan bastards.* My sword hummed with the need to devour the depraved souls of these barbarians.

It sliced through them with ease as Mal thudded to the

ground, using talons and his enormous beak to shred through their flesh.

Pain rippled through my shoulder as I ripped the dagger free. Tossing it aside as I rotated my arm. Wincing at the burn it caused. Thankfully, I still had full movement, and I lifted my sword following the trail of destruction Mal left in his wake.

The battle ended swiftly. Ustraya hadn't stood a chance. The only one left was the soldier at my feet as I carved my message into his chest.

"Determine if there are more troops in Stidahl. Then make sure he makes it to the border." I seethed, ignoring the blanched faces of the men as they stared at the bloody message.

"Do you think there are more out there?" Kalen stepped through the mounds of bodies, with Saki at his back.

"I have a feeling this is just a distraction." I grimaced, rotating my arm again, as I wiped the fresh blood away with a rag.

Kalen's gaze flicked to my shoulder. "You should ask her to…" I raise my hand, cutting him off.

"*No*," I said, with a growl rumbling in my chest. "She wouldn't even if I *demanded* it." I heaved myself onto Mal's back, watching the smug grin creasing Kalen's face as he mounted Saki. "Don't look at me like that."

Mal's wings beat powerfully as he soared into the sky, circling the camp before descending with a thud. I clambered off as Saki trailed behind him.

I stalked to the rim of the platform, looking down at the chaos below. At first light, we'd gather and prepare our fallen for a warrior's send off. No doubt soon after, the city folk would begin scavenging whatever treasures they could find amongst Ustraya's dead.

"They almost got one over on us today. What barbarians use women to fight their battles?" Kalen rubbed his chin as he leant against the stone supply building.

"*Damn cowards*." But it had taken us off guard. "I pictured *her* out there…"

"Who? Tempest?" I gave a nod before walking away. *The little Nephilim got under my skin.* Every time I was near her, feelings I had accepted I would never feel flared to life within me. "You wouldn't have if you had seen her galloping bareback across the meadow in No Man's Land. She isn't your typical damsel in distress." *No… she certainly wasn't.*

"I get the feeling if she wants to kill us, she'll stare us in the eyes as she does it." I chuckled, shaking my head as we started for the stairs.

We reached the Garden Of Souls, which seemed desolate without her in it. I glanced at the wall I had pinned her against, where I'd felt her wetness on my leg, betraying her arousal.

"Shit." Kalen tilted his head towards the two guards. Their gaze dropped as one discreetly positioned his swollen hand behind him. *What had she done?*

I barrelled past them, slamming the door open, and my eyes fell on Tempest. They had tied her slender ankles to the chair legs and secured her already bound hands to the armrest. They had struck her, bloodying her lip and swelling her other cheek. *Someone had touched her, and they were about to die!*

The bath was waiting, and the scent of jasmine wafted with tendrils of steam. Carlia knelt, waiting submissively, with her hands palm up on her knees.

She was beautiful, but she paled compared to the alluring sight of the woman next door. If only Tempest had not been born a monster. I could have claimed her as my own, and allowed myself to be tempted by the warmth and desire that radiated from her.

"You're hurt?" Carlia gasped, redirecting my focus towards her. She was a seductress in her own right. Her body had lain beneath mine many times before, but not even she had drawn an orgasm from me.

"I need stitches," I grumbled as she hurried to her feet. Gently helping me to undress. Her soft hands ran across my chest, exploring every inch of me.

"Relax in the tub and I will fetch the kit." I immersed myself in the hot water until she returned. She leant across the bath as I permitted her to clean the wound on my shoulder.

Her touch was gentle as she sutured me. Once she finished, her plump lips skimmed the wound. "All better." Carlia fluttered her lashes as her kisses rose, trailing a path up my neck.

"Thank you." As I stroked her hair, water ran down her back and she giggled. I cared for these women. They were good to me, offering themselves, even knowing I would never love them back. "You're so beautiful," I murmured as I shut my eyes, and Tempest was there. Her hands brushing against my chest as her lips grazed the curvature of my mouth. *I was losing my fucking sanity.*

"She's special to you, isn't she?" My eyes flew open as Carlia sat back on her heels, meeting my icy gaze. My body tensed. *If she knew too much, I would kill her.* I didn't understand my need to keep Tempest hidden, but no one would take her from me. "I see the way she looks at you, just as conflicted as you are. You hate her, yet she stirs something in you. We *all* see it." She gave a heavy sigh.

"She is my *prisoner* and often, more *trouble* than she is worth." I slipped deeper into the water. "Clean me, woman." I smirked.

Carlia provocatively bit her lip as she coated a cloth in sweet-smelling lotion. "Maybe it is her you should take to your bed?" She looked fleetingly to the room above where Reema waited for me.

"She will never feel my cock between her legs." I scowled. "She's *not* to be trusted."

Carlia frowned as she continued. "Yet you deemed her trustworthy enough to be left with us."

"Yeah, and look how that turned out."

"She put herself between us and those guards. *We* convinced her to get some rest, and she took the brunt of the backlash. If you ask me... she earned my trust."

"Well, I didn't." I lay my head back in the tub as Carlia pouted. *Gods, these women are driving me crazy.*

"Want to know what I think?" she asked, running the cloth between my legs. Batting her lashes as she leant in so her breath fanned my face.

"Not really," I grumbled.

"*Tough.* I think you've judged each other based on *what* you are... not *who* you are. She seems like a good person, and I believe you sense it too. You're just too stubborn to admit it." She shot me a mischievous grin as she ran the cloth over my erect cock.

I hissed as her hand replaced the rag, gripping the shaft. "She is my *enemy*." I let Carlia push me back as she slowly pulsed her hand.

"Is *she*? Who decided that? You? Her? Your *Father*?" Her smirk added to her beauty, but it infuriated me.

"She *just* is." I grabbed the cloth and wiped the dried blood from my face. "Enough about her," I commanded.

"You would have kissed me by now," she said, wily.

"As you wish." I sat up, wrapping my hand around her waist and pulling her fully clothed into the bath. She shrieked in surprise and I pressed my lips against hers as I claimed her.

CHAPTER TWENTY

Fayolan

I gripped the doorknob to my bedroom, my knuckles white, and my cock throbbing with unsatiated need. I'd never felt like this before, and I doubted Reema would quell the raging torrent of sexual desire.

Swinging the door open, I took in her beauty. Her curved hips as she lay on her side. Plump breasts rising and falling with every breath. Her chestnut eyes glistened as she watched me appraising her body. Her auburn hair fell over her shoulders in voluptuous waves, highlighting the glow of her dark complexion.

My cock twitched, approving of the beauty before me…or needing to fuck after Tempest played havoc in my fantasy.

"Do you intend to stand there staring all night?" Reema purred, rubbing the bed beside her seductively. Her gaze trailed down my muscled chest, halting with a gasp as she observed my pulsing dick. "I've never seen you like this before. *Maybe* it's because of the alluring beauty downstairs."

"Let's avoid talking about her… I have all I want right here."

"Are you trying to convince me or yourself?" She grinned wickedly as she rubbed her hand over the silk sheets.

"*Oh*, I don't need convincing," I lied. Even now, as I imagined what I would do to Reema, a certain little Nephilim made my heart race and my dick harder. "Now come to me, *woman*." I smirked.

Reema slid from the bed, wiggling her hips as she crossed to me. Biting her lip sensually as she ran her fingers up my back, weaving them into my hair.

Reema tasted divine as my mouth crashed into hers, claiming her. She pulled away with a seductive smile as she transformed before me. Her skin phased and morphed, paling to the bronzed olive of Tempest's. Reema shrunk in height, and her breasts grew minutely to match the Nephilim's busty curves.

"*Dammit*," I cursed beneath my breath, unable to find the words to make her change back. "What are you doing to me, Reema?"

"I wanted to see you look at me the way you do her." Reema reached up on tiptoes, kissing me again. "Would you prefer if I changed back?"

"I…" *Gods if I said no, it would hurt her and I would allow no one to cause her pain, not even me.*

"It's okay," Reema said, as if she had heard my thoughts. *I need to banish the Nephilim from my thoughts. Maybe fucking Reema like this would be enough to free me from Tempest's seductive spell.*

"Don't change." *I'm going to hell.* I grabbed Reema's waist, pulling her closer. "This will not be gentle," I warned.

She smirked, planting kisses on my neck. "Good. Tell me Fayolan… what is it you wish to do to her?" Reema's breath caressed me as she nipped at my neck.

"I want to feel every inch of her body." I lowered my hands, letting them explore Reema. "And I want to fuck her until my touch no longer hurts her." My voice went hoarse as Reema responded, gripping my cock and jerking her hand with a burning intensity.

"What else?"

My breath hitched as my gaze locked with hers. "I want to ravish her body until her legs tremble and she gives herself to me. I would bind her and she'd cry out my name as I showed her how pleasurable pain could be."

Reema's heart raced as she whispered huskily into my ear. "Show me."

I pushed Reema onto the bed, spreading her legs as I positioned myself between them. Pulling a silk scarf from the aether, I wrapped it tight around her eyes, hiding the part of her face that ruined the illusion. "She has chestnut hair so dark it's almost black," I purred, and Reema changed. *Close enough.* "Gods help me."

I took her slender wrists in one hand, pinning them to the bed, and a squeal left her lips. "Do you like me like this, Fayolan?" her voice rasped. "I can sound like her, too."

"No. I want her to hear *you* screaming my name." I hoped Tempest would be jealous. *Would she even care? Or would she simply be angry I'd disturbed her sleep?*

My fingers intertwined with Reema's as I weighed her down. Lowering my head so my lips skimmed against hers, as I sucked it into my mouth. I bit down, eliciting a squeal without causing her any pain.

"Are you sure about this?" I asked.

"Shut up and fuck me," she demanded.

My cock was so hard I did not take the time to prepare her. Reema screamed out my name as my shaft filled her, but she could not take all of me. None of the women I had bedded could.

Pulling out, I slammed into Reema again, keeping her hands pinned to the bed. My tongue slid into her mouth as my thrusts became harder and faster. Ploughing into Reema until her juices coated my cock, making it glide just a little deeper. It was still not enough.

With a hiss of frustration, I pulled out, flipping Reema so her pert ass was in the air. My hand ran over the unmarred skin on her back as I pictured the scars and the way Tempest fought my touch.

"Do you want more?" I asked as I grabbed Reema's hair.

"Gods yes," Reema cried, and I pushed her head into the pillow as I hammered her from behind. Each deep… forceful… thrust… making her scream. "*Fayolan.*"

My fingers played with her clit, turning the pain into an intense pleasure that had her cunt clenching my cock. As she erupted around me again.

"Cum for me," she begged, but still release eluded me. Although I was closer than *ever* before. I was on the edge of the orgasm I craved.

I fucked Reema until she panted, her skin slick with sweat. She had done well, screaming my name loud enough that Tempest would have heard every cry of bliss I drew from her.

"I'm done, Fayolan," Reema said with a grin as my cock remained hard within her. I pulled out, rolling to the side as she shimmered, returning to her own beautiful visage.

"Sorry… I…"

Reema chuckled, placing a finger across my lips to silence me. "Do not apologise. That was unbelievable. I'm almost a little jealous of her," she breathed.

I rolled towards her and cupped her chin, kissing her softly. "You shouldn't be. Death awaits her."

Reema frowned as she pulled away from me. "What? You're going to kill her?"

"She is a monster, Reema." With a heavy heart, I leant in and reached out to bring her closer.

"You don't truly believe that?" she asked, scrambling away from me.

"Why not? It's the truth, no matter how much I want to pretend it isn't."

"Then you do not deserve her." Reema clambered from the bed, pulling the sheet with her as she stormed out of the room, violently slamming the door behind her. *I'd never seen her react this way.*

Tempest... the Gods damned woman was going to drive me insane. *Could I actually stay away from the temptress? Would I be able to end her when she consumes my mind the way she does?*

My cock still throbbed painfully. I massaged the shaft, picturing Tempest's hand laced around my cock. Her wicked lips skimming against the tip as I pumped faster. Her gaze locking with mine as her tongue did sinful things to my dick. *Fuck!*

My whole body shook as I unloaded. My breath caught in my chest with each pulsating release. *I really was a prick.* The first time I had ever cum was to thoughts of the Nephilim licking my cock clean as I came undone.

As if to punish me, my dick did not soften, and the ache remained. *What if only Tempest could satiate me? Could I let her go without at least trying to claim the beautiful creature? To see if she could make me explode in pure ecstasy?*

"Fayolan!" Kalen hammered on the door. I jumped up, grabbing a pair of trousers from the aether. "Hurry."

I bolted for the door, swinging it open. "What's going on?" *Tempest!* Shoving past him, I bolted down the stairs, not waiting for his reply.

Tempest remained in the chair I'd left her in, her face frozen and streaked with tears as she stared vacantly ahead. I dropped to my knees, brushing her cheek with my thumb, but she could not see me.

"It's a spirit. She'll be fine." I shrugged.

"It's not just one." Kalen scowled.

Tempest gasped as she came back to herself. "No! Please stop!" she begged before she went rigid again. *Dammit.*

"How many?" I asked, spinning on Kalen.

"That's about eight. All she managed to tell me was it was soldiers." *Shit.* The spirits from the battle were flooding to her.

"There're fucking hundreds of them out there," I cursed as I grabbed her shoulders, shaking her to rouse her.

"It won't work, I tried. You need to get her out of here," Kalen snapped.

"It's too dangerous to leave Fayspire tonight." He knew it as much as I did.

He banged his fist into the wall as Tempest cried out again. "Then do *something*!"

"Like *what*?" My wings burst from my back, reacting to her cries. I lifted her from the chair, holding her against my chest as I cocooned us within them.

My shadows pulsed and writhed, engulfing her as they fed off the spirits. I could feel their hunger as they protected her, engorging themselves.

"Fayolan…"

"Stay back," I yelled at Kalen before he could get too close. "I'm not in control of my shadows and I don't know if they can tell friend from foe." All I knew is they desired to protect the Nephilim at all costs.

"Fayolan, you're" Tempest's words faded away as she closed her eyes. Her body going limp in my arms. *At least she wasn't suffering anymore.*

I got to my feet, keeping her tucked safely within my

wings. A crowd had gathered, but Kalen was keeping them back.

"Inaya, change the sheets in my room. Now," I bellowed, and she handed the boy to Reema as she took off running.

"Everyone out of the way." The women scattered as I charged after Inaya. Waiting impatiently as she ripped off the sheet covered in Reema's juices.

"Is there any way I can help?" she asked, tucking the clean sheet under the mattress.

"No. I'm doing everything I can." I slumped onto the bed, holding Tempest against me. She slumbered peacefully as my shadows kept the desperate spirits at bay.

Inaya backed away, her hand resting on the handle as she glanced at me once more. "I'll leave you to it."

I watched over Tempest until the warmth of her body made me sleepy. Keeping her cradled against me, I lowered myself beside her. It felt so right, holding her protectively, as if she had belonged there all along. *So, how could killing her be what I was supposed to do?*

CHAPTER TWENTY-ONE

Tempest

The alluring aroma of citrus and pine comforted me as I woke. Cocooned in darkness with powerful arms wrapped around me, holding me against a wall of solid muscle.

The pain of being touched registered, and I jerked my elbow back. "Get off me."

Fayolan groaned, rolling away. "Relax, I was stopping the spirits from entering you." He clambered off the bed, taking his warmth with him.

I turned my gaze from the half-naked man before my eyes could begin their treacherous route across his body. "Gods, this room stinks of sex."

"Reema didn't seem to mind it." Fayolan shot me a smirk as he materialised a shirt from the aether.

"Of course she didn't. The whole of Fayspire heard *her* screaming your name. Although the funny thing is… You never once called hers. Did you not enjoy her *voluptuous* body?" I asked, grinning as a growl rumbled from Fayolan's chest.

"What's the matter, *Tempest*? *Jealous*?" He gave a sly grin.

I snorted, with a sideways glance in his direction. "Death incarnate is *really* not my type."

"Let me guess, copper-haired, blue-eyed *boys* are more your thing. I mean, we both know you can't handle a *real* man."

I clenched my fists at the mention of Serrin. My palms becoming slick with sweat as my nails dug in. "He's more of a *man* than you'll *ever* be, Fayolan. A monster like you could *never* compare to him."

He exposed his teeth in a fierce snarl as he closed in on me, backing me into a corner. "A little girl like *you* knows nothing of what a *man* like me can do. The pleasure I could give you with a *single* touch."

His breath brushed against me as he leant nearer. Pushing me against the wall with his body as he placed his palms flat on either side of my head, boxing me in. "Has the boy made you feel like I do when kissing you?" His mouth teased against the corner of mine.

My lips quivered as I forced myself to speak, fighting the urge to return his kiss. "Serrin has made me feel things you *never* could, Death. He's satiated my needs and left me *begging* for more." I lied... Fayolan had gone further than any man, but I would never admit it.

"We'll see. Maybe if I *fuck* that needy pussy of yours, you will rethink the *pretty* boy."

"As if I would let you get anywhere near..." A groan escaped my lips as his fingers trailed across my stomach.

"*Remember*, Pet... I felt how *wet* you were for me last night." Fayolan smirked as he backed away, giving me just enough space to edge towards the door. "Now go take a bath. You fucking reek."

"*Asshole!*" I slammed the door behind me, resting my back against it as I seethed. *How dare he… I mean… Gods…* I hated him so much I wanted to punch him in his smug face. But even now, my treacherous body reacted to him. The ache between my legs growing as it consumed me.

I pushed off the door, storming down the corridor to search for a bath. *I'd need an ice-cold one.*

"Oh good, you're up." Reema smiled as she stepped from a room, steam billowing around her.

"I was looking for a bath," I mumbled.

"I ran this one for you just now. We had a feeling you might need it." She stepped aside, letting me peer in. Blue petals from the garden floated around the tub.

"You did this for *me*?" I asked.

Reema nodded with a smile. "Inaya insisted after what you did for her son."

"This isn't necessary. I did what any healer would've. I couldn't just sit by and watch a child suffer."

"You're not used to being fussed over, are you?" Reema chuckled.

"Not really." I shrugged as I swirled my fingers through the warm scented water, scooping up a petal. "What are they? We don't grow these where I come from."

"They're moon flowers. They have healing properties." Reema smiled as she lifted a basket filled with them. "It's rumoured those who see spirits see them glow at night."

I pictured how they had stolen my breath in awe as we crossed the Garden Of Souls. "They do… it's a beautiful sight."

"You see spirits?" she asked.

"Yes. They sing to me."

Reema's jaw dropped. "What a blessing."

"It *can* be a curse. Some spirits carry warnings… which had I heeded… maybe I would not be in this *mess*." *A prisoner to Death himself.*

"Well, I'm glad you found your way here. I think things are going to work out for you," Reema said, winking like she knew something I didn't. "Now, wash up and meet us downstairs. Inaya has been cooking all morning."

She closed the door with a faint click, and I lowered my cloak. Letting it drop to the floor. I ripped the veil from my face, glimpsing my reflection in the water.

My swollen cheeks had turned a deep purple and dried blood still trailed from the corner of my lip. I sighed, releasing my dress and dipping a toe into the bath. Letting out a groan. *It was perfect.*

I hurried to wash before submerging myself under the water. The bone deep ache in my body eased almost instantly.

My head rested back against the tub as a commotion arose. Inaya burst in, slamming the door closed as she grabbed a towel and tossed it at me. "Cover your eyes and hair. *Now.*"

"What's going on?" I asked, trying to keep my scars hidden beneath the water as I covered up.

"Reema," she called through the door.

She scurried in, securing us in the bathing room. "We need your help, Tempest. Where are your clothes?" Reema asked as she began stripping her own.

"Somebody needs to tell me what the *hell's* going on?" I scrambled from the bath, grabbing my pile of clothes.

Inaya snatched them from my hands, hurriedly tossing them to Reema. "Pilla went to the guards. She told them you were a Nephilim. Now they are downstairs demanding your execution." *Oh shit.*

"They won't cross Fayolan though… *right?*" I stammered.

"They outnumber him tenfold. Their Captain insists on seeing you, which is where *I* come in," Reema said as she crossed the room. She could not hide her shock as she noticed my scars. "I know you don't like to be touched, but unfortunately, it's the only way." Her hand pressed against my chest and magic flowed into me, changing my body.

"Put these on." Inaya shoved a mesh dress identical to hers into my hands. "*Hurry.*"

I stumbled into the dress, catching sight of myself in the mirror. *Holy shit.* Reema had swapped our appearance. "That's amazing." She now resembled me except for her eyes and hair, which no longer marked me as Nephilim.

"Bind my hands," Reema ordered.

Inaya held up a rope, and without hesitation, she complied. "Keep your head down and follow my lead."

I trailed the two women from the bathing room. Down to the entrance room of the harem. Inaya shoved Reema forward before dropping to her knees on a scatter cushion.

"This is the one?" The guard captain pushed Pilla forward.

She grinned as she examined Reema, bruises and all. "Yeah, that's her," Pilla said gleefully. *Gods… what the fuck did I do to upset her?*

Fayolan snarled in his attempt to cross to Reema's side, only to have six guards raise their swords at him.

"Get. Out. Of. My. Way!" Fayolan gripped the point of a sword, ripping it from the soldier's hand and sending it scattering towards us.

I reached out, gripping its hilt, sliding it towards me as I kept my eyes on Fayolan.

"Don't," Inaya hissed under her breath and Fayolan's head snapped towards us. *Oops!* He glared at me, issuing a silent warning, and I released the sword, shoving it away.

"Keep your *whores* under control or I will have to take care of them." The Captain smirked.

"Touch them, and I *will* kill you *all*." Fayolan crossed his arms, flashing his teeth in a scowl as he moved to Reema's side. "You answer to me and this insult will not go unpunished."

"I answer to the *King* and if she is a Nephilim, it is my duty to execute her."

"When you see how mistaken you are, it will be you that pays the ultimate price." Fayolan looked at Kalen, who was blocking the exit. "As will you, *Pilla*."

The Captain chuckled as he reached towards the veil, but Fayolan slapped his hand away. "She doesn't like to be touched." I watched with bated breath as he tenderly lowered Reema's hood, lifting the veil from her face.

Pilla shrieked as she realised the fate that now beheld her. She had crossed Fayolan and lost. She was completely unaware that if it hadn't been for Reema, she wouldn't have.

"How did you heal the child?" The Captain sneered, his face reddening as he realised how fucked he was.

Reema smirked, just like I would have done. "I have a small amount of healing magic. Not enough to join the healers, but I can save a sickly babe."

She turned to Pilla with a venomous scowl. "The Prince gave you everything you could ever want, and this is how you repay him?" It was strange hearing my voice coming from Reema.

Pilla dropped to her knees at Fayolan's feet. "Please… I beg you. I was only trying to protect you. I thought she was… *dangerous*."

Her pleas went ignored as Fayolan shot forward. "There is no forgiveness for *treachery*!" His black sword materialised as he swung it, removing Pilla's head from her shoulders. It rolled to a stop at my feet, her mouth frozen in a silent scream.

I slapped my hand against my mouth as I gagged and the other women cried out, scrambling back. I dipped my head, staring at the floor as Pilla's spirit wailed.

"Who is second in command?" Fayolan's voice was stony and cold as he stared across the men.

One guard stepped forward. "I am, Dark Prince." He was the biggest man in the room, but he stumbled over his words.

"Your Captain has caused a lot of trouble here today. I will not have people hunting down my prisoner. Make sure you quash the rumours. You've seen with your own eyes that she's not a Nephilim. Her size alone should have told you that."

"Yes, Dark Prince," the guard stammered, dipping his head.

"As for you, Captain… You have been relieved of duty and will spend the last of your days on the walls of this city. You'll serve as a reminder of what happens when you *dare* to challenge me," Fayolan barked as he stepped over Pilla's body.

The Captain stumbled back, gripping his sword. But Kalen's hand snaked out, snatching it from his grasp. "I wouldn't do that if I were you."

Fayolan flicked his gaze back to the second in command. "Congratulations on making Captain. Oh, and strip his skin *before* hanging him above the gates to rot. I want him kept alive." Fayolan's grin made me shudder as he pointed his dagger towards the dishonoured captain.

"It was a mistake… It was all that girl's fault. She swore to me she had seen her eyes and hair and watched as she weaved a spell over you." He pleaded for his life as they dragged him from the Harem.

"The rest of you *get* out." Fayolan sneered at the remaining men. Without hesitating, they bolted for the door.

"*Not* you." Fayolan smirked as the last six men tried to leave. "You *dared* raise your weapons against *me*."

Kalen moved in, blocking the door, and I froze as the men scattered. Five drawing their swords as the last darted towards me, his still lying discarded at my feet.

"Stay behind me." Fayolan stepped before Reema, protecting her as the fighting broke out. Inaya and Carlia bolted for the stairs, but I was not quick enough. I spun to chase them, but the sharp edge of a sword grazed my throat.

"*Stop* or I *kill* her." Hands grabbed me, forcing me to face Fayolan, making a shield out of my body.

"That would be foolish," Fayolan nudged Reema towards Kalen as he stepped over several bodies, making his way towards me.

"I *mean* it. I'll slit her throat," the guard behind me warned, but Fayolan kept moving closer. Slowly hunting his prey.

"And once she is dead… what will protect you from me, then?" I could feel Fayolan's warm breath against my cheek as he drew nearer. He moved so fast I barely registered his hand shoot out and grip the sword. A taloned wing brushed past me, impaling the guard to the wall.

"Are you hurt?" Fayolan lowered the sword as he scanned my body.

"I'm fine."

"Good. Now go to my room and *fucking* wait whilst I clean up this mess. Do you *think* you can manage that?" I nodded as I edged away from him.

"You too," Fayolan snapped at Reema. She reached out and grabbed the sleeve of my dress, hauling me towards the stairs.

She closed the door behind us as I placed my back against

the wall. I could never regret what I'd done. But people had died because of it.

"I'm so sorry," I gasped as my head rushed with images of what had just happened. "It's all my fault."

"Shut up." Reema firmly gripped my shoulders, compelling me to face her. "This is *all* on Pilla. She knew full well that what happens within these walls stays inside them. She was fucking jealous, and she turned you in even after saving Inaya's son. Pilla always was a hateful bitch." *That explained a lot.*

"Thank you for what you did for me." I relaxed and Reema released me.

"Carlia is unaware of my abilities, and I'd like to keep it that way. If Pilla had known of my magic, everything would have turned out very different."

"You keep mine and I'll keep yours," I said.

I could hear raised voices from below and I winced as Reema dropped onto the side of the bed. "How mad do you reckon he is?"

"I don't know, but I'd wager we're in a whole heap of shit." I almost chuckled. It was peculiar talking to a copy of myself.

The door banged against the wall, making us both jump as Fayolan stormed in, slamming it closed behind him. His lips curled back into a snarl as he rounded on me. "Cover up."

Reema darted to my side and Fayolan snatched the veil and cloak from her hands, placing them over me.

"Change back. *Now*," he demanded.

Reema nodded as she obeyed, touching my chest again as we both morphed back into ourselves. "This wasn't her…"

"One of my men is coming to take you to Solis." Fayolan cut her off. Reema dipped her head without a single flicker of emotion.

"You have caused me a *great* deal of trouble, Tempest, and I cannot let you go unpunished."

I backed away, but Fayolan had me cornered, grabbing my wrists. "You brought this on yourself." He threw me onto the bed, straddling my waist as he fought to control me.

"Leave us, Reema," Fayolan barked without even glancing at her. She scurried away, sealing the door behind her, leaving me alone with *Death*.

I kept struggling against him, but Fayolan was too strong. He fastened my wrists to the bedposts with rope before doing the same with my ankles.

"What do you intend to do with me?" I asked, as he methodically checked and tightened each rope to stop me from wiggling. Fayolan used a cloth to gag me as he headed towards the door.

"Stay here and be a good little girl. I will be back for you later."

CHAPTER TWENTY-TWO

M y eyes shot open as the mattress dipped. Fayolan climbed onto the bed, his body offering me warmth as he straddled my waist. "Time for your punishment, Tempest," he rasped in a husky tone. "I'm going to ask you questions and you *will* answer them. And I'll have to discipline you if you don't."

I yanked at the ropes, desperate to get away from him, but it was useless. Fayolan moved quickly, tightening them to the point of causing me pain before removing the cloth from my mouth.

"Asshole!" I cursed as a cry burst from my lips.

Fayolan grinned as he stared intently down at me. "We will start with an easy one." He removed the veil as he asked, "How old are you?"

I snapped my mouth shut, my lips curling into a snarl. Refusing to give him even the tiniest piece of me.

"Fine, have it your way. Don't say I didn't warn you."

With a swift flick of Fayolan's wrist, a dagger glinted in his hand. He ran its pointed tip lightly down the mesh dress I was wearing. With a sharp tug, he ripped it away from me, exposing my body. "Last chance, Tempest. How old are you?"

"*Bite* me," I hissed as I writhed beneath him.

"As you wish," Fayolan said, shooting me a cocky smirk. He lowered his head, the loose strands of his hair brushing against my skin. His warm breath caressed me as he grazed his teeth across my neck. I squealed as he sank his fangs in, sending pain shooting through me.

My jaw tightened as I spat out, "Twenty-three." Fayolan's chest vibrated with a chuckle as he pulled away from me, sitting up so our bodies were no longer touching. My blood stained his lips, but he did not wipe it away.

"Good. Now, let's see… How many of your kind lived in the village?"

"There were two of us, but you *bastards* killed her." I scowled at him, but deep down I couldn't deny it was my fault Morgaan was dead. "She was kind, and *you* murdered her."

"Watch your tongue," Fayolan warned as his shadows danced around him. "The boy from your village… are you in love with him?"

"Did you kill him?" My lip quivered, terrified of what he would say.

"That is not an answer." Fayolan's smirk deepened as his fingers trailed a fiery path across my skin. "Do. You. Love. Him?" *Why did he even care?*

"In a way," I said, just to stop him touching me. I wasn't *in* love with him. He was like a brother to me.

"What is that supposed to mean? Either you do or you don't. It's that simple." His hands trailed towards my breasts, sending a swell of heat unfurling in my stomach.

"Love is anything but simple." I hissed against the pain. "There are so many types of love. I guess… *in a way*, I love Serrin. But I have never experienced *true* love… I don't even know if I am capable of it. Maybe if I wasn't so broken, I could have loved him more."

"No, I did not *kill* the boy. I made a deal with you, and I never go back on my word." I exhaled sharply, the tension in my body easing.

Fayolan lifted his fingers as he studied me. "Look at me Tempest." I did as he commanded. His face was cold and emotionless as he tilted his head as if something were bothering him. "So… you *fucked* him, anyway?"

"That is *none* of your business." I instantly regretted my words as Fayolan's fingers reached my breasts. Catching a nipple between them as he pinched it firmly.

"Answer me?" Fayolan's nostrils flared as he spoke.

"*No*, I never slept with him," I said, but Fayolan pinched the other nipple. "I *answered*."

"And I don't believe you." He lowered his head and drew my nipple between his teeth with a hiss. Sharp pain turned to heat as he rolled it between them.

"I *fucked* him." I lied, just to make him stop. Fayolan responded by running his tongue over my nipple as he pulled back. Wetness pooled between my thighs as they ached.

"Now *that* I believe, little *seductress*," he said breathily. "How's your face?" He glanced at the swelling.

"Fine." His hand slid between my legs, running through my slick, sensitive folds. I strained at his touch, but each movement only increased the intoxicating sensation. I gasped as the pain morphed into something else… *Pleasure!* "It hurts, but the bath helped." I moaned, fighting to remain composed as my body tried to fall apart.

"Do you wish me dead?"

"*Yes*. With my *whole* heart and soul," I spat in defiance. But despite my feelings… *I kept saving him.*

"Tell me Nephilim… are you considering giving it a shot?" His fingers moved in mesmerising circles, eliciting a passionate moan from me.

"No. I'm not a fool."

Fayolan smiled victoriously. He lifted his fingers to his mouth, running his tongue over them. Savouring the taste of my juices in a way that had my body screaming for his tongue to return and finish what he'd started. There was no escaping the ache he stirred within me.

"We'll pick this up another time," Fayolan said with a dark chuckle. "We'll be leaving at first light, so get some sleep."

Fayolan's shadows spread out, materialising a bowl of fragrant broth on the small cabinet beside the bed. "Reema will be in shortly to assist you." His voice was gentle as he pulled a blanket over me. Before he returned the veil to my face and wrapped a scarf around my hair, concealing it. "At least try to behave."

"Don't trip and fall on your sword," I hissed, my voice oozing with sarcasm.

With a chuckle, Fayolan glanced back towards me. "If I did, you would waste away. *Bound* to my bed." He grinned callously.

"I would rather meet my end than endure another moment with you."

"Do not make me gag you again." He shot me one final, menacing scowl before closing the door behind him.

I lay bound beneath the blanket; the rope stretching my arms and legs out painfully as Reema hurried in. A glower spread over her face as she took in the scene before her.

"Are you hungry?" she asked as she knelt beside me. Lifting my head and positioning a pillow behind it.

"Starving," I said, trying to smile.

"Hurry up, Reema," a gruff male voice called through the door. Followed by a fist pounding on it.

"I'll be out when I'm ready, *Braedon*," she snapped as she lifted the bowl and offered me a spoonful.

The door creaked, and I was met with the most striking grey eyes I'd ever seen. *Gods, was everyone around Fayolan unnaturally beautiful?*

"Holy shit," he cursed, looking over me as if he could see through the veil. His gaze trailed down my body and I shuddered.

"She is not part of the harem," Reema snapped, as she ran a hand through her sleek brown hair.

"Shit." He whirled, turning his back. "He's *fucking* her, isn't he?" Braedon muttered.

"He is *not*!" I barked, and Reema shot me a playful grin.

"Says the woman tied to his bed," Braedon mumbled as he returned his attention to Reema.

"We need to get a move on. What's taking so long?"

The smile slipped from Reema's face as Breadon crossed his arms impatiently. Even if she didn't want to leave, Fayolan was not asking, and he wasn't the type of man you refused. Unless you were one stubborn, pissed off Nephilim like me. Maybe things would go smoother if I conformed like Reema did.

The room closed in on me as I realised this was the best I could hope for. A future where I was a bird trapped in a cage, unable to spread my wings. This was probably my only chance to change my fate… *And like hell, I would waste it.*

"I need to use the restroom," I grumbled, and Braedon shot me an awkward glance. "Please? Or Fayolan will be in for a nasty surprise when he comes back and sees me lying in my own filth."

Braedon sighed as he glanced to Reema. "Fayolan's kept

her locked up all day," she said. He appeared uneasy as he edged closer, averting his gaze as he released me.

"You will not leave my sight," Braedon warned, and I nodded, gripping the blanket and wrapping it around myself. I walked slowly with Braedon at my back as Reema followed. "Leave the door open. You've got five minutes."

"Thank you." I hurried inside, leaving the door ajar as I glanced around the room. Fortunately, both the window and I were out of sight.

Lifting the toilet lid, I turned the tap on to a dribble as I scanned the room, searching for clothes. To my dismay, there was nothing but sheets. *It would have to do.*

Reema's voice wafted into the bathroom as she distracted Breadon. Regardless of whether she'd done it on purpose, I hoped they would not punish her for my actions.

I twisted one sheet into a dress that fit snugly around me, covering me just enough that it almost passed as an actual outfit.

I hurried to knot several other sheets together as I leant out the window, checking no guards patrolled below. Fastening one end of the sheets to a heavy dresser, I tossed the other outside.

"Hurry," Braedon called.

"Almost done." I flushed the toilet and turned the tap on full to hide the noise of my escape. *Here goes...*

I didn't have time to check the sheets would hold my weight, and my adrenaline surged as I climbed onto the windowsill.

With my breath held, I swung my body down, letting the makeshift rope feel my weight. *Thank the Gods.* It held firm.

The moment my feet touched the ground, I hurried towards the Garden Of Souls. The spirits had offered to hide me once, and I prayed they could help.

I reached the garden and darted beneath the archways as I looked for the beautiful spirit.

"Are you ready, Little Nephilim?" she sang, emerging from behind the fountain.

"Can you help me?"

She phased towards me, reaching out with a translucent arm. Mist swirled around her, causing a chill to run up my spine. *"Take my hand..."* her melodic voice echoed around me.

The moment our fingers touched; pain radiated through me. I clasped my free hand over my mouth to stifle a scream. The mist surrounding her became tangible, slamming into me and knocking me back.

"What the…" I gasped as I looked upon the spirit as she smiled. *She was corporeal!* Her skin was no longer transparent and swirling like mist. "What have you done to me?"

"I brought you into my realm, but you must hurry," she warned, glancing back towards Fayolan's harem. *"The one in there can see you. He lives in both the realm of the living and the dead."*

"Fayolan isn't there," I assured her, but she shook her head.

"You are free from Death, but the man that set you free... he can still see you." Dammit. I'd been right when I thought he had seen through the veil, and by now, he would have noticed me missing. *"His magic is the only thing I cannot protect you from. Go now. Run."*

I did not hesitate as I fled through the garden, her voice trailing behind me. *"Be warned Nephilim, the moment you cross the barrier to your home, you will no longer be hidden."*

Without slowing down, I hurried through the open gate, rushing down the stairs as fast as my legs would carry me. My bare feet slapping against the cold cobblestones.

I reached the street below, trying to recall the layout as they crisscrossed the city. Glancing up at the tower, I searched for the largest platform. The one that pointed towards the ridge.

A loud squawk drew my attention to the skies as a giant gryphon circled above, and its rider scoured the city. *Fayolan. Did he already know I was running?*

I didn't stick around to find out as I ran further into the maze of cobbled streets. I got lost multiple times trying to navigate the city, as I headed for the gates that would lead me home.

Finally, I spotted the way to freedom but guards hurried, closing them before I could escape. I watched as Fayolan's men drew swords, searching through the crowds that gathered.

I angled my head downwards as a guard strolled towards me. He walked past me without a second look.

"The war is over. Why are the gates closed?" a woman asked above the growing noise.

"A prisoner has escaped. Return to your business. There is no need for alarm." Gasps sounded around me as more city folk began yelling questions.

"Are they dangerous?"

"Should we lock the doors?"

My stomach turned in knots as I sensed Fayolan nearby. I had no doubt in my mind that he was hiding in the shadows, waiting for me to approach the gates.

This was it… he'd trapped me within the city. *Maybe if I hid long enough, Fayolan would give up and open the gates. The idea was senseless. Death was hunting me and he would not let me go that easily.*

I turned reluctantly from the gates as the crowds dispersed. Following behind them as I headed deeper into the city.

CHAPTER TWENTY-THREE

Men hoisted the guard's captain onto the wall. His screams almost hid the ping of the hammer, driving spikes through him. It was a horrific way to die, left to starve and rot while the ravens feasted on his flesh. Leaving just enough of him to remain alive.

This was all Tempest's fault… *I hated her for disobeying me.* Her actions led to this. She was reckless and naïve to the danger *I* posed to her.

We circled the macabre scene below one more time. Mal squawked beneath me, hungry for the feast that hung on the wall.

"Not yet, my friend." I ruffled his feathers. "He has not suffered enough." He'd been foolish, still believing my father's orders trumped mine. Worse still, he had dared to raise arms against me.

My father only drew breath because I had no desire to rule. I liked the freedom of war…. The death that surrounded me, feeding from the depthless shadows that I knew only the Nephilim could see.

I had caught Tempest staring at them more than once and I'd waited for the look of fear or disgust to crease her beautiful face, but it never came. I chuckled at the thought. She was the sole person who could appreciate me for who I truly was. Yet I wanted to strangle the life out of her.

I pictured my hands wrapped around her dainty neck. Applying just enough pressure to make her panic as she realised how fucked she was. Maybe then Tempest would behave. "Take me down, boy."

Mal banked away from the wall towards the platform. I scanned the city as we flew overhead. Something seemed off. The streets were unusually empty. I stared down, unease settled over me as if I could feel someone watching me.

With a deafening squawk, Mal landed, sending handlers scurrying away from him. He puffed up his chest and ruffled his feathers as he huffed at me. "You will get to feast on him soon enough, Mal." I would make Tempest watch… showing her the consequences of defying me.

"Fetch me the finest deer and feed my beast." I glared towards one handler. Fear creased his face, and his body quaked as he stared at Mal. "Now. Or it will be you he feasts on." The man took off running.

"Fayo," Braedon called as he materialised on the platform, sending all the gryphon into a frenzy. Only Mal and Saki remained calm.

"For fuck's sake, Brae," I cursed, whirling to face him. His face was ashen, and his hands clenched at his side. I didn't think I had ever seen him looking so dishevelled as his hair hung over his face. *Something was wrong.*

"What has she done?" I asked with a scowl.

"She's gone." Braedon winced as he edged away.

"Gone *where*?" My shadows darkened around me as my heart raced.

"I don't know." He stepped back again as I edged closer.

"What do you mean you don't know? I left her tied to my *bed*!" My fingers wrapped around the hilt of my dagger, struggling against the urge to kill him where he stood.

"She needed the restroom…" Of course, the clever Nephilim would work her wiles on him. My wings unfurled as I shoved past Braedon and charged off the platform, taking to the skies.

"Get the gates closed," I bellowed down at him. "No one gets in or out." *You won't escape me, little Nephilim, and when I find you… I'll make fucking sure you never dare to run from me again.*

I swooped low, dropping to the wall where I could watch for her. Crouching down, I scanned the street below. Citizens milled around, an uproar arising as they became trapped inside.

Kalen displaced before me, looking slightly dizzy. "I hate when you do that Brae." He cursed, blinking as he refocused. "What's going on?"

"Our little prisoner escaped." I scowled towards Braedon.

"Seriously? We left her with you for five minutes and you set her free." Kalen shook his head.

"It's not my fault. You didn't tell me who she was and what she was capable of. Hell, you had her tied naked to your bed. I just assumed she was…" Braedon glanced towards me, his words trailing off as a growl rumbled in my chest.

"Did Reema help her? Does she even still look like herself?" I asked through gritted teeth.

Braedon shook her head. "No, Reema was with me. Although I can't be sure she wasn't a distraction." At least I could breathe a little easier, knowing Tempest still looked the same. She would be safe as long as she had not been foolish enough to remove her scarf and veil.

"What's the plan?" Kalen let out a deep sigh as he swept his fingers through his hair.

"She can't escape, but if the guards find her first..." Both men vanished before I uttered the last words... *she was dead.*

Braedon released Kalen at the gate as they navigated through the crowds. Searching beneath every hood as they went.

I would give her until nightfall to appear before ordering a full lockdown. With the streets deserted, she'd have no place to hide.

I remained watching as the crowds dispersed, pushed back from the gates by my guards. But as I waited, the Nephilim failed to appear and attempt to leave Fayspire. *How curious.*

Braedon and Kalen moved deeper into the city to search and I sat back, certain she would make her way here. *Maybe she'd got lost.* I chuckled at the thought. I could picture the purse of her lips and the frown on her face.

Gryphon squawked from the platform way above me. *She wouldn't have... Dammit, she was going to attempt to fly Saki and escape.*

I shot towards the platform. My wings beating furiously as I cursed myself for being a complacent fool. The gryphon came into view and I let out the breath I did not realise I had been holding.

Mal was causing a ruckus as the poor handler tried to find enough space to place a deer. The other gryphons were terrified and joined in, adding to the commotion.

"Give it to me," I commanded as I strolled towards the man. I snatched the deer from him, tossing it at Mal's feet. Even I was not stupid enough to put myself between the ferocious creature and his meal.

"Thank you, my Prince," the man muttered, bowing as I stared down at him. *Pitiful.*

A slight breeze brushed past me. "You'd better have good news for me." I turned my head to glance at Braedon.

"I found her," he said, gripping my shoulder, transporting us to the marketplace before I could blink. He pointed towards an empty bench facing the altar of the sun.

"Is this a *fucking* joke?" I hissed as I grabbed his throat, lifting him from the ground as if he weren't a full-grown man.

"She has displaced into the spirit realm," he said with a sly smirk. I lowered him down as I glanced back.

"How is that even possible?"

Braedon shrugged. "Let me show you." His magic slammed into me, and I gasped as Tempest became visible. Wrapped in a sheet, she stared at the priestess that led the prayers. Occasionally, she glanced into the crowds of worshipers.

"She hasn't uttered a single word. She just watches."

"Maybe Tempest doesn't know our prayers. She's from No Man's Land." I watched as a curse slipped from her lips, her brows furrowing as she clenched her fists beside her.

"Can she see us?" I asked. I needed to get closer to her. To hear the sinful words fall from her rosy lips.

"Yep."

"Dammit," I murmured under my breath as I watched her. Even from the shadows, I did not miss the tear that rolled down her cheek. She wiped it away before it could fall.

"So, what's the story? It's not like you to keep one of her kind alive. You should just get rid of her," Braedon urged, but as I growled, he shot her a confused look.

"She will die when I am certain I know her secrets. The Nephilim has planted doubt in my mind... she is not at all what I expected," I said through clenched teeth. "Something doesn't add up about her."

"Kalen said as much. I hear she saved you both from sirens."

I went to answer, but as Tempest got to her feet, I sealed my lips shut. With a quick glance around, the Nephilim moved from the bench, heading deeper into the busy market.

We followed behind her, keeping our distance, watching her scan every stall she passed. She stopped at one laden with beautiful gowns. Edging closer to a mannequin, she reached out as if she were about to touch the shimmering pink lace.

At the last moment, she pulled her fingers away tentatively. Her gaze remaining locked with the gown as her shoulders slumped. *She would never wear it... It had no sleeves.*

She sighed as she pulled her gaze away. The shame of her body was etched across her beautiful face. I would kill Lacellus for it once I found the lecherous bastard.

Tempest continued down the rows of stalls, but a hulking figure in the shadows drew my attention. *Fuck.* "Stay on her. Don't lose her again." Braedon nodded as I moved to the stall with the dress, beckoning the owner over.

"My Prince," she stammered as I stood before her.

"Can you add sleeves to this?" *Gods what was I thinking?*

"Of course," she said. All I could picture was how much fun I would have removing it from Tempest's alluring body.

"Have it delivered to my residence by nightfall." Holding out the bag of coin, she nodded and called to a younger girl.

"Watch the stall. I'll be gone all afternoon."

Now, back to business. Kalen still lingered, a grimace on his face as I approached. "So, we're buying her pretty clothes now?"

"Who said it was for Tempest?" I snapped. "I assume you aren't lurking around just to talk about dresses."

"No..." he glanced around. "We have a problem at the

gate." He snarled as he tilted his head for me to follow him as he ducked under the balconies that circled the marketplace. With a final glance back, I cursed. Tempest was lost among the crowds. "This had better be important."

Kalen nodded with a scowl, making my shoulders slump. "Your father's men are at the gate demanding entrance."

"*Gods*, what do they *want*?" I turned away from the market, leaving Braedon to watch the Nephilim.

"Ustrayan soldiers have made it further west towards Solis." I exhaled as I spread my wings.

"Tempest is to remain under wraps," I ordered. Kalen nodded, stepping back to avoid being caught by my taloned wings as I took to the air. My muscles rippled with every flap, straining as I shot towards the commotion.

The ground trembled beneath me as I landed. "Open the gates." The guards obeyed, letting my father's horsemen into the city.

I narrowed my eyes at the old general leading the men. Grey hair cascaded around his shoulders as he removed his helm. His steely gaze falling on me.

"Care to explain *this*?" Lacellus's father spat as he spoke. I scowled as I edged closer to his horse. My shoulders rolling as I spread my wings imposingly behind me.

"I don't answer to *you*, old man," I hissed. "The last idiot that made demands of me met his fate on that wall." He lowered his head. The stench of his fear was disgusting. Palleon was as weak as my pathetic father.

"They rarely deny us entrance," he said with a disapproving scowl, changing the subject.

"A dangerous prisoner has escaped, so *I* shut down the city. Maybe you should all retreat to the grand hall. He is *vicious*." I smirked as I lied.

"Well, if you deem it best, who am I to argue?" Palleon cocked his head smugly. "I assume it was you behind the massacre outside?" He lifted an Ustrayan soldier's helm with the head still inside. A chunk of flesh fell near my feet, blood splattering my boot.

"Who else?" I lifted my gaze to his with a smirk that made Palleon shrink back in his saddle. "It's what you and my father raised me for, correct?"

Palleon looked away, wearing his fear and shame like a cloak. It suited him. They had created a monster and one day it would seek its revenge.

When he gave no sign of responding, I turned my back on him. Another insult, as I openly showed he was no threat to me.

I led the men behind me towards the great hall. I was itching to return to my little Nephilim, but I needed to get them out of the way first. They would try to take her life if they knew, forcing me to kill them all.

CHAPTER TWENTY-FOUR

My shoulders slumped as I looked away from the dress. I would never be beautiful enough to wear something this exquisite. I probably wouldn't live long enough to either.

Fayolan was watching me. I had glimpsed him as I sat by the altar cursing the Gods. He'd seen me wipe a tear of anger from my cheek. Prayers didn't bring comfort to people like me.

Braedon trailed along behind me, keeping his distance as he observed my every move. I wound through the market, marvelling at the trinkets, fragrant spices, and clothes fit for a queen. *Maeve and Mother would love it here.*

Grief slammed through me as I remembered their fates. For the briefest of moments, I'd forgotten... that they were gone... that I was a prisoner. Even now, as I stalked the streets, I knew I was on borrowed time.

Everything in Fayspire seemed so foreign… so clean. I had not seen a single beggar on the streets. No children covered in layers of grime and dirt. Even our village had vagrants that would pass through. But here, no one appeared to suffer from poverty or hardships.

Music mixed with the sound of people milling around the market, bartering for goods, or catching up on the latest gossip. It appeared all the citizens were content. *How's it possible for a place like this to exist under Death's command?*

No one paid any attention as I waded through the market. I drew closer to the music where a large crowd had gathered and their jeers filled the air. As I edged nearer, people turned away from the musicians, playing at the side of a large, cobbled street.

I slid to the side, finding shelter by shops with large decorative window displays. I manoeuvred through the streets, squeezing through the crowds as I followed the jeers. *If I could just get a little closer.*

A firm hand clamped around my arm, snatching me back abruptly. "Get off me." I spun, baring my teeth as I expected to see Fayolan, but Braedon's piercing gaze met mine instead.

"Let me go," I said, trying to pull away from him as his touch burned me. His grip tightened as he glanced over my head at whatever was drawing a crowd.

"You don't want to see that," he warned amidst screams and cheers.

"I said…" I used all of my strength to pull free of his grasp.

"Gods," Braedon cursed as he gave chase, but I was smaller and slipped through the crowd until I reached a podium raised in the centre of a square.

Men stood bound and flayed upon it, but a set of dull blue

eyes ripped a scream from my throat. *Serrin!* I pressed my hand against my mouth to silence the sound, moving backward until I brushed against a solid chest.

"I warned you," Braedon whispered into my ear as I stared up at Serrin. A guard walked down the line, forcing each man to their knees. "You can't help them."

Braedon tried to pull me away, but I caught Serrin's gaze. *He stared as if he knew I was here.*

"I have to…" I threw my elbow back into Braedon's ribs. His grip loosened as he huffed, and I darted forward. I shrieked as the head of an Ustrayan soldier rolled to the floor. The man's blood coated a blade, making my stomach churn as the crowd cheered.

I was almost free of the hordes of people as Braedon reached me. His arm wrapped around my waist, lifting me from the ground as I thrashed. "Fucking *stop*!" Braedon roared, as his other arm pinned mine to my chest.

"Serrin isn't one of *them*," I cried as I struggled. "I have to help him. He isn't an enemy."

My surrounding's changed instantly, and we stood in the Garden Of Souls. A queasy feeling had me vomiting as Braedon dumped me brutishly onto the ground.

"You didn't need to see that," he said as he grabbed a rope and stalked towards me.

"Take me back! I have to save him." I bolted towards the gate, but Braedon appeared before me. "They're going to *kill* him."

I darted away as he got closer, but Braedon vanished. Before I knew what was happening, his arms reached around me from behind. Gripping my hands as he bound my wrists. He pulled the rope so tight it cut into them, rubbing the still healing skin.

"There is nothing you can do." He tore off his shirt and

wound it around my mouth, muffling my desperate pleas to let me return. Braedon secured the other end of the rope to one of the ornate stone archways and vanished again. *Bastard!*

Gripping the rope, I placed my feet on the archway, endeavouring to pull free. My heart cracked with each jeer that sounded in the distance. *Would they even care that Serrin was innocent?*

Braedon appeared before me, darting forward as he tore the rope from my hands, gripping my shoulders, forcing me to look at him. I gasped as he sighed. "I'm sorry, Tempest…" The look of pity in his eye was all the confirmation I needed. *Serrin was dead.*

A scream tore from my lungs, silenced by the gag. My legs felt weak and gave way as I collapsed to the floor. *It wasn't fair… I had lost too much! The Gods had taken more than I could bear.*

My heart shattered as it all hit me at once. I had no one left. They had all died because of me. My soul fractured beyond repair as I screamed out again. Unable to hide my grief any longer.

"Get up." Braedon seized my arm, hoisting me to my feet. I lashed out, my nails raking down his face, and he cursed as he shoved me away.

"I will let that one slide, *bitch*, but the next time you try to strike me… I will kill you myself." He snarled before disappearing again.

Alone in the garden, I finally broke. Letting my tears free as my grief consumed me. I'd fought to stay strong in front of Fayolan, but I no longer had anything to fight for.

Darkness fell on the city, and the cheers faded away. The captives were dead—*Serrin was gone.* Fayolan had lied to me… he'd promised Serrin would live.

The night pressed in on me as the light within me

dimmed, taking with it any hope I had left. I prayed Serrin knew I was here, waiting for him to take me with him.

When Braedon returned, I kept my head down. I couldn't stomach looking at him. *I could have done something. Anything to save Serrin, and he robbed me of the chance. He was as bad as Fayolan.*

CHAPTER TWENTY-FIVE

Fayolan

The lamps flickered as I walked through the empty streets. My shadows stretched out around me as I delayed the inevitable.

Braedon had come to me, frantic that Tempest had lost her mind. She'd seen someone on the executioner's block, but we were too late.

The stupid boy should have listened to me. Reed and I had put on a show to scare them both, beating him before Reed left him in the village. But the damn fool was in love and it got him killed.

The second time Braedon returned, he had gouges down his cheek. *I would have to punish her for that as well.* I could have just flown back and dragged the Nephilim into my room and taught her a lesson she wouldn't forget. But the knots in my stomach held me back.

I had promised her I would let him live, and now she

would think I lied. *Why do I even care?* She was really starting to get under my skin and I fucking hated it.

"Is the bird back in her cage?" Kalen leant against the stairs of the looming tower. He pushed off as I rounded on him.

"Did you *know* the boy was here?" I slammed his back against the wall as he growled.

"*What* boy?" His brow furrowed as I got in his face.

"The boy from the village."

Kalen glanced up at the tower. "Did he find her?" he asked.

"No. She found *him* on the block. I failed to reach him in time."

"*Fuck.*" He shoved me off him, kicking a bucket that lay abandoned in the street.

"Braedon got her away before it happened."

"Does *that* make it any *better*?" he asked, without looking at me. His shoulders heaving as his fists clenched at his side.

"*Watch* your tone. She is our prisoner, and she'll join him soon enough. Wasn't it you that wanted me to kill her all this time? Don't let her get inside your head."

Kalen was a fierce warrior, but something in him was changing. He did not look at her with the same hatred.

"I haven't forgotten. I'd kill her right now with my bare hands if you asked me too… but I'm not sure I would ever forgive you."

His words hit me like a punch in the gut as he stalked away. "We leave at first light," I yelled after him.

Kalen glanced back, dipping his head with the respect he would always show me. Even if he hated me right now.

My shoulders were heavy as I climbed the steps to the Garden Of Souls. Braedon's magic had worn off and I could not see or hear Tempest. The rope that bound her, however, remained unmoving on the ground.

I scaled the outskirts of the garden until I found Braedon leaning against the wall. His eyes glazed with emotion while he gazed at her.

"How is she?" I asked, and only then did his attention lift to me.

"She has not stopped sobbing," he mumbled, stuffing his hands into his pockets.

"She's crying?" I'd never seen Tempest truly cry.

"See for yourself." Braedon's magic was harsh and uncontrolled as it crashed into me. He turned to walk away, but I grabbed his arm.

"Are you okay?"

"Yeah."

I should have known better than to leave her with Braedon. I'd been the one to find him on the day he lost his sister. He was just a boy and as he clung to her lifeless body; I had felt his grief. Just a glimpse, but I would never forget it.

He turned back to Tempest, his face devoid of all emotion. Her shoulders shook with every sob as she hugged her knees to her chest. She looked broken.

My gut clenched. I was almost certain I would have saved the boy to spare her this pain. Although part of me doubted myself. I was a heartless bastard… *we both knew it.*

The moonlight flooded over Tempest as if the Gods themselves were watching her. The scarf around her head had fallen, no doubt in the struggle with Braedon, and the light reflected off the deep midnight blue that ran through her hair.

Tempest's head shot up, and a scream left her lips. One so powerful even the gag could not silence it. Wide-eyed, she stared ahead. *The boy had come to her.*

"Bring her back, *now*!" I roared as I bolted towards Tempest. Clasping her cheeks, forcing her to look at me as I dropped in front of her.

The gag around her mouth fell away and her body tensed

at Braedon's hand, clasping her shoulder. Pulling her violently back into our realm. She did not flinch or cry out at his touch. Her grief was all she could feel as it consumed her.

Something tugged at my heart, and it thundered in my chest. *Was Tempest doing this to me?*

"Fayo?" Braedon stared at me. "Are you alright?"

"I'm *fine*," I hissed, turning back to Tempest. Hatred swelled in me at the idea of *her* making me feel.

"Take me with you," Tempest sobbed. I gripped her cheeks tighter with my rough, calloused hands, uncaring if she despised my touch. Even if it hurt her, I was not letting her go.

"The boy cannot have you," I murmured. Keeping her focused on me. Her tearful eyes clamped shut.

"Please let me go with him," she begged. Her shoulders slumped as a cold breeze wrapped around me. "I don't want to stay," she whispered. The chill in the air vanished and her delicate cheeks beneath my fingers added to the warmth that swelled through me.

"I'm getting the *fuck* out of here," Braedon grumbled as he walked away. He did not wait for me to respond as he slunk into the shadows.

"Don't leave me behind, Serrin." Tempest drew my attention back to her. I took a seat and let my hands fall beside me. Looking up as I stared, watching the stars glimmering in the midnight sky.

My father had told me that my mother would sit beneath them, talking to me as I lay in her womb. He'd loved her beyond all reason, and he blamed me for her death.

He often told me she only needed a Nephilim because a vile monster grew in her womb, tainting her with my evil. For years, I had believed him. I became the monster he always said I was. Now I bring death to any that cross him. *The King's faithful assassin.*

Tempest lowered her head into her arms as she trembled beside me. Just like I had done as a child when my grief and guilt became more than I could bear.

"You will survive this," I murmured, running my hand down Tempest's long, sleek hair.

"I'll never survive losing him… or Maeve… or my village. And I *definitely* won't survive *you*." Her words were bitter as she shrunk into herself. No doubt searching for the quiet place in her mind where nothing could hurt her.

I had no words of consolation to offer her. Nor did I care to. She was as much of a monster as me. *There's no comfort for creatures like us.*

I glanced down at Tempest as her head lifted. The accusation in her eyes pierced through me. She blamed me for the boy's stupidity, and if I was being honest, letting her hate me made my life easier.

We sat in silence as my guilt gnawed away at me. Having feelings was the last thing I wanted, but around the Nephilim, it seemed unavoidable.

I would wait until tomorrow to punish her. She'd learn to think twice before running from me again. I would make sure of it. She belonged to me and it's about time she accepted it.

CHAPTER TWENTY-SIX

I woke leaning against something solid, my cheek sore from whatever I had used as a pillow. An icy breeze sent a shiver through my body, and I pulled myself upright to see what I had been sleeping on.

I was still in the Garden Of Souls, with Fayolan sat beside me. He remained still, gazing at the view as if I had not fallen asleep against his shoulder.

His hair billowed in the gentle breeze as he remained lost in thought, unaware I had moved away from him. My heart remained fractured. My soul fraying at the edges as I pictured Serrin's spirit refusing to take me with him.

He wanted me to live, but his words burned deep into my very being. *He is not what you think. The Dark Prince is your salvation. How could he believe that after Fayolan sent him to his death?*

"You're awake?" Fayolan murmured. His body remained still and his gaze locked ahead.

"You stayed outside all night with me?" The sun was just beginning to rise above the buildings, casting a warm glow over the garden.

"I didn't want to leave you alone." Fayolan sighed as he stretched.

"Let me guess… Just in case I ran again." I snorted, looking away. "There isn't any point now, anyway."

"If *that's* what you think… *sure.*" *Of course it was. After all, to him… I'm just a prisoner.* I knew Fayolan well enough that nothing he did was for my benefit, but this seemed different.

"It's time to go." I jumped as Kalen came to a halt behind us. His words stopping me from hurling an insult I would probably regret later.

Without speaking, Fayolan stood up and took hold of the rope still connected to the archway. Wrapping it around his wrist as he hoisted me up.

"You need to change," he said dryly, jerking me back towards his harem.

I hadn't noticed the blanket that hung around my shoulders until it fell to my feet. I bent to retrieve it, but Fayolan yanked me forward again. This time much harder.

"What's your…" I silenced myself as his lips twisted up into a snarl and his chest heaved. I had already pushed him further than I should have with my pointless escape attempt. Now wasn't the time to push my luck. I could almost hear Serrin's cocky voice in my mind as pointed out the obvious. *Despite everything, he stayed with you through the night.*

Fayolan remained silent as he removed the rope and shoved me into his room. Slamming the door behind us, he stalked to the window, showing me his back.

A dress appeared on the bed and I snatched it up, fumbling to keep the sheet covering my modesty. In the end I gave up and dropped it to the floor since Fayolan remained turned away.

"I'm done," I mumbled beneath my breath. Fayolan spun with a dark smirk, tightening his grip on the rope as he advanced towards me.

I gasped as his arm shot out, pulling me towards him while he traced his thumb along my neck. "If you insist on behaving like a disobedient dog, then I will treat you like one." Fayolan's breath brushed against my neck as he slipped the rope round my throat, fashioning a collar.

"What are you doing?" I tried to break away, but Fayolan pulled it tighter.

"When you *learn* not to run… I'll remove the leash." He sneered as he stepped back, wrapping the remaining rope around his hand.

"I can't breathe."

Fayolan ran his fingers beneath the collar, checking the tightness. "Stop being dramatic. *You* caused this…"

"If it were *you* in my shoes, would you not have done the same?" I glared at him as he froze for just a second.

"I'd never *be* in the same situation. *You* should've run that day by the lake, as *far* as you could. Instead, you walked *right* into my clutches."

"Because I *had* too. Unlike *you*, I have people I care about so deeply that I risked myself for them. I know that is a strange concept for you. I doubt you've cared for anyone in your life."

Fayolan was fast as he slammed me back against the door. Pinning me beneath his heaving chest. His face reddening as he stared down at me.

"You know nothing about me, Little Nephilim. So, stop *pretending* you do. *Gods*, I could have snapped your pretty little neck the first moment you were in my grasp."

"Then *why* didn't you?" I yelled.

Fayolan snorted and relaxed his hold on me. "Is that why you keep pushing me?" he asked as he let out a deep exhale. "To force me to kill you?"

"*No*, I just…" I wasn't entirely sure why I did it. Or why *he* affected me so much.

"Just what?"

"I won't let you see me as weak. I won't let *anyone* see me like that. Not again."

Fayolan's hand ran down my cheek as he studied me. As if seeing me with fresh eyes. "I've not once seen you that way, *Pet*. Stubborn and foolish maybe… but never weak."

I sighed as Fayolan stepped away, producing a cloak and wrapping it around me. Hiding my hair beneath the hood. "Come on. We've delayed long enough already."

He led me by the neck as we left his harem and passed through the Garden Of Souls. My mind was running over our fight—*had I misjudged him?*

The gates were open wide as we approached and I thanked the Gods that I wore a veil. My cheeks flushed red as people stared at the collar, pointing and making snide remarks. I stared at the ground, praying it would swallow me whole and end my shame.

"You ride with me, Pet." I glanced up to see two horses. Kalen sat atop one with a serious look as Fayolan placed his hands on my hips. I hissed as he dumped me into the saddle.

"You'd better get used to my touch, Tempest. This is your punishment for running… and for Braedon. You are lucky he *pitied* you or he would have killed you for striking him."

I bit back a sarcastic retort as he mounted behind me, pulling me against his rigid chest. Pain tingled through me as our bodies touched, and I sunk my teeth into my lip to keep from crying out. I refused to let Fayolan see he was winning.

The gates swung open, and Fayolan's arms encircled my

waist as he gripped the reins. And Kalen gave a subtle shake of his head as he watched us.

Guards stepped aside to let us pass. Their gaze lingered on the rope twisted around my throat. Amusement lighting their eyes. *Assholes.*

"Fayolan," a man called. His body stiffened as he pulled me closer.

"Keep looking forward." Fayolan shifted behind me as he turned back.

"You're leaving so soon?" the man snapped.

"Are you questioning me, Palleon?" Fayolan released a low mocking whistle which sent an icy shiver down my body. His arms tensed as he slid me closer.

"No Dark Prince. Of course not," Palleon placated. "I hear you have quite the beauty with you." He changed the subject, but the growl that vibrated Fayolan's chest was a sign he'd just made the situation worse. "It will excite your father to play with her." Palleon's voice lowered in an attempt to rile Fayolan.

"My father knows better than to *touch* what is mine."

"He does not answer to you, *boy*," Palleon reminded him sternly.

Fayolan chuckled menacingly, making my breath lodge in my throat. It came rushing out as he kicked the horse's flank, jolting us forward. "Oh..." he said, still feigning amusement. "Where is your son? I need a... *word* with him." I shuddered at Fayolan's tone.

Palleon paused before giving a cautious reply. "If I see him, I will tell him you're looking for him." *Warn him more like.* I didn't know what Fayolan wanted with his son, but the tension in the air hinted at something ominous.

Fayolan turned his back on him as we rode through the gates. A crowd had gathered outside, staring at the wall above. Unease filled my stomach as they noticed us and they all turned to stare.

Fayolan leant in, whispering in my ear as he pointed up. "This is what your antics have caused."

I gasped as I saw the Captain of the Guard hanging above. They'd pinned his arms against the wall with massive spikes and his head hung limp. "*Never* make me do this again, Pet. Or next time *you* will join them."

"I'm so sorry," I whispered beneath my breath as I fought the bile rising in my stomach.

"I know you are, but sorry won't save him."

"Please end it," I sighed.

Fayolan gave a shrill whistle, making me jump. Two gryphons took to the sky from the lofty tower. I recognised Saki, but the other enormous beast truly terrified me.

They moved elegantly as they circled the wall. Their shrill cries had the crowd jeering until the noise roused the Captain. His piercing screams echoed around us as he spotted the two gryphons dropping for the kill.

I turned my head away as they plunged towards him. "Do *not* close your eyes." Fayolan's hand shot up, gripping my chin, forcing me to watch. I released a cry as Saki ripped the captain's leg from his body before shooting back into the air.

The other beast raked its claws through the captain's chest as I struggled against Fayolan's powerful grip. "Watch what *your* actions caused."

The gryphons took their time dismembering the captain as he wailed. "Please stop this."

"If you want it to end, then *do* it yourself," Fayolan snapped as he shoved a bow into my hands. They trembled as I notched the single arrow he had given me, taking aim as I waited for the gryphon to move out of range.

My chest felt tight, whilst I battled the nausea that swelled in me. *Could I really take a life outside of battle? Even though it would end his suffering?* "What's the matter, Pet? Too afraid to clean up your own mess?"

"No." I released the arrow, letting it sail through the air, piercing the guard captain's heart and ending his torment. Cutting off his screams.

I filled the silence with the sound of my retching over the horse's side. Fayolan took the bow, stroking my back as I expelled the contents of my stomach.

"Killing is never easy, no matter how good your intentions are. But eventually you get used to it." *I never wanted to be okay with it.*

Fayolan released a shrill whistle, and Saki and the other gryphon rose again, heading away from Fayspire.

As I sat up, Fayolan handed me a rag before tugging on the reins of the horse. Steering away from the city as Kalen pulled in beside us. His face remained hard and unyielding as we left the jeering crowd behind.

These two men were used to death. It did not horrify them to see a man ripped apart. It saddened me that this was their normality.

"Here, drink this." Fayolan held out a flask, and I swirled the wine around my mouth before spitting it out. Thankfully, it rid me of the acrid taste of vomit.

"Thank you," I mumbled, handing it back to him. Fayolan pulled me back into his chest, and I fought to move away. He chuckled and tightened his grip. "It hurts," I groaned.

"*Good.*" Fayolan held me closer. "I told you before to get used to feeling my touch. Because I'm not going anywhere and neither are you." I inhaled sharply at his words as they sent heat coursing through my body.

His hand cupped my breast, and I froze. His fingers trailing over my dress, where my nipple hardened at his touch. *Gods help me.*

"Tell me… what's your opinion of Fayspire?" Fayolan's

question threw me, and when I failed to answer, he pinched my nipple, rolling it between his fingers. I hissed and pulled away, but Fayolan was stronger and he squeezed tighter.

"At first, I thought it was beautiful. There were no beggars. Everyone seemed happy and well taken care of," I answered, and he eased his grip. Fayolan caressed the nipple, soothing the pain.

"In Stidahl, every person plays a role, no matter how small. No one goes without. We provide for our people and in return they work hard." I understood now how everyone in Fayspire had seemed so happy. They all had a job to do and in return they lived comfortably with no fear of poverty or hardships. "What do you think now?"

"Now I think it's filled with a hidden ugliness. Your people are as bloodthirsty as you."

Fayolan continued to caress my breast as he chuckled. "They are not like me, Tempest. They simply acknowledge there are consequences for crime. You have seen the brutality and horrors people are capable of committing, yet you condemn those that would see them pay for it."

"Not *all* of them were guilty," I said through gritted teeth.

Fayolan's body tensed at my words. "I warned the boy he *would* die if he tried to follow you."

His callous tone made me shiver. "You *promised* you would let him live."

"I didn't know he was there," he mumbled.

"Would you have saved him if you did?" I asked, even though I was certain I knew the answer.

"I don't know." His hand lowered from my breasts as he whispered against my ear. "I saw you by the altar of the sun. You didn't join in the prayers… do you not like the Gods?"

I snorted as I ground my teeth. "Why *should* I? What have they ever done for me?"

"They are your kin, are they not?" *What a stupid notion.*

"The Gods created us and then condemned us. They are *no* family of mine." I waited for Fayolan to throw some insult at me about being a monster, but he sighed heavily.

"That might be the first thing we have in common, Pet. Your father and mine… Both powerful assholes that aren't worth the air they breathe." I didn't realise how much Fayolan hated his father. *I guess there's a lot I don't know about him.*

"Fayolan… Can I ask you something?"

"Yeah."

"What was your reason for staying with me last night?"

He chuckled, holding me just a little tighter. "I thought you had it all figured out in that pretty little head of yours."

"So did I."

CHAPTER TWENTY-SEVEN

I stared ahead as smoke rose in the distance. The sun had long since dipped behind the horizon, and a campfire danced. Illuminating three silhouettes sat around it.

"I will only warn you once, Tempest… Behave yourself. These are *my* people and I would take your life over one of theirs," Fayolan warned.

His voice caressed my ear as he leant over me. "Play nice, and I won't have to punish you further." His hand snaked around my waist, finding its way to my breast once again.

"I get it," I snapped. Biting my lip to hide the screams that had threatened to escape all day as his touch burned against my skin.

The silhouettes got to their feet as we headed straight towards the campfire.

"You took your time, *Fayo*," a woman said. Her soft, sensual voice wafted around us, enticing him. "Is that *it*? The monster?" She stepped closer.

The flickering light from the fire chased away the shadows that hid her startling white hair and icy blue eyes. She glared at me with a look that had me shrinking back into Fayolan's embrace.

"Calm down, Nix," Fayolan said, grinning as he dismounted.

"Oh, you're no *fun*," Nix said, pouting as she edged closer to Fayolan. Her large breasts pressing against his chest as Fayolan looked down, meeting her piercing gaze.

"I can be *plenty* of fun, Nix." Fayolan's lips curled into a sexy smirk that had heat unfurling in my core and an ache between my thighs.

"Jealous, Tempest?" His gaze shot to mine and my cheeks flushed a deep red, betraying my body's reaction to him.

I hardened my expression as I composed myself. "Who you are *fucking* is none of my business."

"I hear you are quite the beauty… maybe you would like to warm my bed?" Nix smirked as her eyes roamed hungrily over me as she edged closer. Her sultry chuckle made my cheeks heat again.

"Keep your hands to yourself, Nix *baby*," Braedon said, grinning as he moved out of the shadows. His hands gripped her hips as he pulled her back towards the fire. "She is not for you."

My gaze turned to the third man. I stared in disbelief at Reed, and I moved before my brain even registered it.

"*Murderer*!" I screamed, launching myself off the horse. Everyone stared as I lunged at Reed, and he stood looking confused.

Fayolan's muscular arms trapped my waist, lifting me from the ground, kicking and thrashing. Desperate to reach Reed.

"*Enough*, Tempest." Fayolan's grip tightened as he fought to contain me.

"He *murdered* Serrin… Even after I…" Disgust and self-loathing stole my voice as I continued to fight against Fayolan.

"Say the words, *Tempest*," Fayolan growled as he continued to hold me. "When you *what*?"

"It was all a lie… You are a liar, and he is a *murderer*!"

"What the *fuck* have I missed?" Reed still stared at me.

"The boy was in Fayspire." Fayolan's voice was tense in his effort to keep control of me. *I wasn't about to make it easy for him.*

"Shit." Braedon moved closer, using his colossal frame to block the murderer from my view. I wriggled an arm free from Fayolan's grasp, jolting my elbow back into his ribs.

Fayolan slammed me into the solid ground, knocking the wind from my lungs. Using his weight to pin me down.

"Reed, *back* off." Fayolan's breath fanned my cheek whilst he spoke.

"He returned the boy as *I* ordered, but he did not heed my warning. The *fool* returned for *you* and got himself recaptured. By the time we discovered him, it was too late."

"*Liar*," I spat, trying to wriggle free of Fayolan. "I *kissed* you… I did what *you* asked of me. I paid for his freedom. We had an agreement, but you tricked me."

My thrashing calmed. I felt dirty knowing I had done it for nothing. *Fuck, I'd given Fayolan what I'd never been able to give anyone… and it had all been a cruel lie.*

"I took the boy home," Reed argued.

Fayolan shot him a warning look as he gripped me tighter. "Remember, *Nephilim*, it was not the only time you kissed me." His weight eased as I tired, and the fight left me. But still his hands remained, pinning my wrists to the ground.

"A *mistake* on my part. Next time I will let the sirens *rip* your flesh from your bones." I shifted my focus away from him. My chest rose and fell heavily as I bit my lip. Tasting the coppery tang of my blood as I fought to stop myself from completely losing control.

"Of course, you kissed *it*." Nix flapped her arms to her side with a scowl.

"Not now, Nix," Fayolan warned. Gripping the rope, he manoeuvred my hands. Binding them tightly to the leash at my neck so I could not move them.

He hoisted me violently to my feet, knocking my veil from my face. I stared as it fell haplessly to the ground.

"Would you look at those *eyes?* No wonder you had *it* hidden away beneath that cloak. Men would be banging on your door, Fayo, just to get a taste of her. Hell, *I* might be first in line." She winked at me with a chuckle as Fayolan growled.

He jerked me forward towards the fire, catching me as I stumbled, and forcing me to my knees at his feet. Before dropping to a log near the fire with a heavy sigh.

Fayolan gripped the rough rope collar and pulled me back so I sat nestled between his legs, on the cold hard ground. "Are you finished now, Tempest?"

"Yes," I snapped as I gazed into the fire.

"Are you sure? If not, maybe I'll let Nix have you for the night." *Was he being serious?*

"I'm sure," I muttered, turning my attention back to the group. Kalen remained close by, his body tense as if he were ready to pounce on me should the need arise. Reed sat across from the fire, never moving his attention from me as he twirled a dagger menacingly between his fingers. I found myself transfixed watching him… *Wouldn't it be a shame if the knife slipped and he cut off a finger or two? I could hope at least.*

"So, Fayo…" Nix said, drawling his name sexually. "When do I get my kiss?" She pouted her lips, battering her lashes shamelessly.

"It would be improper to kiss a lady in such a crude manor," Fayolan teased.

Braedon snorted as he bit back a laugh. "I don't see a lady here."

"Are *you* a lady?" Nix asked me as she leant closer. With a wicked smirk that dared me to answer.

"With the language that comes out of her pretty mouth… *definitely* not a lady," Kalen said with a devilish grin.

"No… she is a monster," Fayolan mumbled as if he simply meant to think the words. Yet still they seemed to cut deep.

"Reed doesn't treat me like a lady," Nix said, running her tongue over her lips hungrily.

"And you love it," Reed said, finally looking away from me. A weight lifted as if I could finally breathe again now that he no longer focused on me. "You like it dirty, babe."

Nix chuckled huskily as she edged closer to him. Giving up on pursuing Fayolan for now, at least.

"Before you get too distracted. I'm counting on you to track someone down for me, and ensure he's waiting when I get back to Solis." The tone in Fayolan's voice made me shudder. There's no mistaking his intentions.

Fayolan's body tensed and his fingers grasped the rope leash, causing me to gasp for air.

"Who?" Reed scoffed. Whoever it was, Fayolan wanted him dead and the others all knew it, too.

"Lacellus," Fayolan uttered. My heart stopped. That name stirred something within me. It scared me and a tear splashed on my cheek. *Why did I feel sick at the mention of this man?*

Fayolan's hand made me jump as he eased his grip on the rope and tenderly lifted my chin. Forcing me to face him. "Do you know that name?" he asked softly.

"I don't know."

"Yet the sound of it makes you cry," Fayolan mused as he

wiped the lone tear from my cheek. "Not much frightens you, does it? Don't worry, Pet… he won't live long."

Sweat beaded on my forehead as he held my gaze, as if he possessed the power to read my thoughts.

"Huh hum." Kalen coughed, drawing Fayolan's attention from me. Fayolan released my chin as his hand brushed soothingly down my hair. Something in the soft, comforting gesture made me settle back into him. Fayolan's touch seemed like a promise that he would protect me from Lacellus. *Whoever he was.*

"What condition would you like him in?" Reed smirked as he crossed towards us.

"I want to savour my time with him. Make sure he is waiting and… *unsuspecting.*"

Reed nodded, but as his attention fell to me, his grin slipped away. He crouched before me, so our faces were level. "I swear I handed the boy back to his people," Reed said with a calm, soft voice. "I even had Nix heal him up a bit."

Fayolan tensed at Reed's words. Catching my hair in his clenched fist. I yelped in pain.

"Sorry," Fayolan mumbled, stroking my hair and easing the sting.

"I left him with a woman and a babe." Reed looked me dead in the eye as I processed what he was saying. "A pretty little blonde and a woman fierce enough to bring the Gods to their knees. The boy's father was there too."

My breath hitched as I realised what he was telling me. "She…" My words trailed off. I could never allow Fayolan to know about my mother and surviving sister. Reed dipped his head in a subtle nod, confirming he'd left my mother and Lily alive.

"Palleon knows I'm looking for him." Fayolan cut in and the smirk returned to Reed's lips as he got up.

"What's he in for?" Nix grinned. "Let me guess… murder?"

"*No*," Fayolan said with a snarl.

"Okay… Defecting?" Nix made another attempt.

"No." Fayolan's voice deepened as he growled.

"She's gonna keep guessing until you tell her," Braedon chuckled.

"Crimes against a child." Fayolan snapped a twig in his free hand as the camp fell into a silence I hadn't experienced since we got here.

"I'm so sorry, Fayolan," Nix said as she dipped her head. Her flirtatious tone was gone.

"Just find him," Fayolan commanded, putting an end to the discussion.

Everything slowed as Reed approached the fire. I inhaled deeply as his lips twisted into a sneer. Wispy tendrils of smoke billowed from his mouth as if he were a mighty dragon and not just a man.

I edged closer towards Reed as he stood by the fire. Something about them was calling to me. Enthralling me as he worked his magic, becoming one with the flames that danced in the night.

"Look at me." Fayolan's voice sounded distant. Reed was captivating; I couldn't look away. My heart quickened as my desire to get closer took over. "*Now*, Tempest."

Fayolan's hands rested on my cheeks as he pulled my face towards him. The pain freed me from the insatiable need to get closer to Reed… *to touch him.*

"What is he doing?" I rasped. My mouth was dry, as if Reed's fire magic had sucked all the moisture from it.

"Hunting," Fayolan said, sending a shiver running down my spine. I wanted to look back, but Fayolan tightened his grip, holding my gaze as we waited.

"Got the little *wyvern*," Reed said, grinning as he glanced towards us. Fayolan's grip relaxed, but his gaze remained locked on me. "He's in Kahwood." Reed's words pulled Fayolan's attention from me.

"Bring him to Solis. No doubt Palleon has already sent a rider to warn him." Fayolan sneered as if his name was so foul it disgusted him.

Braedon stood up with a menacing smirk, mirroring Reed's expression. These men were eager for blood and it excited them. Braedon's hands shot out, grabbing Reed's shoulders with a rough grip. "Let's finish this quickly."

"He has a whore nestled between his legs. A pretty one, too. Maybe she will suck your cock if you ask her nicely," Reed teased Braedon crassly.

"Once she sees what a real man's dick looks like, she will beg me to fuck her," Braedon laughed as he grabbed his crotch grotesquely.

"You can wet your cock once he is safely in Solis." Fayolan scowled, and without another word, Braedon, and Reed were gone. Leaving the air shimmering where they had stood moments ago.

"Well, that turned dark." Nix chuckled. "I reckon it's about time you got the ale flowing, Fayolan."

He swiped his hand, and a keg appeared beside her with several wooden tankards. Nix clapped her hands with a grin as she hurried to fill each cup, handing them around to Fayolan and Kalen.

"You're really going to get drunk at a time like this?" *Surely I wasn't the only one that thought drinking was a bad idea.*

"*Aww…* Fayo… *it* really cares about you." Nix beamed as she mocked me.

"No, I just don't fancy getting *murdered* in my sleep," I said, glaring at her.

"Oh *hunny*, being killed should be the least of your

worries. Ustrayans are barbaric, and a woman like you would fetch a pretty penny."

I shuddered at the eerie calm in her voice. "Are you saying Ustrayans keep slaves?"

Nix nodded as she watched me intently. "Yeah, they used to sneak into Stidahl and ravage the nearest villages. They took the strongest stock and killed everyone else."

"Why hasn't anyone stopped them?" I asked.

"It's not our place. I mean, we tightened the border security to protect our people, but whether Ustraya has slaves really is none of our concern." It sounded so callous put that way, but Nix was right.

"Do you keep slaves here? In Stidahl?"

"No, but maybe I could make an exception for you, Pet." Fayolan smirked, swigging his ale as I gave him a filthy look.

"Get me another drink, *woman*," Kalen said to Nix with a wink. Thankfully, changing the subject.

The three of them continued to laugh and joke as Nix handed out plates of food. The aroma was delicious, making my stomach rumble. Reminding me I had not eaten in days.

With my hands still bound to my throat, all I could do was stare at the plate sat beside Fayolan as he continued to drink. With each tankard, the ale's effect became more apparent. I had never witnessed Fayolan looking so carefree. *Annoyingly, it suited him.*

Fayolan finished eating before picking up my plate. He taunted me with the scraps of meat, lowering them to my mouth, and snatching them away before I could take a bite.

"I'm not hungry anymore," I said, turning my head away from him, but my stomach growled, exposing my lie.

Fayolan grinned as he dangled another delicious smelling piece of meat before me. "Beg me."

I refused to degrade myself, no matter how hungry I was. "I'd rather starve."

"At least ask nicely," Kalen said, shooting me a warning glance.

"*Fine…* Please, can I have some food?" I tried to curb the sarcasm in my voice, but from the way Kalen rolled his eyes, I had not done it very well.

Fayolan chuckled and allowed me to eat. Holding each delicious scrap of meat to my lips. "Is that better, *Pet*?" he asked, mocking me.

"It's delicious, thank you." I directed my gratitude towards Nix.

Fayolan slurped at his booze and burped. *Disgusting pig!* He leant over me. The stench of ale on his breath was nauseating. "Drink." He sloppily shoved a tankard into my face. It slammed into my lips. Causing blood to drip into my mouth as the ale sloshed over me.

"*Animal,*" I hissed. Fayolan launched the ale aside as he glared at me. His hand gripped my cheeks, and his nails viciously dug into my skin. He lowered his face even closer to mine.

"I was *trying* to be nice." He spat on the ground beside me and I shrieked as his grip tightened.

"Stop, Fayolan." Nix stormed across the camp. "You made her bleed, you big *oaf*." The moment her fingers touched me, warmth radiated through me, stopping the blood flowing from my lip.

Fayolan relaxed as he watched, his thumb rough as it brushed against my mouth. He released my cheeks as Nix healed his nail marks as well.

"It would be unfortunate to leave scars on such a beautiful face." She winked. Her gaze roamed to my breasts. Fayolan hissed through gritted teeth, and she stumbled away with a devilish laugh.

A bed roll appeared before us. Fayolan fell onto it, unable to control his body in his inebriated state, dragging me down.

I yelped as he pulled me into him. *Gods, if Ustrayans found us tonight… there's no hope.*

"Sleep," Fayolan ordered. He was unpredictable in this state and my body tensed. I was defenceless if his hands sought to punish me further. "You smell like the moonflowers in the Garden Of Souls," he whispered.

I suppressed my breath until Fayolan snored softly. His breath fanned my neck as he drifted off into an inebriated sleep. I remained still, cradled in his arms. The only comfort was his body's warmth against the spring chill in the air.

CHAPTER TWENTY-EIGHT

A hand covered my mouth as someone violently hauled me from the ground. My chest heaved as powerful arms dragged me away from the smouldering campfire.

"Hush." Fayolan's words brushed against my ear. *Thank the Gods, it's him and not the Ustrayans.* He pulled me into a small grove of trees as hooves thundered towards us.

Kalen led our horses deeper into the small copse as Fayolan held me tight against his chest. No hint of ale remained on his breath or clung to his clothes.

"What's going on?" I garbled into Fayolan's hand in my quest for answers.

"We have visitors," Fayolan whispered as he angled my head so I could see ten men on horses charging straight towards our camp. Reed was still asleep near the fire and Fayolan flicked his hand, making our bedrolls vanish as if we had never been there.

The men slowed to a halt beside the fire, which bathed them in light. An older man dismounted and strolled to Reed, nudging him awake with the toe of his boot.

I was certain Reed had been conscious the entire time, but he played his part well. Grumbling as he roused himself. If I hadn't known Fayolan and his companions better, I may have believed his act, too.

"Where is he?" the man demanded. I instantly recognised his voice... *Palleon*. His son was Lacellus. *Did he already know Fayolan had retrieved him?*

"Where's who?" Reed asked. His voice sounded groggy as he deliberately knocked over his half-full tankard of ale. Drawing Palleon's attention to it.

"Your Lord and Master," Palleon spat. "He headed this way with a pretty young whore sitting on his cock." I tensed as Fayolan muffled a growl that escaped me.

"He mentioned wanting to get her to Solis. She's the newest addition to his harem," Reed said with a mocking tone as he stumbled to his feet.

"Which way did he go?" Palleon asked with a sneer of distaste etched across his pompous face.

Reed spun, pointing in multiple directions. "Uh...That way," he said, settling on a dirt road heading away from Fayspire.

"How far ahead is he?"

"If you want to catch up, you better *hurry*. He was in a rush to wet his cock in her *succulent* cunt." Reed ignored Palleon's patronising snort. "Can't say I wouldn't mind riding that piece of ass once he's done with her." He groped his cock as he feigned losing his balance. My nostrils flared as Fayolan tightened his grip on my mouth.

"It's all an act, *Pet*. Calm down," Fayolan said as his lips brushed my ear. But I couldn't shake the niggling feeling that Fayolan had planned to dump me in his harem all along.

"Very well. Kill them!" Palleon commanded as he hauled himself into the saddle. Flanked by six of his men, he took off, following the false trail Reed had given him.

The remaining three men dismounted, drawing swords as they entered the camp. Unaware of the danger they had crossed into.

"Close your eyes," Fayolan whispered, and I clamped them shut obediently. The sound of the first man's cry made my heart race.

"What the *fuck?*" another roared, only for more screams to ring out around us. I shrunk back from the clamour, seeking comfort in Fayolan's embrace.

My body trembled, and his arm lowered, holding me tenderly against him, whispering softly. Drawing my attention from the horrors happening before us. "It will all be over soon, Pet."

When Silence fell, Fayolan released me, taking a step back. *Just remembered I'm a monster, did you, Death?*

"Come on." Fayolan led me down to the camp where Nix, Braedon, and Reed stalked towards us. Stepping around the mutilated bodies of the three men.

"You're looking a little pale, Nephilim," Braedon smirked as he walked past me to stop at Fayolan's side.

"I guess I owe you twenty golds, Fayo. I honestly believed Palleon had at least enough sense to know better than to cross you," Reed said. He chuckled as he pulled some coins from his pocket, dropping them into Fayolan's hand.

"You made a bet about whether someone would try to kill you? Even then, you thought getting drunk was a good idea?" *They were insane?*

"It's more fun that way," Nix said with a callous grin as she pulled a dagger from the body at her feet. "Gods it makes me want to cum." Her icy gaze locked with mine as she lifted the blade to her lips, running her tongue through the dripping blood.

I shrunk away as she neared, chuckling creepily. "Don't be frightened, Little Monster. I won't bite." She cocked her head as she reached out, almost touching me. "Unless you want me to."

"Enough, Nix," Fayolan said, as a sinister growl emanated from within him.

"She *needs* help," I muttered beneath my breath, but he heard. He threw his head back and barked out a laugh. His smile was breathtaking and his eyes lit with a humour I had never observed in them before.

Pull yourself together, Tempest. I dropped my gaze to the floor before Fayolan could notice me staring. *Breathe!* He was my enemy. Falling for him is out of the question. Death was destined to be alone. *No one could love a monster... right?*

"Get this mess cleaned up." Fayolan rolled his eyes as he picked his way through the chaos of the campsite. Stepping over body parts without a flicker of emotion. Once again, he reverted to the cold bringer of death. "Then follow the others. I want to know what that *bastard*'s up to."

Reed nodded as he flashed me a soft smile. "I'm sorry about what I said. Palleon has always seen me as a drunken lout and it works to my advantage to keep him believing it."

"*Glad* I could be of help." Reed chuckled as sarcasm tainted my words.

"Come on." Fayolan nudged me towards the horses. "I'm taking you home."

"It's not *my* home," I retorted under my breath, only for him to shove me again.

Kalen shook his head as he handed Fayolan the reins. Once more we found ourselves sharing a saddle, my back pressed against Fayolan's chest as we rode from the camp.

We travelled for over a week. The signs of Ustrayan soldiers trampling through the serene landscape had Fayolan on edge.

We stopped on the brow of a hill, and my mouth opened at the beautiful scenery. The grass faded as it gave way to russet dust and sand, and trees scattered across the landscape. Adding some colour to its rusty palette. Even the sun intensified the awe-inspiring sight as its heat made the landscape shimmer and flicker.

"Solis is just beyond that lake," Fayolan said, pointing out across the horizon. The thought of the vast body of water ahead stirred a sense of dread within me.

"We're going to cross that?" My hands grew moist as I gripped the saddle.

"No. Sometimes the most beautiful things in Stidahl are the deadliest." Fayolan trailed his fingers sensually through my hair. "Just like you, this land is unforgiving and dangerous. Stay by my side, Pet, and you might survive this place."

"Maybe death would be a kindness," Kalen mumbled beneath his breath. Both Fayolan and I snapped our heads to stare at him. *Was that what he wanted? For me to die?* He shrugged as he met Fayolan's gaze. "Solis is no place for *her* kind and you know it."

My fists balled at my side. I could still feel the sting of his belt on my face and the shame it caused me, as if it had happened just yesterday. Yet still his words cut deep.

"I wasn't suggesting he kill you." Kalen sighed, glancing down. "I merely meant that life would be dangerous for you in Solis."

"*Enough*." Fayolan jerked the reins, and the horse jolted forward, descending into the dusty desert below.

By the time we reached the lake, the sun was dipping. Kalen skulked off the moment we stopped.

"We'll camp here tonight." Fayolan called after Kalen only to receive a half-hearted salute. There was an unmistakable shift in their dynamic, and a sinking feeling in my gut pointed to me as the cause.

Run Little Nephilim, you cannot win this battle. I gasped as the wind picked up, bringing a startling warning with it. I did not jump as thunder rumbled above us.

"*Fuck!*" Fayolan flicked his hands, materialising three tents around us with a fire crackling in the centre under a wooden shelter.

"It won't last long." I glanced up at the sky. This storm almost felt unnatural. It appeared from nowhere and static tingled along my arms.

The first drop of rain splashed refreshingly on my cheek, bringing a smile to my face.

"Get inside," Fayolan yelled above a second clap of thunder, but I laughed. Lifting my hands, welcoming the rain.

"Scared of a little *storm*, Death?" I raised a brow as I challenged him to admit it. "They speak to me, you know."

"What does?" Fayolan flicked hair from his face as the rain picked up, soaking us through.

"The storm." I grinned as thunder rolled again. "It brings a warning. Something is coming… a battle we can't win." I shouldn't have told him, but even with the approaching storm, I couldn't shake off the uneasy feeling in the pit of my stomach.

The rain hammered down; the wind swirling around me as it tried to blow me away. To freedom, or away from war, I was unsure either way. I anchored myself by digging my heels into the ground.

Run! The wind screamed as it ripped at the skirt of my dress. *Something's here*! The sky illuminated with lightning, and Fayolan cursed. A sword appearing in his hand.

"In the tent," he bellowed, and the roar I thought was a roll of thunder became clearer. *Soldiers!*

CHAPTER TWENTY-NINE

Fayolan

Tempest's warning came too late. Lightning filled the sky, illuminating the Ustrayan men as they charged towards us.

"Get in the tent," I ordered.

The Nephilim stood firm, her small fists curled at her side as the rain pelted her. "Give me a bow," she demanded. Before I could argue, lightning lit the sky and I could see around thirty men gaining on us. *Dammit!* The possibility of us both being overwhelmed was high, but I couldn't stand by and watch her die helplessly.

"Fine." My magic flared, removing the rope around her neck as I handed her a bow. Before I could blink, she had already shot her first arrow. It found its mark, taking down the first soldier. "This is a fight for your life. There is no room for remorse. Kill them before they do worse to you."

I could not take my eyes off Tempest as she fired again. She was fierce even when she should be cowering in fear.

The storm seemed to have awakened something within her, and she moved with a newfound intensity. Giving her the strength to kill without being affected by it. Her hands did not tremble as a third arrow hit its target.

"Do you expect me to do *all* the work?" The Nephilim didn't even glance at me as she smirked.

"Oh, that's how it is?" I grinned as I accepted her unspoken challenge. She was already three kills ahead of me.

I charged forward, careful to stay out of Tempest's line of fire. My ebony sword sang as it sliced through the stomach of the first man I crossed. As I reached a second, my heart was pounding.

I was about to land a fatal blow when an arrow brushed past my cheek, piercing through the heart of my prey. I spun to catch her grinning.

"Oops," she chuckled. *Gods*, she had the heart of a warrior, even if she did not realise it. "Watch out!" Her mouth parted, and a scream tore through the air.

Everything slowed as she raised her bow. I jabbed my sword back, puncturing through armour as a man grunted behind me. My sword became heavy as his dead weight dragged it to the ground.

I chuckled as she released a held breath. Spinning from her, using my foot to push the soldier off my blade. *Dammit! There's still too many of them.*

"Kalen!" I roared above the clamour and thunder. All I could do was pray he hadn't gone too far.

The sight of fallen men spurred me on, my sword thirsting for more, but I could feel myself being overpowered. When one man fell, a replacement stepped up. There was no end in sight, and alone, I wouldn't be enough to keep them from reaching the Nephilim.

"Fayolan," Tempest cried out. "They're coming from

behind." Men had appeared from around the lake and she turned her attention to them, edging back towards me.

She wouldn't thank me for what I was about to do. The Ustrayan bastards had us trapped like animals, herding us to the centre so they could make their kill.

"Get in the lake!" I yelled as my wings unfurled, and I took to the skies.

"You're leaving me?" I could see the fear splashed across her face as she spun frantically, not knowing where to aim. I scanned for Kalen and spotted him running towards us, but he would not make it in time. *Fuck!*

I swooped low, my sword cleaving a path through the soldiers. Its hum was deafening as my shadows wrapped around it, joining in its ravenous feast.

My wings caught an updraft, and I rose higher again. Just as I was about to drop, Tempest cried out. Her back was to the lake and her arm muscles strained while attempting to hold the bow still.

"The lake!" I roared, but she shook her head, refusing to budge.

"No, I can't…" *Damn, that woman would be the death of me!* I swooped towards Tempest, wrapping my arms around her front as I hauled her into the air. She flailed, trying to get a grip on me, but all she managed was to scratch my arms with her nails.

"Calm down. I won't drop you." *Yet!* I manoeuvred her carefully, so she faced me. Panic shone in her eyes as I carried her deeper over the lake.

I scanned for the nets that kept the monsters that lived within its murky depths at bay. She tried to cling on, realising what I was about to do.

"*Don't* you dare!" Tempest dug her nails into the flesh on my back.

"Sorry, Pet." I grinned as her mouth opened, but her words failed her.

"Fayolan, I can't…"

My lips crashed into hers, silencing her pleas. Just one kiss that had the desire to protect her roaring to life in my chest. I pulled away and released her.

Tempest screamed as she plummeted into the safety of the lake. Time was of the essence as Braedon displaced into the centre of the Ustrayan troops with Kalen, Nix, and Reed at his side. *Now I can fight undistracted by the Nephilim.*

I dipped low, carving a path for the others as they killed without mercy. Nix was in her element. The promise of death projected in the grin on her face. That woman terrified me. *Gods, she almost made my cock hard.*

Braedon vanished and reappeared. Slicing his twin swords violently through a man's neck before disappearing again, avoiding a fatal blow. He moved so fast that no one saw him coming until it was too late.

Kalen was the strongest of them all. He roared as he grabbed a soldier by his helm, crushing his head with his bare hands. The iron caved in under his brute strength.

Reed unleashed a firestorm of black flames through the men. Careful not to hit Nix as she continued her deadly rampage.

I descended, my wings cutting through the air, just above Reed's flames. My sharp talon penetrated a man's shoulder, dragging him through the fire. His screams only fed the deadly intent of my shadows.

A shrill whistle caused a group of men to peel off, heading straight for the lake.

"Kalen, with me." He braced as I swooped towards him. Extending his arm so I could grab it, lifting him off the ground. "Keep them from the lake."

I shot a glance towards the crystal-clear water, but

Tempest was nowhere to be seen. Without a second thought, I released Kalen, not caring whether he was out of harm's way.

I glided towards the spot I had dropped her, searching for her as my heart thundered in my chest. *Where was she? She couldn't have swum to shore so fast.*

Lightning flashed, illuminating the lake. *There!* I spotted her sinking deep beneath the surface. *She can't swim. Fucking idiot!* It should have been obvious. Tempest had refused to bathe in deep water every time I ordered her to do so.

I plunged towards the lake when pain shot through my back. My wings faltered as I lost all control of them, plummeting towards Tempest. My vision blurred as the water rose to meet me.

I hit with such force the air fled from my lungs. All I could do was try to reach Tempest. To give her a chance to survive this. Her face contorted in despair when she realised I could not save her.

Tempest's body convulsed as she tried desperately to get to me. I reached out, pulling her close as I pressed my lips to hers. Giving her my last breath.

My eyes felt heavy. I had no control of my body as I released Tempest. She fought to swim, flailing her arms and legs, but the current dragged her deeper. She was in a panic, her fingers digging into my shoulders, desperate to propel us both towards the surface.

Silly Girl! She was attempting to save me again. Tempest was just too small and exhausted from the battle. I was powerless as the darkness overtook me. *Death had come for us both!*

CHAPTER THIRTY

My lungs burned as I kept my breath held. Fayolan reached out for me as his blood turned the water crimson. A large bolt protruded through his chest.

I lost control of my body as it started convulsing. *This was it... we would not make it.*

My skin tingled when our fingers brushed, and Fayolan drew me in. His lips met mine, filling my lungs as he gave me the last of his air. *Silly man!* He was trying to save me once again.

I used all of my remaining strength to push him towards the surface. His body was too big, too heavy, and it trapped me beneath him as he sank. *Dammit! Why was I so weak?* I couldn't heal him whilst I clung to the edge of death.

My hand caressed Fayolan's cheek as his eyes closed. His heart slowed as my magic instinctively searched out his injuries.

The burn in my chest was unbearable as the air in my lungs ran out. My body convulsed, and blackness devoured me. *In the end, death came to claim me.*

Pressure on my chest dragged me from the darkness. My eyes sprang open as water spewed from my lungs. I coughed and spluttered, rolling over to expel it all.

"I can't heal him. It's too much damage," Nix said. Her voice seemed distant as I battled to focus. *Fayolan… was he still alive?*

"No, but *she* can." A hand slapped my face as Kalen gripped my arms, dragging my throbbing body upright. "You thought you would be *free* if he died?" His face was mere inches from mine as he yelled. The grip of his hands tightened painfully. "Well *guess* again, Nephilim!"

His next slap sent me reeling back. Warm blood dribbled down my cheek. "I *couldn't* save him." I tried to protest as I raised my throbbing arms defensively, but Kalen batted them aside with ease.

"*Yes*, you could. You just *chose* not to."

The fog in my mind cleared, and my anger flared. Kalen was wasting time when I should be healing Fayolan. *He had tried to save me when he realised he was going to die! I owed him this.*

"If I'd died whilst healing Fayolan, he would have too." Everyone spun to face me, and Kalen stopped his hand from striking me again.

"Explain." His face reddened as he scowled down at me.

"If a Nephilim is not strong enough to heal the wounded

person, we both perish. We can't stop once we've started. And with our death, all the injuries return at once, killing the patient. I was drowning. I *can't* swim and if I had tried to heal a wound as severe as that…"

"You would have killed him." Kalen sighed—his shoulders slumped as the information sank in.

I nodded as I rose from the ground. The storm still raged around us. The lightning revealed the true extent of Fayolan's wound.

Nix gasped, giving a strangled cry. "Are you strong enough to heal him?" Tears dripped down her cheeks. I had never seen her looking so… *human.*

"I hope so." Perhaps I could draw on the storm to aid me. I'd never attempted it before. But just maybe it would be enough to help me save Fayolan. "If I do this, I need you all to leave."

I knew how terrifying I looked when healing, and if one of them attacked me, we would all die. Because I was certain Fayolan would kill me if anything happened to one of them.

"We are *not* leaving Fayolan *unprotected* with *you.*" Kalen glared at me. *Gods, I didn't have time to convince him otherwise.*

"*Fine.* But I can't risk anyone interfering. *You,*" I pointed at Kalen. "Follow my rules and *everyone* else leaves. Healing is dangerous for anyone around me."

They all began yelling as I scrambled to Fayolan's side. His chest fluttered as if he could not draw breath, but as I placed my hands on his pecks, I could feel he was fighting to live. "You don't do things by half, do you?" I whispered. "Don't worry, everything will be alright."

"*Dammit!*" Nix yelled as Braedon grabbed her. The three of them disappeared, leaving me with Kalen.

He raised his dagger, pointing it at me as he crouched beside Fayolan. "Do it. *Now.*"

"He doesn't have much time, so listen carefully, because I'll only say this once. No matter what happens, you *do not* touch me. If I die, so does he, so keep me alive."

Kalen nodded as I allowed my magic to spread. "I hope you do not scare easily." I shot him a wicked smirk.

"Why?" he asked, but I didn't answer. He had no inkling of what he was about to witness. I released my magic, pushing it into Fayolan.

My body transformed. Wings burst from my back, and my skin glowed with a blue shimmer. My healing magic worked its way through Fayolan, seeking all of his injuries. *This was going to hurt.*

"*Holy shit*!" Kalen stuttered when he made eye contact with me.

"Are you scared?"

"No." His face told a different story.

"You will be." I chuckled. But as the first wave of pain hit, I held back a scream. "Remove the bolt." I panted against the strain as he pulled it free, tossing it aside like it had burned him. *Shit, he had inadvertently felt my magic.* "Be careful*! If you'd touched me, you would be *dead* already."

The pain that surged through my chest was so intense that it felt like my ribcage was being pried apart. A scream tore from me as my body mimicked tearing flesh and shattering bones.

"Gods," Kalen cursed, stepping back as the thick, black tar oozed from my eyes, ears, nose, and mouth. Sometimes even the bravest of men cowered at the sight of a Nephilim healing.

"Are you *good*?" I asked through gritted teeth. Kalen clung to his dagger so tight his knuckles turned white. He jolted out of his stupor, tossing it aside as if he didn't trust himself not to use it.

Another scream ripped from me. My body tensing as I

battled against the agonising pain to keep my hands on Fayolan.

His internal damage was severe, but luckily, the barbed bolt had missed his heart. His lung had not been so lucky. I gasped for breath, pulling the injury into myself, as I experienced the feeling of mine collapsing.

Sweat coated my body. Even the icy rain could not calm the fever that tried to claim me. *I can't do this! Even I wasn't strong enough.*

"If you can hear me, I need your help. *Please* lend me your power." I wasn't sure the storm could even aid me. Another clap of thunder was its only response..

"What's happening?" Kalen edged closer as he focused on me. His skin was pale and his hands trembling.

"I will not make it. Not alone." Words were becoming harder as my teeth ground together.

"What can I do?" *There's nothing he could do other than pray we both survived this.*

"*Please!*" I cried out in one last desperate plea. *It can't end. Not like this.*

"Take my power, child." I froze as a male voice boomed through the thunder. "The storm will feed your magic."

Lightning crashed to earth around me, sending raw static magic through my body. My hair swirled around me as my strength returned. *Gods, it fucking worked!*

Kalen winced at every agonised scream. Understanding finally struck him as he figured out what was happening.

I shook and cried more inky tears, blurring my vision. "*Come on.* Death!" Relief flooded me as his heartbeat responded, becoming stronger. I swayed, my pain trying to drag me into the depths of unconsciousness, but I clung on. *Just a little more!*

Fayolan's lips parted as he sucked in a deep breath. His eyes did not open, even as I brushed my fingers over his chest. The wound had fully healed, leaving no trace behind.

The world shifted, and I fell back, pulling my magic inside. My wings curled under my skin, now a golden olive once again. My chest heaved as I fought for air. The fatal injuries I'd absorbed were still playing havoc within me.

Kalen was fast, ripping Fayolan's shirt as he inspected him. I simply lay unable to move, just trying to fight the pain.

"What can I do?" Kalen rushed to my side. "Can I touch you now?" I nodded. My magic had depleted, so I could no longer transfer the injuries to him.

He removed his bloodied shirt, dipping it into the lake beside us. He was gentle as he wiped the black from my face, cleaning his shirt again before mopping the sweat pooled on my brow. "What happens now?"

"Fayolan will dream of the future he now has." I tried to smile, but I knew what awaited me was not so pleasant.

"And you?" His brow furrowed.

I gave a husky chuckle as I stared up at the sky. "I'll relive his injuries as if I had received them."

"Really?"

"Ironic isn't it. You all deem us to be monsters. But still we heal, regardless of the cost to ourselves. I've heard tales of Nephilim being driven mad by the dreams."

Kalen brushed aside a lock of hair that was falling across my forehead as he gazed down at me. "Could the Nephilim who killed the Queen have been mad?"

"I doubt it. I don't see the King letting a *crazy* person near the Queen. *Do you?*"

"No. Maybe he didn't know she was."

"There's no point trying to figure it out. Only one person knows the whole truth, and I doubt he will ever admit to lying." I winced as another jolt of pain shot through me.

"Let's get you inside." Kalen scooped me off the ground.

My body hung limp in his arms as he carried me to the tent. At least the pain of healing hid that of his touch. "I'll be right back as soon as I've got Fayolan settled."

I relaxed back into the bedroll as Kalen released me and headed to the tent flap. "Tempest?" He turned his head back to me.

"Yeah?" I grumbled as the room swirled around me.

"How long will it hurt?"

"The worst will pass by morning." He nodded, his lips twisting like it pained him to see me like this. *I don't want his pity.* He would not have spared me this agony even if I had told him about it.

I concealed my gaze, focusing on getting air to my lungs. Slow, shallow breaths were all I could manage. Kalen sighed, and the tent flap rustled as he left me alone.

Moments later, I heard voices outside. The others had returned to watch over Fayolan. I was too tired to listen in. Besides, I didn't care what any of them had to say. *I was a monster to them… until they needed me.*

Kalen stuck to his promise, returning with a blanket and a water pouch for me. His gaze roamed over me as he covered me in furs.

"Why don't you tell Fayolan?" he asked.

"Tell him what?" I croaked weakly.

Too feeble to sit up and drink the water. Kalen lifted my head, helping me to quench my thirst.

"If he knew that the death of a Nephilim whilst healing kills the patient too, he might see what you are."

"A *monster*?" I clenched my teeth as more pain radiated through me.

"I don't believe that. When you heal, you are even more beautiful. You aren't a monster, Tempest." My eyes grew heavy and I let them close. "You're an angel." I barely registered his words of reverence as I drifted away. To nightmares that would have me thrashing in my sleep.

"*Where* the *fuck* is she?" Fayolan roared. The tent's flap flung open, and he glared down at me.

The moonlight flowed around him, accentuating every bulging muscle as his body heaved. "What did you do to me?" His shadows pulsed, trying to snuff out all the light.

"I saved you." I instantly regretted my words. *Something's wrong with him*. His pupils dilated and swirling tattoos had now appeared on his chest and arms. I could have sworn they were moving.

"What else did you do?"

"I don't know what you're talking about... I didn't do anything." I flinched as Fayolan stepped towards me. But he stalked closer until he backed me into the corner.

"I dreamt of *you*," he snarled. "The feel of your skin against mine." His hand shot out, grabbing my ankle. "The taste of your cunt as it came for me." I yelped as Fayolan dragged me across the ground. He straddled me, pinning me beneath his weight. "It felt so good as my dick pounded your sweet flesh."

His hand's trailed up my legs, pushing my dress aside as he reached my thighs.

"I don't control your dreams. When a Nephilim heals you, you see your future." I tried to shuffle back. But with each sweeping touch of his fingers against my skin, heat flared between my legs.

"Stop lying to me, Tempest. *Gods,* you're so fucking wet

for me. You have been making me want you since we first met." He peered down at me with a scowl.

"I haven't. Nephilim don't even have that power." Even though I spoke the truth, my traitorous body wanted him to keep touching me.

"No? Then tell me to stop, Tempest. Say you don't want this and I will leave right now." Fayolan's eyes were a mixture of fury and desire. I knew if I didn't find the strength to utter those words, he would ruin me.

"Why are you doing this?" *That's not what I had in mind to say.* I should have told him I didn't want this… *shouldn't I?* Fayolan's thumb rubbed against my clit, his fingers massaging a spot I had never experienced before. My mind clouded, and a moan escaped my lips. *I was so screwed!*

CHAPTER THIRTY-ONE

I *would teach Tempest to implant dreams in my mind!* She dared to make me long for her.

Her eyes sparkled even in the dark confines of the tent, as my fingers became coated in her juices. She moaned as her clit swelled with the need for me to fill her.

"I'm waiting, Pet. Do you want this or not?" Her body shuddered as a groan escaped her rosy lips. *Hell, I could scent her arousal in the air.*

"I…" Her words failed as her eyes rolled and her back arched. She was so sensitive even the gentlest touch had her losing control.

"Have it your way." I pulled back, but her hands shot up. Her nails digging into my back as she held me in place. "I need you to say it, Pet." I would never claim an unwilling woman. But Tempest kept me rooted in place, a gesture that spoke volumes.

"Last chance. Say the words." Her heart pounded as she

stared up at me. Her hands trembling as she nibbled on her bottom lip. Gods I wanted her so badly, but this was her trap. And I was about to spring it.

"I didn't put a spell on you," she mumbled, but her grip on me remained firm.

"You haven't given me an answer." My fingers circled against her clit again as she remained silent. "All it takes is one word."

"Don't…" she groaned as I pulled my fingers through her folds.

"Say it!"

"Don't go." Her body shuddered as I kissed her, claiming her succulent lips. Forcing my tongue into her mouth.

Something in my mind screamed for me to stop, but I wanted her. *The Nephilim had made sure I craved her.* Her eagerness matched mine. I could see it in the flush of her cheeks and the quiver of her needy cunt.

"This is a onetime thing." It would be the last time I caved to her wiles. I'd give her what she wanted and then I could walk away. Free of her spell. I could wipe her from my mind, knowing she was nothing special. Just another needy woman using sex as a weapon.

Tempest wanted to hate me, but the slight buck of her hips said otherwise. Her groans were like music to my ears as my hand roamed to her breast. They were perfect. Her nipples were already hard as I pinched one through her dress.

"Gods," she hissed.

"There are no Gods here, Pet." My lips found hers again, caressing them softly as I stole her breath. Tempest's hands rose, her palms pressing against my chest as if she considered pushing me away. I chuckled, nipping her lip, stealing another moan from her.

"Having second thoughts?" She met my gaze as her hands continued to explore my body. I freed her nipple, moving to the other as I rolled it between my fingers. The small hiss that escaped her had my cock throbbing.

She'd never been more beautiful than at that instant. If I didn't know better, I would almost think she lacked experience. Her movements were timid and unsure.

"Fayolan…" she murmured as her back arched. Chuckling, I shifted my weight onto my heels. Freeing my cock from my leather trousers. Her eyes grew larger as she gasped.

"Clearly, the boy didn't have what I am offering. I'm going to fill you until you scream out my name." I smirked as her gaze lifted to meet mine. Her breath hitched, and her heart beat so wildly, I could hear it.

"Just shut up and kiss me." Tempest's voice was husky as she licked her lips hungrily.

"Keep talking like that and when we get to Solis, I might keep you chained to my bed and show you how a *real* man fucks."

I leant over her, the tip of my cock rubbing through her wetness. Gods, I knew I should open her up first. Using my fingers to prepare her for what I had to offer. But I could barely contain myself.

I needed to fill her—to hear her scream as she realised what she had been missing. "I will wipe everyone else from your mind. So, all you remember is how good I feel inside you as I fuck your tantalising pussy."

She moaned as my cock worked her sensitive flesh, and she rubbed her greedy cunt against me. "Last chance, Pet. Tell me now if you don't want this. You have to the count of three." I gave her one last opportunity to stop this. "One… Two… Three…"

Her mouth opened. Her tongue licked her lips as if they were too dry to allow words to form. "Fayolan, I've never…" I cut off her words as I slammed into her. The scream that erupted from her was not what I'd expected.

"Gods you're so *tight*." I stilled, giving her a chance to adjust to my cock within her. I still had more to give, but tears glistened in her eyes as she bit her lower lip. "Don't hold back. I want to hear you. The screams, the moans, all of it."

Gradually, I rocked my hips, using my cock to spread her wider, forcing in deeper as she whimpered my name. I drew out slowly and her groans made me crave her even more. I ploughed into her tight, wet pussy again.

This time, her cries were a mix of pain and something euphoric that had my cock pulsing within her. "Can you take more?"

"I think so," she said, her legs spreading to give me more access. Lowering my body against hers, I trapped her beneath me. Thrusting more of my hard, throbbing shaft into her. I wasn't sure she could take all of me. Her previous lovers were clearly lacking if she could not handle what I wanted to give her.

I slowed, thrusting in and out, letting her wetness coat my cock so it could glide deeper with ease. Her pained scream became one of bliss as she rocked her hips, drawing me in as she relaxed.

"Ready?" I asked. Her fists uncurled as she held my stare. Dipping her head, allowing me to speed up. My cock had never been as hard as it was now, buried inside her. Searching for the sweet spot that would have her screaming for me.

Her back arched, accentuating the beautiful curve of her body. I was losing my mind. My heart racing in time with hers as my control slipped.

"Fayolan…" Tempest's head rolled back as she cried out my name. *Gods be damned, I'm in heaven and it's because of her.*

My lips claimed hers, tasting her as she kissed back. Her breasts pressing against me as she cried out again. Her nipples rubbing against my chest as she lost control of her body.

"Fuck it." I picked up the pace, thrusting harder as she made delectable noises. My arms strained as I held myself above her. "Cum with me, Little Nephilim."

"Fayolan," she screamed as she shattered around me, coming undone. Her juices drenched my cock, and I thrust again. Our lips locking in a torrent of emotion as I filled her with my seed.

"Shit," I groaned as my body tensed. After a few more thrusts, I released everything I had inside of her.

I panted as my arms gave out. My whole body trembled as Tempest gasped for air beneath me. "Good girl." I brushed a loose strand of hair from her face. "You are so beautiful."

Her smile was radiant, but a single tear slid down her cheek. I kissed it away before trailing them down her neck. "Did I hurt you?"

"Not really. That was…" Her words trailed off as she took a deep breath, trying to compose herself. Slick sweat coated her body, and I chuckled as I got up.

My cock was still hard, twitching as it begged for more. Tempest's gaze flicked downward, and her jaw dropped. She gave a stifled cry. Barely audible beneath her laboured breaths and the thrumming of my heart.

I glanced down, frowning as I saw the blood coating my cock. *Idiot!* I'd known the boy must have been lacking, but I had fucked her with no preparation. *Bastard! What had I done?*

"I'm sorry." I could not bear to look at her as she bit her bottom lip. Her hands tremored, as she lowered her dress. Sitting up as her gaze sank to the floor. "I should have been gentler. Please say something, Pet."

"It's okay." Her words were barely above a whisper. She

didn't even spare me a look. Her beautiful smile was gone and her lips trembled as she held back sobs.

I spun on my heels, fleeing from the tent. I'd been angry at her, but I never intended to hurt her. Tempest had cried out my name as she groaned and rocked her hips to let me fill her. If I'd known she was in pain, I would have stopped.

Kalen and the others sat around the campfire, and I crossed to them. But still, I could hear Tempest's soft sobs. Never once had I left a woman in tears and I felt like a piece of shit for it.

"The Nephilim might need healing," I grumbled to Nix as she glanced in Tempest's direction. She smirked with a sly wink as she made her way to the tent. But Kalen stared into the flames of the fire with a scowl. "*What*?" Now's not the time for him to provoke me, not when I could feel my patience wearing thin and my temper ready to explode.

"You *really* are a bastard. No wonder she doesn't tell you…" His words trailed off as he sighed angrily.

"Doesn't tell me what?"

"Do you know what? It doesn't even matter. You're not ready to hear the truth. Nothing Tempest says will ever ring true with you." Kalen got to his feet, storming away from me.

Anger nestled deep in my stomach, but something else twisted within me. Stopping me from following and beating him until he confessed what he knew.

"You *fucking* asshole!" Nix stormed from the tent, pointing her finger at me as her face reddened. Her ice-cold eyes trained on me as she looked ready to murder me.

"What did *you* do?" Reed winced as her gaze shot to him.

"It's not my fault she couldn't handle my cock."

"You fucked a virgin with no prep. You just *crammed* it in, ripping her to shreds." I felt sick as her words sunk in.

"She wasn't… she told me she slept with the boy."

Nix's nostrils flared as her fingers teased around the

dagger strapped to her hip. "Was that before or *during* you torturing the poor girl?"

Shit! Tempest had tried to tell me she had never slept with anyone. Of course, she hadn't—the Nephilim allowed no one to touch her. I brought my hand up to my face, dragging it down my cheek as I groaned. Battling the torrent of guilt coursing through me.

"Maybe she should stop being stubborn and heal herself." I regretted my words the moment they left my mouth.

"Just get me some warm water and a cloth. You should know better, Fayolan." Nix was right to chastise me. I stared for a moment as she turned away from me, barking orders at Reed.

"That was fucking cold, man," Reed said, looking awkward as he tousled his hair. *What had got into them all? She's not a woman—she's a monster. Just like me!*

I pulled a bowl of hot steaming water from the aether along with a cloth and a small vial of healing salts. Shoving them into Reed's arms as he refused to meet my gaze. "Not even *she* deserved that," he grumbled as he stalked away.

I trained my attention on Kalen, needing a distraction from my inner turmoil. It's about time he started talking.

"What hasn't the Nephilim told me? *Other* than she's a maiden." I scowled as he spun, straightening his shoulders as he squared up to me. His chest heaving as he clenched his fists. *Brave… stupid, but brave.*

"I learnt a lot when she *saved* your life." Kalen flashed his teeth as he spoke. "Did you know Nephilim cannot stop healing once they've started? Or if the injuries are too severe, both the Nephilim and the patient will not survive. Also, if you kill a Nephilim during healing, the patient dies, too."

His words were like a dagger to the heart. My father had said he killed the Nephilim *after* it murdered my mother.

"He *fucking* lied!" And I believed it like a naïve little

child. "What I don't get is why?" *If she had died whilst trying to save my mother, then why hide it? What would he gain from blaming a whole species for something out of their control?*

"Why don't you ask *him*?" Kalen shrugged as he backed off. His shoulders slumped as he calmed. "You think she is beautiful now…" He flicked his gaze towards Tempest's tent. "Wait till you see her heal." He stalked away, dismissing himself.

"Where are you going?" I stared at his back. I don't think I ever remembered him being this pissed off at me.

"To give her better dreams. You *bitch* and moan about seeing your future because it's not what you wanted. Do you know what she sees in her sleep?"

"No."

"She relives your injuries. But instead of you being impaled… *it's her*." There's nothing I could say to that. No insult or curse I could hurl at him. Instead, I followed him to Tempest's tent without uttering a word.

Nix stormed from inside as we got there. Throwing the blood covered cloth at me. Kalen chuckled as he slipped inside, leaving me leant against the opening.

Tempest's eyes were closed, whimpers escaped as she tossed and turned. Kalen lowered beside her, and a growl escaped before I could stop it. Seeing him so close to her rankled me. I'd hoped fucking the Nephilim would have freed me from her grasp. But all it achieved was making things worse.

His magic flowed from his fingers in green, wispy smoke as he touched her temple. She stilled, her face a picture of innocence as she fell into a peaceful slumber.

CHAPTER THIRTY-TWO

Tempest

I groaned as I woke. My dreams had been peaceful, and I guessed Kalen had something to do with it. I could still feel the tingle of his magic in the air.

Every muscle in my body ached. Sweat clung to me like a second skin, and I could not ignore the soreness between my legs. My cheeks flushed as I remembered the night with Fayolan. *How could I even face him now?*

He'd offered me a chance to say no. To prove I hadn't been manipulating him. But for the first time in so long, someone had touched me and turned it into something pleasurable. I'd wanted it. *No… I'd needed it.*

Foolishly, I'd let my mind believe it meant more to him than it had. Setting myself up for a fall when he rejected me.

My stomach cramped, and I cursed as I battled to get up. I ambled towards the tent flap, stumbling as I walked. Each movement caused another sharp, twisting sensation in my gut. My face beaded with sweat, and my hair plastered to my forehead. *Something's wrong.*

"You're up." Kalen shot me a sympathetic smile as he spotted me. "Hungry?" I nodded as the tantalising aroma of meat roasting on the fire reached me.

My heart beat wildly as I caught Fayolan's gaze. I couldn't forget the feel of him inside of me. Or how his touch turned intense pain into pleasure.

My body had wanted him, and my mind had turned to mush as I fell into a bliss so overwhelming I thought I would never surface. That's until he walked away, leaving me bleeding and broken on the floor.

I tore my gaze from him as my cheeks flushed and my nipples hardened. I took a long inhale as I found the courage to cross to the fire.

"Are you feeling better?" Fayolan asked.

"Yeah," I mumbled, fixing my gaze on the ground by my feet. I could feel him watching me as my body heated. My movements were sluggish as I endeavoured to lower myself to the ground.

Fayolan climbed to his feet, offering me his hand. But I pulled away from him. *Gods, I'm barely containing myself as it is.* Just his closeness was enough to set my body on fire.

He snarled at my rejection. But another cramp made me wince, and I fell the last of the way to the solid ground. Cursing under my breath as it sent a violent shock up my spine.

Thankfully, Kalen handed me a plate of steaming food. It smelled delicious, but as I ate a few bites, my stomach churned. Using magic usually made me hungry, but I wasn't sure I could eat at all.

Fayolan edged closer until I could feel the gentle heat of his body. "What's wrong?"

"I guess the healing has taken its toll on me. But I'm fine."

"Good." Fayolan got up. "We have a lot of ground to cover today. Give me your hands."

I sighed as he held up a rope. It took more effort than it should, just to keep them up as he bound them. Admittedly, not nearly as tight as before.

He hauled me up. Everything around me became a blur, and I squinted to refocus. Fayolan failed to notice as my body swayed and a sudden wave of light-headedness threw me off balance.

Kalen's brow furrowed as he nudged Fayolan. Flicking his head towards me. Both men shot me scrutinising glances.

Fayolan's attention turned to my hair, reaching out for a strand at the front, letting it run through his fingers. I swallowed deeply as heat flared in my stomach. *Treacherous body!*

"This is new," he mused. I glimpsed the latest midnight blue streak in my hair. Thicker than the others that scattered through the chestnut brown.

"Every time I heal, I get another." I answered his unspoken question. His brow rose as he inspected my hair.

"It's bigger." He shrugged.

"You were almost beyond saving." His body was now so close to mine I could smell his intoxicating scent. Pine and citrus wafting around me like a blanket.

"You risked your life. Why?"

"It wasn't like I had a choice." I shot a glance at Kalen. But deep down, I knew I'd have done it, anyway. Even if Fayolan believed I had done it to trap him.

I gnawed at my bottom lip while gazing at the floor. Anything was better than chancing seeing his hatred for me reflected from the depths of his golden eyes. I was uncertain if I could handle it after last night.

I fiddled with my fingers nervously as Fayolan stepped closer still. His body almost pressed against mine as he released my hair.

"You're unusually quiet. Are you sure you're okay?" he asked. His voice was uncharacteristically soft, and I spared a quick glance at his stony face.

"Uh, huh." I nodded. Suddenly unable to find words.

"Then *start* walking. We have no horses. *Move.*" Fayolan stepped around me, tugging on the rope. I should have known he hadn't cared about me. Stupidly, I gave myself to him, and he still hated me.

I struggled to move my feet. The ache of my body tried to drag me back down to the ground. Another cramp ripped through me, and I used my arm to apply pressure to my stomach. But I could not ease the pain that was getting worse.

We walked in silence. Fayolan stalked ahead, but Kalen slowed. Staying beside me as his gaze burned into Fayolan's back. Occasionally, his attention would drift to me as I stumbled, or a slight whimper gave away my pain.

We hadn't gone far when my vision blurred again, and I froze, struggling to steady myself. Fayolan stopped dead, scowling as he clutched the rope. He jerked it, but Kalen's hand shot out. Stopping me from being dragged to the floor.

"Have a drink," Kalen commanded, holding out a water pouch. With trembling hands, I tried to raise it to my lips. Pain tore through my stomach, and everything slowed as it fell from my grip. Cold, refreshing water splashed across my legs. My eyes rolled, and the world tilted as I collapsed.

Kalen caught me in his enormous arms before I could hit the ground. "What have you *done*?" He shot a dark glance at Fayolan as I released a pained moan.

"What are you talking about?"

Kalen swept my sweat-soaked hair from my face. "She's got a fever." He sheltered me in his arms as Fayolan descended beside us, brushing Kalen's hand aside. His nostrils flared as he moved his palm to my racing heart.

"Fucking does not cause this. I thought Nephilim didn't get sick." Fayolan stared at me, waiting for confirmation.

"We don't," I grumbled. "Only poison can…" My words faded away as I groaned. "The barb must've been laced with poison."

"So, this is your body simulating the effects?" Kalen asked.

My head swung back as I squeezed my stomach again. "No. It's the one thing we can't heal. It absorbs into our blood, and only the antidote can save us." *Ironic! After everything I'd survived, healing would cause my death.*

"Look." Kalen ripped the bust of my dress. "We need to find that barb."

Fayolan's eyes darkened as he took in my rapidly heaving chest. "I'll fly ahead. You keep her alive, *dammit*." I could have sworn Fayolan's voice cracked with emotion. *My mind must be playing tricks on me.*

Kalen lifted me from the ground as wings burst from Fayolan's back, and he took to the skies. I watched him soar overhead. His silhouette blocked the sun as my vision dimmed.

"Stay awake, Tempest." Kalen shook me softly as he ran. "Don't you dare close those pretty eyes." He struggled to cradle me as I jolted in pain from the worsening cramps. His muscles rippled beneath me as he gripped me tighter.

"It's okay," I said, my voice weak as it tried to fail me. "At least it will be over soon."

"Don't you talk like that. Fayolan won't let you die." I listened as the sound of Fayolan's wings faded away as he left us behind.

I nestled into Kalen's chest. Dying relieved the pain of touch. At least I would not be alone.

CHAPTER THIRTY-THREE

Fayolan

My wings flapped with such fury that my back muscles ached in protest. Without a second thought, I left them behind. Tempest would not die because she saved my life. *I would not allow it.*

My heart pounded as guilt consumed me. *Why didn't I probe Tempest further about her abilities?* Kalen was right. I knew nothing about her. Or the creatures I'd killed without mercy. My heart and mind still warred over whether she was a goddess or a monster.

My father would pay for the lives he tricked me into taking. Even now, I still hated Tempest, as if he had carved it into my bones. All I knew for certain was that I couldn't let her die until I knew the truth.

I couldn't ignore the vivid splash of colour as the world flew past in a blur. All night and this morning, the world appeared as Tempest saw it.

I'd sat and watched the sunrise, in awe of the hues dancing across the sky. My heart warmed, but with it came an ache. Knowing soon the beauty would be gone once again. The effects of fucking Tempest's delicious temple of a body would wear off.

Even after I'd stolen her virginity, she had given me a gift beyond words. One I would treasure in my memories for all eternity.

The sun reflected off the lake, almost blinding me as I searched intently along its banks. The barb had to be here somewhere.

I couldn't erase the image of the black veins edging towards her heart. A glint caught my eye, and I swooped down.

Pulling gloves from the aether, I picked up the blood-soaked barb, avoiding touching the poisonous tip. Lifting it to my nose, I tried to distinguish the poison from the coppery tang. There it was—a familiar acrid stench with a sweet undertone. *Blood Ivy!*

It killed fast and caused immense pain. But I could save Tempest. That was all that mattered. I shot into the sky, discarding the barb as I returned to my little Nephilim.

Kalen cradled her unconscious body in his arms, as if she were his most prized possession. Desire to kill him for touching her roared to life within me, but I pushed it to the darkest recesses of my mind.

I landed at a run, pulling a bottle of roseweed from the aether. "Lay her down," I ordered, and Kalen obeyed. Gently placing her to the ground and taking a step back.

My shadows were thick and swirling around me; although Kalen could not see them, he could sense them. And they scared even the likes of him.

"What is it?" he asked.

"*Blood* Ivy." I popped the cork from the bottle, dropping

to my knees as I rested Tempest's head against my lap. Her breath was a mere whisper against my skin.

I poured the thick liquid through her slightly parted lips, but the Nephilim was too weak to swallow. "*Dammit, Tempest.*" I clasped my hand over her mouth and nose. Seconds felt like hours as I waited for her body to react.

"Come *on*," Kalen urged beneath his breath as he moved closer. Taking her hand and giving it a gentle squeeze. A deep, guttural growl shook my body, and he released her, edging back to appease the beast within me.

Tempest swallowed, and I sighed heavily. My shoulders slumped as some of the tension in my body ebbed away. She would survive, although it would take some time for her to wake up.

"Where the *fuck* did Ustrayans get Blood Ivy?" Kalen pounded his fists into the ground. It's one of our most guarded secrets. A plant with poison so potent that a single drop could kill even the toughest man.

"It seems we've been betrayed." When I discovered who, their head would hang from the gates of Solis.

I slipped my hands beneath Tempest, lifting her tiny frame to me. She was so light that guilt gnawed at me again. I'd not cared for her like I should.

Kalen took the lead as I followed behind, focusing on the woman in my arms. Once I got her to Solis, she would be safe. Even if I had to make good on my promise and chain her to my bed.

"How's she doing?" Kalen glanced back as we walked. Thankfully, her heart rate had slowed back to normal, and her breathing was less laboured.

"She's getting stronger." She was surprisingly tough for her size.

Other Nephilim were over seven feet tall, yet she only just met my chest. She was hardly bigger than a sixteen-year-old girl. But her curves and the life experience that shone in her eyes marked her years. Yet another element in the puzzle of Tempest.

"When we get back to Solis, I'm going to find out who is behind this." Kalen gripped the sword at his waist as he scowled. "Someone is going to *fucking* pay for this." *Oh, I'll make sure of it.*

"Thanks, by the way." I owed Kalen a great debt.

"For what?" He frowned.

"You noticed she was struggling." I'd been so wrapped up in her rejection of me. That I missed all the signs something was wrong.

"*You* would have if you weren't so *distracted*. Whatever is going on with you, *fix* it." *Unfortunately, it's not that simple.*

The sun began to set, and I lifted my head to the sky. Beautiful colours bled together, forming a blanket of reds and oranges that I'd never appreciated before. *It took my breath away.*

Kalen watched me as my feet slowed and I stopped walking. "Fayolan?"

"I can see it," I said as his gaze trailed to the sunset.

"Nix is going to be furious that she missed your reaction." He chuckled as his hostility towards me faded. At least for now.

"I'm sure if I ever see it again, I'll still react the same." He smiled with a nod as he remained watching the sun dip lower. Not moving on until I sighed, turning away. "Let's go."

Soon after night had fallen, we settled in for the night. I slipped into my tent, tenderly placing Tempest on a cot so she was off the ground.

Pulling a chair from the aether, I sat beside her. My fingers trailed through her lustrous hair as I swept it aside to inspect her chest. Thankfully, the black veins were receding.

Tempest stirred at my touch. Her dark lashes flickered as she tried to open her eyes. The moonlight filtering in made them glimmer. My breath caught in my throat as my heart skipped a beat.

Her lips parted, and one word slipped from them. *"Serrin." She still wanted the fucking boy! I was a damned fool to even consider she would ever call out for me.* Lifting myself from the chair, I slunk into the shadows. I didn't want her to witness me like this.

I slipped towards the tent flap as I heard the rustle of her dress. "Fayolan," she called. My fists clenched, and I softened my face as I turned to her.

She tried to lift her frail arm, reaching towards me. "Stay with me… I don't want to die alone." Her voice trembled as a tear glistened, caught in her lashes. "Not even a monster like me deserves that." Her words slammed into me like a punch to the heart. I'd never allowed her to forget what she was.

Spinning away from her, I hid my face. I could not bring myself to witness her tears. Without another word, I left her alone. Too ashamed of myself to stay.

"How is she?" Kalen asked as I skulked to the campfire, pacing back and forth.

"She will *live*." *Why was I so angry with her?* I hated her beyond reason, but the most offensive thing she had done was to open that smart-ass mouth of hers. She constantly surprised me with kindness I didn't deserve.

"Will you stay with her tonight?" he asked. I spared a fleeting glance at the tent.

"Maybe."

He nodded and rested back on his bedroll, letting the fire warm him. He tossed and turned, grunting now and then as he failed to get comfortable. Something was clearly bothering him.

"Would you like to talk about it?" I asked.

Kalen sighed, pulling himself up. "I hit *her*. Back at the lake. Hell, I was furious she hadn't healed you in the water. I didn't know she couldn't." He'd struck her before, but she'd done nothing wrong this time.

"You're getting attached, Kalen. She is still a prisoner." I may not agree with the reason for my father's condemnation of her people, but I did not have all the answers yet. Until then, nothing would change. I knew I'd blurred the lines, but he needed to remember what she was. *We both did!*

"I've told you before. Kill her or let her go." Kalen rolled away from me.

"I will. Once I know the truth." Yet, in the depths of my soul, I knew I would have to end her, if she became more of a wedge between Kalen and I. His loyalty was worth more than her life.

CHAPTER THIRTY-FOUR

I did not sleep after Fayolan left me alone, fearing I would die. I exhaled in defeat as the sun's rays peeked through the tent flap.

The cool morning breeze lightly swept over me as I slipped outside. Both men had succumbed to exhaustion. But Fayolan remained facing me. *No doubt ensuring I did not run.*

My body was sore, and the cramps continued to throb, although they had lost their intensity. My skin was clammy and damp from the fever that broke during the night. *Ugh, I feel gross.*

The lake glistened invitingly, so I crept past the campfire. Desperate not to disturb the men as I made my way to the shoreline. To wash the horrors of the last couple of days from my body.

I sprawled on the bank to pull off my boots. Wiggling my toes as I dipped them into the icy water making me shiver. *Just get in before you chicken out.* I chastised myself.

Taking a deep breath, I cast one last glance at the sleeping men. No one stirred. I quietly slipped out of my dress and into the lake's shallows. Stumbling deeper than I planned. I gasped as the chill of the water splashed up to my chest. "*Shit!*"

I was deep enough to lower my head beneath the water to clean the grime from my hair. My foot slipped, and disorientation washed over me. I couldn't determine which way was up. *How could I have been so stupid?*

My heart raced as I flailed pathetically, trying to regain my footing. But the moment arms wrapped around me, the pain snapped me back to my senses.

Fayolan dragged me above the waterline. The inviting warmth of his body pressed against my back as I gulped for air. He held me upright until my feet firmly planted on the lakebed.

"Thank you," I said hurriedly, pulling my body away from his. His touch had become far too enticing.

"No problem," he grunted as he held out a clean dress. I snatched it from his hands, clutching it to my chest. *Gods I was naked!*

"Thanks again. For the clothes."

"Stay out of the lake," he commanded. He shook his head and droplets sprayed over him as his hair settled back into place. Pebbles crunched beneath his feet as he led me from the lake.

I froze as he scooped his shirt from the ground. His back rippled as rivulets of water cascaded over his powerful muscles. The heat between my legs flared to life with a vengeance. Images flashed in my mind of him between my thighs, his cock filling me, and the sinful things I wished he would do with his tongue… *I'm going to hell!*

With a deep breath, I turned away before he could see my flushed cheeks. *Why does my captor have to be so damned handsome?*

My fingers traced the material of the dress as I waited for him to return to the campfire. I lingered in the water just a moment more. If I lived long enough, maybe I could learn to swim.

I slipped from the lake, pulling the dress on before joining Kalen and Fayolan by the fire. Ignoring the sharp cramp as I gingerly lowered myself down.

Fayolan passed me a small bottle with a swirling pink liquid inside. Rolling his eyes as I stared at it suspiciously. "Drink. It'll help rid the effects of the poison quicker and ease the pain."

I popped the cork and downed the sickly sweet liquid. "Gods that's vile." I coughed, wiping the residue from my lips. "Yeah, I think I'd rather die than taste that again." I cupped my mouth as the liquid tried to come back up.

Fayolan sneered as he tossed a plate in my direction. *So... we're back to hating each other again, I guess?* I didn't have any trouble doing that. I'd thought I was about to die, and lowered myself to asking him to stay with me. But he turned his back and walked away.

An awkward, stony silence filled the camp as we ate. I didn't fail to notice my meal was more nutritious than any I had received so far. Maybe Fayolan had seen my spine beginning to protrude through my skin. Or the way my eyes have sunk, making me look almost sickly.

"Are you done?" he asked as I became too full to eat another bite. I nodded, holding the plate out towards him. "Good."

A rope manifested in his grasp as he reached towards the plate. I scowled and released it, letting it fall to the ground. It shattered, satisfyingly, at my feet. Eliciting a throaty growl from Fayolan.

"*Oops…*" I said dryly, closing the gap between us. The shards crunching beneath my boots. I held up my wrists, glaring through my thick lashes to meet his gaze. His jaw was tense and his teeth bared. "I won't run. I have *nowhere* to go. *You* made sure of that."

"Are you done?" His nostrils flared, as did the ominous shadows around him. We locked into a silent battle of wills. Neither of us wanted to be the first to avert our gaze.

A small smile played on his lips as he stepped closer, forcing me to crane my neck to maintain eye contact.

Fayolan was so close I felt the gentle caress of his breath on my face. One more step and our bodies would rub together. We both knew I'd back away at the pain of his touch. *I won't let him win this time.* I inhaled sharply as I stood taller.

His hand shot out, gripping my neck. "Do not challenge me. I already like the idea of you permanently chained to my bed. You will be completely at my mercy." He leant in closer. "Now, walk before I change my mind and shove my cock in that wicked mouth of yours." He pushed me away, and I released the breath I forgot I'd been holding.

Bastard! I would bite it off before I let him get one more second of pleasure from me. My gaze bore a hole in his broad back as we moved away from the lake.

The ground became softer, dust and dirt giving way to more russet sand, that rippled into the distance. Enormous dunes stood between us and our next camp. I might hate Stidahl, but even I could not deny its beauty.

I was unsure how far we were from Solis, but reaching it could not come soon enough. Exhaustion wracked my body, which weakened with each passing day.

The sun was brutal as its heat beat down on us. Fayolan's

shirt clung to his back as sweat beaded on the base of his neck. I wiped my brow with my sleeve. If this was spring in Stidahl, I would hate to be trudging through this unforgiving land in the middle of summer.

I winced up at the sky, shielding my eyes from the sun. Not even a wispy cloud in sight. This land was as captivating and deadly as the man my body craved. So much for Serrin's prediction… *he will be my salvation.*

"I *think* you meant he will be my *downfall*," I muttered softly to myself.

We stopped as the sun reached its zenith. Seeking shade under a small grove of trees. My skin was slick, and grainy sand filled my boots.

"Gods be damned." I pulled them off, emptying the never-ending stream of sand. "Maybe the next outfit could be a little more appropriate for this weather."

Fayolan grunted, launching a water pouch at my feet, spraying me with sand. *Asshole!*

"How gentlemanly."

"Just shut up and drink," he snapped. I brushed as much off the pouch as possible, but a few grains still clung to the rim as I drank. The cold, refreshing water was a blessing for my parched throat, so I wouldn't complain.

I tilted my head back, letting the water trickle down my face and neck. A small groan escaped, and Fayolan's head snapped to me. His gaze followed the rivulets of water down my chest and onto the bodice of my dress. *I hope you like the view, Death. It's the only one you'll get.*

"Kalen?" I asked, offering him the pouch, but he shook his head, holding up his own.

After taking one last sip, I tossed the pouch at Fayolan's feet as he had mine. I'd not bothered to replace the lid. The sand turned a deep orange as the liquid spewed round his boots. Judging from the glower on his face, I may have gone a bit too far.

"Hungry?" Fayolan asked as he got up. A plate appearing in his hand. He dropped it at my feet, spoiling the delicious fruit, which was now covered in sand. "Eat."

My head snapped up at his command. *Like fuck I would.* I jutted my chin up defiantly. "I've *lost* my appetite."

Fayolan remained stood over me. His movements were slow and lazy as he fumbled with his belt. "Eat the fruit… or you will eat *this*." He undid his trousers, freeing his already erect cock. He gripped its hardened shaft close to my face, thrusting it derisively towards me.

"This will be fine." I scowled as I snatched up the plate, grabbing a piece of fruit. It made a horrendous crunching noise when I bit into it. But I would not let him win by brushing it off first.

"Yum…" I moaned, feigning pleasure as I wiped a trickle of juice from the edge of my mouth. Fayolan's gaze lowered to my throat as I swallowed. "Please get your dick out of my face." My voice came out husky, and he chuckled.

"What's the matter? It didn't seem to offend you the other night."

"I fear I would find it to be a disappointment after this." I held up another sand-coated piece of fruit. Sinking my teeth into it as I remained staring up at him. I gave a sensual moan as I watched his reaction through lowered lashes.

"Keep it up, Pet. You won't be smarting off once your jaw is aching," he warned as he buttoned his trousers and stalked away. "Get moving."

I tossed the last of the ruined fruit as I grabbed my boots and slung them over my shoulder. The warm sand eased my aching feet as I scurried after Fayolan. We did not speak another word as we climbed the dunes.

By nightfall, a chilly breeze made me shiver and my teeth chatter. But I refused to ask to stop. Regardless of how much I desired to nestle in front of a roaring fire.

CHAPTER THIRTY-FIVE

I crept nearer to the campfire as the chill set into my bones. A plate of warm meat and veg rested on my lap. Whilst I rubbed my hands over my arms, trying to ease the ache from my scars.

The stars glimmered above on a field of blue velvet. This part of the world never ceased to amaze me. You would not find beauty like this in No Man's Land. I lay back as I let my mind drift. Even if for just one moment I could forget where and who I was with.

Kalen rested nearby. He'd barely uttered two words to either Fayolan or me all day. He huffed as he caught me staring. It seemed broken, brooding men were the norm around Fayolan.

Not that I was any better. I was beyond broken, and I doubted anyone could piece me back together. *Maybe they all had their own trauma?*

Although Fayolan was a prince, I doubted he suffered

much as a child. I could picture him intimidating his staff and acting with the same arrogance that was expected of the nobility.

At least Lily would have a chance to live a normal life. Without me around, my mother was free to move back into civilisation. *What if she didn't?* Maybe she would remain in No Man's Land in case I made it home.

If only I could get a message to her, telling her to move on without me. How would I find the words to tell her about Maeve?

A tear fell as I thought of her. *I deserved whatever happened to me. I failed to save her.* Would Fayolan have spared Maeve if I'd told him the truth about who she was? Or would he have killed her on the spot?

I clenched my fists as I fought back more tears. Fearing that once I started crying, I would never stop. I rolled away from the stars, hiding my face in my arm. I refused to allow Fayolan see me like this.

His leathers creaked as he moved, but I kept my head buried, too exhausted to deal with his snide comments. He placed a warm blanket over me without uttering a word. I tensed, praying he did not touch me. Thankfully, he walked away, leaving me to my moment of weakness.

I woke to the delicious aroma of a full cooked breakfast. I held back groans as I ate every morsel under Fayolan's intense gaze. The moment I finished, the plate vanished in a plume of smoke and Fayolan stood. Stalking away without binding my hands.

Kalen matched his pace as I scrambled after them. Both men were tense as they spoke in hushed voices.

Something was going on and it made me feel on edge—Not knowing what was coming. I sped up, gaining on them. If I was in danger, my best bet was with them.

We crested the top of the dune, and black plumes of billowing smoke rose to the sky. A small city below us burned, but I could not see signs of anyone trying to douse the flames. Or survivors hovering outside the gates to watch as their home crumbled.

"Oh, Gods…" My hand clasped over my mouth, stifling a cry. Ustrayan soldiers must have been here.

"You two wait here. I'll check it out," Fayolan commanded.

"I should go with you," I said. Speaking before I could process the words.

"It's too dangerous," Fayolan said as he stared into the distance.

"I can help. And with Kalen there as well, you can both defeat any soldiers."

Fayolan spun to face me, raising an eyebrow. "*You* want to help?"

"Of course, I do. Those people are innocent." They may be my enemies, but I was not a monster. No matter what Fayolan thought of me.

"You wear the veil and hood." Fayolan materialised a thin cloak.

"It won't make a difference," Kalen said with a snort.

"Care to explain?"

"Oh, you'll see soon enough." Kalen smirked, heading down the dune toward the town.

"Do exactly as I tell you, or I will *punish* you." Fayolan remained still until I got the hint and began walking. He remained close. Never more than a few steps behind me.

We walked until the stench of burning and death tainted the air, making me gag. The town loomed ahead, with its solid wooden walls still intact.

"How did the Ustrayans get in?" I asked. Glancing around nervously. If not for the smoke and the Gods-awful stench. There would've been no sign any conflict occurred here.

"I'm not sure. Stay alert." Fayolan stepped around me. Sword in hand as he edged towards the gate.

"Keep close to me." Kalen crowded me.

My gaze did not leave Fayolan's back as he pushed on the enormous gates. They remained immovable, not budging an inch.

"They're barred from the inside." Fayolan's fist banged against the wood as his wings unfurled, ripping through yet another set of leather jerkins.

"I don't like this," Kalen muttered beneath his breath.

I watched as Fayolan vanished over the top of the wall, and Kalen lifted his sword as he waited.

"What's taking so long? Do you think Fayolan's alright?"

"That's *his* people behind that gate. Gods knows what those barbarians did to them." I could not bear thinking about it.

"What if he goes off alone?"

Kalen raised an eyebrow as he glanced at me. "Don't tell me you're worried about him?"

"*No*! I just meant… you know… I can't heal anyone if he leaves me out here. That's all."

Finally, the gates creaked and groaned, drawing Kalen's attention away from me. Fayolan looked pale, and Kalen swung out his arm, halting me from taking another step towards him.

"There's something awry," he warned. I froze, waiting with bated breath as Fayolan stumbled towards us.

"What if he's hurt?"

"He's not." I'd never seen Fayolan looking so shaken. *What had happened within those walls?*

"There will be a lot of spirits in there," Fayolan ground out between his bared teeth.

Instinctively, I took a step away. Fayolan's shadows reached out to me, and I slammed my eyes closed. Counting in my head. One…breathe in. Two…breathe out. It took me to the count of six to find the courage to open them again.

"If you're scared, just *stay* here. I don't have time to coddle you," Fayolan said. I crossed my fingers in a rude symbol. His nostrils flared at the crude gesture.

Fayolan stepped closer. His fingers gripped the pommel of his sword so hard that the veins in his hands were visible. Tension radiated off him as his jaw ticked, and he crowded my personal space.

"Fayolan, stop." Kalen pulled me behind him, using his enormous body as a shield. "Now is not the time."

Fayolan seethed but backed up. "*Move.*"

Kalen let me past, keeping himself between Fayolan and I as we headed towards the gate. Fighting the panic rising within me as I forced myself to keep going. *If anyone survived, they would need me.*

Kalen walked slightly ahead of me but as I stepped into the city. Bodies of men, women, and children littered the streets. Their faces bore the horrors of their deaths, and their spirits moaned in anguish.

Fayolan's hand clamped over my mouth, muffling a scream before I could release it. "You need to be quiet," he whispered. I nodded my understanding, and he freed me. Inclining his head for me to carry on, deeper into the city.

My palms became clammy as I glanced over each body. Searching for those without a spirit standing over them. Their souls remained in a state of confusion.

"This only *just* happened," I whispered. "We were delayed up because of me."

"Don't start thinking like that. It'll eat you up inside. Besides, it wasn't your fault." Fayolan signalled for me to continue.

Images of my village being raided plagued my mind. It happened so fast. One moment everything was peaceful, and the next… there was only death. "I don't think I can do this."

"*Yes,* you can." Fayolan gripped my hand, breaking through the memories.

"How? I'm not tough like you."

"Get angry. Let it take hold of you, then there will be no room for fear." He was right. I clenched my fists and pulled away from him.

The two men separated, scanning the burning buildings whilst I trailed behind. The wooden houses became more dilapidated the nearer we got to the centre. *Someone had attacked from within the city.*

"How could enough Ustrayans, to cause this amount of damage, get in without raising alarms? These people are unarmed as if the attack had been a surprise."

Fayolan pointed to one untouched building surrounded by others that had crumpled to the ground. "Seems a little out-of-place doesn't it?"

Kalen took the lead, drawing his sword as he moved with caution. He slipped inside through the unlocked door, trying not to make a sound. Then it hit me…

"They barred the gates from the *inside*. They're still *here*." I spun to Fayolan—my eyes wide as I pictured the small army it would have taken to rampage this city.

"Hey." Fayolan shook me as I lost my composure. "Tempest." He clasped my cheeks. The pain snapping me from my stupor.

"They're still in the city, aren't they?"

Fayolan's face softened. "It looks like it. But we won't be caught off guard this time." I stared at him as he stroked his thumb down my cheek. "Understand?"

I nodded, pulling myself together. "Yes," I squeaked as he removed his hand. "Can I please have a bow?" His shadows coalesced in his palm as he pulled one from the aether. "Thank you."

"It's all clear," Kalen said as he slipped from the building. "We have a problem." He presented a stack of papers to Fayolan. He snatched them, a tense snarl stretching across his face as he quickly flicked through them.

I caught a glimpse as he studied one page. They were plans for an attack on the Capital.

"So Ustraya is making a play for Solis?" I asked, but the grimace on Kalen's face said otherwise.

"Look at the official seal." He pointed to a wax stamp at the top of the page.

"I don't understand?"

"It wasn't Ustraya trying to mount a siege." Fayolan scrunched the papers in his hand. "It was the council of this city."

I gasped as I stared around. "Please tell me they didn't attack their own people?" I felt sick at the thought.

"I doubt it. It looks like they welcomed the Ustrayan soldiers. Poor fools probably thought they could count on them for backup. The council were their first victims."

"Why would they turn against their king? Against you?" I asked, but no one answered.

CHAPTER THIRTY-SIX

Fayolan

I scattered the papers across the ground. Damn fools had thought Ustraya would *actually* side with them… that crossing *me* was a good move. "We need to keep going." I stepped away from Tempest.

Her hands shook, and she fought to hide the quiver of her lips. I couldn't tell if my wrath scared her or the men that likely lay in wait for us.

She followed Kalen, keeping her gaze down as she searched the bodies for spirits. Only the odd flicker of her lashes betrayed the horror she witnessed. *It's easier for me. All I hear is the silence of death.*

Kalen stalked ahead, twirling his sword in anticipation. He was almost as bloodthirsty as me. All my elites were. Each had their own reasons for relishing in death.

"No," Tempest gasped, darting away from us. *She was running again!* I gave chase as she wound down the street, avoiding the bodies in her path. She was surprisingly fast for someone so small and underfed. I lifted my sword, ready to launch it, when she skidded to a stop, dropping to her knees.

"Here we *go*," Kalen smirked as he prowled closer. His weapon poised, ready to protect her. She ripped off her veil, placing her hands on a young boy's chest.

Blood pooled from a sloppy slash across his throat. It had not been deep enough to kill him quickly. Sick *bastards!* I was going to enjoy devouring their souls.

Kalen positioned himself in front of the Nephilim, as if he thought I would hurt her. *What could be so bad that he considered I'd attack her for saving a child? Had something happened when he witnessed her heal me?*

Tempest cried out, and I swung my gaze back to her. My heart was in my throat when beautiful wings unfurled from her back. Not feathered like mine, and far more delicate look-ing. Like a colourful stained-glass window.

Soft pinks, purples, and greens tinted the almost translu-cent wings. Tempest's skin shimmered blue, refracting the sun, making her look iridescent.

The hood covering her head fell back. Exposing her hair as it flowed around her, as if caught in a breeze. She was magnificent. *Gods, how much more vibrant would she be if I had kissed her first?*

Tempest's neck stiffened as she wailed in agony. It pained me to hear. I stepped towards her, but Kalen snarled, blocking my path.

Another cry jolted her body. Black tar-like liquid dripped from her eyes and nose. It should repulse me, but my cock jerked, hardening, so it pressed against my trousers.

She writhed in pain as the inky tears fell faster, cascading down her cheeks. *It's destroying her!* I darted forward to pull her away from the boy.

"Don't touch her," Kalen warned as he shoved me back.

"It's killing her." *Can he not see what it's doing to Tempest?*

He pushed me again, forcing me to back up. "Healing *you* almost killed her. She's got this." He scowled as he raised his sword. "This is nothing compared to what she went through to save you." Now I could understand why he'd been so pissed at me that night.

Tempest's head spun to the right as heavy boots pounded against the cobblestones. A soldier burst into view from the alley beside her. His sword sliced through the air, aiming for her neck.

"*Tempest!*" I roared. Shoving Kalen aside as I charged towards her.

She narrowed her eyes as the sword swerved towards her. She ducked, removing one hand from the boy. Clasping the soldier's hand as his blade missed its mark. He stopped dead. The sword falling from his grip as he cried out in pain.

"Stop!" Kalen flung me back. "Don't touch her."

The soldier's scream mingled with hers. His face contorting as a slit opened across his throat. *She could transfer wounds to another!* All this time, she had told me Nephilim could not use their powers to kill.

I watched the man writhe and fall to the ground. Gurgling through the slash that matched the one from the boy's throat. Who now showed no physical sign of having suffered injuries, not even a scar.

Tempest pulled her blood-soaked hands from the boy. Her hair cascaded around her shoulders once again. She lifted her head and met my gaze as her wings curled into her back.

"You *lied* to me." I shoved Kalen off me as I tackled the Nephilim. My fingers dug into her cheeks, causing her to cry out as I drew blood. "You told me Nephilim cannot *kill* with their magic."

"It's the *truth*," she spat at me. "I told Kalen what would happen if anyone touched me during healing. Why do you think he *forced* you to stay back? I can't just inflict injuries on people whenever I *fucking* feel like it. When we use our magic, we are vulnerable to attack. This is our only means of protection."

"How can I trust anything a *monster* like you says?" I saw the pain of my words flash in her eyes. I regretted them the moment they slipped from my lips.

"Because *you* are still *breathing*," she snarled. "We. Don't. Kill."

"One of you *murdered* my mother, so don't tell me you can't."

"It's not possible." Tempest scowled as she struggled to escape from beneath me. "Not if she was healing her." The truth rang through her words. She truly believed it to be impossible.

"Clearly, *lying* comes easily to your kind." I pulled a rope from the aether and fought to grip her wrists. She wriggled, desperately trying to break free as I straddled her. "Keep still."

Tempest hissed at me like a wild animal caught in a hunter's trap. *I'd been a fucking idiot.* I'd softened towards her. Even started to believe my father had made it all up. But now… I had seen her use her power to kill with my own eyes. She deceived me once, but she'd not do so again.

"Fayolan…" Kalen advanced towards me.

"Do not interfere. I *won't* have insubordination." I dragged Tempest to her feet. Twisting the rope around her waist, trapping her arms in an X across her chest. She cried out, almost dropping to her knees.

"The healing is still taking its toll on her body." Kalen remained back. He knew better than to question me now.

"Walk on your own or I'll carry you." I had no sympathy for her. *Liar! Monster! Killer!* That's what I had called the Nephilim, even though those names matched me better.

The boy murmured. Kalen was careful as he lifted him off the ground, grunting as he stood up. Placing him over his shoulder to free up his sword hand. He balanced the tip of the blade on the Ustrayan's neck. With a solid thrust, the gurgling ceased.

"We need to clear the city and move on." I used the point of my sword to nudge Tempest forward. She held her chin high as she walked ahead.

Survivors trickled out of hiding as we searched through the ruins of the city. They had found shelter inside an abandoned warehouse, and there hadn't been enough time to hide Tempest's hair.

She found eight more injured survivors trapped in a collapsed building. I made a point to stand by her side, sword in hand, pressing it against her neck as she healed. She was my prisoner, and I had her under control.

As Tempest healed the last man, her body swayed, having endured more than it should have. The black liquid now coated her face, spilling from her eyes, ears, nose, and mouth.

I caught her before she collapsed, lifting her into my arms after re-securing her hands.

The city folk murmured around us. Before we left, I would make sure Kalen mesmerised them, making them forget her.

"They're this way." A boy pointed to a nearby cluster of houses.

"Show me." I followed behind him as he led us to the building he had seen the Ustrayans.

"Do you hear that?" Kalen sneered as laughter wafted through an open window. The bastards were celebrating.

"*Burn* it down!" It's a horrible way to die, but I was fresh out of mercy.

Kalen handed off the boy, grabbing nearby wooden debris as he barked orders. Those able-bodied survivors hurried to help. Silently, barring the doors and windows closed from the outside.

"What if there's innocent people in there?" Tempest stirred in my arms.

"I can't risk alerting the Ustrayans. Gods knows how many of them there are. I won't put those we've already saved in the firing line."

I stood back as Kalen tossed oil along the wooden building. There would be no escape. They would pay for the deaths they caused here.

Kalen created a spark, and a ferocious flame licked up the walls. Smoke billowed around us, filling the street.

I eased Tempest to the floor beside me. Her eyes fluttered closed from exhaustion as I brushed a stray hair from her face. She saved my people, even after I accused her of being a liar and a monster. Regardless of the risk to her own life.

I pulled daggers from the aether, standing over her as I prepared for Ustrayans attempting to jump from the upper floors. Sure enough, panicked yells replaced the laughter.

"Get back." I waved my arm as chairs and other furniture flew through the windows. Glass cascaded over us as the city folk scrambled out of the way.

"To the left." Kalen pointed as the first Ustrayan tried to escape. I cricked my neck, releasing a dagger. It planted into the soldier's chest, making him stumble backward. Serving as a warning to anyone else.

Soon, the screams died off. Those that had been desperate enough to escape fell to my blade. The stench of burnt flesh defiled my nose, but it excited the beast within me. The second soul inside of me. One so depraved of humanity that it craved violent, bloody, death.

"Help me," a woman screamed as she stumbled towards

us. She clutched a small child in her arms, swathed in a blanket. "Please save my daughter."

Her gaze locked on Tempest, who stirred at my feet.

"I can't," she breathed as she tried to sit up. "I don't have the strength."

"What if you transferred the injuries straight into another person?" Kalen asked as the woman dropped to her knees before Tempest.

CHAPTER THIRTY-SEVEN

"Take *my* life," the mother begged, while attempting to shove the child into Tempest's arms.

"No. Your child will die anyway without a parent to care for them." I wouldn't allow such a reckless exchange of life.

"Take mine." An old man stumbled forward. "My damn health is failing me, anyway."

"No," Tempest said. Her voice was strained as she fought just to remain conscious. "I won't murder an innocent man."

"I'm dying anyway, child. At least let my death mean something."

"Please," the woman begged. Tempest shook her head, letting out a small sob. They were asking her to go against everything she believed in.

"Maybe we could search for one of those barbarians?" Kalen suggested.

"There's no time." Even I could see the child was moments from death.

"I'm sorry." I grabbed Tempest's wrists, sending the rope back to the aether.

"No. Don't do this," Tempest cried as I spread her arms wide. The woman brought her child forward, holding her towards Tempest's outstretched hand.

The man hobbled closer, taking the Nephilim's other hand. Gripping it tight as Tempest tried to pull away. "I'll never forgive you for this."

"Do it," I commanded as I forced Tempest's hand onto the child. "Now!"

Tempest screamed as her magic acted on instinct. Locking her in place as I released her to avoid being caught by her power.

"Please, don't make me do this." It was too late, the healing had already begun. Her magic was weak, but it sent a static shock up my arm. *She may never forgive me.*

Her body jerked as she passed the wounds from the child into the ailing man. Her wings unfurled, knocking me back as I avoided touching them.

I braced. The moment Tempest had finished, she crumpled in my arms.

"Thank you for your sacrifice," I said to the man as Kalen moved in, ending his suffering. An oppressive silence hung in the air. Everyone stared at Tempest as she lay limp in my arms. I had saved a child, yet it filled me with a sense of regret.

"I can never repay you." The woman sobbed as she scooped up her daughter. Who now had a full life ahead of her.

"That was the last one. You'll kill her if you force her to heal anymore," Kalen said, gazing down at Tempest. "She needs to rest. We're not far from The Sacred Maple. I say we head there."

"Let's go." He was right. Tempest had nothing left to give. I cradled against me as she mumbled and cried in her sleep. Nightmares of death plaguing her as she dreamt.

"Kalen. Can you help her?" He nodded solemnly. "I can't carry her whilst she is thrashing like this." At least that was what I told him.

Kalen touched her temple, sending tendrils of magic into her mind. She stilled; her face no longer contorted in pain as she slumbered peacefully.

We backtracked through the city to the open gates. "Now that's a sight for sore eyes." Kalen grinned as a squadron of my troops came into view.

"That it is. You know what to do." I hid Tempest beneath a blanket as Kalen slipped through the villagers. Shaking hands, patting others on the back, or touching their arm. His magic flowed unnoticed, wiping Tempest from their minds.

"Don't tell me I missed all the fun." The squadron's captain saluted as he stepped aside.

"Have half your men sweep the city. The other half escort the survivors to the nearest village."

"You heard your Prince. Get to it." They bowed their heads and branched off.

We would follow the city folk as far as the inn. I had frequented it many times. Nix had a particular fondness for it. She often visited the bar keep's daughter… *and* his son.

It stood only a short walk away, and relief flooded me when I saw it untouched by the savages invading my land. "Take the survivors to safety and get your squadron back to Solis. War is heading our way."

I clutched Tempest to my chest as Kalen held the door.

"Fayo!" Lilith's shrill cry echoed through the tavern. She caught sight of Tempest, still hidden beneath the blanket.

Only her arms streaked with black ooze were visible. "What the *fuck* have you been up to?"

"Ustrayan soldiers attacked Wrossa," I said. She gasped as she took in both mine and Kalen's dishevelled state. "I need a room and someone to bathe her." I glanced down at Tempest.

Lilith dipped her head and scurried behind the bar, grabbing a key. As I followed her up the stairs, murmurs filtered up behind us. The threat of war on their doorstep created a sobering atmosphere.

"In here." Lilith ushered us inside my usual room on the third floor. The familiar aroma of lavender offered a sense of home to the secluded attic.

Tempest let out a moan as I laid her down on the bed. "I need someone discreet, Lil." I caught hold of Lilith's arm just as she was about to leave. It's not as if I couldn't have bathed Tempest myself, but she'd be livid if she found out.

Lilith spared Tempest one final glance. A few strands of her hair had fallen free of the blanket. "I'll be right back." She smiled softly as she scurried away.

Kalen entered behind me and closed the door, flipping the latch, locking the world out. He dropped onto a small wooden stool in the room's corner. It looked like children's furniture against him and groaned under his massive frame.

"Do you think other cities have tried to ally with Ustraya?" he asked grimly. His brows furrowed.

"It will not *end* well *if* they have." Rebellion was a plague I would not tolerate. My father sat idly by as his people conspired against him.

"You didn't tell me how much healing hurt Tempest." I hadn't meant for my words to sound so much like an accusation.

"You didn't ask."

"Well, I am now." I lowered myself onto an armchair in the corner of the small room nearest to Tempest.

"When I watched her back at the lake. I think her body imitated *your* injuries."

"Wait, so you're telling me if she heals a broken leg. Then she feels as if her bones are breaking."

"I think so."

Knock. Knock. "It's just me," Lilith called through the door. Kalen freed the latch, and she strolled in with her arms laden with bathing supplies. The scent of fragrant-smelling soaps followed her as she headed to the adjoining bathroom. "You could have *started* running the bath, at least."

"That's what I have you for, Lil." I smirked as she shot me a curse. It rolled easily off her tongue, just like Tempest.

"Bring her in," she said after filling the tub with essential oils and warm water.

"Moonflowers would have been better," I whispered into Tempest's hair as I carried her into the bathing room. I made her clothes vanish in an instant, revealing her scarred arms and back.

"Gods. What the *fuck* has this poor girl been through?" Lilith's smile vanished, and a pitiful frown replaced it.

"The man responsible is at the top of my kill list. Don't worry." My fingers were gentle as I traced the length of one of Tempest's scars. "She hates physical contact. If she wakes, stop."

"I'll take care of her, I promise." I eased Tempest into the bath. Resting her head against the back of the tub. "She is so small. I thought her kind were giants."

"They are," I muttered. "She's to be kept secret." I did not worry about Lilith. Her loyalty to me was renowned. She knew my darkest secrets and she would lay her life down before she spilled one.

"She's beautiful. I always pictured them as hideous creatures that would steal children from their beds if they were naughty." Her lips quirked up in amusement. Nephilim had become a thing of nightmares. A tale that parents used to scare their offspring into behaving.

"There's a lot I'm learning we're mistaken about." I watched as Lilith lifted Tempest's ravaged arm. Tenderly wiping the cloth over her. Every time I saw the marks on her skin, my rage towards her abuser surged.

I'd never experienced dreams before Tempest. Not one nightmare plagued me. I was soulless, like my father told me often as a child.

Now, what *they* did to her haunts me in my dreams. I hated being helpless, watching this beautiful woman being flogged night after night. I watch it happen but can't intervene.

"Are you planning on standing there all night *creeping* on her?" Lilith snapped me out of my musings.

"Just be gentle with her." I sighed, turning away, closing the door behind me.

I collapsed onto the bed, kicking my boots off and lay back.

"Nix is here," Kalen said, holding a piece of parchment. I snatched it from him, cursing as I read it.

"You couldn't have given me this before I got comfortable? I have to go. Tempest could use a few days to regain her strength. She won't survive in Solis like this. Stay here and keep her out of *fucking* trouble." I placed a bundle of rope on the table, along with extra weapons. "Tie her to the damned bed if you have to." I stuffed my aching feet back into my boots.

Kalen lounged back in his chair, twirling a dagger, staring at the bathing room door. "How long will you be gone?"

"Hopefully, no longer than three days. It seems my father has made moves against me. He's lucky that, for now, his plans are only imaginings. The moment he takes action, I will end his miserable existence."

"Son of a bitch finally grew a pair," Kalen chuckled. He detested my father as intensely as I did.

I stormed down to the tavern to find Nix at the bar, winking frivolously at Wilem. He had the same soft hazel eyes as Lilith. The family resemblance was striking.

"You ready?" I inclined my head towards the exit.

"Do you really need to ask?" she laughed coldly as she headed for the door. Nix enjoyed taking care of business. The time had come to deal with Palleon and his cohort of fools.

CHAPTER THIRTY-EIGHT

Sunlight streamed into the room, rousing me. I lay on a proper bed, my body sinking into it as it moulded around me.

"Awake at last," Kalen murmured. I struggled to push myself up. Fighting the aching exhaustion that consumed me.

The scent of freshly washed hair lingered in the air as I noticed my neatly braided locks. Even my clothes had changed.

"*Who* the fuck…" Kalen's chuckle cut me off.

"*Lilith*, the innkeeper's daughter. Fayolan thought you'd be pissed off if *he* did it." Kalen grimed.

"It's not like *Death* to care how he'll make me feel." I glanced around the small room, but Fayolan was absent. "Where is he, anyway?" I crinkled my nose with distaste. *Lilith probably serviced his needs, too.*

"Fayolan had urgent business he needed to attend to. Until he returns, *you're* to remain in this room. Do *not* make me use these." His hand brushed over a pile of ropes nestled on the table beside him. "Are you hungry?"

"Starving." My stomach growled in response.

Kalen lumbered to the door, sparing a quick glance back. "Stay there." He pointed to the bed.

"It's not like I have anywhere *else* to go." I pulled my knees into my chest, glaring at the wall. Kalen did not respond. The slight click of the door locking was the only sign he'd left.

I shuffled across the bed to the window, taking a peek outside. The sun was high in the sky. I must have slept all night and into the day.

The view was breathtaking. The sand had eased off, giving way to dusty ground with grass desperately trying to sprout. Towering trees scattered around, offering shade to a small pond, which attracted the local wildlife.

I watched as a bird fluttered from the shrubbery. It's colourful feathered plumes swirled as it landed near the water. I stared as it hopped along, searching through some fallen leaves.

I wished I could hear its song. This small wooden room was eerily silent. I could not even hear noise from the inn below. I sighed as the beautiful bird got spooked, taking flight.

The lock clicked, and I glanced towards the door as Kalen stepped in with a large tray laden with bowls and a couple chalices.

"That smells delicious." The delicate aroma made my mouth water. I scrambled from the bed as Kalen chuckled.

"It's one of the best meals here. Besides, I figured after yesterday you'd need something extra hearty." He slid a bowl of broth across the table just as I sat down.

My taste buds burst into life, and I groaned. "It reminds me of home." I sighed as I thought of my family.

"I need to talk to you about your sis…"

Knock. Knock. Kalen raised his finger to his mouth to shush me as he gripped the dagger sheathed at his hip.

"I thought you might like some fresh bread," a woman called. Her voice was soft and almost musical.

Kalen released the dagger as a smile teased at the edges of his lips. "Behave," he warned as he flung the door wide open.

"Kalen." The woman dipped her head curtly as she scurried into the room, carrying a basket full of steaming bread. Her cheeks flushed as the two of them locked eyes. It reminded me of how sometimes Fayolan had that effect on me. *Ridiculous as it sounds, that man was growing on me.*

"You're awake." She smiled warmly as she flicked a stray strand of dark blonde hair behind her ears. She looked feminine with her hair pinned neatly into place, but she had a confidence about her. I could tell she was more than capable of holding her own. "When these lug heads brought you in last night, I was so worried." *She must be Lilith.*

My cheeks heated, knowing she'd seen me naked… and the scars that marred my skin. "Thank you for helping me yesterday."

"It was no bother." She held out the basket, and I took a crusty roll. "I had words with these brutes about treating you better. Sometimes Fayolan forgets his manners."

"Enough, Lil." Kalen cut her off. I stifled a laugh as she shot him a chastising look. They acted like an old married couple.

"Why don't you come to the bar later? I'm sure after putting up with these two thugs, you could do with some female company." *Did she not realise I was Death's prisoner?*

"Tempest will stay in this room." I shoved a piece of broth coated bread in my mouth as Lilith and Kalen stared off. *Wow, this couldn't get more awkward.*

"It's fine. Thanks for the offer." I tried to ease the tension.

"No, it's not." Lilith cut in.

"Gods you're insufferable, *woman*." Kalen inhaled a deep breath as his nostrils flared. She certainly knew how to get under his skin.

Lilith pouted until she noticed the ropes on the table. Her lips pinched as she reached towards them. "I didn't realise someone left these here. Why don't I take them?"

Kalen's hand slammed down. The bang against the table made us both jump. "*Enough*, Lilith. You know better than to interfere with Fayolan's prisoners."

"Maybe *Fayolan* would like whips and chains, too. I have *plenty*." She shot me an apologetic look as she stormed towards the door. "Oh, and *Kalen…* when Nix returns, *send* her to my room." She slammed the door behind her without another word.

From the grimace on Kalen's face, her words had been designed to hurt him. And it had worked. You could cut the tension with a knife.

"She's as much of a smartass as you. Fayolan would kill me if I left *you* two together for long," he grumbled. "*Damned* women."

"Someone's a little tetchy today." Kalen ignored my taunting as he ripped into a piece of bread. "I think I like her."

All day I sat by the window watching people coming and going. They were so carefree and full of life. I used to frequent the taverns with Serrin. It helped me to unwind and let loose. One of many things I had taken for granted.

Night fell, and still, I remained at the window. My thoughts drifting to my fate.

"Kalen?" I asked without tearing my eyes away.

"Yeah."

"What is going to happen to me?"

"I don't know," he breathed.

"He's going to kill me, isn't he?" I asked, but the room fell silent. I stared at the moon, soaking up its beauty… maybe for the last time.

"I don't know. Get some rest, Tempest. You need to get your strength back before we get to Solis."

I climbed back onto the bed. When death came, I would face Fayolan without a single drop of fear. I would not give him the satisfaction.

The next two days came and went. And Kalen finally allowed Lilith to sit with me by the window.

"Did Kalen tell you anything about this place?" Lilith asked.

"No. He's not been very *chatty* since we got here." In fact, he had been sulking since their confrontation the other night.

"That's probably my fault. I took things a little too far." She spared him a fleeting glance, only to receive a grunt from Kalen. "Let me tell you about the Sacred Maple. You see that tree out there?" Lilith pointed to a large, gnarled maple. It looked so out of place here. "Well, legend says it's been here since the creation of this world."

"How can it be *that* old?"

"Some believe it's imbued with the power of the Gods and will live on until the end of time." It sounded almost too fantastical to be true. "So, when my ancestors built the original tavern. They named it after the sacred maple. Over generations, the building has changed, but the name remains."

"That's such a lovely story. But do you believe it?" She paused in thought, staring out at the old tree.

"Of course. Many have attempted to chop it down, to no avail. Still, it stands stronger than ever."

"It's a load of bullshit, if you ask me." Kalen chimed in.

"Good job I wasn't then," Lilith smarted off. I stifled a laugh with my hand.

"So, Tempest, tell me about your home."

My heart ached at the thought, but maybe talking about it would ease my pain. "I live in No Man's Land."

"Really? I've heard that place is drab and filled with cutthroats and criminals." Lilith sighed. "I'm sorry, that was rude of me."

"It's okay. Most of the people from my village were exiles. Some, like me, were hiding."

"Where did your family originate from?" Lilith smiled warmly as I stared out the window again.

"Solis. My mother lived there when the King put the kill order on all Nephilim. About eight years later, she met my father and fell pregnant with me, so she ran to keep me safe."

"I'm so sorry. It must have been hard."

"Not really. I'd give anything to have just one more day there with my family." But it was impossible. Even the Gods can't reverse time.

"Maybe you'll eventually call this place home. Well, it's getting late, so I'd better go."

"Thanks for today, Lilith."

"It's been my pleasure." She winked before striding past Kalen without so much as a farewell.

Night had already descended, and I slipped into the bathing room. Filling the tub with hot water and some healing oils, Lilith had left me. She had found a moonflower one after I told her how much I liked the Garden Of Souls.

I dipped my head below the water, letting the silence fill

me with peace. Fayolan would return soon, so I would enjoy my bath whilst I could. I emerged from the water, resting my head on the back of the tub.

A loud bang filled the room as a door swung open forcefully.

CHAPTER THIRTY-NINE

Tempest

I froze! A thud echoed… followed by silence. I lifted myself from the water, grabbing a towel to cover myself.

"Kalen?" I called out softly. *Nothing.* My hands quaked as I snuck closer to the door.

I reached out, brushing my fingers against the knob. With each beat of my heart, I searched for the courage to swing it open. *Get a grip! It's probably just Fayolan returning in a bad mood.*

The door flung inwards, sending me reeling across the room. My head collided with the bath, and my vision dimmed.

"There *it* is. Grab it." Rough hands yanked me from the ground.

"*Kalen*!" The towel fell as I kicked and screamed.

"No one's going to help you, Nephilim," a man said. He tightened his hold on me as he spoke.

"Get the fuck off me." I resisted the pain while trying to ward them off.

"Come on. Let's get out of here before *he* comes back." A second man grabbed my arm, trying to help get me under control. They carried me, naked, from the bathing room. Both men struggled to keep hold of my slick, wet body.

Kalen lay unconscious on the floor. Blood seeped from his head. *No!* I writhed as I fought harder to escape them. Kalen could not help me now. *Unless…*

"Let me heal him. He won't wake up… *Please*."

"Nice try, Nephilim. You think we don't know you can transfer his injuries to us?" The first man laughed, hauling me away from Kalen.

I grabbed the doorframe, my nails digging into the splintered wood. "You *fucking* bastards!" I lost my grip, doubling over as a fist slammed into my stomach.

Calloused hands were all over my body, dragging me down the stairs. My leg kicked out, catching one man in the temple with a satisfying thud. He yanked my head towards him by a handful of hair.

"Do that again, *bitch*, and I will *fuck* that cunt of yours raw before we kill you."

"You can try, *asshole*. But I *won't* stop *fighting* you." Fayolan would be here soon. I just had to hold out until then.

My body bounced off every step as they dragged me down into the tavern by my hair. A gash sliced across my cheek from a boot to the face.

"Tempest." My eye was so swollen I could barely see Lilith on her knees. Struggling to break free as three men held her down.

"You're all going to fucking die!" she screamed.

"Shut your mouth, *wench*." A man yanked her head back, her braid wrapped in his hand. "Play nice, *Nephilim*, or I'll end her first." His sword bit into her throat as he held her still.

I caught movement in the mirror that hung above the bar. The Tavern's patrons were bloody and beaten, kneeling bound to each other in a human chain. *All of this to get to me.*

"Let them go." I bared my teeth in a threatening snarl. "If you harm them, the Dark Prince will kill you all."

They forced a horse's bit into my mouth. I snapped at the man as he shoved it deeper, securing it in place.

"Now get moving." A boot to my back sent me flailing out into the frigid night air. The icy wind sliced into my bare, wet skin.

I sprawled across the floor, almost colliding with a horse. I glanced upwards at the man in the saddle. The leather creaked ominously as he leant down to look at me. "What do we have here?" He cracked a sinister smile that sent a chill down my spine.

Men pounced, holding me down as they bound my wrists and threw the end of the rope to the man on horseback. I thrashed and struggled as they hauled me up.

"You." The rider pointed to a man near the door. "Kill them all. Leave no witnesses."

"It would be my pleasure." He laughed, drawing two swords from their scabbards.

"*Kalen!*" I screamed around the bit. He had to wake, or they were all dead.

The horse jolted me forward, and I stumbled, trying to catch myself. The men following us leered at me with a lustful look that made me feel queasy.

A dull ache pulsed in my skull. Blood dribbled down my back from a gash in my head. My throat was sore and dry. My lungs screaming in pain. *This was it. The end for me.*

Hopefully, I would bleed out before they started taking pleasure in abusing my body.

We neared a village, and crowds had gathered outside. Their jeers grew louder when they spotted us. The cold had seeped through to my bones and I stumbled with every step.

"Die you abomination," a woman screamed, and something hard hit my temple. Almost knocking me off my feet. More stones pelted me, accompanied by jeers and hateful slurs. *Freak... Monster... Dark Prince's Whore!*

I refused to cry, holding back my tears as my legs tried to buckle beneath me. I wouldn't give these people the satisfaction of seeing me dragged wailing to my death. If they ravaged my body, I would bite off my tongue before I screamed. I lifted my chin as I focused on steadily moving ahead with each step.

"That's her. The Nephilim." My heart broke as I recognised the voice. The woman whose child I'd saved stood surrounded by the others from the city. "They tried to put a spell on us to make us forget. But I can never forget an abomination like you."

The sinking feeling in my chest threatened to pull me into the depths of despair. I'd saved their lives, and as a token of gratitude, they sentenced me to death.

That hurt more than knowing what was about to happen. I'd done a great service for these people, yet they still condemned me. I locked eyes with them as we walked past, and not one shied away. They showed no hint of guilt or remorse. *They were the real monsters.*

The rider dragged me through the village's dusty streets. A breeze swept around me, accompanied by the shuffling of feet as those gathered scurried aside.

Gods I was better off leaving this world. I was no longer willing to be a part of this race that murdered and hated with such ferocity. I'm not strong enough to survive in a cutthroat world like this.

A wolf's howl pierced the night as a man slunk from the shadows. "Pretty little thing, aren't you?" His gaze explored my body as he circled me. "No wonder the Dark Prince kept you around. I wouldn't mind getting my cock wet. He smiled softly as he closed in. Reaching towards me, pulling the bit from my mouth. "I want the Prince to hear your screams as you die."

I bared my teeth, a hiss escaping my lips. "He is going to have fun killing you all." I smiled coldly as I pictured Fayolan unleashing his fury. "I wonder if he will let you run first. Make you believe you stand a chance before he ends your miserable lives."

"Maybe I will leave your corpse hanging from the walls like he did my brother. Or I could send you to him in pieces." He leant closer, and the moonlight lit his face. He looked just like… *The Captain of Fayspire was his brother.*

"Lock her up until we're ready. I want him to see the flames as he comes for her. He will feel helpless just as I did."

Men dragged me towards the nearest building. Others watched me, their eyes filled with an almost palpable thirst. Inside, they took me to the lower level, where a cage sat waiting.

I braced myself as its door clanged, echoing off the walls as they shoved me inside. I scrambled back, curling up, trying to cover the remaining shreds of my dignity.

Men stood guard, leering as they threw promises to defile me. Though not one attempted to act on it. I remained in a ball, pressing against the cold bars. Even as they stung my skin.

"Fayolan," I said under my breath. "Please find me." What I wouldn't give to see him stride through that door. I wouldn't care if he's covered in blood as long as he was here.

The longer I waited, the more helpless I felt. *Gods I don't even know if Fayolan will bother to come for me.* Perhaps now he would be happily free of me. After all, I'd been nothing but a thorn in his side. Even once I'd seen glimpses of the real him, I pushed him away. The same as I did every-one. It made things simpler that way. If only I'd allowed him in. Things might have been different.

"It's time, sweetheart," the captain's brother cooed with a mocking chuckle. I pressed myself against the back of the cage, trying to stay as far from him as possible.

He bared his teeth in a snarl, grabbing the rope as he heaved it towards him. "You can either come with me now and face your death. Or stay here and I will let them use your body until you are compliant." His head inclined towards the men that guarded me.

This was it, two options. Face the end and be free. Or, let them defile me in the worst of ways and pray it gave Fayolan enough time to get here.

"Decide now," he barked.

I slid forward. I'd rather die than let another man ruin me. Enough had been taken from me, and I would not lose anymore. I scrambled to my feet and held my chin high. I refused to let them see my fear.

My heart raced in my chest as he forcefully pulled me from the building. I could hear the lively chatter of the villagers filling the streets. They watched me pass with smiles of anticipation.

They parted, allowing me to see a raised platform surrounded by large logs. A stake loomed in the centre. My blood ran cold. *The bastards were going to burn me alive!*

"You *fucking* animals!" I dug my heels into the ground.

All my resolve lost as I fought with every fibre of my being. This wasn't just an execution… *it was torture.*

"Not so brave now, are you, Nephilim?"

I cried in panic as hands from the crowds latched onto me, forcing me forward.

"Burn the monster," people screamed as they saw me struggling to escape. "Send her soul to the underworld."

The Captain's brother gripped my arm in his vice-like grip, dragging me on. "Did you honestly believe I would allow a creature like you a quick death? If you're lucky, the smoke will get you first."

"You'll wish you had, because trust me. I'll be waiting for you in hell."

Men waited at the base of the platform, dragging me up the steps by my bound wrists. They shoved me against the stake, forcing my face against it as they cut the rope. I fought against their grip, kicking, and thrashing in a desperate attempt to break free.

"Gods just tie her up already." Before I could stop them, two men spun me to face the crowds. They captured my arms, yanking them painfully behind me and the stake. The rope bit into my skin as they bound me to it.

"Be *still*, whore." My captor yanked my head back by my hair, slamming it into the pillar. Tears filled my eyes as pain exploded in my skull. "You should be *fucking* thankful I did not strip your skin as the Dark Prince did to my brother." Spittle flew from his mouth onto my face.

"You disgusting son of a *bitch*. Fayolan will rip your *fucking* head off for that."

He leant in, licking the spit and tears from my cheek, making me gag. "Watch your tongue, *whore*. There's still time to rid you of your flesh."

The rope circling my body tightened as someone cinched it around the stake. There was no way I could escape now.

Terror clawed at me as I watched the men leaving the platform. If they hadn't pinned me to the pillar, my trembling legs would have given out. My heart pounded against my ribs amidst my fear. Fayolan couldn't save me this time.

"Any last words?" My captor mocked me with a savage grin. *Oh, I had a few…*

"Fayolan, the bringer of death, will reap *all* of your souls and raze your village to the *fucking* ground. You'll pay dearly for what you're about to do."

"*Touching.* It must hurt knowing he hasn't come. I guess saving you wasn't worth his time. But sure, you keep fooling yourself into believing you mean something to him. Fayolan isn't the hero in your story." *No… he was my villain!*

Horror filled me as he stepped away, lifting a burning torch. No hint of mercy shone in his eyes as he lit the oil coated branches.

The air filled with the scent of burning wood as flames erupted around me. I screamed at the top of lungs, but the roaring fire drowned it out.

"*Please*! Help me! This is wrong… Do you not remember that I was the one that saved you?" I stared at those from the city, but they showed no compassion.

I fought desperately against the ropes, trying to avoid the heat crawling towards me. It was no use. This is how my story ends.

"*Gods*." I screamed as the flames licked my skin. The wind snatched the thick black smoke before it could fill my lungs. I pushed frantically onto tip toes to escape the pain.

"Burn the monster," someone in the crowd jeered. I could hear laughter at my agonised screams as the stench of my burning flesh churned my stomach.

"Where is your prince now?" someone spat.

A roll of thunder echoed in the distance. I prayed my

father was watching. Maybe he would take pity on me and end my suffering.

"I am Tempest, daughter of *Sirus*, and I bring his *wrath* upon you. Tonight, I burn, but by morning he will *smite* you all!" Lightning cracked in the sky and the crowds fell silent. My father had heard me and he was watching.

My words of wrath turned to screams once more as the flames lashed against my body. The thick black fumes finally choked me as it filled my lungs. *Just let it be over.*

A small breeze caught the smoke and flames, pulling them into a protective vortex around me. But still it couldn't save me.

Lightning crashed against a building and terrified cries merged with my own. My skin blistered, and my head swam as I hung on the edge of consciousness. I wanted it to take me.

The moisture had vanished from my parched mouth as I whispered one final prayer to my absent father. "Please end this. Kill me now. I can't take anymore."

My head hung limp, and I gave in. Letting the flames consume my body. "I'm sorry Fayolan… I can't wait for you."

"I kept you alive for him," a familiar voice called through the flames. This voice had offered me aid the night I healed Fayolan. "Call out his name, daughter. He has come for you."

I lifted my head and screamed one last time. One word I prayed would end this. "*Fayolan*!"

Something slammed into me from behind. The ropes binding me were burnt and brittle, snapping under the force.

Everything went black.

CHAPTER FORTY

B raedon smirked as we stood over the soon-to-be corpse of Palleon. Body parts littered the ground around him as he begged for his life. *Pathetic bastard.*

I'd made him watch as we tore his companions apart piece by fucking piece. Taking our time to remove every finger, toe, and limb.

"Stop playing with your food," Nix huffed. She'd been in a foul mood since we left The Sacred Maple. She had set her sights on Wilem, and she always got cranky when she needed a good fucking.

"Please, I swear my allegiance to you. It was your father who sent me after you. He's planning to be rid of you." My foot slammed Palleon's face to the floor.

"Don't worry. My father will *soon* learn his place. He rules because *I* allow it. He breathes because *I* allow it." I lifted my foot and stamped on his face again and again. I felt the moment his skull caved in. Blood and brain matter ruining my boots.

"Ohhh," Nix moaned in ecstasy as she licked her lips. Death had the same effect as sex on the wicked woman.

"Make a noise like that again, and I will bend you over and fuck that delicious cunt of yours myself." Desire raged in Reed's eyes as he watched her.

"Ohhhhhh," she moaned again, and he was on her. His hand gripped Nix's throat as he claimed her lips. She ripped at his shirt, her chest heaving as she glanced down at the bodies.

I turned to Braedon. "Take me back." He nodded with a look of relief. He was as fucked up as the rest of us. But Nix and Reed were on another level.

Braedon gripped my arm, and the world shifted. We appeared amongst a cluster of trees by the Inn. "Once they've finished, bring them back." He dipped his head and displaced.

As I glanced around, a sense of foreboding washed over me in the eerie silence. I could not hear the music from the tavern and no candles flickered, lighting the upper rooms.

"*Fayolan*," Lilith cried out. She lingered near the door. She looked pale and crimson streaked her cheeks. "They took her!" My heart stopped beating at the stricken look on her face and the red that stained her dress.

"Where's Kalen?" She gestured towards the Inn. I darted past her, slamming the door open.

He lay unconscious on a table. Wilem held a bloody rag to his temple. Eight bodies littered the floor. Only one man, bound and gagged, still lived.

"We've been trying to get him to talk," Lilith said as she lifted a dagger smeared in his blood. I snatched it from her hands and stalked towards the man. My menacing wings spread out as my shadows flickered eagerly around me.

I ripped the gag down, bending over the man as I gripped his neck. Forcing him to look up at me.

"Where. Is. She?" I drawled as I raised the dagger. The tip hovering just in front of his eye.

"Please have mercy."

"It's too late for that." I pushed the blade into his socket, careful not to go too deep. I wanted him alive. After all, dead men can't spill their secrets. I plucked out his eyeball, and his head grew limp. I slapped his cheek, keeping him with me as I showed him my dagger.

"Where. Is. She?" I asked again as my blade hovered above his other eye.

"They took her to Midscar," he wailed. "You're too late. She'll be dead by now." I spat in his face as I released him, taking a step back.

"You had better pray she is not." I spun, handing the knife back to Lilith. She grinned, flicking the dagger so the eye splattered on the floor. Her dainty foot slammed down, popping it with a satisfying moist squelch. I'd forgotten how lurid she could be.

I turned to Wilem, who had gone pale as he swayed. He lacked Lilith's taste for the gruesome. "Stitch Kalen up," I snapped. "As for him." I jerked my head towards the still wailing man. "Keep him alive. Kalen will want to take his time with him."

While heading towards the door, I spared Lilith one final glance. "How many?"

"Eleven that I know of." With one mighty flap of my wings, I shot into the night sky. The beast within me rattled his cage, desperate to get out. And once I found her—I would unleash him.

He was the dark and depraved part of me I kept locked inside. His magic was so murderous that I could never use it. But tonight… I'd let him tear this world to the ground.

Lightning lit up the sky, and the wind whipped around me. Carrying her words to me. "I am Tempest, daughter of *Sirus*, and I bring his *wrath* upon you. Tonight, I burn, but by morning he will *smite* you all." Daughter of the most powerful and feared son of the Gods. *I should have known.* But he wouldn't get to destroy the village. *That pleasure was mine.*

A plume of thick black smoke rose into the night sky, hiding the stars from view. A block of ice replaced my heart as I caught sight of the colossal fire. Tempest was bound to a stake while the flames seared her skin. *My Gods what the fuck had they done?*

More lightning struck the houses with precision, sending debris and shrapnel cascading into the crowd of onlookers. Tempest had the favour of the Gods, but it failed to save her.

Her screams broke me inside. But as she went silent and her head fell forward, my heart shattered into a million pieces. *I was too late. She was gone!* I soared over the flames, slamming to the ground with such force it quaked beneath me.

My legs became weak, dropping me to one knee. I stared, unable to breathe at the sight of her engulfed in flames.

"*Fayolan!*" she screamed as her head snapped up. I dived forward, my shadows creating a protective cocoon around me as I plunged through the blaze. My arms encircled Tempest, lifting her as the rope securing her crumbled. Her cry of pain shattered my soul.

I released the beast the second my feet touched the ground. Screams tore through the villagers as he peered through my eyes. His shadows took form on my skin like dark tattoos flickering across my body.

I caught sight of the folk Tempest had saved from Wrossa, and their screams died in their throats as the beast released his magic. Only the roaring fire made a noise as bodies fell life-lessly before me.

Instant death was what he wrought. Spreading through the village and beyond. I was determined to burn this fucking world to the ground. To make it truly safe for her.

A groan drew my attention to Tempest. She would never forgive me if I spilt innocent blood. I roared, drawing the power of death back inside. Fighting the beast to return him to his cage.

Seeing Tempest as she whimpered in my arms had him retreating. He wanted her to live, so he relinquished his control so I could save her.

Tempest's body was red and blistered from her toes to her neck. Only her face had escaped the fires of hell.

The sky lit once more as if the Gods themselves were thanking me.

"I am here now, Tempest. No one will touch you again or I will *devour* them." I launched into the sky, letting the cooling wind brush against her skin, easing the burn as she groaned.

"Fayolan," she whispered. A sob threatened to break her. "You came for me."

"Did you think I wouldn't?" My voice rasped as I pushed aside the torrent of hate and fear that tried to destroy me. "You called out to me."

"Did *you* think I wouldn't?" she repeated my words and my heart splintered. The black that had tainted it burst from me, as colour flooded my vision. Both a blessing and a curse as I saw how badly damaged her body was.

If I'd lost her, there would've been nothing left of this world. Tempest was mine to protect. She had *been* since the moment I first laid eyes on her. I was just so damned stubborn it had taken *this*—to make me see it.

I landed as softly as I could. Even so, she grunted at the

jolt. I kicked the door of the Sacred Maple off its hinges. Striding in with Tempest cradled in my arms. Lilith shrieked as she saw her ravaged body.

"Mother *fucker*!" Kalen's fist collided with the face of the man, who now had both eyes gouged out.

"Find Nix," I roared.

With Lilith on my heels, I crossed the tavern, taking three stairs at a time. The door to our room hung from its hinges. Deep grooves marred the door frame where Tempest had fought to stop them taking her.

The tub was still full, with blood dripped down the side.

"Let me clean it." Lilith manoeuvred around me, careful not to touch Tempest. She hurried to drain the bath, scrubbing it clean.

"I'm so sorry, Tempest," I muttered, lowering her into the tub. She cried out as I turned on the tap, cold water flowing over her back. I cupped my hands gently, pouring it over her.

"Please stop," Tempest rasped. Each drop made her body jerk.

"I have to, Pet." Something dark fell into the tub. Shreds of blackened skin hung from my shirt, in plain sight for Tempest to see. I ripped it from my body and continued to pour cold water over her.

She flung her head back as she sobbed. Her breath laboured, and her lungs no doubt burnt from the thick black smoke. "Tempest, I *need* you to heal yourself." She had refused before, but I couldn't bear seeing her like this. I felt sick to my very core.

"I can't," she cried. "Nephilim don't have that ability." *Shit!* She had been telling the truth this whole time.

CHAPTER FORTY-ONE

I had ordered Lilith to leave us. My hands were unsteady as I clutched a pair of tweezers, hovering over a clump of melted rope. I slowed my breath as I pulled the material from Tempest's body.

Normally, I was numb to the screams of pain I inflicted on others. But hers destroyed me, ripping my soul into tiny fragments. "I'm sorry, Pet."

She did not fight my touch as I lay her back. Her head heavy as she succumbed to the pain. "You have to stay awake. Can you do that for me?"

"Please. Don't leave me." Her words were but a whisper. Still, they cut deep. I had been an asshole when she'd been poisoned. Too wrapped up in my jealousy to stay by her side. But that would never happen again.

"I'm not going anywhere." I ran my hand through what little remained of her hair. The sight of the damage inflicted on her body made my stomach churn.

Words could not ease Tempest's suffering. And if Nix did not get her ass here soon, I would kill her myself.

I used more cold water to ease the burns as I pulled a vial from the aether. Three times I had tried to get Tempest to drink the blue swirling liquid, but she coughed and spluttered it up.

I prayed Tempest would keep it down as I held it to her smoke-blackened lips. It would take some of her pain, numbing her body slightly. She groaned as I tilted her head back, pouring the liquid straight down her throat.

My hand grasped firmly over her mouth, stopping her from spitting it back out. She erupted into a coughing fit. It filled me with self-loathing as she struggled against me, hurting herself further.

I lost count of the time I remained by her side. Carefully removing bits of melted rope and damaged skin that hung from her body.

"Nix is here," Lilith yelled up the stairs, and I released Tempest. Her eyes rolled as I lay her back down. She couldn't bear the pain. With Nix here, I could finally let her rest.

"Sleep, Tempest. You're safe now," I soothed as I clasped her hand tenderly in mine.

"Am I?" she mumbled absently before her eyes closed and her body relaxed.

"I'll protect you. I swear it."

"Fucking *bastards*." Nix's nostrils flared as she caught sight of Tempest. "*Move*." She glared at me, but my feet would not follow her commands.

"I'm *not* leaving her side."

Nix cursed as she climbed into the tub. She crouched between Tempest's legs, examining every inch of burnt flesh. Her nose crinkled at the smell. It no longer phased me.

"Are they dead?" she asked, rubbing her hands together.

"Not *one* heart still beats in that village." I gritted my

teeth as I sensed her magic flare. She was not powerful enough to mend the severest of wounds or organs. But I prayed she could at least repair Tempest's skin. "I want *all* the scars gone. Even the ones she had before."

Nix stiffened. "Her skin shows deep damage. Her old ones are already gone. But I swear to the Gods, Fayolan…" she lifted her startling gaze to me. "If I can't save her skin from the burns, and you *shun* her. I will *cut* off your dick and *feed* it to you."

With my fangs bared, I could feel the heat rising in my chest as I scowled at Nix. "I don't want you to heal them for me." My shadows made Nix shrink back. "I want them gone because they hurt *her*. They remind her every day of what men took from her. She hasn't allowed another person to touch her since then."

Nix's expression softened. She could relate to Tempest's suffering. Maybe one day she would tell her story to the Nephilim.

"I was a bitch to her, wasn't I?" She stared down at Tempest, seeing the woman, not the monster they had taught us to despise.

"You're not alone. I refused to acknowledge what was right in front of my eyes, from the very beginning."

Nix began healing, and I lowered my head against the tub, still holding Tempest's hand. So many emotions I'd never experienced flooded me. It drained all my energy. But one thing I knew for certain, regardless of what she was… or whether the Nephilim were monsters… *Tempest* was different.

By the time Nix had finished healing, the sun had risen, and she wobbled on her feet. I slipped my arm under hers, scooping her up as I carried her to her room below.

"Thank you," I muttered, placing her on the bed. Pressing a kiss against her forehead.

"I did it for *her*, not you." She smiled as she closed her eyes. Sleep claimed her instantly. Reed dropped beside her. He would protect her as she gathered her strength.

"Keep the door open." Reed smirked. "The screams will comfort her." I propped it wide with a chair. Kalen was still having fun downstairs with the eyeless man.

My body felt heavy as I climbed the stairs. Tempest still lay sleeping in the tub. I sighed, lowering to the floor beside her as I ran my fingers over her soft, unmarred skin. *Would she resent my touch even more now?*

"How's she doing?" Braedon leant against the door frame. Keeping his gaze solely on me. He knew better than to let it fall upon her naked body.

"Nix has healed her physical injuries, but her mental state is probably in pieces."

"I'm sorry we weren't here. I can't imagine what it was like for her." He had the most compassion among us. Even though he was just as ruthless.

I sighed, brushing her glossy hair behind her ears. "When I got there, I thought she was dead. I never want to feel that way again." I pulled a soft fur blanket from the aether, wrapping it around Tempest as I lifted her from the tub.

"What do you have in mind?" he asked. Solis would be just as perilous for her. He knew it as well as I did.

"I think we need to make a *point*," I said darkly. I gave Braedon his orders. He was grinning from ear to ear when he blinked out of sight.

I eased Tempest onto my bare chest. I yearned for this moment of closeness before she reverted to the haunted woman who despised physical contact.

She snored softly in my arms. The dreams Kalen had given her protected her from the nightmares. With one hand, I stroked down her back soothingly, exploring every curve whilst the other smoothed her hair.

The day passed, and I remained nestled beneath her. The beast's shadow tattoos still marred my skin. A reminder that he was her protector, and he wanted revenge.

"Fayolan?" Lilith nudged open the door, carrying a tray laden with food. "I brought some broth for Tempest." Her throat would still be sore from the harrowing screams that would haunt me for the rest of my life.

"I don't want to wake her." She seemed so peaceful nestled into my chest. It's where she belonged, safe in my arms.

"The poor girl needs to eat." Lilith tried to coax me from beneath Tempest, but my beast was not ready to let her go. Even though he knew she needed food more than she needed us. It scared him because, in truth, neither of us knew how she would react when she woke. Maybe she'd reject us? Or our appearance would frighten her?

"I'll wake her soon. Just leave."

Lilith scowled as she banged the tray on the table. "Fine, I was only trying to help."

"I'm sorry. I just need a little more time. But I'll make sure she eats soon." All I could do was delay the inevitable. I'd just hold her for a few more minutes.

Lilith dipped her head, closing the door with a soft click. Leaving us alone. Everyone lingered close by, but remained out of sight. No one wanted to crowd Tempest. She already hated to be touched. *What would this do to her?*

I slipped from beneath her as she stirred. Moving back into the shadows, giving her time to adjust. Her eyes shot open. Her mouth twisting in fear as she sat in the dark.

"*Fayolan?*" I froze as she called out to me, seeking comfort. Her voice trembled as she searched for me.

I stepped from the shadows, and her panic eased. "I told you... I will not leave you." Her gaze drifted to the inky shadows that moved across my skin. *Would she fear what I had become to save her?*

She swallowed as she edged further back across the bed. *I knew I repulsed her.*

"Fayolan." She glanced down at the space she had created. I moved closer, my breath held, expecting her to cry out and withdraw. But she remained silent, watching me as I placed one knee on the bed.

She inhaled sharply but didn't flinch. My mind urged me to back off, but my curiosity pushed me to see how far she would let me go. I lowered onto the bed.

Still, she remained glued to the spot. She tilted her head and examined me, as if confused by her actions. I tracked her movements, rotating myself to look at her, and then she shifted position.

She knelt, bending towards me as her arm rose. I kept still, so I did not startle her. Her hand stayed poised just before it reached my cheek. I wanted to lean forward. To force the contact as she hesitated, but I wanted her to have the control she needed. I wouldn't take that from her again.

Her eyes found mine, staring deep into my soul as if seeing me as she never had before. She swallowed, and her hand moved. Resting on my cheek. "Thank you… for saving me… and for looking after me."

Before I could respond, she seemed to notice what she had done. She snapped her hand away, staring at it as if it had acted on its own. I shifted my weight, ready to back off and give her space.

"Don't…" She lunged forward, wrapping her arms around my neck as she clung to me. "Please stay." Hearing her words, I could not stop the smile that tugged at the corner of my lips as I cocooned her against me. I'd hold her there as long as she needed.

Her tears fell on my shoulder as her body trembled. "It's okay. You can let it out. I'm here now." I gripped her tighter.

"Thank you." She mumbled her words into my neck. I held her until she stopped crying and sat back. My thumb gently wiped the tears from her cheeks as I smiled softly.

"Feel better?" Tempest nodded in response. "Good, because you need to eat." I slipped off the bed, towards the table, grabbing the food Lilith had left.

When I turned back, Tempest looked hurt, as if I had just rejected her. It pained my soul to see that look in her eyes.

My beast growled, and I returned to the bed, balancing the tray on my lap. Watching her as she drank as much of the broth as she could manage.

I stayed beside Tempest, kicking my boots off as she fell asleep. My back rested against the wall as I watched over her. Only leaving her side to fetch Kalen when her dreams turned into night terrors.

CHAPTER FORTY-TWO

Tempest

My fingers ran over the smooth skin on my arms as I examined my reflection in the mirror. For the first in a long time, my body didn't repulse me. Nix had given me a priceless gift, and I could never thank her enough.

I lifted the dress Fayolan had provided me and bit my lip excitedly as I held it up against me. It was beautiful. Made of the most expensive lace. The first time I saw it, it hung displayed on a mannequin at a stall in Fayspire.

The only difference was that Fayolan had requested the seamstress to add sleeves. It fit me perfectly. I pulled my hair into a bun, freeing a few strands around my face.

I was fighting my nerves as I stared at my reflection. Lilith had insisted we go to the tavern tonight, as tomorrow we would head to Solis. I didn't want to go. Despite saving people, they still turned on me. I just wanted to hide from the world.

Fayolan had promised he had taken steps to ensure my safety, but I could not dispel the fear that penetrated my very soul. Even though he'd remained at my side. Holding me as I pieced myself back together.

It had shocked me when I first placed my hand on his cheek and felt no pain. Just warmth that made me want to be closer to him. He'd even grinned as I told him I desired him to stay. He had the most alluring smile. *When he wasn't being an ass!*

I had asked him about the shadow tattoos that now traversed his skin, but he evaded my questions. All he would say is he'd released the beast within him to save me. He said they would fade soon enough.

It did not matter to me if he had them forever. He was still beautiful. Even if he wasn't mine and *if* we were enemies.

"Are you almost ready?" Fayolan called through the closed door.

"*Coming.*" Things had been easier over the past couple of days. He was no longer trying to frighten me into submission, and I was not rebelling against him. We had found a comfortable middle ground.

I finally pulled myself away from the mirror and yanked the door open, colliding with his solid chest. He was leaning against the frame. His white shirt hugged his toned body, and he had a set of suspenders emphasising his muscular build. My heart leaped into my throat as I took him in.

His eyes roamed over me. The way they devoured me had heat flushing my cheeks.

His hand rose. Halting just beneath my chin. I inhaled a deep breath, expecting him to lift my face, but he remained still.

"Look at me," he husked. I let my eyes meet the fire that swirled in his. "You are beautiful scars or no scars. *Never* shy away from me, Little Monster." His words were gentle and raspy with desire. Even his use of the word monster did not have the usual bite. Instead, it made heat unfurl between my legs.

"You think I'm beautiful, *Death*?" I flicked my lashes in a way my mother would have been ashamed of. The lines between us were blurring; if I crossed them, there would be no return.

"If you keep looking at me like that, I will not be held responsible for my actions. I only have so much restraint." I took a sharp intake of breath as I took a tentative step closer. My mind no longer controlled my actions.

My fingers brushed against Fayolan's washboard stomach before trailing up to his chest. His hands shot out, encasing mine as he pulled them away. As he stepped back, I felt sick; the embarrassment hitting me like a tidal wave trying to sweep me away. "You are not ready, Tempest."

I yanked at my hands, trying to back away. But Fayolan gripped me tighter, and I stumbled, falling against him.

"Why does your touch not hurt anymore? Do you think Nix *fixed* me?"

He released me and cupped my cheek, towering over me. "I don't know." His lips swept against mine. A fleeting touch that made me lose my mind.

Before he could move away, I rose on my tiptoes, nipping his lip, eliciting a sharp hiss. Fayolan teased my mouth open with his tongue. I ached to feel it between my thighs. I was certain he would do wicked things as he devoured me.

"Tempest…" His voice was strained as my hands ran across his torso. Circling his nipples through his shirt. A chuckle escaped me as he let me push him back against the door frame. Biting my bottom lip, I glanced towards the stairs.

"The others are waiting." My voice was husky with the desire for him to fill me with every pulsing inch of him.

I'd almost died, but it had made me realise something I had been denying all along. *I wanted Fayolan to be mine.*

"You don't want to play games with me, Pet. I don't lose." His lips brushed my cheek, planting a subtle kiss. I fell for his distraction. I missed his hand as it slid beneath my dress. Brushing my underwear aside, teasing the bundle of nerves, testing my level of arousal.

"Then we should get going." My voice sounded strained.

Fayolan rubbed his fingers through my slick folds, making me gasp. The jolts of pleasure made me wobble on my feet. He chuckled, pulling his fingers away. The burning look he gave as he glossed my lips with my juices was so intense, I almost forgot to breathe.

"Delicious," he moaned, licking his fingers clean with an enticing groan before ravishing my mouth. I could taste myself in his kiss. A low moan lingered in my throat. Fayolan lifted his head, searching my eyes. "Let's go."

"Are you serious?" He walked out of the room as if nothing had happened, leaving me staring. *Bastard!* My hands clasped the door frame to steady myself.

"Are you coming?" he called back. *Yeah... once I had remembered how to breathe.* I gathered myself and hurried after him.

Once I reached the tavern, the sound of its patrons made me stop dead in my tracks. *There's so many people here. I couldn't go out there.* My hair and eyes were visible to everyone. They would all stare at the monster amongst them.

I took a step back, ready to run up the stairs, pressing myself against the wall. I rested my head as I gazed at the ceiling, trying to calm my nerves. *You can survive this, Tempest.* My mother's words played in my mind. But I was not some naïve eight-year-old girl anymore. I knew how the world saw me.

I sensed Fayolan before I saw him. He grazed the back of his hand against mine. Waiting for me to accept his touch.

"I can't go out there. Not looking like this." My fingers twitched, and I slipped my knuckles between Fayolan's.

"Do you think anyone would *dare* to hurt you whilst you are with *me*?" He raised his brow when I did not answer.

"No," I sighed. "It doesn't mean they won't place a target on my back." He spun smoothly, placing his palms on the wall on both sides of my head. Instantly I missed the warmth of his hand against mine.

"I refuse to hide you away. If I have to kill *everyone* in this *goddamn* place to protect you. I will."

"What if they take me again?"

"There's no place in this world where they can hide you from me." His eyes flared with danger as he spoke. "I almost lost you once, Tempest. I'll fucking die before I let it happen again." The conviction of his words snatched my breath away. A false courage filled me, and I nodded, gripping Fayolan's hand as he stepped away.

He interlaced our fingers and led me into the bar. Kalen, Reed, Nix, and Lilith sat with drinks in hand.

Lilith's laughter trailed off as she caught sight of my hand clutched protectively within Fayolan's. A smile reached her eyes as she banged her hand on the bar.

"Two more," she barked, and the roguishly good-looking bartender hurried, grabbing a couple of goblets as he unstoppered a bottle. He poured wine while his gaze lingered on Nix before settling on me.

I winced, expecting him to recoil in disgust, but he winked seductively as he placed the drinks down. Fayolan led me to an empty stool. His hand remained locked with mine as he helped me to take a seat.

"Are you okay?" He spoke so quietly no one else but me heard.

"I think so." The bar fell silent, and I peered into the goblet as I sensed eyes burning into my back. My fingers tightened around the stem, and I threw it back, gulping the fruity wine in one go.

My vision blurred as Fayolan placed his hand over the goblet and sat beside me. He chuckled as I struggled to meet his eyes.

"Take it slowly." He withheld laughter as I struggled to regain composure. "This wine differs from what you are used to. It's Lilith's special brew." *He was right.* My body warmed as it worked its way through my system.

"I realised this bunch drank so much I needed something stronger." She winked playfully as she snatched up my goblet and banged her fist again on the mahogany bar. I blinked in quick succession to focus.

An old man sitting in the corner stared at me as I coughed, covering my mouth with embarrassment. The tavern was still silent, and Lilith smiled, observing my unease.

"Sillo, get some music playing. It's deader in here than a *fucking* graveyard." She winked at me. "And if you lot have nothing better to do than stare…" She pinned her gaze around the room. "Then pay your tabs and get the *fuck* out!"

Murmurs filled the air as the patrons averted their gazes. Returning to their lighthearted conversations.

Satisfied, Lilith returned to her drink, taking it down in one gulp. She wiped her lips with a smirk as the others did the same. Fayolan rolled his eyes, lifting his goblet with a wink, and downing it.

I laughed as he banged on the bar, as Lilith had. The man behind it refilled all our drinks, leaving mine till last. He leant over the counter. His eyes perused every inch of me as he got closer.

"You are quite the rare sight around these parts." He reached out towards my hair, and I flinched.

Fayolan's hand shot out, trapping the man's wrist. "You can look, but you *do not* touch, Wilem." He bared his teeth in warning.

Wilem smirked as he nodded. His tongue ran across his lips, wetting them as he gave me one more flirtatious wink, and Fayolan released his grip.

"Ignore him." Lilith waved her hand, dismissing him. "My brother is a horrendous flirt, but unfortunately, he lacks the goods to back it up."

Wilem sneered at her playfully as he grabbed his crotch and thrust towards Nix. "I don't hear any complaints?" he smarted off. Lilith rolled her eyes, and Wilem returned his attention to Nix. Who certainly did not seem to think him lacking, as she snapped her teeth at him.

I couldn't help giggling as the wine took hold. I gripped Fayolan's hand tighter as I turned to him. "Thank you for tonight. It feels so normal after everything."

"All of this is *normal* for you?" He laughed as he glanced around at Wilem, Lilith, Nix, and the others.

"Maybe not quite like this. But vagrants and criminals get *pretty* rowdy." I smirked, knowing full well what he thought of the people that resided in No Man's Land.

"Is that *so*? I find it hard to believe when you're sitting here so timid and quiet." He teased me with a smirk.

Nudging him, I lifted my drink. "I'll show you how rowdy I can get." I downed the wine in one as I had the first.

"That sound's like a challenge, Pet."

"Maybe it is." I nibbled my bottom lip as I met his intoxicating gaze. Fayolan was the type of man that liked to win, but I wouldn't make it easy for him.

Music played in the background, and I spun on my stool to watch. Sillo banged on a drum as others joined in the rhythm with fiddles and a flute.

"Do you like music?" Fayolan asked, returning my attention to him.

"I guess." I shrugged.

"Tell me which one is your favourite?" He leant closer, sweeping my hair from my face.

"My favourite what?"

"Song," he said, watching me intently.

"Are you trying to get to know me, *Death*?" A smirk teased at the edges of my lips. "Anyone might think you were going *soft*."

"There is nothing *soft* about me." It must have been the wine controlling me, as my eyes dropped to his bulging crotch. "I *told* you." My cheeks flushed as I took another gulp of the wine. *He was going to be my undoing.*

CHAPTER FORTY-THREE

I stared at Tempest as my desire and the wine controlled my actions. Her cheeks flushed the softest pink as her gaze lifted from the hard bulge in my trousers. She swallowed as she glanced away.

Gods help me get through this night! I prayed as my cock stiffened more. I had to give it to the boy…. How he'd kept his hands to himself when it came to her was beyond me. He must have had constant blue balls. Unlike him, I was not a good man. The first chance I got, I'd claimed her body.

I was a bastard, but I'd never pretended to be otherwise. I'd shown Tempest some of the worst of me. But here she was, holding my hand and smiling at me. It was more than I deserved.

She took another gulp of wine before she turned back to me. "So, Death…" She paused as if changing her mind about speaking. I lifted her chin towards me. Her body tensed, but she met my gaze, locking her eyes with mine. "Do you like music?"

"We train to it, but I would not say I like it." I shrugged indifferently.

"I could change your mind…" she mumbled, pulling away.

"I *bet* you could," I breathed. Tempest's eyes roamed around our group. A smile creased her rosy lips at Nix and Reed's shameless flirting.

"I can't tell which one she wants." Tempest smirked.

"She will end up with both, I expect," Lilith said as she chuckled. "What Nix wants, she often gets."

"Even Lilith," I laughed. Lilith blew me a kiss as she winked.

"Even you?" I nearly missed Tempest's question. Her voice a mere whisper.

"*Jealous*?" I raised an eyebrow. She fiddled with her fingers as she stared at her lap.

"What right do *I* have to be?"

Every right! I should have said it aloud. I could've declared her as mine right then. But I averted my gaze from her. *Tempest isn't ready for that yet. I'd only push her further away.*

She slammed her goblet against the bar as she banged her hand, making Lilith chuckle.

"I like her," Lilith said. "It's decided. I'm coming with you tomorrow."

I almost spat out my drink. "No, *you* are not." I chugged my wine. Somehow, I knew I would need it. "I've not forgotten the day you left. What was it you said to me? I am never coming back, and if I try, I expect you to refuse me."

"I did. But I'm not returning for you." Lilith smirked as her gaze shifted to the small woman behind me. "If you intend to claim her as yours. Then she will need me."

"To the Gods Lilith. You're as big a flirt as your brother." She whacked my arm, shooting a fiery glance in my direction.

"Not like that, *prick*. You know Tempest isn't ready for this world. I will be her shield." I knew Lilith better than to argue. There's also no one I trusted more to keep her safe. "But I am *hers* to command. I do not answer to *you*. I won't spy on Tempest, and before you ask if anything happens between you two… I will protect *her*. Do *not* make me fight against you."

"*Fine!*" I did not like knowing Lilith would turn against me if Tempest did. But she needed someone to protect her, even from me. Besides, I would not lose her now that I had her.

"What did I miss?" Tempest grinned as she finished another goblet of wine. Banging her hand for a refill.

"I think you need to slow it down, Pet." She pouted at me, poking out her tongue.

"Let her have some fun. After everything she's been through, she deserves it." Nix nudged me aside as she grabbed Tempest's drink.

"Wilem, it's rude to keep a girl waiting." Nix grinned as he strutted over with a cocky smirk.

"I'm not so sure it's a good idea. Tempest has a knack for causing trouble even when sober," Kalen laughed as he edged closer to Lilith. She either didn't notice or chose to ignore him.

"If you ask me," Wilem said. "If the woman wants to drink, then let her."

"No one *is* asking you." I grit my teeth, but Tempest squeezed my hand, catching my attention.

As the night went on, she grew increasingly boisterous like the rest of us. She was normally so guarded, but tonight she laughed and conversed with the others. It suited her. Even if it was the wine giving her the courage.

"Li li li la," she sang under her breath, and Lilith's eyes opened wide.

"You know this one?" Lilith asked her. Tempest was too drunk to let her shyness get the better of her, and she nodded.

"It's my go-to drunken ballad." A soft giggle escaped her.

"Come on," Lilith grabbed her hand, but Tempest winced as she felt the pain. *Interesting... So it was only my touch that no longer hurt.*

Tempest stumbled as she fell from the chair. I caught her before she hit her pretty little face on the solid wooden floorboards of the Tavern. The tie holding her bun fell loose, and her hair flowed down her back. I laughed as she threw her head back with a giggle.

Lilith grabbed her hand again. Tempest tensed, but smiled as she dragged her across the bar, ordering Sillo to begin the song again.

"Gods help us," Kalen groaned as Lilith tried to encourage her to sing. Tempest's eyes met mine. The wine failed to conceal her fear. I went to stand as the music stopped, but her lips parted.

"One winter's morn, the wind called," she sang. Her delicate voice wobbling with nerves. "Li li li la." The music started again, and she found her confidence as Lilith beamed. Sillo pounded on his drum to the beat of the song as other musicians joined in.

"The warrior of hearts bold and true.
Li li li la.
She lifted her sword as she felt the tides of war.
Facing man and beast until she fell to her knees.
She called to the storm, praying it came to her aid.

She will be the warrior of myths, far and wide.
One winter's morn, she called.
Li li li la.
The warrior of hearts bold and true.
Li li li la.
The storm heard her calls, bringing the wind lifting her to the
skies.
She was a goddess and commanded the storm.
Who would be the one to bring the end of the war?
She will be the warrior of myths, far and wide.
Li li li la."

As the music stopped, her voice got softer. Her melodic singing tugged at my heart. Lilith stepped beside her, adding harmony to her song. Her eyes rose to look at the ceiling as she battled the tears that glistened in her eyes.

"Stand tall, my warrior queen.
There'll be peace once the war is won.
Be strong as your heart is true.
Freedom is yours to claim.
Fight on."

Silence fell as she finished. My heart was pounding as I focused on her. In that moment, my desire for her was beyond measure.

All eyes were on her as the clapping started. Slow and soft after the emotional a cappella ending of the song.

She stumbled forward as she giggled. Her nerves returned, and she reached out for a goblet of wine, tripping over her feet.

I rushed towards her, catching her and whipping the wine out of her hand.

"Aww," she pouted.

"I'm cutting you off," I said, laughing as I placed my arm beneath Tempest's knees, scooping her up. Tempest shrieked before she nestled into me. "You need to sleep it off." I carried her towards the stairs.

"I can manage," she said as she planted her hands on my chest. "You should stay."

"Come on, man." Reed grinned drunkenly. "The night is still young. There is pussy free for the taking." He slurped his drink, almost falling from his stool at Nix's feet.

"Gods *dammit*," I sighed.

"Go," Tempest said as I set her down. "I don't need you like they do." She pinned me with a warning glance. *Ever the fighter.* Even as she struggled to stand.

"I've got her," Lilith offered her arm to Tempest.

"I don't like people touching me," she slurred her words as she spoke. "But I like you."

Lilith laughed as a smile creased my lips. Tempest was fond of her, which is good if Lilith was to become her shield.

"I can help," Wilem offered, as his eyes locked with mine. The bastard always did like to push my buttons.

I waited at the bottom of the stairs as the women's giggles faded away. Lilith shrieked, followed by a bang as Tempest fell. I rolled my eyes, leaving them to it.

"You are about to lose that *tongue* of yours." I glared at Wilem. He clutched his heart as he feigned looking wounded.

"She needs a man between those succulent thighs of hers. I can picture her sweet voice singing my name as my cock fills her."

He sniggered as I lunged across the bar. Kalen and Nix grabbed me, dragging me back.

A low growl emanated from the depths of my chest. "She

would find it lacking. She has felt a real man between those thighs."

Pain surged at the nape of my head. Everyone chuckled as Nix retreated a bit. She'd struck me so hard her palm turned red.

"*Don't* talk about her like that. She isn't like the girls in your harem or me," she chided. Frustratingly, she was right.

She shot Wilem a warning glance as she raised her hand toward him. "Disrespect her again, and you will *still* have blue balls in the morning," she threatened crassly.

"You're breaking my heart, Nix, baby." Wilem grinned. Everyone knew that as much as Nix fucked whoever was willing—she only accepted three to her bed regularly. Wilem, Reed, and Lilith.

Even though she was a wicked flirt, I'd never crossed that line with Nix. Other than playful flirting, she never tried either. Love makes things messy.

My gaze drew to the stairs as I sighed. My little Nephilim was going to complicate everything. I grabbed a goblet of wine and drank it down. It seemed Tempest had set the bar for tonight.

"I'm beat," Kalen sighed as he downed his last drink. His gaze locked on the stairs, and I grinned, knowing exactly who he sought. He was a fierce warrior, and he had fallen for Lilith the moment he had seen her beat a man for spitting on her new boots.

She was the only woman capable of handling the hulk of a man, but he never had the balls to tie her down. He'd let her leave Solis to run her father's tavern. He even watched as Nix bedded her. She was unaware that Lilith belonged to him.

Lilith did, of course! I was sure she only did it to make him jealous. One day, he would grow a pair and claim her. She was certainly going to make him work for it.

He stumbled up the staircase, and I downed another drink before grabbing Reed's arm.

"You've had enough," I warned, dragging him from the bar.

"You just want to ruin my fun." He pouted like a petulant child. "Nix can take me to bed." He grinned as he fought against me. She rolled her eyes as she finished her drink and stormed across the bar.

"Come on," she grumbled as he almost fell over her. I chuckled as I climbed the stairs behind them.

I left them as Nix shoved Reed into his room, slamming the door behind them. *Thank the Gods, the walls were soundproof.*

As I climbed up to the third floor, my heart started beating faster. I knew Tempest would be fast asleep. My hand rested against the creaky door, trying to calm my throbbing cock, glancing down as it pressed uncomfortably against my trousers. My erection growing at the mere thought of the temptress waiting behind the door. *Not tonight. She needed time.*

CHAPTER FORTY-FOUR

Tempest

The stool in my hands slipped in my sweaty grip. I lifted it over my head, ready to strike. I stared at the door, praying they would not break it down again.

The creaking stairs warned me that someone was almost at my room. My heart hammered in my chest as fear dug its claws into me.

The footsteps halted on the other side of the door. My breath hitched as the handle turned. A scream lodged in my throat as I swung the stool at the intruder's head. A massive hand stopped the stool mid-arc, shaking my bones.

Fayolan stared at me, stunned. "Are you *still* trying to kill me?" He grinned.

"No. I thought you were them. They won't stop until I'm dead."

Fayolan's arms shot out, pulling me against his chest in a tight embrace. "I'm here now." He stroked my hair soothingly as I buried my face in his neck, breathing in his familiar scent.

His wings moved with grace, unfurling from his back. His fiery gaze was almost too intense to bear, as his shadows blocked the moonlight from the window. "Believe me, I will *never* let that happen again."

I sensed a change in his strength as he brought me closer. I looked up…and gasped. The hair on my arms rose as he bared his teeth. Licking his tongue over his growing fangs, the tips of the sharp points glinting in the darkness. "Do you fear me, Tempest?"

The air surrounding me thickened as I hesitated. "Yes."

"So do *they*…and you have far less to fear from me than they do."

I shivered. No one had ever promised to protect me as Fayolan had. A current of comforting warmth washed over me. "I've never cared for anyone the way I do about you. Tempest, I just need you to trust me."

"I do." I traced my fingers gently over his feathered wings, marvelling at how soft they felt. He quivered at my touch. "You're beautiful." Fayolan's body tensed as I wrapped my arms around him. "Does it frighten you when I touch them?"

"No," he rasped huskily. "I *fear* what I will do to you if you continue."

"Do you want to hurt me?" I whispered back. I lifted my face to him, finding a wantonness I had not known I possessed. His skin against mine made me feel so alive.

"Yes," his voice caught in his throat.

"Why?" I leant in closer to his lips.

"Because you make me *feel*," Fayolan murmured as the shadows danced across his face. "I want you to see who I really am, but it terrifies me."

"I know *who* you are." My lips brushed Death's. His

breathing became ragged as he lifted me onto the bed, his resolve breaking. I gently pressed my fingertip against his mouth. Needing him to stop and listen. "I want *this*." My mind was finally free of doubt. *I wanted this man.*

I yelped as his fang nipped the tip of my finger. A hunger intensified in him as he watched my blood trickle down my hand. His tongue licked out, running through the crimson as he savoured the taste of me.

A deep, animalistic groan reverberated in his chest. "You've no idea about the darkness in me. If you did… You would not be throwing yourself at me."

I pulled my hand back and slapped him across the face. "You don't get to decide that for me, *Death*! I won't run from you anymore. I *choose* to stay with you."

Fayolan slammed me up against the wall, trapping me with his enormous body. I clung to him tightly, my legs wrapped around his waist.

Our lips collided with a fierce hunger, as if we had craved the taste of each other our whole lives. His fangs sunk into my bottom lip as he pulled it back. *"Tempest,"* he said through his gritted teeth.

"I know you *want* me," I taunted.

His hand gripped my throat. My breath came in shallow gasps, my lungs aching for air.

"If we do *this*…" he glared into my eyes. "I'll be unable to let you go. Even though you'll despise me. I will *never* let you run. I'll bring you pleasure *and* pain as I *fuck* that delicious body of yours."

To prove his point, a sharp talon sliced into my side. "You don't know the things I want to *do* to you. They may call you a monster. But me… they do not have words for a creature like me."

"*Death*." My voice was strained against his hold on my

throat. "*My* Death." I reached for his talon, raking it up my side, pressing it deeper into my flesh.

"Gods Tempest! If you don't want this, say now." He pulled me from the wall, dangling me in mid-air.

"*Bring* it, Death," I breathed deeply when he lowered me to the bed.

"Listen well, Tempest. My beast doesn't like being challenged. So, be a good girl and do as I *fucking* tell you." He gripped my waist, bringing me to my knees, facing the foot of the bed.

I heard the creak of a rope behind me as Fayolan tied it to the bedpost in front of me. My heart raced when he wrapped it around my thigh. Pulling it tight so I could not back away from him.

My muscle tensed beneath his hands as he secured my other thigh to the other post. His eyes were alight with amusement as he saw me breathe deeply. A smirk played on his lips.

"Shall I keep going?" Fayolan asked in a deep voice that scarcely sounded like his own.

I nodded, and he pulled more earthy smelling rope from the aether. I held my breath in anticipation. He circled behind me, wrapping his hand firmly around my ankle. Spreading my legs wider as he bound it to a post at the head of the bed.

"You're my special girl, aren't you?" His question was rhetorical as he glided his fingers down my leg. I was bound so tight even as my body instinctively tried to pull away, I remained in place. With a dark chuckle, Fayolan tugged on another rope securing the other ankle.

His fingers were like a steel trap around my wrist as he bound it. He leant in close to my ear, his breath fanning my neck. "Forgive me for what I'm about to do." His voice rasped with danger.

"Fayolan…" I gasped as he pulled my arms back. Tying

each to a bedpost behind me, immobilising me in place. *I could not move!* A chill of panic ran through me, but my fear turned to adrenaline. I was powerless, spread out like a meal for him to devour.

Fayolan moved closer, whispering in my ear… one single word. I shivered as his lips brushed my neck.

"I don't understand?"

"Remember that word, Tempest. If you say it, then everything stops. The moment it falls from your *succulent* lips, I will free you and this all ends. That *one* word gives *you* the power, Pet. I want you to know you are safe."

The thing was… I did know it. I'd never felt more protected than I did around Fayolan. He wasn't the hero that would sacrifice me for the greater good. *No, he was the villain willing to let the world burn, just to save me.*

He prowled around the bed, tilting his head as his gaze lingered on my body. My heart beat faster as a small smirk played on his lips. "Look how beautiful you are, all spread out and ready for me."

His eyes turned black for an instant. Something else was inside him… watching me. The pale gold returned to his iris, and he was Fayolan once again.

Death smiled in amusement. With a flick of his wrist, the glint of a dagger shone in his hand. He toyed with it as he prowled closer. My body heat intensified as a needy ache unfurled from the swollen lips between my legs.

He closed the gap between us. He was a predator, and I was the prey caught in his web. *And I craved it.*

"Are you scared, Tempest?" Fayolan's voice was husky. He inhaled deeply, his nostrils flaring as he smelt my arousal.

"Should I be?" I asked breathily. My voice shook. Desire and fear consumed me, leaving me on a precipice that only he had the power to push me over.

"Gods, you're *beautiful*. Even now… bound and

completely at my mercy, you don't shy away. You do not know how long I've waited for you."

My breath caught sharply as the knife's tip broke through the lace of my clothes. A fire ignited in me as he cut it from my body.

"I liked that dress," I pouted.

"I *told* you to be a good girl, Tempest." His eyes flickered darkly. The sharp point of the blade pressed against my cheek. "Don't make me *punish* you."

"I'm sorry." My heart fluttered as I nibbled my lip. Gods there were no words for the emotions this man created within me.

Fayolan lowered the knife, slicing the dress until he could pull it from my body. He maintained a steady gaze as he cut my undergarments away.

"That's better, Pet. Let me worship your body as it deserves. Be good for me and I will tear down those walls you hide behind. There is an entire world of pleasure I desire to show you."

His presence was powerful. I longed for his touch, knowing that if I behaved, he would reward me.

"You are beyond perfection, Tempest." With a brisk flick of his wrist, Fayolan's clothes vanished into the aether. My pussy pulsed as he knelt before me, naked, clenching his jaw as he battled his most primal urges.

His body was fascinating! It was the very first time I'd seen him in all his glory. A black and grey tattoo of shredded skin framed three-dimensional armoured breastplates. A realistic skull on each one faced towards the raven in the centre. Its wings outstretched towards his collarbone. A large dragon scale capped his shoulders, giving way to smaller ones and chain mail. Which cascaded over his bulging muscles, down to his wrists and ankles.

The curve of his hip blended into his Adonis belt. I

gulped as it guided my eyes down to his erection. Memories of it filling me brought a flush to my cheeks. The tip pulsed with promises of things to come. *Gods… Have you sent him to save or destroy me?*

"Hungry?" he asked. "Because I am ravenous." He cupped my face, lingering before pressing his mouth to mine. My lips parted in anticipation. I craved the euphoria that his kisses often brought to me.

Fayolan nibbled on my bottom lip with his fangs. "Are you ready for this, Pet? Remember the word. Because if you don't use it, I plan to teach you to obey me."

"Will it hurt?" He raised an eyebrow. Flicking his hand, he lifted the knife, hovering it by my lips.

His chest rumbled. "Open up." Even as panic flared within me, I did as he asked. The fear only intensified the torrent of need surging through me. Turning into a raging furnace of desire.

Fayolan was cautious as he placed the knife's blade between my teeth. "This will teach you not to run that pretty little mouth of yours." He grinned as he gripped my jaw.

I swallowed, and my tongue caught the ice-cold steel. The coppery tang of blood trickled into my mouth, but I kept it firm between my teeth. "That's my good Little Girl," Fayolan cooed, running his fingers down my breasts. His eyes hovered on my hardened nipples.

"Breathe," he commanded. I gasped as he slid his fingers between my folds. I held back a moan that would cause another cut from the blade.

He eased three fingers inside me. Caressing my clit with his thumb whilst he delved into me. I leant my head back to savour the sensations, swallowing a moan. The knife cut into my tongue again.

Fayolan looked ravenous as a trickle of blood trailed

down my chin. The predator in him caused a chill to run down my back.

"Ready?" he mumbled against my neck, trailing kisses down my shoulder. "You are Daddy's perfect girl, aren't you? Let me in." His fingers pulled away, leaving me with a hollow feeling. I locked my eyes with his, begging him to fill me again.

The glistening tip of his cock dipped into my entrance. He wrapped one hand firmly around the nape of my neck. Stroking my skin reassuringly with his thumb as his fingers returned to my clit. His grip was tight and unrelenting, leaving me unable to look away.

Fayolan pushed in a little further, rocking his hips, easing out before sliding in deeper than before. His cock pulsed inside me, causing the liquid ball of heat in my core to expand throughout my body. The euphoria robbed me of my breath.

"You open so nicely for me." Fayolan moved faster as he groaned. His hips ground against me, working my pussy.

My mind detached from the world. Death's movements were the only thing my thoughts could grasp onto. I went deeper into my soul as he fucked me into a blissful, numb oblivion. Each thrust making the pain a thing of the past.

My body became his to control whilst I moaned for more. Fayolan felt the shift in my threshold and grinned, baring his fangs. He slammed into me, burying his cock to the hilt of my cunt with such force that stars burst behind my eyes.

"Look how well you fit around my dick. You're *fucking* perfect, Tempest." He filled me to the breaking point.

A tingling giddiness built up along every nerve fibre inside me, like a tsunami waiting to come crashing down on me. I couldn't stop the overwhelming tide of emotion rolling over me. I was teetering on the edge of oblivion.

With a nip of my neck, Fayolan threw me over. My back

arched, my head flung back, and darkness engulfed my senses. His juices filled me, and he cried out my name as if making a confession and a prayer.

The sound of it alone made my body spasm in delight. "*Fuck*," he groaned as his body shook, remaining inside me. He pulled me towards him. "You did so well, my special girl," he whispered against my ear, making me shiver at the huskiness in his voice.

He cupped my cheek, teasing the dagger from my mouth. His breath grew ragged as he leant in, his tongue delicately licking the blood from the corner of my mouth.

I tilted my head to his ear and purred… "Oh, Daddy… don't stop."

CHAPTER FORTY-FIVE

Fayolan

"Oh, Daddy… don't stop." Tempest's lips grazed my lobe, caressing it with her tongue. My cock was rock hard again. Still buried deep in her hungry cunt. My body shook as the last of my control left me.

With a quick gesture of my hands, the rope binding Tempest vanished. She fell backwards. My cock slipping from her silken depths.

"Stay still for me, and you'll like how this feels." My voice became dark and husky as I fought the beast for control. He rattled against his cage, desperate to fuck her until she could take no more. *She's mine too…*

Tempest chewed on her bottom lip, making me wild. I'd seen nothing so sexy in my life. My cock jerk between her folds. Her breath quickened; her body needed to be touched.

My lips caressed her sweat-salted skin between nips of her tender flesh. I moved my way down to her glistening pussy. I lusted for the taste of her sweet nectar. Her hips tried to buck as my tongue ran sensually through her heat. "I said be still." I held her down.

My teeth nipped at her sensitive nub, making her cry out. She fought the desire to move as I teased her clit with my tongue. She tasted like heaven, and she was addicting. Especially the soft groans that escaped her slightly parted lips.

"Fayolan…" She locked her eyes with mine as she groaned out my name. Her cunt pulsed as she almost orgasmed again.

"Spread your legs so I can taste you." My tongue ran across her opening, teasing her as I added pressure.

I pressed her hips down as she bucked again, my nails leaving indents in her skin. "Don't make me tie you down." My control was already diminishing, and If I bound her, she would be a fucking mess by the time the beast had finished with her.

I nipped harder at her folds. Her hands trembled as my tongue lashed out, pushing into her, turning the pain into pleasure.

A euphoric high swirled through me as she remained still. Only her moans let me know how close she was to orgasming. I released her hip, grabbing her hand and placed it on her clit. "Show me how you like to play with yourself."

Her fingers moving in shy, inexperienced circular motions. My cock pulsed as I watched her pleasure herself. "That's it. Just a little harder."

I pushed my tongue deeper. My hunger for Tempest had my cock throbbing with the need to fuck her as she screamed out my name. The Gods would feel the might of her orgasm. "I want to hear you as you cum."

I searched for the sweet spot within her and grinned as she flung her head back onto the bed. Unable to remain still as I teased it, making her body convulse around my tongue, squirting cum with only one name on her lips.

"Fayolan." Her breath fluttered. Her desperate moans filled the room as she clutched the bedsheets and writhed.

The tantalising taste of her made my senses come alive. I knew that if she ever ran from me, I would follow her to the furthest reaches of the world. And I would fuck her into blissful submission when I found her.

"That's Daddy's good girl." I placed a gentle kiss on her throbbing clit. She panted, still lost in the orgasm. My lips and tongue made their way up her beguilingly seductive figure. She shuddered with pleasure each time my lips touched her velvet skin.

I kissed below her belly button, and her stomach tightened beneath my touch. She stilled her body as it freed her from the intoxicating high. Her breath hitched as my fingers ran up her sides.

One day, I would see how deep her sinful lust ran in her veins. My lips reached her breasts. They were pert, and as I grazed my fangs over one of her nipples, she inhaled sharply.

Her pussy pulsed, begging for release. I used my body to pin her down. "Do you still remember the word, Pet?"

"Yes." She nodded.

"Good. Because I'm going to see how far you're willing to go for me." My hand clasped over her mouth as I bit down sharply.

Her scream was intoxicating. I pressed my teeth into her skin, not hard enough to draw blood, yet still enough to make her cry out. Her hips rolled beneath me as my tongue stroked over her hard nipple, soothing it. I moved to the other, and she gasped as my fangs brushed teasingly over it.

She attempted to wriggle away from me, but I heard her muffled cries of frustration — knowing she could not escape. Her body was a temple of sin and redemption. *It knew its master!*

I bit harder this time, punishing her for moving. "You can

end this if it's too much. If not, then be still." Her nipple was still between my teeth as I pulled back. I muffled another scream. Her pupils constricted as her desire flared to life within their endless depths.

Deep down, I liked it when she rebelled. Just so I could teach her how pleasurable my pain could be. My hand flicked, pulling small clamps from the aether.

I freed her nipple as I worked it in my fingers, hardening it further. "You will learn to do as you're told," I purred as I placed the first clamp on her nipple, tightening it until she hissed.

Just enough for it to teach her a lesson whilst her cunt quivered in anticipation. The perfect blend of pain and pleasure—exactly what she made me feel from the moment I set eyes on her.

I tightened the second clamp. Losing my mind as Tempest's tongue slid along her bottom lip. The little minx knew how to get my blood pumping.

My lips hungrily claimed hers. I'd taken it easier last time to prepare her, but now—I planned on fucking destroying her. Throwing her into a blissful ravine so deep only my touch could bring her to the surface for air.

I caught her gasp on my lips as I pushed into her. My cock buried to the hilt as her needy cunt clamped around it. "Perfect," I soothed as she groaned, embracing the pain of me stretching her to her limits.

I lowered my hips as I pulled out completely. My tongue parted Tempest's lips as I penetrated her again. I was not gentle, and she took what I offered, her back arching as she groaned. Her breasts rising to tease their pert peaks against my chest.

I swept away her sweat-glistening hair from her eyes. I wanted to see her every emotion reflected at me whilst I fucked her deep within her pulsating cunt. Not a hint of objection came as she stared into mine with unwavering determination. *The Gods made her to be fucked by me!*

"Show me how much you want me. Do not cum until I give you permission. Prove to me what a perfect little girl you are." I shot her a dangerous smirk. Her eyes opened wide as I ploughed into her again. "Do you understand?"

"Yes," she panted as she gripped the sheets tighter.

"Yes, *what*?"

"Daddy," she crooned huskily. Her words sent heat searing through me. A groan tore from me as I pounded her sweet pink flesh.

Tempest screamed out as the tidal waves of pleasure slammed into her. Still, she clung to the edge of bliss as she waited—*like a good girl*.

She was so close, but I stopped. Pulling back, I gripped her ankles and dragged her with me as I climbed from the bed. I wrapped her legs loosely around my waist and lifted her hips.

My breaths came out in short, laboured gasps as I whispered, "Tell me what you want, Tempest?" I ploughed into her without warning. This position allowed me to go deeper, hitting the spot that had her body convulsing on the edge of release.

"Fuck me harder," she cried out. Delirium consumed her as she drowned in sensations no man had ever made her feel. She screamed my name as I obliged her. My cock was ready to unload. "Fuck me," she begged as I thrust ravenously.

"Cum with me."

Her back arched. "Oh Gods…*Fayolan*." My name rolled off her lips as she screamed for me. Her juices cascaded over my cock as I filled her. I thrust a couple more times, unloading within her.

I slid out, my cock already hard again, but she could not

take anymore. Even though she licked her lips hungrily. Her body still trembling as she rode out the orgasm.

Carefully, I lowered her to the bed; the blankets rustling beneath her. Her legs shook as she looked at me, ravenous for more. My lips curved into a gentle smile as I descended from the high. "You did an outstanding job for me, Pet. I'm so proud of you."

"Thank you for letting me in. I've never felt so alive. It was amazing."

"It was my pleasure." I turned to the bathroom, filling the bath with hot, steaming water and essential oils.

I scooped her from the bed. The softness of her skin against my palms made my heart race as I laid her in the tub. A hiss left her lips as the water touched her tender, sore flesh.

"Fayolan," she moaned as I lay her head back against the bath.

"It's my time to look after you. Let me clean you," I murmured, and she inhaled the scent of moonflowers as she relaxed. I grabbed a cloth, gently brushing it against her swollen folds. *She would not thank me in the morning.*

I took my time as I washed every inch of her. Worshipping her body as she deserved. No man had touched her skin as I had—Tasted her or buried themselves inside her, which pleased the beast.

Once I washed her, I scooped her up and carried her to the bed. Placing her beneath the covers.

She looked up at the ceiling. Her eyes tracked me as I stood above her. I was unsure whether she wanted me to sleep beside her after that.

"What are you, Death?" she asked wistfully. She moved over and lifted the cover, inviting me to lie with her.

"I don't know." I shrugged. There had never been a creature like me before.

I dropped to the bed beside Tempest. Relishing in the

comforting warmth of her body as she rolled onto her stomach and propped herself up. The multiple orgasms still addling her mind.

"Tell me…" she murmured. "What exactly is your magic?"

I smiled at her wispy tone. My fingers trailed up her spine, which still protruded more than I liked. *Fuck, I'd need to remedy that.*

I chuckled as she shivered under my touch. "I can pull any object from the aether and send it back."

"Can you send anything there?" Waiting for my answer. She inclined her head while gazing at me.

"No. I can only return what I take from it."

"That makes sense," she breathed. "It would be unfair if you could send anything there." I had given her more answers than I offered to most.

"Now sleep, Tempest." I rolled her over, pulling her back against me as I wrapped my legs around her.

She drifted off in my arms. Unaware of just how happy she had made me. She was beyond words.

CHAPTER FORTY-SIX

Fayolan

Tempest remained sleeping soundly as I woke. My cock still rock hard as it pressed against her. The wine left me with a throbbing head and my body ached from fucking her long into the night.

I pressed a delicate kiss on her forehead. She stirred, but her soft snores continued. Slipping silently off the bed, I pulled my leather armour from the aether. I would need the added protection as I took Tempest home.

Even with the display, Braedon had left, ready for our arrival. I'm certain the people would not take kindly to her. The streets of Solis would run red today.

I crept from the room. Trying to adjust my aching cock as I gingerly made my way down the stairs.

"I knew at least one of us would end up with blue balls." Reed smirked as he spotted me. *He was still drunk!*

"You need to sober the fuck up. If Tempest gets hurt, I will remove your cock."

"*Alright*, man. I was only joking." Reed got up from his stool. "Maybe you *should* fuck her properly, and then you can get her out of your system."

"*If* I fuck her or not is none of your *damn* business. I'm pretty sure *my* cock got wetter than yours last night," I spat. Anger causing my shadows to flair out of control.

"Slick." Nix glowered from behind me.

I spun, and the heat of Tempest's glare burned into me as our eyes met. Her cheeks were scarlet with rage as her lips formed a thin line.

"Asshole!" She squinted as her fists clenched at her side.

"I *never* claimed to be a good man. You should not have offered yourself up if *that's* what you expected."

"Maybe it was just the wine speaking." She spun on her heels, heading for the stairs.

"*Don't* walk away from me, Tempest." She raised her fingers into a vulgar gesture as she continued. Nix tried to block my path as I charged for her, but I pushed her aside.

Tempest whimpered as my fingers laced around her neck, and I dragged her back. The sound of her body colliding with the wall echoed in the room. A small squeal slipped from her as the wind fled from her lungs.

The intensity of her glare bore into me; Her face so close to mine it almost brushed against me. "You need to remember your place, Pet."

"That's right… a piece of meat for you to use and discard as you see fit." Her lips trembled. "I'm *your* prisoner." She lifted her chin in defiance.

"That's not what I meant. You belong with me. I told you last night I care about you and if you gave yourself to me, I wouldn't be able to let you go."

"If you *care,* then why would you humiliate me like this? I'm not a whore from your harem. I thought last night meant…" Her words trailed off and her face softened. "You're right, I forgot my place."

I pulled her into my arms as a tear rolled down her cheek. I held her for a brief moment until she pushed away from me.

"Well, that was tense," Wilem quipped. "You went and embarrassed the poor girl. Shame on you Fayolan."

I launched across the bar as Wilem backed up. "I was only joking." My fist collided with his face, sending him flying back into the shelves of liquor behind him.

"Enough, you idiots." Nix leapt gracefully over the bar, placing herself between Wilem and me. "Both of you knuckleheads deserve a fucking beating."

A bang came from the stairs, followed by a scream of anger. I spun to find Tempest and Lilith gone. Forgetting about Wilem, I turned to follow the women.

"Leave *them* be. Let her get it out of her system before you make it any worse. *Dumbass*."

Another bang echoed as something large came crashing down the stairs.

"You're paying for that." Wilem winced as he stood, rubbing his swollen cheek.

"I'm sure your sister is encouraging her," I said, and he smirked with a knowing nod.

"Are you eating before you go?" Wilem tried to change the subject. I sighed with a shake of my head. We didn't have time. I had to get Tempest safely to Solis.

I cringed, feeling the rumble of another crash as it thudded above us. "Add the damage to my tab." My voice was icy as I stared up above.

"Little firecracker, isn't she? Not your normal type, Fayolan."

No, she wasn't. My usual type did not have my rationale revolting. The little she-devil was going to test my patience at every turn. My control was slipping around her.

"Give it here," Nix dropped onto a stool beside me at the bar, holding out her hand as she waited for me to give her mine. I sighed deeply as her gentle magic healed the cuts on my knuckle. "You can't let her get to you like that. You aren't thinking clearly. Your father is looking for your weakness, and you are about to walk her through the front gates."

Nix sighed as she released me and spun back to the bar. "You can't afford to act irrationally. Both your lives depend on you being focused."

"I told you to kill her or free her." Kalen stood in the doorway. Crossing the tavern with a smirk as he saw Wilem's face. "But you let your dick complicate things, and now you can't do either."

"Not now, Kale." Nix scowled.

A low growl formed on Kalen's lips. "You *fucking* did it again?" He sneered, only to glare at Wilem as he threw his head back, laughing.

It's a good job that I trusted the innkeeper's son to keep his mouth shut when it mattered. We both cringed as another crash shook the ceiling.

Kalen looked up in alarm as Tempest's piercing scream echoed through the air. "Is anyone going to check she is okay?" We all spun to face him. He kept his face composed but clenched his fists and set his jaw, showing the rage simmering beneath the surface.

"It's best to let her vent. You don't want her to carry her anger, trust me." Nix was right. Females could be vicious when scorned. And a woman like Tempest... *she had the claws of a gryphon.*

We sat in silence until Lilith appeared with a soft smile and Tempest at her heels. Her head remained down, quietly seething as she sat beside Nix.

"I'm sorry about the mess." She raised her gaze to meet Wilem's. "I'll have to find a way to make it up to you." She'd chosen her hurtful words carefully as she fluttered her lashes, resting her chin seductively on the back of her hand.

"Whatever you are about to say… I suggest you *don't*." I glowered as Wilem smirked at Tempest. The flirtatious retort lodged in his throat. "We're leaving!"

I clutched her arm tight and yanked her from the bar stool. She fell into me, and I leant in closer. My lips lightly grazing against her earlobe. "Do not make me jealous, Pet. I *would* have killed him if he had flirted back. I don't share what belongs to *me*. And even if you hate me right now… You. Are. *Mine*!"

My hand remained around her arm, leading her from the room before she could cause more damage. She did not realise I was only clinging to reason by a thread. My warning to Wilem had been a courtesy to Lilith. Otherwise, I would have killed him without a shred of remorse.

She wrenched her arm away from me. Although I could see her fear, she remained resolute, her eyes narrowing and her lips forming a fierce snarl. *Hellfire and moon flowers, that's what she was!*

I kept pace as she stormed towards the horses. We lacked enough for her to ride alone. I watched with amusement as she counted them, and her gaze drifted over my elites as they trudged behind us.

I gestured to my horse. Tempest gritted her teeth as she stomped over. Before I could help her, she hauled herself onto the saddle…and hissed in pain.

She was still tender from the fucking I had given her last night. The intoxicating sound of her screaming my name still resounded in my head. A siren's call I could not escape.

She froze as I mounted behind her. My embrace secured her as I took the reins.

"Not going to bind me?" she sassed.

"You will have more than just ropes around those slender

wrists of yours once we reach my room," I said huskily, and her back straightened. "You were so beautifully enchanting, wrapped around my cock. Will you sing my name for me, little bird, when I worship your body?"

She swallowed hard, becoming tense as I pulled her back into me. "You didn't deserve what I said this morning. I'm sorry, Tempest. Sometimes Reed brings out the worst in me."

"I shouldn't have flirted with Wilem. I only wanted to make you see how your words hurt me. Gods, I don't know where I *fit* into your world, and it scares me."

"You *are* my world, Pet," I whispered. My words were only for her.

Tempest placed her dainty hand on mine as Lilith moved beside us. Gone were her barmaid dresses; instead, she wore armour as black as mine. Her grey gelding impatiently shifted beneath her.

"You sure you want to come back?" Lilith gave a stern nod. I was certain this morning had reinforced her desire to protect Tempest. I would rest a little easier knowing that Lilith would be there for her.

Tempest wriggled away from me as my erection pressed into her ass. "You did that." My words caressed her ear. Her body rested against me. I was certain it was only because it offered her comfort from the swollen flesh between her legs. Still, I liked the feel of her nestled into me.

CHAPTER FORTY-SEVEN

Solis came into view as we crested a large dune. I straightened my back, stretching to get a better view. A gigantic wall cocooned the circular city. Keeping its residents safe within. I'd seen nothing so magnificent in my life. To think my family once called it home.

The palace stood proudly in the centre. The sunlight reflecting off the tall cylindrical towers. It resembled something out of a fairy tale my mother read me as a child.

The city's streets spiralled throughout Solis, creating a maze stretching from the palace. They were like waves spreading out in all directions.

Though beautiful, the thought of being trapped within the city walls made me nauseous. The recent chaos in Wrossa crossed my mind. *Things hadn't gone so well for me in Stidahl!*

Fayolan slowed our horse as the others continued their

descent to the city below. My heart raced and my palms became clammy.

"Relax." Fayolan pulled me closer. "No one will hurt you with me at your side. I am going to make it abundantly clear that you *are* protected."

"It's like you said, the most beautiful things in Stidahl are the…"

"*I* am the *deadliest* thing in Stidahl." Of that, I had no shadow of doubt. But it was not enough to calm my nerves.

Fayolan's hand snaked up to my chin, tilting my face as his lips brushed mine in a deep and consuming kiss. My fears melted away as he held me safe in his arms. *I wish this moment could last forever.*

"It's time, Pet." Fayolan released me and I nestled into him. Using his body warmth to ease my worries.

We caught up with the others as they slowed in front of the gates. A row of guards was waiting for us as we approached. Their gaze fixated solely on me.

A lump rose in my throat as Fayolan led us forward. The others fell into line behind us.

"Be a good girl and keep your head up." I did as Fayolan asked. Jutting my chin just enough that I looked strong and unafraid. "Perfect. Just like that." A shiver ran through me at his praise.

One guard from the front line stepped forward and removed his helmet. He smiled as he saluted to Fayolan. "Quite the statement you have made," he said, grinning. "Your father threw a fit."

"Good. As long as the message is received *loud* and *clear*." Fayolan pulled me into him.

"It's bold to bring one of her kind here." The man looked over at me as if I was a monster poised, ready to rip him apart.

"You're not scared of a little woman, right, Thursden?"

Fayolan chided. "Since when have you believed everything my father says?"

"I did not say I believed him. I simply meant if you like the woman…." He nodded toward me. "Bringing her into the dragon's lair is not your smartest of moves."

"*Hence* the message." A hint of darkness tainted Fayolan's playful words. "I assume your people will not be a problem? I'd *hate* to leave more of a mess."

"Of course not. I've made sure they understand." Thursden bowed to Fayolan before stepping aside. He swept his arm in a grand gesture towards the open gate. "Welcome home, Dark Prince. The streets are full. Everyone wants to see you and your Nephilim."

He had not lied. People stood lining the street to see the Dark Prince and his monster. Astonished murmurs and sighs erupted as we passed.

I scanned the crowds until I spotted what Fayolan had done. Men and women hung from large wooden posts. I gasped, clasping my hand to my mouth.

I recognised the first man. He had taken me from The Sacred Maple. He stared ahead through lifeless eyes. His head nailed back for everyone to witness.

The next post held the body of the woman whose daughter I had saved. Her spirit stood beneath her wailing as she watched the crowds.

"You killed *all* of them? Anyone that watched as I…."

"I killed the entire village." He cut me off. "And I'll do the same here if anyone comes for you."

I dropped my head, unable to stomach seeing the display of the dead. Fayolan reached around to lift my chin again. "I told you to keep your head up. You want to be a good girl for me, don't you?"

At his words, heat unfurled within me. So, I focused instead on the beautiful, curved buildings that lined the streets. Their walls built out of smooth, sand-coloured stones. Every single one was elegant.

The roads curled around the sweeping circular city. It really was a maze, and I'd never find my way out if I ever ran. But things were different now. I didn't want to escape.

"Kill the monster!" a man shrieked. Something flew towards me, drawing me from my musings. Fayolan's hand flew out and grabbed the rock, his fingers wrapping tightly around it before it hit me.

The man glared at me with spittle building in the corner of his mouth, confirming all my fears. I was not safe here.

"It's going to be okay." Fayolan spoke softly as he signalled toward the man. Braedon materialised with a dagger glinting in his hand. He ran it across the man's neck. Blood gushed to cobblestones beneath his feet.

"You don't need to do this for me."

"This has to happen, Pet. The people have forgotten who I am, and I cannot forgive that. Just keep those beautiful eyes of yours forward." Fayolan gently gripped my chin, forcing my face up. "The streets will run red for you, Little Nephilim."

I stared ahead as others jeered and threw things, only for Braedon to end them without warning. Each time, screams marked their death.

Once Fayolan got fed up with reminding me to keep my head up, he gripped my chin, slightly digging his nails into my skin. "I think my good girl needs a lesson in doing as she's told." His promise of punishment sent a rush of excitement through my body.

I lost count of how many people died as we crossed the city to the golden gates of the palace. *My prison!*

Guards rushed out to form a blockade, and Fayolan reined in his horse. Kalen and the others hopped off, weapons in hand.

Fayolan dismounted, keeping hold of the reins. "Stay on the horse." In true Fayolan fashion, his wings tore from his back.

His shadows surged into an ominous cloud around him. It seemed I was the only one who could see them encompassing his body. No one else reacted as they reached out towards them.

"Stand down, Prince Fayolan. We only want the Nephilim," one man said. His head hit the ground before I even saw Fayolan move.

"She is mine. *I* claim her. Anyone that tries to harm her dies!" Fayolan's anticipation was palpable as he rolled his shoulders.

The crowd surrounding us grew uneasy. Some people returned to the safety of their homes, whilst others nervously watched the prince. A fragile silence fell over them as Fayolan pulled his sword from the scabbard.

One guard stepped forward, followed by another… both armed with vicious looking weapons.

Fayolan moved so fast that his body was a blur as his shadows swarmed the men. The two guards fell to the floor, their heads rolling to a stop at Fayolan's feet. He skewered one on the tip of his sword before stalking towards me. "Chin up and show no fear, Pet."

Fayolan led our horse through the gates. No one dared challenge him as we entered a courtyard filled with soldiers.

The massive gates swung closed, trapping us inside. "Do you really want me to wipe out your *entire* elite guard?" Fayolan sounded bored. His head tilted up towards the balcony of the palace.

"Give me the Nephilim," a deep, gravelly voice echoed through the courtyard.

"Why do you hide in the shadows, *Father*? Are you *afraid* to show yourself?" Fayolan scoffed in amusement. He manoeuvred his sword playfully, keeping his attention trained above as he displayed the head spiked upon its tip.

A man stepped from the shadows. He was muscular with hair almost as black as Fayolan's. He looked powerful, decked in his finery and golden crown.

The man stared at Fayolan, showing no fear as his gaze wandered to me, perusing my body. "You would die for a monster, Son?"

Fayolan laughed scornfully. "We both know there's not enough men *here* to kill me."

"That may be true," his father mused. "However, you can't stop them all from reaching *her*." As one, all the men in the courtyard trained their deadly weapons on me. Archers ran forward, lining the balcony, taking aim.

Oh! Sure! Don't worry, Tempest! No one will hurt you if I'm by your side! I'm so screwed.

Fayolan's eyes darkened. The shadows boiled around him, making the air thick. Even the King seemed to sense it as a look of unease pulled at his stoic features.

Braedon reached out, and Fayolan snatched his hand, appearing on the balcony behind his father. He grabbed him, dragging him back as he leant in and whispered something in his father's ear.

The king paled. "Set down your weapons," he stammered. "The woman has sanctuary within the palace." Whatever Fayolan said, put the fear of the Gods into the King.

Fayolan reappeared beside me, glaring around until every man had set their weapons down. They looked relieved. Even they weren't foolish enough to believe they would not fall if they attacked.

"What did you tell him?" Lilith smirked as she stepped closer. Using her foot to remove the head still spiked on Fayolan's sword.

"I told him she had the Gods' favour because of who her

father is." *So, the King was a religious man.* I made a mental note to remember that.

"And *who* is her father?" Lilith asked eagerly. She loved to gossip.

"Sirus," I answered for him. Lilith threw her head back and laughed.

"You're lucky he hasn't smitten you already, Fayo." Nix grinned, looking over me approvingly.

"Bring her to me!" The King bellowed before disappearing into the shadows.

Fayolan led the horse deeper into the courtyard before setting me down on the ground.

"Lilith with me." He snapped his fingers. "The rest of you know what to do." Taking my hand in his, he escorted me towards the front entrance of the palace.

The staff glared and whispered as we walked by, and the guards sneered. But if they caught Fayolan's eye, they averted their gaze.

Lilith remained at my side, twirling a dagger playfully in her fingers. Her shoulders were tense, but the smile on her face said otherwise. I was grateful to have her here as my protector.

CHAPTER FORTY-EIGHT

Tempest

We stood staring up at the grand palace entrance. "Let's get through this quickly." Fayolan sighed as he dipped his head, placing a tender kiss on mine. "Then I believe it's time for my good little girl to be taught what happens when she fails to do as she's told." His lips quirked up into a dangerous smirk.

"I might enjoy it." I smiled playfully as Fayolan wrapped his arm around my waist, pulling me closer.

"Oh, I *guarantee* you will." His hand trailed down my side. "I love hearing those beautiful noises you make."

"Gods get a room." Lilith smarted off as she grinned. "You should be lucky it isn't Nix here. She'd want to join you."

"I don't think even *I* could manage her kind of *psycho*. Beside I want to keep my fiery little Nephilim all to myself." Fayolan lifted my hand, placing a soft kiss on the back of it.

"Maybe we should just avoid your father and get to you teaching me a lesson."

Fayolan laughed softly, wrapping his fingers around my hand and guiding me towards a brightly lit corridor. "As tempting as it sounds, Pet. It's best we get this over with. The quicker he learns his place, the better. Besides, there's something I want you to see."

I followed Fayolan as he guided me across the worn red carpet that protected the marble from our filthy boots. It carried on up a flight of stairs, spreading out to a large cross section.

"This way." Fayolan led me to a corridor with decorative stone railings and hand carved pillars. It overlooked a terrace filled with dark purple orchids and ornate statues.

"It's beautiful." I stared below, inhaling the musky floral scents as they wafted towards us.

"This garden belonged to my mother. I thought you would love it as much as she did. I'm told she used to spend hours here reading. Although it was much brighter back then. Since she died, my father let everything fall into darkness. He just stopped caring and now the palace is unkept and gloomy. My mother would be disappointed if she could see it now."

My heart ached for Fayolan. I couldn't imagine never having met my mother. Knowing she loved me, but died before I drew my first breath. "I'm sorry. That sounds so sad."

Fayolan smiled, brushing his hand down my hair, running it through his fingers. "Maybe we could plant some moon flowers."

"Really? But don't you want to keep it the same?" Fayolan chuckled, wrapping his arms affectionately around me.

"From what I've been told about my mother, she would

want me to give it to you. Maybe you can brighten it up for her."

"Thank you." I reached my arms up, cupping his face as I brought it down to meet mine. Placing a tender kiss on his lips. "You don't know what this means to me."

A tear welled in my eye, and as it fell, Fayolan brushed it away with the corner of his mouth. "Come on." He stepped back, leading me away from the garden.

We circled around the terrace before climbing a second set of stairs. Each step closer to the King rattled my nerves, making it harder to breathe. I wanted to run. To find a hidden passage where no one would ever discover me. A palace of this magnitude would surely have many secret doors.

Fayolan's grip on my hand tightened as we walked down a long corridor with ceiling high decorated arches. The windows were stained, casting dark coloured shadows.

Sconces lined the walls, with candles flickering in warning as the throne room loomed ahead. With guards standing between each pillar, watching us with emotionless faces.

My chest heaved with trepidation as we rounded a sweeping corner to face a large arched set of wooden doors. Gold inlaid within them depicted vines similar to the ones that ran up my ear cuff.

I stopped dead, staring as I traced a finger over the intricate design. A shock of magic tingled up my arm. "I've seen these before," I muttered.

"How?" Lilith asked, placing her hand on the door as well. She did not react to the magic. *Maybe she couldn't feel it?*

"A spirit showed them to me in a memory." I edged closer to Fayolan, seeking his warmth.

"According to legends, these doors have been here for millennia. A gift from the Gods themselves. They don't wear as wood should, and the gold never dulls. The kings of ages have remodelled the palace more times than I can remember. But they do not replace those doors," Fayolan said as his finger ran over the cuff on my ear. "From your father?"

"No." I sighed heavily as I thought of Morgaan. "The only gift my father gave me was a crib." I turned my gaze to Fayolan. His eyes softened as he witnessed me warring with my emotion. "The Nephilim from my village gave this to me. Her father gifted it to her."

"It's imbued with the same magic as the door." Fayolan smiled as he released the cuff. "Chin up, Tempest. Do not let my father scare you. I will kill him before he harms you." He squeezed my hand one last time as he swung the doors open.

Silence met us as the King's guards surrounded him. Their iron chest plates gleamed in the sunlight, engraved with his sigil, a symbol of his power and authority. He sat straight on a large golden throne, looking down at us from a slightly raised platform.

Fayolan led me forward as we walked through the room. To the three stone steps leading to the podium.

"Bow before your king!" a man bellowed. I jumped as his voice bounced off the walls. I went to lower myself, but Fayolan grabbed me, shaking his head in warning.

"He is not *your* King." I stood, sweat beading on my forehead as Fayolan spread his wings and bowed mockingly. Lilith dropped to her knee but kept her gaze on Fayolan. A slight that made the king scowl.

"Such *disrespect*, son, after the kindness *I* have afforded you." Standing up, Fayolan's father sneered and casually strolled down the steps.

"Do not think for *one* moment that I take your gesture as kindness. You are a *god-fearing* man, and her lineage *scares* you," Fayolan said with a menacing snigger.

"Does it not scare you, Son?" The King did not look at

Fayolan as he moved in on me. Circling me under his scrutinising gaze. Fayolan chuckled again.

"I fear *no-one*. Not even the Gods can kill me, or they would have done it the moment I took my first breath."

"She's small for her kind," the King mused as he continued to circle. He towered over me just like Fayolan, but the king was not nearly as terrifying. He was just a man. "Does she even possess the power of her kind?"

"Does it matter?" Fayolan took a step towards me. My heart raced as I noticed the ripple in his muscles as he trained his eyes on me.

"Her kind *killed* your mother. *Of course*, it matters," the King said, spit flying from his mouth. He halted, sighing as he calmed himself, slipping the mask of indifference back over his face. "She is a pretty little thing. Unlike *that* creature…" His words trailed off in a dramatic silence.

The King shot forward. His arm snaked around my waist as he drew me close. Grimacing, even as his lust filled eyes bore into me. His fingers threaded through my hair as he inspected the blue strands within it.

"Release her before I relieve you of your *head*!" The room's echo amplified Fayolan's deep voice. Guards drew swords at his threat, but the King chuckled as he leant closer. His breath made my skin crawl as it fanned me.

"When my son tires of you. You'll warm my bed. That is the *cost* of your sanctuary." He swept a strand of hair behind my ear. "My son always gets bored with his *whores*."

Fayolan ripped me from his father's clutches with a deadly glare. He encircled his arms around me as he pressed my back into his heaving chest. His muscles twitched as he tensed.

"*Call* her a whore, again," Fayolan baited through gritted teeth.

"I assumed that's what she was. She has the looks for it." The King shrugged indifferently.

"We've had a long journey and I need to clean up, so please excuse us." Fayolan forcefully steered me towards the doors, leaving no doubt it was not a request. "*Oh*, one more thing." He stopped, spinning back to his father. "I have a gift for you." He gave a shrill whistle, and the throne room doors swung open.

Kalen walked in with a sickening grin. A sack hung from his hands. Something inside had soaked it with blood.

I watched as he confidently strode across the marble floor towards the King. He released the sack, and it fell with a dull thud at his feet.

"*Next* time you plot against me, it will be *your*s!" Fayolan sneered as the mutilated head of Palleon fell from the bag. The King's face blanched as he peered down at it.

Lilith got to her feet. She discreetly sheathed the dagger I hadn't noticed her clutching. She followed us as Fayolan led us from the throne room and down another set of stairs to a second set of decorative doors.

Two men dressed in Fayolan's elite guard armour waited outside. They dipped their heads as they opened the door for us. Shock spread across their faces as they noticed me.

Fayolan didn't react as he guided me inside. "No one enters this room. This woman is to be protected with your lives."

The heavy doors clicked shut behind us. I gasped at the beautiful room with a daybed and a large, comfy bench. Cushions lined it adding to the luxury.

Two sets of doors led from the room, and Fayolan swung one open with a smile. "This is yours," he said, and I edged closer to peek inside.

Fayolan had decorated it lavishly with elegant wall sconces and other candles scattered around the room. A writing desk sat nestled beneath a large arched window with a small sill. And a giant fourposter bed sat in the middle of the enormous suite. It looked fit for a king.

"My room is over there." Fayolan pointed to the second door. I stepped towards it, but he pulled me back. "You're not ready for that room yet. If you ever enter there, Pet, know I will ravish your beautiful body as I see fit. I delight in turning your pain into pleasure." His voice darkened. "Once inside, only your safe word will allow you to leave until I am done with you. The locks alone will see to that." I retreated from the door that now appeared ominous.

"*Lilith*," Fayolan barked, his eyes not leaving me. "Wait outside. I have a lesson to teach." I squealed at the dominating rasp in his voice.

His tongue lashed out to lick his lips hungrily. "Get on your knees for me, Pet. You're going to like how good this feels."

CHAPTER FORTY-NINE

Regardless of whether I wanted to, the pure animalistic need in me made my legs quiver and give way. The baritone in Fayolan's voice sent shivers of excitement through my entire body.

"Gods I love the way you look when you're on your knees for me. Wait here, just like that." He crossed to his room, using his shadows to block my view inside.

Curiosity tore at me. I wanted to get to know Fayolan and learn his darkest sins and desires. My body heated as my imagination ran wild with the thought of the dangers lurking in his room.

Fayolan chuckled as he closed the door, three items held in his hands. "This is a taste of what's in there. I will reward good behaviour, Pet. But failing to do as I ask will result in punishments," he promised in a sultry voice.

He looked down at me, his eyes burning with the shadows

he kept locked inside. Desire and arousal poured from them. "Show me what a good girl you are and undress for Daddy."

I stumbled to my feet. My hands tremored with desire as I fumbled with the cords at the front of my gown. I wanted to look down to see what I was doing, but Fayolan's burning gaze locked me in place. *I don't think I could look any less sexy if I tried.*

This god of a man could be about to *fuck* me or *kill* me. I would never know his true intent as my body and mind caved to every dangerous seduction. Yet I never felt as safe around anyone else as I did Fayolan.

The way he praised me as if I was the most valuable thing in his world. Or the promise of punishment, if I was naughty, made me want to both obey and rebel. *Pull yourself together, Tempest.*

Fayolan watched as I sensually ran my fingers under the dress and slipped it off my shoulders, flicking my hips to slow their downward descent. The most beautiful smile formed across his mouth.

"Is this how you like it, Daddy?" Something flickered in his devouring stare, sending heat pooling between my legs.

"You are beyond perfection, Pet. You're so innocent and sexy. Gods I've never seen a creature as alluring as you. Only you have the power to make my cock hard with a single look."

I felt a rush of adrenaline as I stepped out of the dress and freed myself from my underwear. Fayolan's gaze followed the curve of my figure as he finally moved, stalking behind me.

His calloused hand grazed against my slick folds as he explored my body. "Such a good girl. Look how wet you are for me and I haven't even touched you yet."

My breath hitched at his words. A groan escaping as his fingers trailed to my breasts. "Face forward for me." Fayolan gently angled my chin, his hand caressing my neck. "This will teach you to keep your pretty head up."

He lifted a rope collar around my neck. Hovering it in front of my face so I could see it. My heart skipped a beat as I fixated on it.

Three strands of cord secured a long piece of metal in the centre. It had two sharp points at either end, like a miniature pitchfork. "Will you wear this for me?"

"Yes." My voice trembled as the thought alone made my pussy throb.

He placed the sharp points on the base of my throat and the other under my chin. It forced my head up as it dug into my flesh.

Fayolan pulled the rope tight around my neck, securing it in place. It cut off my breath just enough that I could still inhale small amounts of air. "Beautiful," he whispered sweetly to me.

His fingers trailed around the collar as he circled to my front, inspecting his handiwork. Embarrassment rose in me, and I tried to look down. The points dug in, making me hiss.

"Look at me, Tempest." I met his gaze. His eyes held a tenderness as he leant in, his lips brushing mine with a feather-light touch. "Please, don't shy away from me. Do you realise what you do to me?"

The scent of pine and citrus mixed with the sweetness of his kiss as his arms embraced me. I could feel his chest rise and fall with each breath as my breasts pressed against him.

"You make my heart race." Fayolan lifted my hand to his chiselled chest so I could feel it hammering. "Around you, I lose all self-control. I want you so badly it *fucking* hurts."

"I..." The metal dug further into my neck as I attempted to speak.

Fayolan's thumb brushed against my chin, sending warmth through me. He brought it to his lips. My blood smeared across it. His tongue darted out, licking it clean. "I like it when you bleed for me."

My lips parted, and a small, breathy moan escaped. In one swift motion, he scooped me up and placed me on the daybed.

My heart was pounding as he locked my ankles into a set of wooden stocks, leaving me vulnerable to his every whim. With a firm tug, Fayolan tightened the clasps, binding them to the bed with a thick rope.

"Are you ready for more? Be still for me, Pet, and you'll get a reward," he said, sending an excited chill through me.

When Fayolan touched me, I felt a teasing warmth that spread from my leg to the rest of my body. He slowly made his way to the base of the bed. His hands explored the soles of my feet, causing me to squirm with delight. I wanted to watch him, but the collar forced my head back, staring at the ceiling as I waited.

Swish! The cane contacted the tender flesh on the underside of my foot. I gasped at the sharp pain, but as Fayolan's hand caressed my foot, my pussy clenched. The sting melting away into a pool of molten heat between my thighs.

"Gods," I groaned.

"Did that feel nice?" Fayolan rasped. He had no idea of the euphoric feeling it caused. "Shall I do it again?"

"Please, Daddy… I've been a *bad* girl." The sultry husk in my voice shocked even me. Somehow, Fayolan drew the slutty side of me out. I ran my tongue over my lips as if to prove my point.

"How could I say no when you asked so nicely? Now count for me, my naughty little girl." Fayolan slapped the cane across my soles again.

"One," I rasped through dry lips.

"Louder, Tempest." The way my name rolled off his tongue had my pussy quivering.

"One." His touch on my soles was like a balm, easing the ache. I surrendered to the tidal wave of bliss, counting each swish as it came. "Two."

"There's my good little girl," he mused as his hands eased the discomfort. "You're taking your punishment so well."

Swish! "Three." I hungered for the biting crop so he would send me spiralling into the depths of pleasure.

Swish! "Four." *Swish!* "Five." I cried out, my head falling back as my core pulsed with need.

"One more. You've done such a good job enduring for me, Pet. As your reward, I will fill that needy cunt of yours. Would you like that?"

"More than anything, Daddy."

Swish! The cane cut a little deeper this time. Drawing a hiss from my lips as I groaned out his name. "*Fayolan.*"

With each stroke of his fingers on my soles, a delightful shiver ran up my spine. My pussy pulsed as the consuming heat inside of me became unbearable.

"You did so well for me, Tempest. I'm so proud of you." Slowly, he removed the stocks, tossing them aside as he magicked his clothes back into the aether. His virile cock throbbing. Needing me just as much as I did him.

He effortlessly lifted me and lowered us both onto the daybed. Leaning back, I heard him inhale sharply as I hovered precariously over him. His cock rested against my entrance. Becoming slick in my wetness.

My knees met the bed as two fingers pushed inside me. He chuckled as my back arched. Each sweeping movement had my legs shaking as his cock teased me. "What is it you want, Tempest?" He cocked an eyebrow as he pushed in a third finger.

"I want you." My lips trembled.

"Show me how much," he said with a wicked grin as he

removed his hand. Gripping his cock and holding it to my throbbing entrance.

I lowered myself down as he pushed into me. Stretching and filling me with his cock and fingers. His hands gripped my hips as he pushed me lower. My clit rubbed against his body as he buried himself to the hilt. "Gods your body was made for me."

I felt complete with Fayolan inside me, as if he was the part I had never known I was missing. His hands released me as I rocked my hips, eliciting a sensual groan from him.

I fought against my shaking legs to lift myself off his cock before lowering. Slowly at first, as I adjusted to his girth within me. But with each thrust, my clit found pleasure.

I moved faster, rocking my hips so his dick found the spot inside that had me screaming out. Ignoring the blood that trickled down my neck as the collar bit into me.

"Such a *fucking* good girl." Fayolan sat up, lacing his fingers through my hair. He yanked my head back as I slammed onto him, pushing myself as close to him as I could. Greedily consuming every fucking inch he had to give me.

His lips caressed my neck, planting kisses as I built up speed. Finding a rhythm that made his chest heave and pupils dilate.

I grabbed his hand, lowering it to my nub as I held it there, adding to my pleasure as I rode him. "*Oh*, you're *deliciously* slutty today, Pet," Fayolan breathed, staring deep into my eyes as he rubbed his finger through my slick folds.

I released a small moan as he pulled his hand back. "Don't stop."

His fingers were like velvet as they pressed against my mouth, coating it with the taste of my own juices. "Those beautiful lips of yours are made for being kissed by me." He claimed me, muffling my moans. His passion stealing my breath away as he deepened the kiss.

"Open that pretty mouth for me, Pet." I did as Fayolan asked. Letting him push the slick coated fingers inside, closing my lips around them. "I *said* open your *fucking* mouth."

His fingers pressed deep into my throat, making me gag as I rose and fell on his mammoth cock. Fayolan fucked my face with them. A deep primal growl rumbled in his chest as he found my throat, cutting off my air.

"That's it. Just like that." He thrust again, sending my mind spiralling. I breathed in deeply as Fayolan removed his hand. "Keep being my good little girl and soon, I may let you taste me." My pussy clamped around his cock at the thought.

"Thank you, Daddy."

Fayolan grabbed my hips as he pounded into me. I was so full I could not take anymore. Each thrust had me screaming out as an orgasm tore through me. My body convulsed. Only his grip kept me upright. Slamming deep into me again as he unloaded with such force, he roared my name. "*Tempest*!"

Fayolan kept me from fully immersing in the bliss as I swayed. Spinning me around, my hair still gripped in his hand as he leant me forward. I gasped as he ploughed into me from behind.

Each thrust was so forceful his fingers pulled at my hair, leaving a searing pain on my scalp. His other hand made its way to my breasts, pinching a nipple with a slight twist.

"Fuck," I groaned. And he obliged. Pounding me with such force, the world around me shattered into a million shards floating in a sea of euphoria.

I fell apart as he kept thrusting, extending the orgasm that threatened to devour me. My vision darkened as he released inside me again.

"So, *fucking* perfect." Fayolan pulled me into his arms, wrapping his body around me and freeing the collar from my neck. "Did you find it as enjoyable as I did?"

"It was perfect. I never thought I would give control to another living being. Especially not a man. But with you, I feel safe. You build me up instead of tearing me down."

Fayolan smiled, planting a delicate kiss on my forehead. "I know sometimes I can be an asshole. I just never believed I'd find my equal… yet here you are. Feisty, beautiful, and all mine."

Our fingers entwined as he enveloped me in his warm embrace. I could feel his heart racing as I nestled into him. If we could only remain like this forever.

"Fayolan?" I breathed a deep sigh. "Are you my salvation or my downfall?"

"Both." He kissed me again. "I will lift you higher than ever before, whilst taking you to the brink of darkness." His words swam in my rapture-hazed mind. He manoeuvred under me, positioning me at his side.

"Where are you going?"

Fayolan chuckled, rising to his feet. Something dark flickered across his face. "I have a rat to catch. I won't be long. There's a bathing pool just through there. Relax and clean up. But for the love of the Gods, *stay* in this fucking room."

"Aww, but I wanted to wander alone through this strange palace. In a city where pretty much everyone wants me dead." I pouted playfully.

"You're going to be the death of me, Pet. I simply want you to be safe. You mean too much to me to lose you. I don't think I could bear it."

All I could do was watch, speechless, as Fayolan stalked away. His back straight and his shoulders tensed. I missed his warmth already. I craved more of him. Wanting to see inside his soul. To uncover the man hidden beneath the shadows of death.

As he slipped from the room, my legs started moving,

chasing after him. I reached the door when his growl reverberated from outside.

"It smells of sex in there. I thought she wasn't your
whore," his father's voice echoed.

"*Why* are you here?" Fayolan asked. I could not see him,
but the air had thickened with tension.

"Be careful, son. I am still your *king*. I could order you to
take her to my bed."

"You have misunderstood the level that I *feel* for that
woman. And the lengths I'll go to protect her. If you lay one
fucking finger on her, I will *kill* you. We both know you are
only king because *I* allow it." Fayolan's words sent my heart
racing. "Just *fucking* try it and see!"

I jumped back, pushing my naked body against the wall
as the door swung open. Holding my breath as I waited to see
if the King was brave enough to cross Fayolan.

"I didn't *fucking* think so." A growl rumbled from deep in
Fayolan's chest.

The door closed as the King's footsteps faded away. "It
seems we have a rodent problem I must deal with. Nix, watch
Tempest. If he comes near her. *Kill* him!"

"With pleasure," she chimed.

I dashed into the bathing room as soon as she entered.

"*Holy* shit." Nix gasped. *Gods, Fayolan's toys were still
on the floor.* "Are you okay?"

"Just going to take a bath," I called, cheeks flushing.

CHAPTER FIFTY

Fayolan

I watched my father as he skulked away. Tempest thought I did not hear her behind the door as I threatened him. But I knew she was listening. Her clumsy footsteps gave her away.

Part of me hoped my father would cross into our room. Just so I could tear him apart and show her how far I will go to protect her. I never craved the throne, but I would claim it. *For her!*

My soul felt divided, as if my heart and mind were in conflict. Pulling me in opposite directions. I was reluctant to leave Tempest's side with my father trying to get to her. But I couldn't rest knowing her abuser still walked free. I wanted to be the one to chase her nightmares away.

Gods the lengths I would go to spend eternity holding her. But she was safe with Nix, and the beast inside of me rattled against his cage. But I wouldn't let him out… Lacellus was going to die *slowly*.

"Gods give me strength." I stalked away from my quarters, fighting the urge to run back and spread her slender legs, after the way Tempest had ridden me. Her confidence had grown as she took all of me, throwing us both into an orgasm that shattered my soul. *Gods, that woman undid me in all the best ways.*

"Fayolan." Kalen bolted up the stairs towards me. "He's ready." I grinned, rolling my neck, making it crack.

I followed him to the lowest level of the Palace. The part I felt most at home, surrounded by the shadows of death. The wails of the scum down here were music to my ears. Most people would hate it here, but I found solace.

Lacellus was waiting in the part of the dungeon that I kept the most despicable scum. Those depraved individuals I wanted to take my time with. Once I had planned to bring Tempest here, but now the thought repulsed me.

I heard Lacellus before I strolled into his cell. Kalen had chained him to a large cross. Pure fear contorted his face as his focus landed on me. Staring through the same vile eyes that perused an eight-year-old-girl as he tortured her.

I snarled in disgust as his foul stench assaulted me. He'd fucking pissed himself. We hadn't even begun yet.

"Thank the Gods you're here," he cried out. "There is no need for… *this*. There has to be some mistake." His desperation sickened me.

I crossed to a table laden with tools that would break any man's spirit. I hovered my fingers over them as my chest heaved, and I shot him a smirk full of contempt.

"Did the young Nephilim try to convince you to let her go?" I tilted my head. My excitement poured from me in waves. "Did she beg you to stop?" I already knew the answer. I just wanted to see the fear in his eyes when he realised how dire his situation was.

"What *Nephilim*?" His confusion was still ripe.

"The one you found fifteen years ago in No Man's Land. Did she scream when your barbed whip cut into her flesh?"

He gasped as his body shook. He was like his father, all bark, and no bite. "Did you enjoy it? I know how intoxicating her fear is," I said as I lifted a clamp off the table, twirling it in my fingers. "*Well*?" I asked. "Her screams must have been *exhilarating*."

"I would have a hard-on for days if I could hear her now. I bet she is beautiful." He smiled, mistaking the danger in my questions… the trap I had led him into.

Kalen snarled, darting towards Lacellus as he plunged a dagger into his trousers. Cutting them from his body.

Exposing his pathetic, flaccid prick as Kalen gripped his balls. "What are you doing?"

I chuckled as I stalked closer. "Do you know what this place is? It's where I bring *disgusting* pieces of shit like you." I placed a clamp around his balls, tightening them until his eyes rolled.

"Stay with me, *Lacellus*." I winked, slapping his face as I mocked him. Breathing in the delectable scent of excruciating pain and fear.

"She's a *fucking* Nephilim," he hissed through gritted teeth.

"Yes, she is… She's *my* fucking Nephilim." I tilted my head, and Kalen stalked forward, smirking as he grabbed a pear-shaped device.

"I never touched her like that." He whimpered as Kalen stalked behind him.

Grabbing a chair, I placed it backwards, straddling it. Watching Kalen insert the device. Eliciting a scream from the rodent that would curdle most people's blood. But not mine. I relished in it.

I sat back and watched as Kalen had his fun. All of this

was for Tempest, and I wished I could bring her here to witness it. But she wasn't like me and this would horrify her. I would not subject her to it.

Hours passed, and we kept him conscious. Kalen was a master of torture, and Lacellus had already pleaded for death several times.

"If I get out of here, I will fuck her so hard she's *ruined*. I will leave her a bloody mess!" he screamed, trying to bait us into killing him.

"You wouldn't do much damage with that unimpressive *cock*. I doubt she'd even feel it after me filling her." I smirked.

Eventually, I grew bored with his whimpering as we took turns to break the pathetic excuse for a Fae. I left him in Kalen's capable hands as I skulked away.

I'd already left Tempest too long. But I hadn't set foot in the Palace for months. Reluctantly, I turned and headed towards the training ground.

The chants and songs made my heart beat faster as I neared. Jumping over the barriers, I crossed to find Lilith causing hell. The men disapproved of women's presence in the arena. They believed it to be bad luck. *Superstitious bastards*. Little did they know she could best all of them.

"Fucking fight me and find out." She scowled.

"Now, now, Lil. You know there's not one amongst them that would pose a challenge."

She grinned, surveying me as I pulled off my shirt. My muscles rippled with strength. "Finally." She smirked. I grabbed a sword as I watched her circling. She was lithe but agile, and if I let her get close, I was done.

I flexed my wrist, twirling my weapon as I rolled my shoulders. She lunged, two small swords spinning as she ducked and parried.

She'd obviously kept up with her training, but was still no match for me. I defended, throwing out the odd attack to catch her off guard.

"Fucking fight me." She knew I was holding back.

"As you wish." I lunged. Her swords blocked mine, but she missed my elbow as I swung it around, knocking her to the ground.

She beamed as she clambered to her feet, bouncing with excitement as I let her come to me. Men backed away to avoid the steel we both wielded with deadly ferocity.

Sweat ran down my back as she pushed in closer. Challenging me as she let out whatever pent-up anger she had.

"*Fayolan*!" Nix called, and I spun. Lilith collided with me, knocking us both to the ground. I hastily got up, my gaze quickly moving around, attempting to find Tempest.

"Where. Is. She?"

"She ran. Something spooked her, and she bolted." *Fuck!*

My heart hammered as I thought of Tempest being found by my father. I'd been a fucking fool to leave her. I'd been so focused on getting revenge that I screwed up.

Nix took off, and I launched myself over the arena barrier with Lilith at my heels.

I neared our room when I heard her voice, and my heart calmed.

"Do not finish that sentence, Maeve," she hissed. I edged closer to the small passageway that most didn't know existed. I kept to the shadows as my gaze fell on her and the girl she had claimed was from her village.

Tempest's fists balled up at her side as the two stood, faces almost touching.

"You aren't the boss of me, Tempest. Mum and Lily are dead, and it's all your fault!"

A deep guttural growl rumbled my chest. Both of them jumped as they spun to face me. "You are in *big* trouble."

"You fucking *lied* to me!" Tempest's words sliced through my heart.

CHAPTER FIFTY-ONE

Tempest

Nix paced as she grew bored with babysitting me. She hadn't noticed my gaze drifting to the spirit that floated aimlessly behind her. The woman's delicate face and startling beauty were oddly familiar.

Her hair flowed around her, laced with moon flowers. A wave of warmth swept over me as she noticed me staring.

"Come, Little Nephilim," she sang. Her voice was angelic. *"You need to show my son the truth."*

"Leave me alone," I mumbled quietly to myself. I was already worried about Fayolan—I needed nothing else to fret over.

"Excuse me?" Nix frowned, spinning on me. I hadn't meant for her to hear me.

"Sorry. Not you." I tried to smile, but the mystical spirit was floating towards me. She held out her trembling hands, blood dripping from them. This spirit was unlike any I'd ever encountered.

"Please, Nephilim. The tides of war are upon this city, and you can save them all. See the truth and be free."

She reached out. So close I could see the tears that glistened as they ran down her cheeks. I stilled, and the moment she touched me, it drew me from my body into her memories.

Damn spirits! Cramps ripped through my stomach. I was lying on a bed, dying. Blood pooled between my legs, and I cried out as I fought against the pain. A hand landed on my swollen stomach, pressing down as frantic voices discussed my condition.

"You *will* heal her." The King banged his fist. "Bring them in." I looked on with dread as the door swung inward and guards marched into the room with six people between them.

They looked terrified. Three men, two women and a Nephilim child. She must have been only seventeen. "Heal her, or I kill them."

He nodded, and one guard sliced a sword across the first man's throat. I let out a gurgled scream when he hit the ground.

"Galeren. Stop this madness," I pleaded. *Could I be witnessing Fayolan's mother's death? She must have been the spirit that brought me here, to understand how she died.*

"I won't lose you. Fayolan needs his mother," he said. His sorrow splashed across his face.

"Heal her," he commanded, and another man fell.

"I've already told you I'm not strong enough. If the Queen's injuries kill me mid-healing, she dies and maybe the babe, too," the Nephilim explained as tears rolled down her pallid cheeks.

"I don't care. The boy is worth nothing if I lose her," Galeren hissed. Too lost in his grief to care about his own son's life. I shared in his wife's heartbreak.

"Kill the girl," he said, without a flicker of remorse.

"*No!*" I screamed. His wife's pleas fell on deaf ears as a sword hovered above the girl's throat. She cried out, her innocent eyes going wide as she trembled.

"*Okay*," the Nephilim said. Her healing magic flowed into me. It was in vain. The Queen had ruptured, haemorrhaging beyond repair. My eyes grew heavy as the healing began, but I knew the outcome already.

The moment the Nephilim died, the injuries slammed into me with such force my consciousness waned.

"*Kill* them all!" Galeren roared. The queen lost her life to the sound of death. Silence prevailed as the girl's wail cut off, leaving a grim emptiness. The Queen gave up. Praying for her son to die with her, sparing him from this cruel world.

"*He does not know what he is. Show him, Little Nephilim. He is born of death. The first of his kind. Tell him he's not a monster. He is a reaper.*" Her voice faded as I slammed back into my body.

I shrieked as I clambered from the daybed. She was still floating before me. "*Run to Fayolan, Little Nephilim. His father is coming for him now. Tell him to protect Xavier. He will know what that means.*"

I bolted from the room without another moment's hesitation.

"*Tempest!*" Nix gave chase. Fayolan's mother twisted and turned, leading me through several small tunnel-like corridors. Her spiritual glow illuminated my path, guiding me through the darkness.

Nix's voice disappeared. I'd lost her. My heart thundered and my muscles burned as I pushed myself. I had to find Fayolan to save him.

Every breath hurt, but I wouldn't stop. I had a newfound urge to protect him. Not one flickering shadow of doubt lingered in my gut.

I rounded a corner, slamming straight into someone. Shrieks filled the air, and we tumbled to the ground.

"Get *off* me," Maeve said, her brow furrowing as she glared at me.

"Look, it's *her*," another girl squealed. "The Prince's whore." *I was getting sick of people calling me that!*

I staggered up, ready to keep running, but my feet would not move. *Maeve was alive!*

"Maeve." I took a step towards her.

"Get *away* from me." She backed up with a look of disgust that ripped my heart in two. The surrounding girls smirked as Maeve's words cut through me.

"Do you know *it*?" one asked.

Maeve stared at me with hatred, shaking her head in denial. "I've never seen her before."

I huffed as I grabbed her dress, crunching the fabric between my fingers. Pulling her back into the hidden corridor.

"I don't have time for this, Maeve. I *love* you!"

"*Liar*! You *left* me with them."

"I thought you were *dead*. I tried to protect you, but…"

"Go now, Nephilim. Time is running out," Fayolan's mother wailed. Her tears were luminous as the blood stained the ground around her feet.

"Maeve, I have to go, but promise me we can talk," I said.

"I don't *ever* want to see you again. I should have known the Prince's *whore* was the monster I grew up with. Your kind is…."

"Do *not* finish that sentence, Maeve." I stepped closer. Her face was so close to me I could feel her heaving breath mixing with mine.

"You aren't the boss of me, *Tempest*. Mum and Lily are dead, and it's all your *fault*!"

A growl made us both jump as Fayolan stepped from the shadows. At least he was safe for now.

"You're in *big* trouble..." he glared at us both. Maeve squeaked in fear, clasping her hand to her mouth.

"You fucking *lied* to me!" I stepped towards him. "You told me Kalen killed her."

"We will discuss this later." His arms encircled me, drawing me closer.

"You let him *touch* you." Maeve's hurt shone through her no longer soft eyes. "You really are a...."

The air surrounding us thickened as Fayolan pulled me protectively behind him. Shrouding Maeve in his shadows.

"You had better not finish that sentence, Little *Girl.*" Fayolan towered over her.

Maeve scrambled to back up against the cold brick wall. Desperately, she searched for an escape but found only blackness. "You live thanks to Tempest. Because she would have broken if you had died."

Maeve's throat tightened as she looked up at him. Her slender body shook with fear.

"Let her go," I sighed as I reached out and placed my hand tenderly on his arm.

"Go, Maeve." This time, she bolted. Fayolan's darkness receded to allow her to flee.

I turned back to Fayolan. "Thank..."

Fayolan's clothes rustled as his hand shot out, pulling me into his warm embrace. "Please don't *ever* do that again. I was so scared I would lose you." Fayolan's voice was soft as he held me tight. His heart raced, pounding against my ear.

"I'm sorry for worrying you."

My feet swept off the ground as Fayolan lifted me into his arms. His grip remained firm, as if scared I may vanish.

He carried me to his quarters, growling at the guards as

they scurried out of his way. "I'll deal with you later." The men saluted, dropping their heads.

Fayolan lowered onto the bench, placing me gently on his lap. Burying his head in the crook of my neck. His heavy breath caressing my skin. "The night those villagers took you from me… I broke, thinking I'd lost you. I never want to feel like that again."

Tears welled in my eyes as I clung to him. He'd never been so honest about his feelings and it hurt to know I had caused him such pain. I had to tell him why I'd disobeyed him.

"Sorry for leaving, but I had to find you," I sobbed, struggling to find the words. "I know what happened to your mother. *Fayolan*, I know what you are." The words fell from me in a sudden flurry. Fayolan lifted his head, staring at me as he wiped the tears from my cheeks.

"You saw her, didn't you?" I nodded.

"She showed me everything. Your father is ready to act. He wants you dead. Your mother was leading me to you when I bumped into Maeve."

His grip lessened as he pressed me against his heaving chest. While he held me, I could feel his fingertips barely grazing my skin, as if I might shatter with too much pressure. "You need to stop risking your life for me."

"Your mother told me Galeren is coming to kill you. And that you need to protect Xavier. She said you'd know what that means."

My arms wrapped around Fayolan as I nestled into him. I gulped nervously as the words I wanted to hide from him escaped. "I don't want to *lose* you." A stray tear fell to his shoulder as I hid my face in his sinewy neck.

His heart raced, the thud reverberating through my chest as he pressed me against him. "That'll never happen." His hand stroked through my hair, sending a wave of relaxation through my body.

He eased back. His lips kissing away my tears. Warmth radiated from him as we settled on the bench.

I melted into his embrace, feeling the softness of his chest against my cheek. The rhythm of his heart was a soothing melody that calmed my soul. His hand moved across my back in a slow, soothing motion, his eyes fixed on me.

"You look like her," I said wispily as she continued to sing her warnings.

"Is she still here?" he asked, and I gave a nod.

"Apparently, she will not leave me alone until you are safe." I groaned as a small headache sparked in my mind.

"We will sleep tonight, and tomorrow I will take care of my father," he soothed. Hopefully, then she would move on and let me get some peace.

CHAPTER FIFTY-TWO

Tempest

I woke in my bed with powerful arms encasing me. Fayolan's warmth flowed through me as his heady scent comforted me. I had not noticed the subtle hint of fire and brimstone that mixed with the citrus and pine.

Last night I had woken disoriented and panicking until he wrapped his body around me. Offering solace in my fight against the shadows.

In my nightmares, a man I recognised… whose face I would never forget… led a city against me. Whilst the spirits whispered of a weapon made of bone and souls that could kill even the Gods. I shuddered as I pictured it.

The man who had given me my scars fifteen years ago now held the weapon that could kill Fayolan. In my dreams, it devoured my soul as it fed from my despair.

Fayolan clasped me tight within his muscular arms as he drew me near. "Morning, Little Nephilim." His golden eyes transfixed me as his fingertips swept a strand of hair from my face, tucking it behind my ear.

"Morning," I muttered as a familiar melodic voice wafted from the room beside us. "Your *mother* is still here." I groaned as he pressed his soft lips against my neck.

"Then she is in for a shock." His wicked grin had my heart fluttering with dark anticipation. Fayolan was a shadow that hid in the deep recesses of my soul. His kind of pain brought me pleasure I could never have imagined.

"*Stop.*" I brushed my fingers against his cheek to make him look at me. His mother's warning was clear. "Your father is going to act today. He has something that he plans to turn against you." My throat tightened as his body tensed.

"Will you show me what happened? To my mother." I nodded. Part of me wanted to shield him from the pain, but he had the right to know... It was his burden to bear.

"*It's not a memory I wish for you,*" his mother sang as she settled behind him on the bed. Her delicate hand brushed against his cheek. An affectionate gesture I had refused my own mother. Even now, I was not sure I could let her touch me.

"She said she doesn't wish you to see it." I lifted my hand, running it down the spot on his cheek where her wispy hand had been. "But the decision is yours." I lowered my gaze from his.

Sorrow flooded through me. This was a two-pronged gift. If Fayolan saw her death, it would forever haunt him. If he didn't, he'd never discover the truth of my kind. Forever seeing me as a monster. Despite that, I would never force the choice on him. It had to be his, and I would live with it either way.

"Fayolan!" Kalen hammered on the bedroom door.

"This had better be good." Fayolan kissed me again, drawing me into him as his hard cock pressed against me.

"The rodent escaped."

Fayolan cursed as he pulled away. "Get dressed, Pet." He pointed towards a large ornate wardrobe in the corner of my room.

His armour appeared on the bed, and he slipped his trousers on as he called to Kalen. "I'm coming."

He stormed shirtless from the room. I watched the stiffness in his back as he retreated. Fayolan would never admit it. But this situation with his father was weighing heavily on him.

I hurled myself off the bed. My body finally submitting to my commands. Fayolan had filled the wardrobe with elegant gowns, nothing like I would have worn before. Not one dress had sleeves. Most were just a wisp of material. My body was no longer scarred, but the memories were still there.

Fayolan's impatient sigh wafted from the other room. "Just pick *one*."

I covered my eyes and grabbed the nearest dress. It was beautiful, made of a pale blue satin that reminded me of steel. It hugged my body, cascading to the floor around my feet. The back of the dress consisted of a few thin straps with most of my skin exposed.

Golden coils cinched the material at my shoulders. And the tight-fitting dress pushed my rounded breasts up on display. It appeared too elegant for a creature like me. As I slipped into the dress, it moulded to my body, accentuating every curve.

I glimpsed into the mirror, gasping at my reflection. I was a fraud. A commoner dressed as a queen.

"Breathtaking." My head shot up to see Lilith smiling into the mirror behind me.

"It's not me," I grumbled as my eyes dropped to the floor.

"I think it's perfect for you. It shows your station." Lilith beamed as she stepped closer, her hand raising my gaze back to the mirror.

"What station? The Dark Prince's *Whore*... that's what they call me."

"Only because they are jealous." She had a dangerous glint in her eyes.

"My *own* sister said as much. Is that what I am? His whore?"

"Fayolan has never allowed a woman to sleep in his quarters. Or spent the night holding her. He fucks them and leaves. And never here, only in his harems. You are *not* his whore," she stated firmly as she took my hand. Jolting me as she dragged me towards the bedroom door.

I dug my heels in. Anxiety spiked in me, yet Lilith was steadfast as she yanked me out of the room behind her. She propelled me on, the door shutting with a reverberating thud, preventing me from bolting.

"Wow!" Nix's face lit up with a wide, beaming grin when she saw me. She let out a sultry whistle, her eyes like shards of ice as they scanned my body.

An eerie silence descended as the group focused on me. But none so much as Fayolan. His gaze lingered on me, taking in each detail as though he were memorising it. The corners of his mouth twitched as a mischievous smile crossed his lips.

"Haven't you all got more *important* things to do than make the poor girl uncomfortable?" Lilith shot them a stern look.

"Oh, I can think of a few things," Fayolan whispered, pulling me into his side. "Did you deliberately dress so deliciously sexy for me?" My cheeks flushed, even knowing the others could not hear his sultry words. "I am going to have fun undressing you later, Pet."

"Promises, promises." I smirked, nestling into him. He planted a kiss atop my head before turning towards the others.

"We know my father plans to move today. The fact that he freed Lacellus is all the proof of his betrayal that we need." Fayolan's hands tremored with barely controlled rage. "No doubt he plans to exploit Tempest to reach me." I shuddered at his words. Fayolan now had a weakness. I hated myself for it.

"I say we find him now and end him." Nix spoke as if she were bored. She stared at her nails as she yawned.

"I won't leave Tempest unprotected." Fayolan glanced at me.

"I think you should." My mouth moved before I engaged my brain. "Splitting you from your elites is probably what your father is hoping to do." I met Fayolan's gaze, gripping his hand tightly in mine. "Go fight him, and I will stay here. You have guards on the door, and I am not completely defenceless."

"We should leave her with Lilith and several guards outside. We've seen Tempest's more than capable with a bow," Kalen added.

"If you stay here, you aim at that door, and if it opens without us announcing ourselves, you *fire*," Fayolan said with a deep rasp.

"What if I accidentally shoot one of you?"

Fayolan scowled towards his elites. "If we come in without announcing ourselves, we *deserve* that arrow."

Fayolan flicked his hand, smoke coating it while extending to reveal a large ornate bow. He watched me as I stood up, resting it in my palms. Testing its weight, pulling the strings to feel their tension.

"I will wait with you. I *am* your shield," Lilith said as she gripped the dagger sheathed at her side.

"The King has a sword of bone and souls," Fayolan's mother sang. *"A weapon strong enough to end even a creature of death."* The image of the sword from my nightmares stole through my mind. *She had made me see it!*

"No." They all turned to face me. "The King has a weapon to use against you. Lilith should be there with you." My hands trembled even when Fayolan held them a little tighter. "He has a sword capable of killing you."

"Have you not realised, Little Nephilim… *nothing* can kill me. That is my curse." Fayolan smirked. I froze. All the times I had saved his life, he had known he would not die. Yet Kalen's fear had been real back at the lake when I healed Fayolan.

"But…"

"This lot worry that one day something will kill me." Fayolan grinned, shooting a pointed look at Kalen, who shrugged with a roll of his eyes.

"This sword can kill even *Death."* I stood my ground. "I've seen it. Last night in my dreams." I held my head high as I watched Fayolan. "This weapon *can* kill you!" His eyes penetrated mine as he nodded, accepting my fear.

"It explains why your father has suddenly grown some balls." Reed glowered.

"He let me think he was after Tempest, so I would run in with only half my elite guard." A deep rumble vibrated Fayolan's chest as he spoke.

"And if we're mistaken, and he *is* after her?" Lilith played the advocate.

"Then I hold my own until you return," I said, lifting the bow in a demonstration. "If I have to hide… I will." I glanced to the hidden bathing room.

"Regardless, Lilith stays here. If I'm worrying about you, I won't be focused on fighting." Fayolan stroked my cheek.

He leant in, kissing me one last time. *Why did it seem like a goodbye?*

I took position with my bow as they filed out. My hands gripped the ornate wooden shaft. I remained poised before the door. Please come back to me… *Death!*

CHAPTER FIFTY-THREE

Fayolan

The click of the door had a shudder running down my spine. Doubt coursed through me, even knowing Lilith would be there to watch over Tempest.

"If *anything* happens to me… Get. Her. Out!" My chest filled with a low, resonating rumble. "Take her away to somewhere safe and protect her. *Swear* to me that if I give you the order to leave me. You'll do it."

"We can't do that. We all swore to fight to the death at your side." Reed clasped his arm across his chest.

"It's not a request. As your Prince and soon to be king, I order it. My father will track her to the farthest corners of this world. You are the *only* ones I can trust to keep her safe."

"Then you'd better not die on us." Nix grinned.

"I have no intention of letting my father win." I hated the fear that rose inside of me. Not for me, but for the intoxicating siren behind the door. My chest ached to stay with her. My mind was unfocused as I stepped away.

Braedon returned with eight more guards. Their weapons clanking against their armour as they marched in to protect the room that held my most precious and alluring treasure.

I'd never been so sure about anyone as I was the tiny Nephilim. Tempest was my world and even now heading to war. My cock hardened at the thought of her and the beautiful sounds she made as she gave control to me. Allowing me to worship her, drowning the temptress in tantalising pleasure.

"Get your head on straight, *damn it*!" Nix clipped my head to make a point. "You want to keep her alive, then *fucking* concentrate."

I bared my fangs with a nod as I slammed the barriers of my mind up, blocking out all thoughts of Tempest. Rolling my shoulders, I centred myself. My twin soul-devouring swords appeared in my hands as I stalked down the corridor.

I could scent the tang of iron and steel, mixing with sweat as we headed towards my father's throne room. We neared the stairs, and I snarled. The blood-curdling sound drew the attention of the men who stood waiting. Blocking my way.

"When will your father learn his men are no match for us?" Reed grinned as he swung his scimitar lazily. *Blood-thirsty brute!*

A deadly grin spread across my lips. I strolled forward. This would be over so quick, the thought bored me. The stench of fear assaulted us. My father's men were mere children compared to us. He lacked the strength to command them, as I did my armies.

My elites spread out. I flexed my arms, limbering up my muscled body. My feet adjusted, and I lifted my swords, ready.

"Kill them *all*!" I bellowed. My elites ran forward, their weapons swinging in controlled formations. Every movement was precise and echoed through the room with sharp clarity. We'd fought side by side countless times, and the sweeping staircase was little more than a hindrance.

My heart hummed in time with my swords as they sliced through flesh, meeting no resistance as they found gaps in the heavy steel armour. My father's second mistake. Men wearing such restricting gear trying to fight in a cramped space. *Easy pickings.*

My shadows swelled as we manoeuvred over the fallen corpses. A well-refined unit, using our swords and momentum to heft our kills behind us. I glanced back, expecting an attack from the rear, but only an ever-growing pile of bodies flanked us.

"Something is off," Nix said, cleaving a path up the stairs. Blood splattered her face like war paint. Her eyes twinkled with murderous intent as she slashed and lunged. The moment steel clanked behind us, and I felt easier.

"Braedon, watch our backs," I commanded, and he peeled away, stopping my father's men advancing up the stairs. My breath was steady, my swing strong as I cleaved through the men.

Sweat dripped down my spine as I pushed on. Finally, breaching the stairs. My wings spread, and I charged. Talons ripping at flesh. Swords slicing gratingly into bone. My muscles roared as I closed in on the throne room doors.

A fist slammed into my cheek, sending me reeling backwards. I had not seen it coming. I dodged a second swing, bringing my sword up and slicing it across the man's stomach. His body crumbled, the life slipping from his eyes as they glazed over. I strutted over his body, spitting on him as I redirected my attention to the throne room door.

"Anyone else think this was too easy?" Kalen stepped beside me. I cracked my knuckles as I stormed forward.

My fingers gripped the gold-inlaid doors, shoving them open with no resistance. *The room was fucking empty.*

"*Tempest!*" Time slowed as I realised what a fucking idiot I'd been. Having a sword that could kill me was only effective if you could get close enough to use it. My father needed Tempest to lure me into a trap.

I launched into the air with one powerful beat of my wings. Gripping Nix's wrist, hauling her with me as I went. Braedon grabbed Reed and Kalen as he displaced.

The stench of blood filled the corridor, and I knew my men were dead before I saw their mangled corpses. I was too late.

Kalen kicked the doors open, and I roared as I took in the destruction. Tempest and Lilith had put up a fight.

Four men lay dead, with arrows embedded deep in their bodies. Another three had every bone in their body broken. Lilith had unleashed her magic, and it'd still not been enough. She lay unconscious with a dagger protruding from her abdomen.

"She's alive," Nix confirmed. "Hang on a little longer, Lil." We all knew she'd want us to find Tempest. It was deemed a dishonour for a shield to outlive the person they swore to protect.

The door to my bedroom lay splintered on the ground, smashed in, and the scent of Tempest's blood wafted from within.

"There isn't enough to be fatal. The King wants her alive." Kalen banged his fist against the wall as he snarled.

"He's taken her to his room." I didn't need to track him to know he'd made good on his threat.

Braedon reached out, and we linked hands, appearing almost instantly at my father's chambers. Tempest's wild screams clawed at my heart. My mind became feral as I merged with the beast that dwelled within me.

Claws burst through the flesh of my fingers. The pain was nothing more than a mere tingle in my insatiable rage. My fangs elongated and sharpened, becoming almost canine.

As my wings grew, my back rippled with the power of their movements. Their talons sharpened to a deadly point. Even the soft black feathers hardened, becoming like steel blades.

"Stay the *fuck* back." Without hesitation, my elites stepped aside. I faced around thirty men standing between me and Tempest's desperate screams.

I could scent the fear dripping off the soldiers waiting for death to claim them. There would be no chance for them. No offer for them to leave unharmed.

A sword scraped across my side, but my body felt no pain. An animalistic sound rumbled through me into the ground, making it tremble beneath my feet.

The world dimmed. I was a predator, and my prey was falling at my feet. My wings cleaved through armour like silk. The metallic tang of blood excited the beast as I let him out to play.

I could not release his magic to kill them all in one go for fear of hurting Tempest and my elites. The beast didn't want me to either. He wanted to maim and slaughter with his bare hands.

I tossed my swords down, letting him have his wish as we moved closer to Tempest. Each muffled scream had my blood roaring in my ears until I could hear nothing else.

Mutilated bodies lay at my feet as I stalked towards my father's quarters. One man remained standing between me and those doors. I closed in on him. Blood dripped from my claws as I leant closer. His body trembled as he backed into a wall.

"*Open* them." I snarled like some half-crazed beast. He trembled as he shook his head. I laughed, a wicked bone-chilling sound as I lifted a claw. Raking it down his cheek as the blood smeared down his face. "*Now!*"

He spun, rapping on the door as if his life depended on it. The fool was dead anyway, but the beast liked them to have hope before he pounced.

"It's done." His voice trembled, but he knocked harder. "Open up."

"King's orders. They remain closed until he's finished." Again, I chuckled as my hand shot out. The guard's head thudded to the floor.

My claws dug into the doors as I dragged them through the hardwood. The sound echoed through the halls and I could hear men panicking on the other side.

"Open. The. Door. Or I *kill* you, and hunt down your families," I said in a voice that wasn't mine. One so deep the Gods themselves would fear it. "One…" I counted as I listened to their panicked voices. "Two…" They moved towards the door. "Three…"

The heavy wooden barricade groaned, and the doors swung inward. I strolled through with a smirk that had the men running.

Tempest's screams stopped. Fear coursed through me at the silence, and I nodded for my elites to finish the men.

Without a sound, they spread out to cover more ground. Disposing of them as I stalked across the living quarter. I could hear my father's voice coming from the other side. *No trace of panic sounded in his voice… he did not realise I was here. How poetic that he would not see me coming.*

I eased open the door. Not a creak sounded as my father ranted at Tempest. His back was to me, hiding her from view.

Five men surrounded Tempest, and no one noticed me. Their attention was on the small hands and feet stretched wide and bound to the four-bed posts.

"By the time he finds you, I will have broken your frail

body and simple mind. His affection for you will be his undo-ing," my father gloated, and I struck.

No regret... No grief... just blinding rage and hatred. My wing protruded from his chest. His heart still beating as it hovered before him. I never wanted the throne, but I'll take it for *her*!

CHAPTER FIFTY-FOUR

The chilling clash of metal made my blood run cold. *Had Fayolan fallen?* My chest heaved, the aching pain in my heart intensifying. I rolled my fingers as they tightened around the bow. An arrow notched and ready as I took deep breaths, pushing aside my worry for Fayolan. My arms strained as I struggled against the tremble that tried to consume me.

"Are you ready? We take as many of these mother fuckers down with us." Lilith scowled towards the doors.

"You got it." I took a slow breath. Closing my eyes momentarily as I centred myself. *Fayolan was alive. I could feel it. Now I had to survive for him.*

The door creaked open, and my first arrow whizzed towards it. A man grunted as he fell to the ground. Magic sizzled in the air as Lilith blasted a second soldier. His body broke and contorted. Each snap caused vomit to rise in my throat.

I grabbed a second arrow, taking a sharp inhale as I sent it towards another of the king's men.

"Run, Tempest." Lilith sent another blast of magic towards the soldiers, but there were just too many of them.

With each defeat, the next man inched closer to us. I shot off two more arrows, but despite my efforts, they didn't make a difference.

"Go now!" Lilith shoved me back. Placing herself between me and the king's guard. *Fuck!* I cursed under my breath, realising I had nowhere to hide. The men would see wherever I fled.

Fayolan's words replayed in my thoughts. *Once you enter that room, there will be no escape!* My legs started moving, and the bow clattered to the floor with a deafening thud. I slammed into Fayolan's bedroom door hard. Praying it would open.

As it gave way, I stumbled forward. "Come on, Lilith." I spun just in time to see her fall. A dagger piercing her abdomen. *No!*

"Close that *fucking* door," Lilith commanded, as she let out one last blast of magic. She was beyond my help, and I felt powerless.

I slammed the door with a loud bang, silencing the men's yells. Tears burned in my eyes as I frantically searched for locks. *I failed Lilith. Running instead of standing and fighting at her side.*

My fingers wrapped around a steel latch, feeling its cool surface as I clicked it shut. I located three more locks, their mechanisms creaking as I slid them closed.

Something rammed into the door, and I stumbled as it trembled beneath the force. I shuffled back until I tripped over something behind me. Catching myself, I spun, taking in the room.

Wooden panels adorned the walls, and multiple devices

and instruments were hanging from them. There were gags…
so many that my throat tightened as I swallowed. Some filled
your mouth and others held it open.

Clamps of varying sizes hung together. Some had weights
attached and other's chains. Some even looked big enough to
place a whole-body part inside.

Sharp instruments littered the area. Items that resembled
cocks. Large shiny hooks with balls of varying sizes and
shapes at the end. Whips of every kind that made me shudder.
This place looked like a torture chamber.

Fayolan's bed was a four-poster with a cage beneath it.
An enormous wooden cross with shackles attached loomed in
the corner. Along with other items of furniture that made me
shudder again. Racks and stands and things I had no words to
describe.

He's going to destroy me in here. Yet the now familiar
ache between my thighs returned. I wanted to let Fayolan
bring me to his room. His kind of pleasure and pain had me
weak at the knees.

Another thud drew me back to my senses. Sharp decorative knives hung from another wall. I grabbed two, gripping
them tight as I waited. Each time the door flexed and creaked,
my blood roared.

The first lock came undone with a clatter, falling to the
ground before me. I shivered uneasily. My palms became
clammy with sweat.

With a thunderous crack, the door flew open; the hinges
breaking as it fell inward. I dived back. The ground shuddered beneath me as it thudded to the floor where I had just
stood.

Grim, snarling faces flicked between me and the knives
clutched in my trembling hands. The men's snarls softened to
grins when they realised I was not a trained warrior.

I raised the daggers, sweat pouring off my face in an attempt to shroud my terror.

Every creaking step reverberated as they crossed the threshold, making my jaw tighten. I tilted my chin up as I parted my legs, steadying them. I darted forward, using the surprise attack to slice at the nearest man.

He anticipated my onslaught, and his fist swung out as I advanced. An intense pain surged through my nose as the impact of his punch caused me to crash to the floor. Blood pooled around me as a calloused hand tightened around my ankles, and a body pressed me down.

I heard them laughing as they used rope to bind my wrists and pull me towards them. Their touch on my skin was like fire, and I screamed and twisted away from them in agony.

"Stop the bleeding," a familiar voice snarled. I froze in terror. He's the man whose face haunted my nightmares since I was eight years old.

"Sorry, Lacellus. The *bitch* was trying to cut me up." *Lacellus! He's the man Fayolan's been after.*

"The King wants to fuck her pretty little cunt. He won't appreciate her blood staining his bed… not until he draws it." His salacious words made my stomach churn.

They shoved a shirt to my nose as they yanked me upright with a force that jarred my body. The five colossal men converged on me as they tugged me from Fayolan's room.

I endeavoured to stand my ground, but a hand seized my hair as Lacellus hauled me into his sinewy body. "Once he is done with you, *Nephilim*," he spat the word. "The King has vowed to give me whatever remains of you."

A wave of nausea coursed through my body as I uttered a plaintive cry, my memories flooding my mind. With his iron grip tightening in my hair, he dragged me along as I fought to keep my feet on the ground.

"*Lilith!*" I struggled against his hold on me. Her body lay crumpled on the ground, but she was still breathing. *Just!*

"Shut up and keep moving." Lacellus yanked at my hair again, forcing me deeper into the palace.

"Fayolan is going to kill you!" I strove to remain steadfast, despite my soul being sapped of courage. His only answer was a dark, mirthless chuckle.

We reached a large door with guards standing outside. Their suggestive grins lingered on my skin as they parted to let us pass.

Lacellus halted me as he ordered the shirt removed from my nose. The bleeding had stopped, and he grabbed my chin, tilting my face to check the damage.

He directed a cold, intimidating glare at the man who had punched my face. "You're fortunate it's not broken."

A second set of doors stood open, and I struggled against Lacellus as he pulled me towards them. The smell of incense and sex assaulted me as we neared. "Behave, and you might survive him," he said into my ear as he shoved me into the large, darkly decorated room.

The King sat on the edge of his four-poster bed, its black worn silk curtains billowed in the breeze. Galeren's piercing gaze swept over me as his men advanced.

The ripping sound of my dress being torn from me had me stiffening as they exposed my naked body. The King's eyes were like a weight on me as I heard the slithering sound of his tongue on his lips.

"Did she put up much of a fight?" Galeren asked.

"She took out a few men, but we overpowered her easily once we delt with the lesser Fae witch." Lacellus smirked as he shoved me closer towards the King. "She's a feisty one, though, so watch yourself."

I tightly pressed my lips together, hardening my expression as Galeren sauntered to his feet. Each slow step closing the gap between us had my mind screaming. I tried to fight against Lacellus' iron-clad grip.

"For a monster, you are intoxicating." Galeren reached out, running his fingers through my hair, casting a shadow over me. "So small and frail." He leant over me, his breath brushing against my face.

"*Fuck* you!" My head swung forward, catching his chin with a crack. His hand shot out, wrapping around my throat as he lowered his mouth to mine. The foul scent of liquor suffocated me as he bit into my lip.

"Secure her." He released me, shoving me towards the bed.

Lacellus and the other men grabbed me, their grips unrelenting, as I cried out and twisted. I screamed from the depths of my throat as they slammed me onto the mattress.

"I see why my *delinquent* son likes you." Galeren watched with a smug smirk as I lay in front of him. The rope cut my skin as I struggled to get free.

"Fayolan will have your head for this," I spat, as Lacellus stepped aside. Backing off so the king could move closer.

"I would not worry about my *son* when you're tied to *my* bed." His hands snaked out, drawing a scream of pain as he gripped my feet before running up my legs. "I'll enjoy taking my time with you. I'm going to hurt you, and I will fuck that sweet cunt of yours until I have destroyed it. Your mind will be in pieces by the time I'm done with you."

"I don't care what you do to me. As long as Fayolan lives, I'll survive this." I knew it with all of my heart. Fayolan would piece me back together if the king broke me.

"We'll see how tough you are once I'm having fun with you." Galeren climbed onto the bed, his clothes rubbing against me as he pressed his bulge into my stomach. "Does it feel good against your tender flesh? Or is it just my beast of a son that gets your cunt wet?"

He rotated his hips, grinding between my legs as his hands snaked into my hair. He gripped it tight as he pinned my head against the bed.

"You don't live up to your son." I spat in his face. Galeren let out a thunderous roar as he raised off me and smashed his fists into my gut and ribs. A beating was preferable to what he had planned for me. I just needed to hang on for Fayolan.

"My son is a *fucking* disappointment. You will learn it soon enough." He inclined his head, his teeth sinking into my skin, making me cry out as I wrestled to pull away. "You taste delicious."

"My father will make you pay for this," I screamed as he bit into my flesh again.

"I went to great lengths to procure you. The Gods have blessed me and they will not stop me from taking your wretched body as I see fit."

Galeren smirked, my blood dribbling from his mouth as he lowered to my breast, sinking his sharp teeth into me. "Fayolan will fall apart when he sees what I have done to you, and then I will strike him down." He claimed the other breast before biting into my side.

"Fayolan will not *fall* to you. He is a *reaper*." I screamed as Galeren bit me again. Groaning grotesquely as he tasted me, his tongue running over the teeth marks. His head trailed lower, biting his way to my inner thighs. The louder I wailed, the more thrilled he became.

"He may be a reaper, but I have the one sword that can kill the unkillable." His eyes darted to Lacellus, who uncovered a blade made of bone. Shadows slithered over it. The cries of the damned souls attached to it made my ears throb.

"Not so cocky now, are you? All I needed was to wait for something that Fayolan cared enough about to get within striking distance. Then you unwittingly played into my hands. All of this is on you."

Galeren cackled as he drew back, smearing the crimson from his lips as he stood up. His ravenous eyes assessed the bites that littered my body. As if I were a piece of art he had created.

"You're foolish to think this will work. Fayolan will destroy the world to get to me. Do you really think you stand a chance against his rage?" *He'd told me as much himself.*

"I know my *son*… he will come charging in here thinking he is indestructible. That's when we will catch him off guard."

Galeren's fingers deftly worked the buttons on his chest, before he tossed the shirt aside and fumbled with his belt. I screamed as I thrashed around, desperately trying to loosen the ropes that kept me captive.

Galeren lowered his trousers, gripping his hardened cock. Licking his lower lip as he admired the bites on my thighs and my exposed pussy.

I sealed my eyes shut, but could not block out the sound of his grunts as he jerked himself off. My skin crawled, and I tried to swallow the fear and nausea swirling in my stomach. *Fayolan would come…*

"*Watch* me," Galeren ordered, and I opened my eyes. My face twisted into a scowl as I forced the angry words that lingered on my tongue back down my throat. "Tighten the ropes and secure her head."

Lacellus smirked, straddling my waist as he wrapped some cord around my neck, pulling it tight. My cries subsided as I strained to draw breath. With a firm yank, he fastened the rope to the bedpost behind me and secured it.

Galeren's icy fingers grazed my skin. I jerked my head away, and the rope cut off my air. "Stay still, Nephilim." He gripped my face, making me meet his gaze. "I wouldn't want you to miss out on our fun."

"*Fuck you!*"

Lacellus's hand grasped my breast, his nails piercing my flesh as he seethed. His face contorted with fury, turning a deep crimson. "Stupid slut. Show your king some respect."

"*My* king isn't here," I rasped as the rope constricted my throat. "Fayolan's the *only* man I recognise as such."

Galeren slapped his hand across my face. "Gag the stupid *whore*."

"It's time you felt a real cock in your cunt. You'll scream my name as your *king* once I am done with you." He struck me again.

Lacellus hastened to tie a cloth around my mouth, the fabric rough against my lips. Before clambering off me as Galeren drew nearer. A pearl of cum already slipping from his rancid cock.

Galeren watched me struggle with an amused smirk, and my throat constricted as I tried to scream. "By the time he finds you, I will have broken your frail body and simple mind. His affection for you will be his undoing."

Blood splattered my face, and my eyes opened wide as a taloned wing burst through his chest. I stared in shock as his heart persisted to beat outside his body. *Fayolan had come.*

The nearby men leapt into action. Four of them drew swords, stalking towards Fayolan. Whilst Lacellus sprinted to me, his eyes wild with urgency. A knife cut through the rope as he hauled me from the bed.

"*Move.*" A sharp point dug into me as he dragged me back to a wooden door hidden behind a tapestry.

I glanced at Fayolan as he fought, the sound of clashing swords ringing in my ears as his muscles rippled beneath his leather armour. He was so lost in the fight that he hadn't noticed me being dragged away into the darkness.

CHAPTER FIFTY-FIVE

Lacellus hauled me through the wooden door. As he silenced me, pressing his hand over my mouth, the dagger continued to nick my side. "Stay quiet."

The door softly clicked behind us, blocking out any light. Whilst an icy breeze whipped against my broken, naked body, sending a chill through me.

I strained my eyes, but I couldn't make out anything in the darkness. Shoved forward by Lacellus as he fumbled through the pitch black, I bounced off a rough stone wall.

"Fayolan's pet fire mage won't be able to track us in the dark. I just need enough time to get you into position. *You're going to help me lure him in.*" *As if I would ever betray Fayolan. Especially for Lacellus.*

He slammed me forward again, and I crashed into another wall. The gag in my mouth muffling my cry as the force made my eyes water.

"This way." Lacellus jerked me to the side, finding

another corridor. There's no chance I'd remember my way out of this dark maze. "The King showed me this place. He said it was where he planned on keeping you. But I made sure it has everything we'll need."

Lacellus's breath was icy as it fanned around my neck, making my hair stand on end. "We're almost there." He shoved me down yet another pitch-black corridor. It unfurled into a cold room with no sunlight. Only a few sconces lighting the room.

Lacellus slammed me against a wooden cross, ripping the gag from my mouth. The point of his knife dug into my side as I thrashed and kicked in my desperation to escape.

"The more you fight me, the worse this will be for you. And *trust* me when I say it's *already* going to be bad." He locked manacles around my wrist. Using the rope still wound around my neck to secure my head up, forcing me to face him.

"It's not too late to let me go. You could run and get a head start. Because we *both* know Fayolan is coming for you." I could not help the chuckle that escaped me. "He knows what you did to me fifteen years ago." Even when we still hated each other, Fayolan had gone after Lacellus... *for me.*

"Oh, I'm *counting* on him charging in. So lost in his rage that I can get the drop on him." Lacellus smirked, crossing to a large wooden chest nestled within the shadows, cast by the flickering sconces.

"He's not a fool."

Lacellus laughed as he turned to me. "Fayolan taught me a few things in his little torture room. He *proudly* showed off his favourite toys and demonstrated their use with a *smile*. I wonder if he will react the same when I use them on you? I warned him what I would do if I got my hands on you, so don't tell me he isn't a fool."

A hand sized metal object scraped against the chest as he lifted it before me, making me shudder. It had a curved shape, similar to that of a pear. His eyes lit up as he crossed the room, his fingers reaching out as he ran them between my legs.

"I would say this won't hurt. But I intend to ensure it does."

"You *bastard*," I cried out, trying to wiggle away, but he was fast, pushing the object inside me. Pain erupted between my legs as he forced it deeper.

Lacellus twisted the bottom of the device, and it expanded. Each turn made it feel like he was ripping me apart inside, stretching me until my screams stopped and my vision darkened.

He released it as he stepped back, admiring his work. "I see the satisfaction." The vile look of delight etched on his face made my stomach turn.

Tears ran down my cheeks, mixing with the dust from the ground as he searched for another item. "You're a *fucking* monster."

Lacellus bared his teeth as he bolted towards me, digging his nails into my cheeks. His face almost touching mine. "*No*. That's where you're mistaken. Fayolan is the monster. He's a sick sadistic prick and this world will be far better off without him in it."

He lifted a metal clamp with a menacing grin. I tried again to evade him, but the pear-shaped device inside of me sent waves of pain through my body, immobilising me. I sobbed as he gripped my breasts, sliding them within the pinching grip of the clamp.

The sound of his sneering laughter was unbearable as he wound it tighter. My breasts roared with pain, and my legs buckled beneath me. My body trembled as I grappled to stay upright.

"Fucking *bastard*," I cried out.

"You should never have run from me all those years ago, Tempest. Now you will be Fayolan's downfall. But don't worry. I'll look after you once he's gone."

I felt sick as he slid the sword from the cloth he had shrouded it in. "Where did you even get that?"

"That's not important, *Nephilim*. Fayolan *will* track you down, so we have little time. When he finds you like *this*... I will strike. And since he *took* care of his father... I'll claim the throne, and *you* will be at *my* mercy."

Lacellus blew out all but one of the flames, the hiss echoed loud in the darkness. Lacellus sniggered and retreated into the shadows. My heart tightened as I waited. My awareness waned as the contraptions broke my body.

Run, Fayolan... stay away!

My groans of agony echoed throughout the room as I drifted in and out of consciousness. While Lacellus watched me with a grim sense of satisfaction. The souls attached to the sword of bone singing of death.

"Call for him, *Nephilim*." He grinned, watching me.

"*No*." I wouldn't do it. I'd die before I helped Lacellus hurt Fayolan.

Lacellus emerged from the darkness like a lightning bolt, as his rage intensified. "Scream out his name." His nails dug into my skin, and his eyes burned with rage. "If he doesn't come for you, I will fuck that swollen cunt. Burying myself inside you so deep, you forget everyone but me."

"I won't do it," I sobbed as he held the device implanted

in me, twisting it anew. A powerful scream erupted from my lungs, so loud it reverberated off the walls.

"Call to him." His fingers shook with anger as he hovered them over the device, the roar of his voice echoing as he turned it again.

"*Fayolan*!" A scream tore from me, and he flashed a smirk as he faded into the shadows. "I'm *so* sorry."

CHAPTER FIFTY-SIX

Fayolan

The last man fell at my feet. I'd splattered the room with blood, and the beast howled with pleasure. I tucked in my wings, turning to the bed. *Shit!* It lay empty, the rope severed where it had been binding Tempest. I scowled at the coarse texture of it against my skin.

Lacellus had left his distinct scent on the bed, mingling with the coppery aroma of her blood. "Fucking *rodent*." Bile rose in my throat when I imagined Tempest in his clutches again.

I fought against the beast. He wanted to tear the palace apart and kill everyone in sight. But now was not the time. *I have to stay calm. Lacellus will keep her alive... for now.* "Reed, fucking find her."

He trampled through the pools of blood. Sending flames shooting into the fireplace. I paced, staring around the room, looking for any clue where the rat had taken her.

He could not have escaped past my elites. Which meant

my father had a secret tunnel I was not aware of. I could think of only one person who would know for sure. *Xavier!*

"*Dammit.*" Reed grimaced. "Wherever Tempest is, there are no flames." Of course, Lacellus had planned ahead.

"The sword of bones isn't here either. If it even *exists*." Nix flipped a mangled body with her foot, searching his robes for the weapon.

"Lacellus has it, and he's going to use Tempest as bait." I grimaced. The beast roared from deep within me, causing the palace's foundations to shake. "Nix, take Lilith to the healers. The rest of you spread out and have the palace locked down. No one leaves until I've found her."

"Where are *you* going?" Kalen asked, scowling when I moved towards the door.

"I'm going to find the *one* person who knows this palace better than I do. We could spend hours hunting for secret passages. Tempest might not have that long."

My wings stretched out as I ascended, soaring through the palace until I reached the dungeons. There was a hidden section that even my father had not known about. I rapped on the door, but got no response.

"Xavier?" Silence… "I'm coming in." Typically, the one time I needed him, he'd vanished. My mother's message played in my mind. *Keep Xavier safe.*

I booted the door, sending it flying open. The dank, musty air greeted me. How he preferred it down here was beyond me. "Xavier?"

There was no time to waste, so I swiftly crossed to the rack filled with intricately sketched maps. At least he kept his space organised, and I found the rolled-up parchment for my father's chambers easily. It was covered in dust, making me cough as pulled it from the shelves.

"It's not nice to sneak up on people like that." I grinned as

Xavier's black wolf edged out of the shadows. "I need a favour. These tunnels, do they lead out of the palace?"

"Yes." The wolf's bones twisted and snapped, reforming back into the man.

"I need your help. Make sure no one gets out. I'm going to enter the tunnels here and search for a rodent that has stolen something precious to me."

"You lost the Nephilim already?" Of course, he already knew. For someone that dwelled in the dungeons, he was always the most informed. "I noticed Lacellus lurking here before you returned. I'd follow this route."

Xavier grabbed a quill and marked the tunnels I needed to take. "Oh, and if he should try to leave?"

"*Kill* him!"

Xavier grinned as he slunk back into the shadows. The growl of his wolf echoed around me as I bolted for the door. Taking flight as I returned to my father's room.

His corpse still lay crumpled on the ground, coated in blood. I spat on his body as I stepped over him. *What a pathetic fool.*

I spotted the old worn tapestry hanging beside the bed. Someone had smeared some of the blood splatter coating it. I ripped it from the wall, leaning against the wooden panels behind it. A gust of air escaped as it creaked open. Pulling a torch from the aether, I stepped inside.

It was deathly cold within the dark, wet tunnels. The stale air tickled my nose as I followed Xavier's map. It was like a maze, and without it; I had no hope of navigating them. My father had done well to hide the labyrinth of secret passages from me.

As I negotiated through the darkness, my fingers glided over the slimy texture of the damp stone. A scream echoed around me, coming from all directions.

I felt nauseous as I heard Tempest's pain to my very core. The beast lost his mind as I suppressed the memories of her scarred body. After what Kalen and I had done to Lacellus, he would seek revenge on her. He better pray she is still alive once I get there. *I can delay death for a considerable amount of time.*

"*Fayolan!*" The anguish in Tempest's scream made me draw a sharp breath. I fumbled in the blackness even as an urgent tugging inside my mind told me to stop. *It's a trap.*

I quickened my pace at the sound of her sorrowful sobs. My heart thumped as a lump formed in my throat. "I'm coming, Pet."

The tunnel opened into a room shrouded in shadow. Only one flickering sconce illuminated her.

Tempest's head lolled. A clamp tightened around her breasts had rendered them a mottled purple. My eyes drifted down her body. A roar escaping as I saw the device embedded between her legs and the bite marks that trailed from her neck to her inner thighs. My fists tightened, and my stomach churned. A wave of nausea overtook me as the darkness consumed me.

The beast seized control of my body, rushing to her side. Her scream reverberated as her eyes lifted and her face contorted in fear. "*Run!*"

I was too slow to react as her eyes darted behind me, my sword clanging as I whipped around. Lacellus grinned as he charged, the bone sword piercing through my chest.

"*Bastard.*" I scowled, spinning on my heels as I battled to remain conscious. My wings lashed out, jolting the bone sword with every attempt to strike down Lacellus. My swings were slow, and he evaded with ease. Soon my arms became heavy and my swords clattered to the ground at my feet.

His laugh was sickening as he ducked into the shadows. "You seem sluggish, Fayolan. Not to worry, it'll all be over soon. For *you* at least. The same can't be said for the beautiful *Nephilim*. She's *mine* now."

"*Never*!" I roared, using the last of my waning strength to lunge. My hands wrapped around Lacellus' throat. My weight dragging him down beneath me. "I won't die until *you* have."

"*Fayolan*," Tempest cried out. Her voice trembled with fear.

"You're safe now." I squeezed my hands as tight as my failing body would allow. Watching as Lacellus' eyes bulged and his lips turned purple. I ignored the pain as he clawed at me. Punching my ribs and kicking his legs.

I had little strength left. My body swayed as my vision dimmed. I just had to hold on a little longer. The moment he stopped fighting and his arms fell limp to the ground, I pulled a hunting knife from the aether. My aim was off as I tumbled forward, missing his heart. *Dammit!*

"Please get up, Fayolan!" Tempest cried. "I'm so sorry. This is all my fault." *Silly girl... I started all of this long before she was born.*

A dizzying darkness overcame me as my body caved. Crumpling to the floor as I lost the fight to remain conscious.

CHAPTER FIFTY-SEVEN

Tempest

I watched in horror as Fayolan crumpled to the ground before me, and my heart ripped in two. His body was motionless, and the sword of bone and souls reverberated as it jutted from his chest.

"*Fayolan!*" My lungs were tight and my breath shallow as I stared, praying he would get to his feet. *He couldn't die... I would not allow it.*

With all my might, I kicked at the hilt of the sword, hoping to dislodge it from his chest, but it wouldn't budge. My toes barely scraped against it. "*Dammit.*" I couldn't heal Fayolan with it still lodged inside of him.

My gaze fell on Lacellus. I couldn't tell if he was dead. My heart was beating fast as I tried once more to remove the sword. If he woke before I healed Fayolan, it was all over. "*Come on!*" I screamed, fighting the pain as I kicked out again.

My toes grazed Fayolan's hand, and I shut my eyes tight.

Fighting the tremor that ran up my spine. *I would die trying to save him if that's what it took.*

"Don't heal him yet," a deep, familiar voice rumbled around me. The hairs on my neck stood on end as a man appeared from the depths of the shadows. A strong magical aura emanated from him, capturing my breath. The power he exuded illuminated his skin as mine did when I healed and long chestnut hair cascaded down his back.

"I won't let him die." I stifled my cries, my throat tightening as I sobbed.

"Daughter, I need your permission to take the sword." He eyed me with a smirk as I gasped. "Tempest, this sword can bring death to even the unkillable. You must verbally give it to me, or I cannot lay a finger on it."

Staring with a hooded expression, his eyes flickered with power as he waited for me to speak.

"What will you do with the sword?" I held his stare as he smirked.

"I will hide it away. It's too dangerous to be in the hands of mortals or Gods." I could sense the tension in his words and knew he was lying. But it didn't matter.

"Promise me you won't wield it against Fayolan or anyone we care about."

"I promise," he said. It was the first truth to come out of his mouth.

"I give you the sword."

"Love makes us do rash things. I hope he is worth saving." My father smiled, making me feel uneasy as he gripped the hilt and pulled it free.

He vanished, and I let my healing magic free. My wings ripped from my back, and I roared as I pulled Fayolan's injuries into me. My head snapped back against the cross as the device dug deeper into my body. But I persevered through the pain.

Fayolan's injuries took their toll, and my vision became hazy, but I could hear the slow beat of his heart. Once… twice… It grew stronger, and my magic pulled back. My wings folded away, and the darkness devoured me.

Fayolan's voice stirred me from my sleep like a gust of wind, calling out my name. "Tempest." My eyes shot open as he clambered to his feet.

With the lightest of touches, he lifted my face to meet his, his eyes searching mine. "It's over now."

"I'm *so* sorry." My voice shook as his thumb brushed away a tear. "I led you here. I tried not to, but I…"

"Hush." Fayolan planted a tender kiss on my lips, silencing me. "Do you think I wouldn't have come for you, anyway?"

"You shouldn't have. I almost lost you."

Fayolan rested his forehead against mine, his hands freeing the rope around my neck as he stared deep into my eyes. "Listen to me. There's *nothing* in this world that will *ever* stop me from coming for you. I'll lay down my life before that ever happens. Do you understand me?"

A tear slid down my cheek. "You might not think so when you learn what I did to save you." Guilt made bile rise in my throat. "I gave the sword to my father."

Fayolan let out a deep breath. His lips swept across my cheek. "I don't care what you did. I would have done the same to save you."

My heart melted. "You would?"

"I'd have let him run me through with it if it meant saving you. Now, you must stay still. I'll be as gentle as I can."

His hand lowered to the device between my legs. I screamed out, even though he tried to be delicate as he twisted it.

Fayolan reached out and grasped my cheek with his free hand, offering me comfort. "Deep breaths, Tempie." He twisted it again, his gaze unwavering as a sharp, piercing sound erupted from me.

He cupped my cheek tighter as his face came closer to mine. His mouth grazing my earlobe. "Look at me, Pet." Our lips met, sending a shiver of pleasure through me, enough to distract me from the pain.

Once the device shifted beneath his fingertips, Fayolan drew it out in one soft sweeping motion. "I've got you." He flung it aside with a deep growl.

His hands were gentle as he removed the clamps around my breasts and undid the restraints from my wrists. His arms were like a shelter, and I clung to him as his chest heaved against mine.

"How long have we been down here?" A mumble escaped my lips as he manoeuvred my body. Slipping his shoulder under my arm to prop me up.

"I doubt we have been here long. The others would have found us already." He urged me forward, but my legs shook beneath me as I stumbled. "I've got you. Lean on me."

Fayolan's arms were heavy around my waist, and I could feel his exhaustion as we made our way through the long, winding tunnels. I stumbled, and my hand smacked against the wall, sending vibrations through my arm.

Fayolan kept his grip firm as we stumbled through the pitch-black darkness. I felt a rivulet of blood streaming down my thighs as we walked.

"We're almost there."

Relief swept through me as I heard familiar muffled voices. My path now lit by a soft, golden glow emanating from the king's room.

"They're here." Braedon's voice echoed through the tunnel as he peered inside. Gripping me as Fayolan almost buckled beneath me.

"*Fuck!*" Nix pointed at my shaking legs. "What did he *fucking* do?" She hurried to help support my almost dead weight. Ignoring my wince of pain.

Kalen and Reed hurried to Fayolan's side, holding him up. "Close your eyes, Tempest," Fayolan warned, but it came too late.

A deep crimson stained the walls, and the coppery stench of blood filled the air, making my stomach churn. I gasped at the horrific sight.

Nix guided me forward, and I tumbled. Braedon's powerful arms encircled me, lifting me into his chest. He held me against him as the room we were in disappeared. My head swirled as he settled me onto the daybed.

"I'll be right back." He vanished, returning with the others in tow. Fayolan pulled away from them, and the weight of a blanket settled across my broken body as he dropped to the floor beside me.

"Get the healers." His fingers grazed my neck, tracing the shape of the jagged bite mark left by his father. Blood stained them as he lifted them away from me.

"Where's Lilith?" I asked, trying to get up, but Fayolan held me down firmly.

"She's with the healers. She'll be fine." Nix smiled as she edged a little closer.

"Is there anything I can do?" She glanced to Fayolan.

"I left the fucking rodent back there. I'm not even sure he's dead. Follow this map and make certain he is."

His shadows moved around him, dark shapes creating an

eerie feeling as he watched me through unfamiliar eyes. Something else looked back at me, and I found comfort in its lethal embrace.

The bedroom doors swung open and five Fae stepped into Fayolan's quarters. The hooded robes they wore couldn't quite conceal the prominent points of their ears.

As they glared at me with distaste, I felt the oppressive weight of their magic.

"Why have you summoned us?" One male stepped forward. His presence alone filled the room. His gaze was as piercing as steel, his eyes a startling shade of grey. He drew his lips into a tight, disapproving line as his eyebrows knitted together in a scowl.

His body was enormous and intimidating for a healer, with huge biceps and broad shoulders. The fabric of his robe strained against his bulging muscles.

"Heal her, Marcell." Fayolan's hands clenched. His jaw went rigid, and the shadows undulated around him.

"She is Nephilim. She can heal herself." Marcell held his chin high, his nostrils flaring as he peered down towards me. "The King will…."

"The King is *dead*!" Fayolan's scowl deepened as he stood up. He spread his wings with force, creating a gust of wind that ruffled his feathers. He squared his shoulders, narrowing his eyes. "That makes *me* king, and I *order* you to heal her."

Marcell sneered as he examined the room, taking in the tarnished armour of Fayolan and his elites. He rolled up his sleeves, his muscles flexing as he took a determined stride towards me.

"I should heal you first. Then I'll examine her injuries."

"She already healed me." Fayolan grimaced.

"As you wish, my King. May I?" Marcell reached down

towards the blanket. I nodded, my hands shaking, as Fayolan's growl reverberated through the room.

"We will need some space." A woman stepped forward. A reassuring smile touched her lips as she placed her hand on Fayolan's shoulders. Her gentle guidance attempting to move him away from my side.

Fayolan did not move, his powerful arms supporting me as he lifted me. His hard chest pressed against my back as he slid underneath me.

As the healers gathered around, my head reclined against his shoulder, and the blanket shifted as they examined my wounds.

"Avanthe, if you'd be so kind." Marcell signalled towards the base of the daybed.

When she saw the blood seeping between my thighs, she recoiled. "I need a better look," she glanced at Fayolan. I winced in pain as he wrapped his hands around my thighs, spreading my legs for her.

"Deep breaths, Pet. This will all be over soon, I promise." Fayolan entwined his fingers with mine. Placing a kiss on my head. "Let us take care of you."

"She's lost a lot of blood," Marcell said. He winced as he looked over the destruction, as Avanthe's face drained of colour. "She is going to want to sleep through this," he said as his magic pushed into me, and my eyelids grew heavy.

"I won't leave you." Fayolan kissed my temple. "Sleep."

CHAPTER FIFTY-EIGHT

I stared into the wardrobe, running the mix of fabrics through my fingers. I had to select the ideal dress. Something that would catch Fayolan off guard.

"Perfect." I smiled as I grabbed a beautiful magenta dress that matched my eyes. I slid it on and the fabric swished around my leg. The delicate lace bodice hugged my curves and pushed my breasts up in a way Fayolan admired.

I rushed to brush my hair, letting the silky locks fall over my bare shoulders. My gaze drifted to the glimmering bangles that Fayolan had left for me. He had been like a ghost since I woke up from my healing. Even my bed was cold from the lack of his warmth.

"You look beautiful, Daughter." I jumped, spinning to see my father standing in the doorway. The morning light high-lighted his features, giving him a divine radiance.

"I don't see you in twenty-three years, and now you've

graced me twice in just a couple of days. I should feel *honoured*."

My father chortled, looking unphased by my lack of respect. "I've always watched over you, Tempie. You just weren't ready to see me."

"*Don't* call me that. You haven't earned the right. You are merely a sperm donor that abandoned me and my mother the first *chance* you got." I turned away, clenching my fists as my chest heaved. "What do you *want*? I gave you the *damn* sword."

With a firm hand on my shoulder, he turned me to face him. His power was almost tangible, leaving a trail of goose-bumps across my skin.

"I came to warn you, Daughter. The Gods are restless, and you have drawn their gaze upon you. Tread carefully, as even I cannot protect you from them. I am bound to their commands." His words carried a weight of unease.

"Is that it? Will you vanish for another twenty-three years?" I bit out.

"I know you feel I have let you down, but I had my reasons for leaving. There are rules I must follow, and I cannot interfere in the affairs of mortals. I already did so with your mother and the Gods wanted me to pay for it. I left so they would not claim either of you as my penance."

"You interfered with Fayolan." I scowled.

"He is not mortal, and I sense that neither are you. He has surrounded himself with outcasts, and not one is what they seem. Immortality is not a gift easily given, and it *always* comes at a cost," he mused. *Whatever that was supposed to mean?*

"It seems I owe you my thanks," I sighed. "For saving him."

"Do not thank me yet. I took the sword for my own selfish reasons. It had nothing to do with saving either of you." *Of course, it didn't. How could I be stupid enough to think he came to save me?*

I stepped back as I resisted the urge to slap him. *He did not deserve a shred of emotion from me.* "Just fucking leave. I don't *need* you. Especially when you just want to use me."

He simply watched me with cold indifference. "You have a visitor. Help the boy… there will come a time when you'll need his skills." He vanished without looking back. *The selfish bastard had no love in his heart, even for me. He was incapable of caring for anyone but himself.*

"Tempest," Reema called as she knocked on my bedroom door.

"How did you get in here?" I asked as I swung it open and stepped into the living quarters. "Fayolan left the suite surrounded by heavy guards."

"I'm his harem. I told the guards Fayolan wanted me to warm his bed." She grinned and wrapped her fingers around mine, tugging me towards the sprawling balcony, ignoring my winces of pain.

"Reema, what's going on?" I glared at her as she peered over the balcony. I leant over the edge, glancing downwards, and spotted a boy's small arms straining as he made his way up the palace wall towards us. Carrying a large bundle fastened to his back with rope.

"I found him wandering the corridors. He needs your help. Mace is a good boy. Just a *little* foolhardy."

"He'll kill himself if he falls," I huffed as I leant over the balcony, stretching my hand out to him. We gripped the rope wrapped around his chest, hauling him up and over the stone railings.

He gazed at me with his eyes wide, taking a hesitant step back. "I won't hurt you," I assured. Mace moved his hands down his back, untying the bundle before easing it to the ground.

"I need your help," he said as he lifted the cloth hiding a small gryphon. "He's hurt."

"*Shit.*" I swore under my breath as the bird's piercing squawk startled me. I tousled my hair with my fingers, taking in the boy, no older than fourteen. "Where did you get it?" I asked, and he stood up, squaring his shoulders as he faced me.

"I found him abandoned in the city. He's hurt. Can you heal him… Please?" I lowered beside the gryphon, running my fingers through his soft feathers.

"It's a boy?"

"Yes," he said. He grinned as I moved slowly, lifting the creature's wing, its soft feathers brushing against my skin. I felt the indentations where wire had bitten into the bone, leaving a rough texture.

"He is lucky you found him." I let my magic flow from me. The creature let out a terrified squawk as I treated its wounds without needing to transform. "Hush little gryphon." Fayolan's guards would hear us if I didn't finish this fast.

"You've been claimed by a gryphon?" Mace's gaze dropped to my unmarked hand.

"You can sense that?" In truth I had worried that since Nix had healed me, that Saki's bite had gone. It reassured me to know it was still there.

"They claimed you as kin. You belong to the gryphons now."

"You know a lot about creatures?"

Mace grinned as his face lit up. "I feel them, and they listen to me."

"Is that so?" I mused.

"My mother says it's a gift from the Gods." I smiled warmly, even though I could not agree with him. The Gods were selfish pricks. But if it gave Mace comfort, who was I to say otherwise?

Mace inspected the gryphon as it nuzzled into him. "I brought you some coin. I don't have much, but…" I raised my hand, stopping him.

"There is no fee, Mace." I smiled as he and Reema wrapped the gryphon up. They hauled it onto his back, its weight pressing against his shoulders. He spun toward the balcony, and the corners of my mouth turned up as I rolled my eyes. "*Use* the doors." I lifted my arm, exaggerating, as I pointed to the exit.

I struggled to my feet, the sharp pain in my back causing me to gasp and lean against the wall.

"Are you okay?" Reema asked.

"I'm a little sore from the healing. But it's nothing." I waved her off and stepped away from the wall, my hand trailing along the cool surface as I led them to the door. The groaning and creaking wood echoed through the hall as I opened it, startling the guards.

"What the…" Their lips curled into snarls as they noticed Mace.

"This is my friend, Mace. If he should ever come asking for me, ensure you fetch me right away."

They stepped aside, allowing Reema and Mace to hurry away. A chuckle left my lips. "Where is the King? I have an urgent matter to discuss with him." Like why he seemed to be avoiding me.

They spun around to face me, their voices urgent as they ushered me back into the room. "We will send word. *You* are to stay here." I heaved a sigh as I allowed them to shut me in the room.

I dropped onto a pile of scatter cushions. Being locked in this room with just myself was driving me crazy.

"Looks like I came at just the right time." Lilith smiled as she leant against the doorframe.

"You're better… I'm so sorry for running and hiding."

"You did as I ordered and that's what matters. Don't go blaming yourself. I'm a big girl and a blade to the gut isn't enough to keep me down. So come on, get up." She smiled, tilting her head towards the hallway. "I thought you might like to explore the Palace."

"Does Fayolan…"

"Fayolan does not control you." Lilith cut me off. "Being cooped up in here will drive you insane." I shuffled off the cushions, adjusting my dress as I stood.

With a deep breath, she opened the door, her hand placed gently on the hilt of her sword as the guards tried to block our exit. "I am taking Tempest to the gardens. Join us if you are that *bothered*," she said.

"We were instructed she was to remain here."

Lilith let out a hiss, and the sound of her sword being drawn caught their attention.

"As her healer, I have recommended she get some fresh air." Marcell stood in the corridor, his broad figure seemed to fill the space. His lips curled in an amused smirk. "Do I have to tell the King you refused to follow my instructions as her healer?"

They stepped back as Marcell gestured towards me, his arm outstretched in invitation. I smiled as I stepped beside him, fiddling with my fingers as I dipped my head out of respect.

He realised I did not intend to clasp his arm as Lilith returned her sword to its sheath and surged forward. He walked with us until we rounded the corner. "I'm afraid I had an ulterior motive for coming to see you today." His voice was smooth like butter. "It has been a while since we had a Nephilim roaming the halls of the Palace."

He slowed as he turned to face me. Running his hand through his grey hair as he continued. "I was wondering if you would like to join us in the medical wing. Your knowledge would be invaluable. I'm sure there is a lot we could teach each other."

I don't know what I had expected since coming here. Fayolan had not tried to place me in his harem, but I had no purpose here except to warm his bed. Maybe helping in the medical wing would keep me busy.

"I will consider it. Fayolan requested I stay safe in his quarters." I gazed up into his alluring eyes, studying his features.

"And yet, *here* you are." A mischievous glimmer shone in his eyes.

"I'm not sure I would be very welcome," I pointed out. The King's death weighed heavily on my shoulders, and my existence as a Nephilim only increased the hatred people had for me. Even my sister had contempt for me, so what hope did I have of finding acceptance from anyone else?

"I will let you go, but I sincerely hope you will have the strength to accept my invitation. We'd be lucky to have someone like you on our team." He dipped his head, and a sweet scent of lavender followed him as he walked away from us. Leaving Lilith and me as we made our way to the garden.

CHAPTER FIFTY-NINE

Fayolan

As Marcell slipped away, I watched Lilith lead Tempest into the blooming garden. I stood in the shadows, hesitant to disturb her as she inhaled the fragrant scent of the orchids.

"Are you planning on dragging her back to your quarters?" Kalen asked as he slunk from the darkness.

"Looks like I'm not the only one watching her." I raised my eyebrow cockily at him.

"I came to find you. General Tam has returned." I released a heavy breath as I turned my gaze away from Tempest.

"Where is he?" I needed to put everything into place before word of my father's death reached the city.

"Reed has him waiting in the hall." Kalen returned his gaze to the Nephilim. "You didn't answer my question."

"I'll let her be. But first it's time we learnt the truth about my mother." I emerged from the shadows, and Tempest's head turned to me as if she had sensed my presence the moment I stepped away from the safety of the darkness.

Her lips stretched into a content smile. That look took me aback, and the sensation of my erect cock pressing against the fabric of my trousers was almost unbearable.

"Not such a *good* girl today, are you?" I asked in a low, throaty voice, and I watched as a shiver ran through her body. The sense of dread that I aroused in her captivated her, and I fucking admired that she could handle the shadows of my soul.

"I made her come. She is not an animal to be caged, Fayo." Lilith shot Kalen a sly glance, her lips curling into a smirk.

I chuckled darkly, knowing the pleasure Tempest would take in the reprimand I had in store for her. Hell, I could smell her arousal already as she batted her lashes.

"I'd almost forgotten you existed. Since I haven't seen you in days and my bed is awfully cold at night." Tempest pouted beautifully as she chastised me.

"We can't have that. I'll ensure you never suffer like that again." I smirked. She sent my heart wild. It hammered against my chest as I strolled towards the enticing little Nephilim.

"Make sure that you do." She got to her feet, stepping into my open arms. "Are you okay?" All hints of a smile faded as she looked up at me. "I was worried."

I ran my hand over her hair as I lowered my lips to her head. "It's nothing to worry about. I just have to put plans into motion so I can keep ahead of the situation." In truth, I hadn't slept since I killed my father. Tempest was my only concern. I had to ensure her safety throughout all of this.

I gently kissed the tip of her head as Tempest's grip around my waist grew tighter. "You need to take care of yourself. When was the last time you ate something?" Her voice had the faintest tremble. No one had ever cared for me as much as she did.

I chuckled, lifting her chin so her gaze met mine. "I promise I am perfectly fine. But I *do* have something to ask of you." Our lips met, silencing me as I claimed her.

The taste of the Nephilim was a nectar I could never get enough of. She fell deeper into my embrace. "Will you allow me to see what happened to my mother?

Tempest's gaze darted behind me, and I was certain my mother's spirit lingered. She worried her bottom lip as her face paled. My stomach churned as I asked her to relive it again, but I had to know the truth.

"Okay," she said with a heavy sigh. The weight of her worry was palpable as she inhaled deeply, her shoulders slumping.

Kalen's gentle fingers brushed her temples, and a whimper of agony escaped her lips. He projected my mother's memories, immersing me in the sights and sounds as if I were living them myself. Tempest shivered at his touch, her tears reflecting the luminescent shades of blue and magenta in her eyes. I held her closer, trying to ease her suffering.

"Son of a *bitch*!" I ground my teeth, spitting out a hiss of fury as I watched my father callously order the death of innocent civilians. He forced the Nephilim to heal my mother, even knowing she was not strong enough.

I heard the Nephilim's last breath as she died, taking my mother with her. The last sound around her was the child's screams fading into eerie silence. I felt sick to my stomach.

I'd treated Tempest like a vile creature from the moment I first met, and she didn't deserve it. My father had fed me a pack of lies and I'd stupidly believed them all. Gods, so many innocent Nephilim had died at my hands alone.

"Do you understand?" Tempest spoke in a shaky voice, stuttering with each word. "They welcomed you into this world surrounded by death. The souls of the dead merged with you, creating a spark of energy that ignited within you. You became something this world had never seen before—a being of immortality. You are a *reaper*… a bearer of souls." Her words struck me as I stared down at her with a torrent of emotion.

Tempest's fingers were gentle as they clasped my cheeks. "I'm so sorry," she whispered. Pity had no place in her voice —only understanding.

The surrounding temperature dropped as I stared into her eyes, and a deep cold consumed me. Pushing aside the raw emotions swirling within me. I had to be strong. For Tempest's sake.

"I will be busy today, and it will be dangerous for you to leave the quarters." My words were sharper than I intended them to be. Her lips tightened, and her shoulders sagged as she cast her eyes to the ground. "Keep those *pretty* eyes up."

"Have I done something wrong?" she asked. I almost missed the words. They were so soft.

A mischievous smile tugged at my mouth as I took her hands. "Why would you think that? Give me a few days to deal with my father's demise, and then you will be all mine. I'm still debating tying you to my bed, Pet," I said with a seductive look.

Tempest gazed up at me, biting her bottom lip and releasing a soft moan. My cock tensed, my desire driving the fire coursing through my veins. "What's on your mind, Pet?"

Tempest hesitated, her eyes betraying her fears as she moved backwards, her hand reaching out for something to steady herself. "Am I part of your harem?"

"Is that what you want? To be one of them?" I clenched my jaw, fighting to restrain my frustration at her words. *Is that all Tempest thought she was to me?*

"No. Of course I don't." She sounded so sure as she spoke without hesitation.

"What do *you* want, Tempest?" My fingers slipped under her chin as she attempted to look away. "*Answer* me."

"I want you." My grip tightened as her cheeks flushed red. "*All* of you… and I yearn for you to want *me* too."

"I *do*. More than anything in this Gods forsaken world." She pulled away, shaking her head.

"You crave my body, but it's not enough. I long for you to *love* me the way I…" My face grew tense, and an oppressive silence descended as her words trailed off. *She was asking the impossible from me.*

"I am incapable of love. I'm an actual monster, Tempest. But I promise to offer you all that I am capable of. I belong to you as much as you do to me. The only thing I cannot give you is an emotion I do not possess."

She gasped, her eyes dulling as she stepped back, spinning on her heels and running from the garden.

"Smooth." With a fiery glint in her eye, Lilith trudged behind Tempest. *I was a damned fool!* I hated seeing Tempest upset, but I couldn't bring myself to lie to her. She meant the world to me. More than any woman from my harem. I didn't just crave her body. More than anything, *I wanted to love her.*

I snapped my fingers at Kalen, and my angry footsteps echoed off the garden walls as I stormed away. What more could I do to show Tempest how much I care for her?

"For what it's worth, I think you're wrong. You don't know what love feels like because you've never had it. The fear when you nearly lost her. The desire to end the world to keep her safe… It may not be as deep as she can feel, but you *love* that woman." Kalen walked past me with a knowing look as I halted.

"That was just my possessive nature. Hell, I'd give my life to feel it for just a moment. So, I could tell her from the bottom of my heart that I loved her." But to do so now would be a lie, and Tempest meant more to me than that.

"I've met no one with such a keen eye for detail that can be so glaringly blind at the same time. I guess for now I'll give you one piece of advice. Stop telling Tempest you will never love her. Sometimes you are too honest."

"I won't lie to her." She deserved better.

"I didn't say to lie. Just maybe not be so blatant. The poor girl is still trying to figure out where she belongs in your world and saying things like that aren't helping. Maybe focus more on showing her how much she means to you."

"I'm an idiot, aren't I?"

"You said it, not me." Kalen chuckled as we reached the great hall.

Tam sat waiting, slumped in a chair. His battle-worn helm rested on the table, smeared with blood. He saluted as I signalled for him to remain seated. "Have you much to report?" I asked.

"We found five legions of Ustrayan soldiers. I believe the No Man's Land battle was a distraction so they could launch a strike on Solis. There is no sign of Horik's dominant forces, and I believe this was simply a means to test our defences."

"I don't disagree," I sighed, pushing Tempest from my mind as I watched him. "We have another issue I need to deal with." I could feel his eyes on me, like a physical weight, as he strived to read me. "My father is dead."

A smirk teased his lips as he brushed his fingers through his hair. "That's quite a mess you've got on your hands."

"Do I have your allegiance?" If Tam were to turn against me, it would greatly weaken my army. It would be a loss I couldn't afford.

He leant back, his feet resting on the table as he got comfortable. He always was a cocky bastard. "Did *you* kill him?"

"Yes."

"About *fucking* time." He relaxed his shoulders as he continued watching me. "Not one man in this army didn't wish to see you claim the throne. Your father was a pompous *fuck* who cared little for his men or his people. But I have to ask… what are your plans with the Nephilim? People are uncomfortable with her… proximity to you." He chose his words carefully, despite my glare.

"My father lied about the Nephilim. He killed my mother and accused them to keep the blame from himself. I have seen it with my own eyes. Word is to be spread that Nephilim are no longer to be harmed. Any caught doing so will face death."

His eyes darkened as he lowered his feet, drawing himself forward as he rested his elbows on his knees. "You realise how this looks? You claim a Nephilim as your bed mate and then murder your father, taking his crown…"

"The Nephilim is mine, and yes, I have claimed her. But she has nothing to do with anything else. My father conspired against me with Palleon and Lacellus. All three are now dead. Besides, I have proof that my father lied."

I watched as he skimmed his rough fingers over his chin.

"The Nephilim are innocent. I would not allow monsters to live just because I found a good *fuck*." I was not the forgiving type, and he knew it better than most.

He snorted as he reached out for his helm. "You have my support, but not all will like the rules protecting the Nephilim," he said as he lumbered to his feet. "What's the plan?"

"We are going to hang my father from the battlements. I need your men ready to disable his guard and replace them. You will send any of my father's men that wish to pledge loyalty to me to your camps for re-training. I want to hit each major city and town before an uprising is possible. With

Ustraya making a move, I cannot afford to fight a war on both fronts. It's imperative you act fast and make an example of any that think to cross me."

Tam smirked, reaching his arm out and clasping mine. "I will see to it, my King," he said with a respectful dip of his head. "How long until you address the people?"

"I want my father's guards neutralised within the hour. Braedon will be at your disposal to get you around Solis. I want this settled within a week."

"My pleasure." The same darkness radiating through my elites flickered across his features as he strolled leisurely from the room.

I sat for a moment, deep in thought. I had one further task to put in motion before my grand speech to the people. *It was time to show Tempest what she means to me.*

I slipped from the great hall, descending into the lowest levels of the palace where the servants dwelled. I hadn't ventured down here since I was a child.

"My Prince?" A woman dropped to her knees as she spotted me ambling down the corridor.

"Please fetch the heads of staff. I have a few requests. So I'll wait in the kitchens." I chuckled as she scrambled to her feet, scurrying away with a look of shock etched across her face. It's time we brightened up the palace, starting with moonflowers. I wanted it to feel like home... for me and my Nephilim!

CHAPTER SIXTY

Tempest strolled towards me, her hair shimmering in the sunlight. Her gaze locked with mine, no doubt to avoid the mutilated body of my father. She clutched the sides of her sensual yet revealing dress. Digging her nails into the elegant tulle fabric to still her trembling hands.

"You look beautiful." I smiled, wrapping my arms around her waist. I lifted a moonflower, tucking it softly behind her ear. The scent of it mingled with her own, creating an intoxicating aroma.

She smiled softly, looking up as she brushed a stray hair from my face. "You don't look so bad yourself, my King." She curtsied slightly, looking up at me through her thick lashes.

Scooping her into my arms, I turned her body away from my father's corpse. "I'm glad you came. I didn't handle things well earlier. Will you forgive me?"

Tempest blinked as a smile pulled at the corner of her lips. "No, I was out of line. I need you to know, Fayolan, I accept you for who you are, regardless of whether you can love me. I won't lie and say it doesn't hurt, but I'm okay with it as long as I get to be by your side."

Her words warmed me. "I swear to you right now that I will be the type of man you deserve. I know you might not always understand or like my actions. But I will be better… for you." She wrapped her tiny fingers around my hand, squeezing them gently.

"You're *not* a monster, Fayolan. You were raised by one who wanted to turn you into a heartless weapon. But he's gone now and you're free to be the kind of man you choose. Your life belongs to you now."

She had a remarkable capacity for forgiveness, always seeing light in the darkness. If anyone could teach me to love, it would be her.

"Huh hum," Kalen coughed, drawing our attention. When Tempest was around, I forgot everything around me. Only she existed.

"I'm sorry." Tempest took a small step back. "What's going on?"

"It's time the people of Solis know the truth. You were *never* a monster. My father was." Her eyes opened wide, and I grasped her trembling hand in mine, feeling the warmth of her skin.

"Are you sure you want to do this?" Tempest glanced towards the battlements where I intended to make my speech.

"I've never been more certain of anything in my life. So chin up, Pet. Let's change the world… together."

We made our way towards the battlements, and the vibrations of the people below reverberated in my chest. My elites spread around us, with Kalen taking position on my right. Whilst Lilith and Nix hovered protectively at Tempest's left.

Reed and Braedon solemnly carried my father's body forward, using ropes to haul him up for all to see. A shock wave rippled through the crowd as Solis saw their king, followed by a chorus of gasps and screams.

"General Tam and his men are in position," Kalen said.

"Then it's time." With Tempest at my side, I stepped towards the wall, our footsteps echoing off the stone. I felt the heavy pressure of the crowd's silence as they waited for me to speak. Tempest gave my hand a reassuring squeeze as I coughed, drawing the people's attention to me.

"The King is dead," I announced. "He failed not only his people but his own son. He plotted my murder with two of his trusted advisors." Gasps filled the air, and I let them settle before I continued.

"Your King did not care that Ustraya sent its armies into our lands, wiping out several villages and cities. You're all aware of the brutality shown towards our people. He failed you... but *I* will *not*!"

Tempest's body shook as she stared at the mass of people in the city below. I gripped her hand tighter, reassuring her before she had the chance to flee. I was not done yet.

"We have defeated the Ustrayans that strayed into our lands. My armies have claimed victory for now, but war is upon us, and we need to act."

The murmuring of the people below quickly grew to a loud roar. Cheers and jeers echoed through the crowd. I raised my hand to silence them.

"It's time." Lilith gave a mischievous wink as I gathered Tempest into my arms.

"What's happening?" Tempest asked, as Kalen stepped forward.

"Close your eyes for just a minute, Pet. It's important for them all to see the truth. I covered her ears with my arms, turning her into me.

Kalen stepped forward, projecting my mother's last moments above the city for all to see. The people fell silent as they watched. Whether they would believe it or think it some wild trick, I couldn't tell. But there would be no avoiding punishment for those that chose to act out.

"As you have seen, my father accused the Nephilim of murdering my mother… your beloved queen. This was a lie! The King killed her. He blamed the Nephilim to hide his own guilt." Tempest bravely turned towards the crowds. Letting them see her as I continued my address.

"From this day forward, anyone who kills, hunts, or harms a Nephilim will face the severest punishments. It is time to accept the truth about my father's lies. The Nephilim are healers, not killers. They are innocent of the accusations my father spun, and they may very well change the tides of the upcoming war."

The people began to jeer and shout. Even seeing the truth couldn't reverse years of hatred.

"This Nephilim beside me saved the lives of countless of our people. She never once cared that they hated her or wanted her dead. She saved my life even though I had captured her. This is what the Nephilim are. We have all hunted and murdered innocent healers; we are *all* guilty. It ends now. Stidahl *will* welcome the Nephilim."

I stared below and saw men pushing forward in a wave of rage, their yells echoing. Tams men acted with no leniency as they cut through those that opposed my edict.

"I am the King of Stidahl, and my word is final. Any that disobey me will fall. I will not show mercy. There's no place for revolts when we're at war."

Tam and his crew lugged the bodies away, and a hush descended. They would hang them from the battlements as a stark warning.

"Keep watch of the city tonight. I want ears everywhere.

We *must* deal with those that stir unrest," I said, and Kalen, Braedon, and Reed slunk into the shadows.

"Bring Thursden to me." I glanced towards Nix. I didn't wait for her to move as I pulled Tempest away from the battlements. Her lip quivered as she held my hand like a lifeline, her knuckles whitening.

"I'm sorry you had to witness that. But I needed you to see that I'm making changes for the better." *Idiot!* Tempest dropped her head, looking at the floor. "That's not what I meant to say."

"Did you free them for me or because it's the right thing to do?" she asked.

"I am not a virtuous man, Tempest. I did it for you, but only because I knew the truth."

Her lips moved as she struggled to form her thoughts into words. "Thank you for freeing my people. I guess the reason doesn't matter." She bowed her head with politeness and stepped away. My hand felt cold without hers. "You must be busy. I'll return to your quarters."

"Tempest, I need you by my side. I can't do this without you. Give me two more days, Tempest and I will show that needy cunt of yours *who* it belongs to."

I resisted the desire to pull her back and embed my pulsing cock into her as I caught the scent of her arousal. She devoured me with a craving so powerful it tormented me.

Tempest stormed away, her head jerking to give me a brief, furious glance. A fire ignited in her eyes, fuelled by her own desires.

Once she was out of sight, I hastened to the throne room. Seeing my father's empty seat was odd, knowing it now belonged to me. I would replace it with my own. If I were like him, I would tear the palace to the ground and build it up in my image. But I did not care about such frivolous things.

"My King." Thursden smirked as I spun to face him. "It

has been a long time coming."

"I never wanted this, and you know it." My voice rumbled as I pointed to the throne. "I need your men out in Solis tonight. We cannot afford to let the seeds of unrest sow roots within my kingdom."

I stretched my wings and stood tall, ensuring he felt my presence. My shadows were uneasy, waiting for the peace to end.

"I will arrange a large uniformed patrol and send men into the taverns. A small group of guards may be problematic. How would you like me to deal with them?" Thursden was highly skilled—able to detect the rat in a den full of cutthroats. If he had concerns, I would be a fool to ignore them.

"Do you think you can pull them in line?" I asked and saw his muscles tighten as his shoulders rose.

"I think they can do a lot of damage before I do. The Nephilim is not *helping* your cause."

My jaw ticked as my fists clenched. "Then do what you need to. The Nephilim stays, and anyone that attempts to get to her will be fed to the gryphons." My shadows swirled around me, reaching out for Thursden as the beast rattled his cage.

"I'll make sure my men uphold your orders. I do not accept insubordination amongst my ranks. Those that pose a risk will die tonight." I dipped my head as he banged his fist across his chest and took his leave.

As I crossed the room, the chandelier's light illuminated my way, and I climbed the steps to my father's throne. My mother's still stood dutifully beside his.

My shadows had consumed his soul so he would not torment Tempest in his death. It seemed a fitting end, knowing he would never rest in peace.

"You know they will never accept her as your queen,"

Nix said softly. I skimmed my fingers across my mother's palladium throne. The sharp edges were a reminder of the fierce woman she was.

"Then I will marry a woman to be my queen." My gaze fell upon Nix.

Her icy eyes softened, and her shoulders slumped as she released a deep, weary sigh. "Do you think Tempest will be okay with that?" She gave a nonchalant shrug as she ambled towards me.

"It will break her heart. But she'll learn to accept it."

Nix shook her head in dismay as she reached out and slid her hand up my arm. "Fayo… she will be miserable. Is that what you want? She will *truly* be your whore."

My muscles tensed, and I jerked myself away from Nix. The hurt shone across her face. "A queen will have one purpose… to birth me an heir and look pretty upon my mother's throne. Tempest will have everything else I can offer. She will *never* be a *whore* because she's my *woman*."

My fingers gripped my mother's throne tightly as I fought my anger. It bit into my palm. Blood oozed over the cold metal. *Fuck!*

"She'll run Fayolan, and you know it. She is falling in love with you." Nix's words pierced my heart. I knew she was right, but I'd do whatever it took to keep Tempest safe.

"Then I will hunt her down. No matter how often it takes until she realises how special she is to me. Taking another woman as my queen is a political tactic at most."

I heard the rapid beating of my heart as my hand rose to my chest. Something was different. The words I had spoken filled my chest with a heavy ache.

"Tempest is stubborn. She will never stop, and in the end, she will hate you."

"*Shut* up." I hissed as the ache worsened, as if my heart were breaking.

"*Fayolan*!" Nix rushed forward as I leant against my mother's throne to stop myself falling. "I'll get the healers."

"*No!*" I bared my teeth. "They cannot help me." I had never experienced such pain, but a warmth filled me as Tempest entered my mind.

One moment I stood in the throne room and the next I was seeing through her eyes. She was in my quarters. Her bare feet padded against the marble floor as she paced the room.

"It's not that simple," Lilith said. Tempest stood before her, looking down as she lounged on the daybed.

"It is that simple. He told me so many times he was not a nice man. I've accepted he will never love me, but am I asking too much? To hope that he'll care for my people too? And not just because of me. I want him to *believe* they are innocent in all of this. If he can't... he will never stop seeing me as a monster." Tempest let out a frustrated sigh as she returned to pacing.

"Fayolan does not see you like that. That night in the bar, he held your hand. He openly showed affection to you, and he has never cared enough to do that before," Lilith explained.

"Yes, and he spent the night he rescued me, caring for me, but despite that, it did not mean to him what it meant to me." Her fingers lifted to her cheek as she wiped a tear away.

"Fayolan?" Nix shook my arm. I jolted, returning to my body. "Where did you go?"

"Tell Tempest that I am leaving to help General Tam. I will be back in two nights. Tell her to wear something nice. I have a surprise for her." I didn't linger for her answer as I stormed from the room.

I darted to the closest balcony, the cool breeze blowing through my feathers as I flew away. *It was impossible—no matter how much I wanted to, a monster like me could never love.*

CHAPTER SIXTY-ONE

Tempest

The cloth wrapped around my eyes had me on edge as I heard the door slip open. Fayolan's boots were soft as he edged closer. His intoxicating scent filled my nostrils as he stopped before me.

"Give me your hand," he said in a hushed, husky voice.

"Where are we going?" I asked as he assisted me to my feet. His arm curved around my waist, and the warmth of his touch sent a shiver through me as he guided me forward.

"Stop asking questions, Tempest. It's a surprise." My name gracefully flowed from his mouth, and I shuddered with anticipation.

The door squeaked as he directed me down the hallway, away from his quarters. With a steady grip, he escorted me to a stairwell, cradling me in his embrace as he lifted me.

"I'm sorry I've been away so long. Things were worse than I anticipated. But now I'm all yours, Pet."

The thought sent heat through my core. Whenever I was

close to Fayolan, I lost any sense of self control I had. Thoughts of him consumed me in his absence. Wishing he would return and hold me tenderly in his arms.

"I'm just glad you're back in one piece. If I recall, you promised not to leave my bed cold at night."

"So, I did." Fayolan chuckled as he pulled me closer into his chest. "Tonight, I will be sure to leave it extra warm. Maybe a bed warmer or two should do the trick."

I playfully thwacked his chest. "I don't think so, Mr... Sorry, shouldn't it be... Daddy?" Fayolan tensed at my words. The moment they left my mouth, I knew he was mine.

Once we had spiralled around the longest staircase I'd ever climbed, Fayolan placed my feet on the floor. "Almost there," he said with a chuckle.

An icy breeze fanned my skin, carrying my hair as we entered the night air. The noises from the city below were a faint hum, just audible over the wind.

His hands moved to my face, the soft fabric falling away as he cradled my cheeks. He was bathed in the moon's pale light as its beams cascaded over him, chasing the shadows away. "I wanted to show you something *I*'ve never been able to see before. The world's always been dull to me... until you." His eyes lifted to the sky. They sparkled with a mixture of awe and sadness.

I exhaled a deep breath, wanting to continue watching him, but I let my eyes raise above the city. I gasped in amazement as I looked at the breathtakingly beautiful sight.

A galaxy full of stars and planets swirled above Solis. They shone brightly, their twinkling light seeming to speak to us from the heavens. A vibrant contrast of purple and blue hues lit the black night sky.

"It's beautiful," I breathed as Fayolan pulled me closer.

He leant over, kissing my head. "That's what I see when I look into your eyes."

"You could never see this before?" I shifted my attention back to him.

"No. Nix has described it, but it's so much more than I could imagine."

I reached out and took his hand, squeezing it softly as I stepped closer. His warmth shielding me from the wind. He gripped me tighter as he chuckled. His gaze stayed riveted on the galaxy.

I stared down at the city that spanned out beneath us. My breath hitching as I gasped, "You can see the whole of Solis from up here!"

We stood on a balcony high in one of the spiral towers of the palace, listening to the distant sounds of the city below. The moonflowers gave it a magical ambiance. Their vines wrapped around the stone railings, offering a soft glow in the moonlight.

"I used to come up here to escape my father. I wanted to share it with you." My soul stirred within me as I whirled to face him. My lips stretched in a wide smile. "You are the only person I've brought here. I promise to give you every part of me I have to give."

"Name me something else you have never given to anyone else?" I asked. My mind was racing as I realised he was trying.

"I never shared a bed overnight with a woman until you."

"You can do better than that," I teased, running my hands down his sides to his waist. I caressed my fingers across the hills and valleys of his muscled body, eliciting a low moan from him. I could feel the tension radiating from his body as I touched him.

"Naughty girl," he rasped as my hands lowered, teasing at the belt around his waist. "I never held another person's hand."

"Tut! Tut!" I bit my lip as I freed the buckle. "I want

more." My fingers slipped within the waistline of his trousers. He hissed as I traced the muscle wall that created a V leading to his throbbing cock.

"I never found release with another woman," he rasped as my fingers ran along his shaft. His eyes swirled as he locked my gaze.

"So, no one has ever tasted your cum?" I asked. His breath hitched as I freed his girthy erection from its restraints, lowering my gaze flirtatiously as I watched my hand work his hardened shaft. His body stiffened as I lowered to my knees. "Then please let me be the first?"

Fayolan's fingers ran through my hair as I leant in, opening my mouth as my tongue ran across the tip of his cock, making him jerk.

"*Fuck.*" He hissed as my lips closed around his erection, and I leant forward. "I've never met anyone like you." I swallowed at his words. His cock slipped to the rear of my mouth. He groaned, and my juices pooled between my legs as I pulled back.

"I refused to allow anyone to so much as lay a finger on me in fifteen years until you. Now I crave your touch," I admitted, before I took him into my mouth. Teasing his cock against the roof of my mouth, coating it in saliva.

His hips moved, demanding I take him deeper as his fingers twisted my hair. His grip was tight and unyielding as he held my head, his power over me unmistakable.

"*Look* at me. Gods you're fucking beautiful with your lips wrapped around my cock." My eyes shot to his, and he groaned as he pressed further down my throat.

He fucked my mouth slowly as I licked my tongue down the shaft. My core heated with every deep thrust, stretching my mouth and throat. Pain and pleasure encompassed me in a swirling deluge of ecstasy.

"That's it… perfect. Just a little more for Daddy. I know you can take it."

I enclosed my arms around the back of Fayolan's legs, pulling him closer. Holding my face flush against him, devouring his entire girthy cock. His legs shook as he groaned, his hand gripping my hair tightly.

"Do you want to taste me, my good little girl?" I released him, taking a deep breath, refilling my lungs with air.

"Yes." My voice was raspy and my desire to please him flared within me.

"I'm going to take you to the edge before I allow it. Will you let me?"

I nodded as he pulled the belt from his waist, wrapping it around my throat. He ran his fingertips teasingly over my skin as he pulled it taut. I struggled to breathe against the strain of its grip around my neck. "Good girl."

His fingers left a trail of warmth on my cheek before they returned to my hair. "Eyes on me."

His enormous cock pressed against my quivering lips. My breath caressed his shaft as it hovered before me. I opened my mouth eagerly. All rational thought was fleeing as my pussy ached to be filled, and my tongue wanted so badly to taste him.

Fayolan thrust his cock deep down my throat. I gagged as he held me flush against him. The delicious groans it elicited from him made my heart race.

"That's it, my special girl." His shadows edged towards me as my vision swam, but still, he held me in place. His cock was within my throat, straining against his belt.

My eyes fluttered when Fayolan pulled back, allowing me to gasp for air. "Can you do that again for me? It felt so fucking good."

I nodded and his hips thrust again, moving fast, teasing

my gag reflex as he panted. Saliva coated his shaft, allowing it to glide deeper down my throat.

Heat flushed my cheeks as my stomach clenched with need. I wanted to taste him, and as he thrust again, Fayolan groaned and filled my mouth with his juices.

I pulsed my head forward to squeeze every drop from him. The taste was heavenly. His eyes were wide, and his pupils dilated as he let me draw another stream of cum. Licking my lips as I watched him through watery lashes. I'd tasted nothing so divine in my life and I wanted more.

CHAPTER SIXTY-TWO

My chest heaved as the adrenaline coursed through my body. I should have hated Fayolan having so much control over me, yet it opened a world of pleasure I never knew existed.

"You're cold." Fayolan noticed the skin on my arms pebbling. I suppressed my shivers, my body aching for the relief only release could bring.

"I want you," I moaned as I rocked on my heels. Still on my knees at his feet as he rubbed his hand over his throbbing shaft.

"Tempest…" Fayolan's body tensed as he stumbled back.

"What's happening?"

"The beast inside of me wants a taste of you, and I can't hold him back any longer. Remember the safe word and know he would never hurt you. He desires you as much as I do."

I stared, unable to comprehend what he was saying. "Fayolan I don't…"

"You should *run*, Tempest." Fayolan smirked. His eyes darkened as something else stared through them. "If I catch you… I'm going to do *bad* things to you." He displayed his elongating fangs as I stayed rooted to the spot. "I said… *Run*!" His voice sounded gravelly as if it was not his. *Something else is controlling his body. The beast is real!*

My pulse pounded as I rose to my feet. Before my mind could catch up, I was already running—the wind rushing past my ears. Fear surged through me, along with a dull ache in every muscle.

"Tempest…" he drawled eerily. He sounded almost demonic as his voice echoed down the tower's spiral stairs.

I clasped a hand over my mouth as a cry hung on my lips. My excitement and fear fought for dominance.

I jumped off the last step, the coarse grains of sandstone grinding against my exposed skin as I collided with the wall. With a wince, I pushed off the bricks, hurrying down the corridor Fayolan had led me down.

"Fuck." He'd blindfolded me on the way here, and I was clueless about where I was going. My legs ached as I sprinted forward, the air burning my lungs with each gasp I took.

My gaze fell on a tapestry that fluttered as if caressed by a gentle breeze. I pulled it back to reveal an ominous corridor. I had no desire for *whatever* drove Fayolan to catch me in the dark.

"Where is my good little girl?" he purred. He was gaining on me.

"If he kills me in *here*, I will make sure I stink the *entire* palace out!" I huffed as I tiptoed behind the tapestry. The fabric brushed against me as I moved. My breath became visible in the air, a chill running down my spine as the breeze swept around me.

Part of me wanted the beast to catch me, as something

wrapped around my heart. Golden threads of magic within me seemed to search for something that beckoned me.

Fayolan's demonic voice drawled, with mock amusement, echoing through the tunnel. "I can *smell* you, Tempest."

I could sense his presence as I fumbled through the darkness, the hairs on my neck standing up. As the corridor became increasingly narrow, a wave of amusement coursed through me, knowing it would slow Fayolan's progress.

My hands brushed against the icy walls as I guided myself forward. Racing down the winding tunnels, my panted breath echoing off the walls until a glimmer of light shone ahead. I ran with all my might towards it. Shivering as I stepped from the icy darkness of the hidden tunnel.

A strange sensation, like a feather, brushed against my thoughts. *Tempest*... I could practically hear the magic in the air, and my fear rose. I took in a long breath, closing my eyes, knowing the only place I could hide was nearby. But part of me did not want to remain hidden once I arrived. *Slut!*

I bolted past the balcony overlooking the exquisite palace garden, the sweet scent of orchids and moonflowers lingering in the air. Fighting for breath, my chest heaved rapidly.

The eyes of the guards landed on me as I ran towards them, their confusion palpable. They parted, and I flew through the quarters, my heart pounding as I ran. I skidded to a terrified stop, my hand trembling as it hovered over the door handle.

"Remember the Prince's warning before you set foot in there," the beast inside Fayolan growled. I felt the weight of my own hands, my fingers unmovable. Frozen in place as my breath clouded the air.

"I know," I said as I threw the door open, the wood cool against my fingertips as I stepped into Fayolan's room. I hurried quickly closing the bolts as I ignored the excitement that wrapped around me like a vice.

"Those locks will not stop me." The door handle twisted, and I backed away. The deep demonic rumble of his voice reverberated around the room.

I leant against the wall as my breath came in ragged bursts. The sound of my blood roared through my ears as I strove to remain calm.

The locks clicked open of their own accord and the door's slow creak tormented me as it opened. Fayolan smirked, watching me through obsidian eyes. "Your scent is delectable," he rasped as he stepped into the room.

Each click of a lock, sealing me inside, made me jump as my hands became clammy. "Do you fear me, Nephilim?" He tilted his head as his eyes roamed my body.

"Should I?" I asked.

"I am a creature of nightmares, and I make even the Gods tremble. But you, my sweet Tempest, are mine, and you are safe with me. I swear never to do more than you can handle, and to atone for it with pleasure."

He stared at me intently as I examined every detail of his face. The tattoo-like shadows on his skin moved like a living thing, coiling around his body. *I'd seen them before!*

"Where is Fayolan?" I asked with a deep swallow. He let out a chuckle, and his clothes vanished with a snap of his fingers. Exposing Fayolan in all of his glory. His own tattoos intertwined with the shadows that crawled across his toned muscles.

"Fayolan is watching. His mind is one with mine, but I control this body for now. The Gods imprisoned me. Tricked me into a noncorporeal form that meant I could not harm them. But they did not foresee a male being born strong enough to house me. Fayolan accepted me as a child, but even he fears what I am."

My breath was unsteady as I pushed away from the wall. My legs propelled me towards the unknown, despite the hint of fear that lingered in the air and screamed for me to flee.

His skin was warm as my fingers caressed his stubbled cheek, and I looked into his captivating, obsidian eyes.

"Can I see him? Just a glimpse to know he's there." I watched his eyes turn a pale gold, followed by a smirk of arrogance spreading across his lips.

"Are you scared of what my beast will do to you?" Fayolan's voice sounded husky as he brushed my hair from my face.

"No more than I am of you. He is a part of you, and I'm asking you to give me all you are. You've seen what lies within me, after all." I lifted myself onto my toes and grazed my lips across his.

"There are rules in this room, Tempest. Especially when *he* is out to play. You willingly entered this room, and you knew what awaited you, but you still hold the power to make it all stop. Say the word, Tempest. So I can be sure you won't let my beast take it too far."

I reached up, placing my hands on Fayolan's cheeks. Whispering the word into his ear.

"Good. You are ours to play with in this room, and if you behave, I promise you will love it here. Rule one, never enter this room clothed...."

He flicked his hand, and my clothes were gone in a moment, leaving me with a tingling sensation. *Of course... he'd pulled my entire wardrobe from the aether.* "Rule two, in this room, you will refer to me as Master... or Daddy." His eyes darkened as the beast struggled to break free. "The beast will not hurt you. Trust him as you do me. Do you understand?"

"Yes."

"That's my good girl." His eyes became veiled with darkness as black shadows engulfed them.

"Fayolan," I gasped, but the beast stared back.

"He is watching you and he feels everything I do. You *broke* one of our rules already." The beast tsked as he gripped my chin, forcing me down to my knees. "Rest your hands on your legs." His tongue ran over his teeth as he inspected me. "Palm *up*." The timbre of his voice was so deep that it sent shivers of desire down my spine.

I flipped my hands, and my gaze flicked up to watch Fayolan as he stalked around the room. His biceps flexed as he ran his hands over objects hanging from the wall.

CHAPTER SIXTY-THREE

The Beast/ Fayolan

Tempest's body trembled as I came to the whips. I knew the fear she felt after what that prick did to her as a child.

"*She is not ready.*" The Fae that housed me growled as he fought for control. He could not sense my true intentions, no matter how hard he tried. I may be dark, but even I was not that cruel.

"*You told her to trust me. Maybe you should do the same.*" I reminded the Fae Prince. "*The Nephilim was made for us. I won't allow her to suffer at my hands.*"

I drew on his power, sending the whips back to the aether. Maybe one day, when she was ready, I would let her feel how pleasurable I could make them feel against her supple skin.

Tempest's shoulders relaxed as I moved on, gauging her level of interest in the other objects around the room. She tilted her head as my hand ran over a leather paddle. It had the word slut carved into it.

"Feeling kinky today, are we, Pet?" Her lips parted, but no words came out, as her cheeks turned the softest red. "Would you like to try it?"

As I held out the paddle, Tempest wrapped her delicate hand around the handle. Her fingers grazing the carved letters as she explored it. She slapped it teasingly against her palm, testing the pain it would cause.

A wicked smile tugged at her lips as she glanced up at me, nibbling on her bottom lip. "Please, Master… be gentle with me."

The sexual glint in her eye had my cock hardening. Such a devious little minx. I didn't miss how she subtly spread her legs a little wider.

"Be still. I want to drink you in with my eyes. Every fucking delicious curve. The Gods created you for me, Pet." *Literally.*

Tempest did not know the truth of her birth. That her father had approached me with a proposal.

He desired offspring with a Fae woman of lower status, but the Gods sought the extinction of Nephilim children. So he made a deal with me. He would tie Tempest's destiny to mine. She would be born the perfect match for me, and I would bind myself to the Fae prince.

I'd be strong enough to protect her from the Gods, and she'd be the mate I could never have hoped for. The creature to balance my darkness with light. He made her to be mine.

Fayolan was also unaware of my agreement with the son of the Gods. I even stopped him from finding release with another woman to ensure that when he found *her*, he would claim her. The mate bond had begun forming, and I would share her with him. He was as much a part of me as I was of him. Together, we were the perfect match for her.

I stood over her, my hand soothingly running through her hair as the midnight blue shimmered. *Did she know she differed from other Nephilim? That her power was far beyond that of her race?* She was born like my host... immortal. But unlike him, she could feel the coldness of death's touch.

Her father had been sneaky. He had not bound her powers as he should have. I could feel it pulsing against my skin as her desire grew. *Such a beautiful monster.*

I lowered to my knees, placing my hand beneath her chin, lifting her face to meet mine. I could see her arousal as I lifted a gag. A leather ball attached to a strap that I would fasten to her head. "Are you going to be my good little girl?" I asked.

"Yes," she panted.

"Yes, *what*?" My fingers wrapped around the paddle as I slipped it from her grasp.

"Yes... Master." Her words were a mere whisper against my neck. My fingers swept over her parted lips as I pulled the strap tight. She was beautiful and all mine.

The belt remained wrapped around her neck, and I lowered my hands as I tightened it. She had adjusted to its pressure. Her cheeks flushed red, and wetness pooled between her thighs as her scent had my cock growing.

I was larger than the Prince, and she gasped as she watched my cock enlarging. "You're going to take all of me, aren't you, my special girl?" I drew in a deep breath, holding my hand out to her. "I want you splayed out like a feast for me to devour. Come with me."

Tempest pushed herself up, the sound of her body stretching, breaking the silence. Her legs almost gave out as she shook with unsatiated desire. I stood towering over her. Today I would make her scream for me. She would leave this room with only my name on her lips.

My hands trailed down her arms, clasping her wrists sharply as I hauled her towards the waiting wooden frame. Its soft mahogany was warm against my touch as I lifted her arms.

Steel manacles hung in each corner. I took my time clamping them around her wrists, holding them high above her so her toes only skimmed the ground.

Placing my legs between hers, I forced them apart. Her weight transferred to her wrists as she fought to touch the ground. I clipped manacles around her ankles and stepped back to admire her.

Her nipples hardened as I splayed her out, unable to move while she watched me. Her eyes devoured me as her gaze lifted from my cock, examining every contour of my muscular body. Lingering on the tattoos that swirled across me.

She moaned as my solid erection pulsed against her stomach. A promise of what was to come. "Is this what you want?" I stroked my cock under her watchful gaze. "I'd love nothing more than to bury myself deep in that pussy of yours, but first, I'm going to teach you a lesson. In here, you're at my mercy and will learn to follow the rules."

I would never force Tempest to enter this room. She'd come here because she wanted to, and that thought made my cock stiffen with the desire to stretch her greedy cunt.

"Does it feel good, sweet girl… to let go and allow me to have control?"

Tempest nodded her head, making an unintelligible noise around the ball gag.

I trailed the paddle down her back as a warning before I slapped it across her pert ass. Tempest let out a sharp moan as her head lolled back.

Again, the paddle left a red mark across her flesh. The word slut barely visible. She groaned in ecstasy with each strike. I used just enough force for it to sting a little, but not to cause her harm.

"Have you learnt your lesson?" I asked.

Tempest shook her head, a smile teasing at the corner of her mouth.

"Naughty little Slut." I slapped the paddle against her ass cheek slightly harder than before. The beautiful noise she made sent a shiver down my spine.

Three more spanks had her head thrown back, her ass red as she lost control, and her juices dripped to the floor beneath her. "I didn't give you *permission* to cum." I spoke through gritted teeth, gripping her neck, forcing her head back.

My cock pulsed against her ass as her fear returned. "From now on, you ask *permission* to cum. I own you in this room, and you will *beg* me for release." I shoved her head back upright, lowering the gag as I ran the paddle over her pert ass. "Let me hear how much you enjoy a spanking."

I slapped the leather paddle against her sensitive flesh four more times. The intoxicating sounds she made had my mind racing. *It's almost time to make her mine…*

"Please," she gasped.

"Please, what?" I slapped the paddle between her legs.

"Please let me cum."

"No!" I lashed the paddle again before running my fingers through the throbbing folds between her legs. She groaned and quivered. Clinging to the edge of reason as she fought the orgasm that tried to tear her apart.

I stalked around her, admiring the soft hues of her skin. Tossing the paddle aside. *Gods, she was a weapon.* One that could drop me to my fucking knees. Maybe that had been the bastard's plan all along. To create the one thing that would bring me to heel.

Her eyes were wild as they lingered on me. Her throat bobbed as she swallowed. A good man would prepare her for the cock that would rip her apart. But I was not a man.

Moving against her, I slipped my hands beneath her arms.

Lifting my hands into her hair as I gripped it tight at her scalp, pulling her head back as my cock pushed into her cunt. She cried out the most exhilarating sound. Her body jolted as I gave her all of me.

I was slow as I pulled out, using her juices to coat my cock before sliding into her again. My instincts took over as I sped up. With each thrust, she screamed out as I ploughed deep inside her.

Fayolan was roaring as he battled for control. But Tempest's moans were loud as her cunt clamped around my cock.

My fangs grew as my true form emerged. Power surged within me, and my back heaved as black wings burst from my skin and my canines extended. My body grew, even as my cock expanded within her.

I allowed Tempest to lift her head. Her eyes widened as she took in all of me.

My muscles bulged, and my skin blackened as deadly claws burst from my fingers. I was a creature of the night. Born before the Gods of this world.

Her features softened as she acknowledged what I was and accepted me. She mumbled, her lips quivering with emotion. "I see *you*."

I slammed into her, pulling her head back, claiming her tantalising cunt as I was about to claim her soul. Binding us for all of eternity. Even death would not separate us.

"Don't you fucking dare." Fayolan realised what I was doing. Her magic mingled with mine as the tether around his heart reached out to her. *"Get back in your cage!"*

He would have succeeded in overpowering me if her magic had not held me there. As if she knew what I planned to do and wanted it.

My head lowered to her neck, fangs grazing against her as I pierced her flesh. My bite mixed with my saliva as I marked her. Our tethers were meeting and binding as our bond snapped into place.

Wings burst from her back as her Nephilim side broke free. Accepting the bonds I'd forged with my bite. The softest shade of blue illuminated her skin, and her hair swayed, appearing as if caught in a gentle breeze. She was a magnificent creature. One of light and darkness.

"Cum for me," I breathed against her neck as she screamed and I thrust again. My juices filled her as she came undone around my cock.

Her body convulsed as my saliva ran through her veins, and I allowed Fayolan to the surface.

Fucking beast! I roared as Tempest fought against the merging of our souls. My cock still thrust within her as I desperately tried to bring her back to me, using her orgasm to draw her into the bliss.

I should have seen it coming. He'd blocked his intentions from me and marked her as ours. Her pain radiated through the threads that now connected us.

"She was already developing the bond. I just strengthened it, making it soul deep. There is nowhere she can run that you cannot find her. Now you can protect what is ours." The beast settled within me.

Tempest groaned, her eyes rolling as I held her against my body. I fucked her harder until her head snapped up. Shadows danced in her eyes. But even they could not dim the iridescent beauty of her irises.

The intensity of her stare was magnetising as she rotated her hips against my cock. I used my magic to free the manacles around her ankles as I hauled her up. Her legs wrapped tight around my waist as she rode me, plunging her clit against me as she devoured my cock. Sucking it inside as I ploughed her.

The beast was right. She could take me and my dark, sadistic desires. She took the pain I offered her and fucked me back with such ferocity, my body blazed with heat.

My dark, looming shadows stretched out, longing to devour her soul. But I pulled away, sensing the tension between us as her lips creased into a frown. The shadows seemed alive as their tendrils curled towards her, and she watched in awe. "They want to feed from you."

Her body tensed as her grip locked me in place, stopping me from retreating. "Then *let* them." She smirked darkly with no flicker of doubt.

I released my shadows, letting them dance around her as they fed. The beast inside me controlled them as they drew moans of bliss from her. "I need to cum… Daddy. *Please.*"

Tempest's pupils dilated as I slipped two fingers inside her, filling her even more. Stretching her with each thrust of my cock as I pounded into her. She screamed out in bliss as I allowed her to topple over the precipice.

I roared as my seed flowed into her. My arms gripped her back as I rode the orgasm with her, and she went limp.

Her head hung back. Her breaths laboured as the belt still restricted her breathing. With a snap of my wrists, I released her from the manacles. Carrying her to my bed, I placed her down. Careful not to hurt her wings. Sweat clung to her forehead as our souls melded.

"Rest Tempest. I'll be watching over you."

"What's happening?"

I had been powerless to do anything but watch as my

beast claimed her. He hadn't considered how she would feel about it. Fucking bastard! *What if she rejected us now?*

"The beast housed inside me marked you. It's going to be alright."

She would have to remain here for the next few days. Her need would be insatiable, as would mine. "I'm sorry, Pet."

CHAPTER SIXTY-FOUR

I gasped as Fayolan lifted me from the bed. Settling me on his monstrous cock. Our bodies were coated in sweat as we took each other repeatedly. Two days passed without either of us leaving Fayolan's room of torture and pleasure.

My breasts bounced as I rolled my hips. I pressed my lips against his as his hands wandered, exploring every inch of me.

My body was flushed with heat that only Fayolan could ease as he pounded into me. His powerful arms, rippling with muscle, held me firmly in place.

Jagged breath fanning against my neck with his unwavering stare on the mark that still marred my flesh. I had a feeling it was permanent. A symbol that I belonged to the beast—to Fayolan.

"*Fuck,*" he roared as our bodies and minds collided. I

could feel his orgasm through our bond as my own rocked me. Gods I couldn't get enough of him as I lost myself again.

I leant against him, my chest heaving as I tried to catch my breath. The thunder of my heart echoed as my mind soared in bliss.

"I can't breathe," I said as Fayolan slipped from inside me. The heat of my body flared as soon as he retreated.

"You need to eat and rest. This will pass, Tempest. Each release will make it easier." He lowered me onto the bed, my body weak as it had succumbed to multiple orgasms.

"What did he do?" I asked as Fayolan flicked his hand and clothes returned to our bodies. The fabric hurt my tender flesh, but it gave me a little more clarity.

"He *disobeyed* me and bound us as *mates*. He had no *fucking* right, but he did it, anyway. I tried to stop him…"

"You didn't *want* me as a mate?"

"It wasn't my wish for him to mark you. It was not his decision alone, and now neither of us can do anything about it. He connected our souls for all of eternity without thinking about us. I'm not sure you understand…You will always belong to me, Tempest. Even death will not free you from our bond."

The beast had claimed me. Fayolan might not have chosen me, but *he* had. "Are you mad at him because he bound you to me *forever*?"

"He acted impulsively. I wasn't given a choice," he said coldly, avoiding my gaze as a plate of food appeared on the table.

"Neither was I… He did this to me, *too*. Do you know how it feels to be bound to someone who doesn't *want* to be?" I sat up and clambered from the bed. "I need some air."

Fayolan shot across the room as I started towards the door. "Let me pass." I gave a frustrated huff as the pain in my soul intensified. I could feel Fayolan's anger towards the beast for binding us. *And it hurt.*

"You *cannot* leave like *this*." His enormous body framed the door. Blocking me from reaching the locks.

"You don't want me, so what does it *matter*?" I seethed. "I told you I *won't* run, but I *need* to be *away* from you right now."

"You can't." He moved closer. "Our souls are still melding; only I can calm the fire that consumes your body." He smirked as he placed a finger on my shoulder. Diminishing the burning fever that wracked me. Despite my reluctance, I forced my feet to take a step back, my groan of protest echoing in the air.

"I will take a cold shower. I just need to… *think*." His finger traced my arm, a fire ignited in my core, and my legs involuntarily tightened.

"And *where* will you go?" he scoffed as he backed off, letting the fever return.

"I'm going to the medical wing. Marcell asked me to help." I had thought little about Marcell's offer. But now I was desperate to find an escape.

I sighed, stepping into Fayolan as if defeated. He ran his hand through my hair, trying to comfort me. I reached up, pulling his head towards mine as I whispered the safe word into his ear.

Fayolan growled, releasing me as he stepped away from the door. "I won't stop you from leaving, Tempest. That word stands for trust and I won't break it. But you're being damned stupid."

I knew he was looking out for me, but right now, I needed space.

"You're to take Lilith with you."

"*Thank* you," I hissed through my teeth, scowling as I clicked the first lock. After fiddling with the others, the door finally opened with a loud groan. I looked back at Fayolan as he lay on the bed, his slow breaths creating a gentle rhythm.

A wicked smile crept across his face as the darkness shifted and shimmered in his pale golden eyes. "You will be back!" The beast preened as I hurried from the room.

The shower did little to ease the burning that consumed me. My desperation had reached its peak, and the thought of returning to Fayolan to plead for help crossed my mind multiple times.

On my descent to the lower levels of the Palace. Lilith showed me the way to the infirmary, and I felt the chilly breeze of the building as we entered. Offering me a moment of relief.

"Are you sure about this?" Lilith's eyes roamed over me, noting the beads of sweat that coated my forehead. I had covered Fayolan's mark with a silk scarf, but the flush of my cheeks was impossible to hide.

"Trust me, I'm fine." I smiled as I opened the door to the infirmary. The tang of chemicals assaulted my nostrils, and my stomach roiled. *My senses had sharpened.*

The infirmary was pristine. Cots lined the main room, wrapped in clean white sheets. Shelves adorned the walls, and a padlocked cabinet housed vials and stoppered bottles.

They outfitted the beds with screens they could pull around them, creating a privacy barrier. An intricately patterned divide already hid one bed in the corner.

"Tempest," Marcell said. A warm, beaming smile illuminated his angular face. He was handsome, but all I could think about was Fayolan and his majestic beast. Two beings residing in one body.

The sound of Lilith's coughing jolted me out of my daze. "Sorry." I grimaced. "I came to see the infirmary."

Marcell ushered me further inside. "Maeve," he called. "She's my newest apprentice." My heart sank as I anxiously waited for her to notice me. She was angry with me, and she had every right to be.

She stepped from a second room. Glowering as she saw me. "What are *you* doing here?"

Marcell's gaze darted between us, and his brow furrowed in confusion. Maeve stood upright, her muscles taut and her hands clenched tight. Remaining across the room, the soft light of the lamps created a gentle glow across her pale skin.

"I invited Tempest to help in the infirmary." Marcell smiled, but Maeve threw her arms up in the air as she cursed.

"So, you're taking *this* from me, too?" She banged her fist on a countertop beside her.

My eyes fixed on her. "Maybe I should go." She was no longer the loving sister I had failed to save. But an angry girl that had nothing but hate for me. And I deserved it.

"You are here by my invite…." Marcell's words became muffled as my vision blurred. I reached out to grab the nearest bed, but my hands met air as my legs buckled. I hit the ground hard and cried as burning pain seared my flesh.

"Don't *touch* her." Maeve darted between Marcell and me as chaos erupted.

"*Fayolan,*" I muttered as my hands reached for the scarf around my neck.

"What is *that*?" Maeve shrieked upon seeing my neck.

Marcell stepped away. "The King has marked her and their souls are still melding. He should *not* have allowed her to come here." He threw his arms into the air. "I cannot touch her. Take her back to him. *Now*!"

Hands slipped beneath me, but unlike Fayolan's, they did not ease the heat.

The room shook as Fayolan roared. The doors slammed against the wall, causing everyone to step back.

His gaze darted to Maeve and his fangs bared as she backed up further. Marcell's arm shot out as he placed it in front of Maeve, protecting her and drawing Fayolan's attention to him.

Fayolan's wings spread as he lifted me into his arms. Wrapping them around me to hide me from view. His chest rumbled as he took deep, ragged breaths.

He stormed from the medical wing. His hands shook as his fingers dug into my arms.

"I'm sorry," I said as he carried me back to his room. The locks clicked before he lowered me onto his bed. He did not speak as ropes wound around my wrists and ankles, pulling tight as he splayed me across the mattress.

"You will *not* leave this room until this is over." His voice was a deep rumble. "Will you let me ease your suffering?"

"Please…" I squeaked as the heat became a searing pain.

His fingers pushed inside me as he pumped his hand, easing the burn, so my vision became focused.

He knelt between my legs, and his wings spread wide as he found the spot that had me groaning.

"What happens when this is all over?" I asked, as I fought to stop the orgasm that threatened to debilitate me. "Will you *still* hate me? I know you don't wish to be mated to me."

His fingers stilled as he pulled them from me torturously. "I never said I did not *want* you, Tempest. Fuck, I've wanted you from the moment I first saw you. Mark or no mark, you belong to me." His fingers sank into me again.

"*But*…" He stopped moving within me, cutting me off, leaving me yearning for more.

"But nothing, Tempest. I would have marked you when

we were ready. He just took the choice from us. I'm not angry that it's *you* I'm bound to. It scared me you might not *want* me."

"Fayolan, I choose *you*. It's always been you."

A smile spread across his lips as he settled between my legs, his fingers running over my folds as his cock pushed against my entrance. "Now let me ease your suffering." He grinned wickedly as he pounded me.

Each dominating thrust had me crying out his name. My back arched. The rope dug into my wrists as I lifted off the bed.

"*Harder*!" I screamed, and he obliged, reaching deeper as he claimed me as his. His beast watching as Fayolan's cock destroyed me.

I clamped my legs, keeping him close as he stroked my clit in swirling motions that had my body jolting as his erection continued to hammer in and out of me. His knees pushed beneath me, lifting my hips, and he plunged even deeper.

I drew my gaze to the shadows that swirled around him, running across my stomach and around my breasts. Everywhere they touched, it felt as if Fayolan was running his fingers, pinching my nipples and stroking my stomach.

"Cum for me." Fayolan worked my clit and his cock filled and stretched me. I collapsed into a bliss so strong all thoughts fled my mind.

My spirit found solace as it melded with his. I heard the beast's growl in my head and a link formed between our minds. With a sigh of contentment, my body relaxed as Fayolan pulled away from me.

"Now, will you eat? Your body is weakening, and we're not *done* yet," he chuckled.

"Um hum," was all I could manage. *He's going to be the ruin of me.*

"Not even death will keep you from me!" his voice caressed my mind.

Fayolan carried me to the bathing room. Our heat had finally subsided, and my body was weak and sore. For three days, we had remained locked in his room. Sleeping and eating between the insatiable sex, which was all that could quell the burning heat.

Fayolan lowered himself into the bath, settling me against his chest.

"Fayolan," I murmured. "What is his name? Your beast…"

"Zakayus. He is ancient, and even the Gods fear him." I leant over, taking in the sight of the neatly folded cloths on the shelves as I grabbed a bottle of liquid soap with a fresh aroma.

"Thank you, Zakayus," I whispered as I poured some fragrant liquid onto the cloth.

"For marking you?" Fayolan asked as he ran a finger over the mark on the crook of my neck.

"For caring enough about me to want to." He relaxed back as I ran the cloth over his chest. His tattoos were no longer dancing with the shadows of the night.

Fayolan rested his arms over the tub as I washed him. "I broke your rules," I mused as my hands lowered down his body. I had screamed his name as we fucked in mindless, animalistic need, and I had left his room without his permission.

"Yes, you did. Maybe I will let you choose your punishment," he rasped. His lips curled up as he leant forward.

"*What* an offer." I raised an eyebrow as I leant into him, washing his back. I explored him as he relaxed against the tub. "What do we do now?" His hands caught my hair and twirled it between his fingers.

"I have a war to prepare for. And *you* will remain safe within the palace walls. Marcell will still want you in the medical wing. With war upon us, we will need all the help we can get."

He released my hair as he took my chin in his hand, his lips brushing against my cheek. "No matter what, Tempest." His gaze remained unwavering. "*You* will always belong with me."

The End... For now!

AFTERWORD

First off, I would like to thank you all for bearing with me and following my writing journey. With every book I've written, I've learnt more, and it has led me here. With your support, I have found the courage to carry on and do what I love.

I have had so much fun creating the world of Tempest and Fayolan, and their story is far from over. I hope you have enjoyed their adventure so far and will follow them as more dangers befall Solis. Can Fayolan find redemption amongst the chaos of war?
Book Two Sins Of The Reaper coming 2024!

Eleana Jaynes
Fantasy author of The Wolf King's Mate Series and The
Healer Chronicles.

The Wolf King's Mate Series
The Wolf King's Goddess
The Wolf King's Lost Mate
The Wolf King's Stolen Queen
The Wolf Queen's Vendetta
The Wolf King's Rampage

The Healer Chronicles
Curse of the Nephilim
Sins of the Reaper - Coming 2024

RAVENSWOOD CREATIVE COALITION

Ravenswood Creative Coalition "Unleashing Creativity, Empowering Independence."

I've partnered with Ravenswood Creative Coalition. We're on a mission to establish a unique and artist-friendly platform akin to Etsy or Fiverr, designed specifically for independent artists and authors of all genres. To find out more or join the coalition please visit www.ravenswoodcreativecoalition.com

www.ingramcontent.com/pod-product-compliance
Lightning Source LLC
Chambersburg PA
CBHW021219060726
47590CB00005B/1558